"We dance round in a ring and suppose,
But the Secret sits in the middle and knows."

- Robert Frost, *The Secret Sits*

H

Mascot Books
560 Herndon Parkway #120
Herndon, VA 20170
info@mascotbooks.com

PRBVG0815A

Library of Congress Control Number: 2015910406

ISBN-13: 978-1-63177-289-4

Printed in the United States

www.mascotbooks.com

Some secrets can destroy you.
Some can set you free.

THE HAGEN FAMILY
SECRET

K. M. ROBERSON

To my steadfast husband,
you have my love always and forever.

Prologue

Daveney

May 2034

I was running as fast as I could, faster than I ever had before. The warm, damp dirt cradled my bare feet in the brief moments they connected as I made my way through the dark woods. I had to find a way out before Leo's father found me.

"Go Daveney! Go now before he returns!" The urgency in Leo's voice scared me, and without looking back, I ran. I couldn't look back, because I was afraid that if I did, I wouldn't be able to leave him there, as I imagined the wrath he would face when his father returned and found me gone.

As I left through one of the side doors of the mansion, I slipped off my high heels and clung to the sides of my formal gown, trying in vain to keep it from catching on the branches I quickly passed by. It was so dark I could hardly see anything, but I continued running, hoping I would find a way out. After a few minutes, I began to hear the sounds of a busy street, so I made my way towards it. As I approached the wall that would free me from my nightmare, I heard the most wonderful sound in the world—it was my mother, and she was calling for me. I moved faster, but before I could cry out to her, I tripped, hitting my head on something hard, and as the pain crept down my body, everything faded away to black.

December 2033

"Daveney? Daveney? Where are you?" I heard my mother call.

"I'm up here, Mom," I yelled, thinking she would find it odd that I was in our attic for the third consecutive day of my holiday break. I was wrong.

"I thought I might find you up here," Mom said, as she climbed the last step of the ladder and pulled herself up into our dusty, warm attic. It was rarely cold in Texas, even in the winter. In fact, earlier that day, I had worn flip-flops during a shopping excursion with my mom, aunt, and cousin. I now sat cross-legged on the floor, with my flip-flops barely hanging on.

"I wanted to look around a little more," I replied. The truth was that I had become fascinated with the treasure trove I had found two days earlier, when I had gone in search of a memento that "represented my family history." It was an assignment for my honors history class. At the time it was given, I thought it was kind of odd and terribly easy, but I soon discovered, looking through some of the things my mom had saved over the years, it was kind of fun and made me want to learn more about my family.

"I thought you were going to use the wedding picture of your grandma and grandpa I gave you?" Mom asked, as she looked around at all of the boxes I had yet to go through.

"I am, but I wanted to see what else was up here." I watched Mom eye one particular box. "Is there something you don't want me to find?" I joked.

"Not at all. In fact, it's time you learned more about our family history," Mom said sweetly, but I could tell she was a little anxious. Even on edge, my mother was one of the most beautiful women I had ever seen in person. She wore her blonde hair long, and I often used hers as an example when trying to manage my own long, dark tresses. She was very stylish, yet appropriate in what she wore, which pleased my younger twin brothers and me greatly. It was nice that she wasn't frumpy, but we didn't want her to be over the top either. She and my dad married right after college, and a year later had me, which made them by far the youngest parents of any of my sixteen year-old peers.

"Really? Have you been hiding some kind of family secret or something?" I asked with a laugh.

Mom didn't respond, which I found odd. She was shuffling through a box I had yet to open. Suddenly, Mom stopped and gasped as she held up a photograph.

"What is it?" I asked, jumping up and going over to see what she had found.

"It's a picture taken before my senior prom." Mom smiled slightly, as she stared at the photograph and gently dusted it off.

I looked over her shoulder and saw seven young women in the picture, not much older than me. They were beautifully dressed in an array of colors. My mother wore a striking red dress and, as we looked at the picture, I made a mental note to ask her later if she still had it put away somewhere. If she did, and it was in good shape, I thought I might want to wear it to my own junior prom at the end of the year. It would be fun to go vintage.

We remained silent as we stared at the picture for a minute. While Mom was still looking at it, I peeked into the box where the picture had come from, and noticed a newspaper clipping with the headline, "SEVERAL AREA SENIORS INJURED IN TOLL ROAD ACCIDENT EN ROUTE TO PROM."

"Mom, what's this?" I asked, showing her the clipping. I had never heard much about Mom's senior prom, and I certainly had never heard about an accident.

Mom took the clipping from me and replied quietly, "There was a major accident on the highway on our way to dinner before the prom." She had a far off look in her eyes, and I could tell she was remembering what had happened.

"That's terrible! Was anyone hurt?" I asked, staring at Mom, who kept her eyes on the clipping.

"There were a lot of people hurt that night, and for some, their lives were never the same," Mom said mysteriously.

I wanted to ask more questions, but I didn't. I just watched her for a moment. Suddenly, she put the picture and the clipping back into the box and closed it. "Come with me, I want to show you something," Mom said, gently leading me out of the attic.

I followed her to the master bedroom closet she shared with my dad, where she pulled down a small box from the top shelf. It was marked "Old Bills." I remembered seeing it over the years whenever I was in there, but had never thought much about it. Mom sat down on the floor and opened the box, and I sat beside her. I saw there were a few leather-bound journals, stuffed with what looked like handwritten letters and other memorabilia.

"What are these?" I asked, reaching for the dark brown leather journal on top.

"These are journals that tell our family history, dating back to your great-great grandparents. The one you are holding is a compilation of the journals my sister Darcy and I kept when we weren't much older than you are now. Pieced together, they detail our senior year of high school, and how we discovered a secret our parents had kept hidden from us. I believe you are old enough now to know the full story. More importantly, I believe you need to know this to prepare you for what may come your way, so you can avoid some of the mistakes we all made." Mom's voice was calm, even though I could see her hand trembling as she touched the journal. "However, I must warn you that there will be parts that are hard to read and even harder to believe. When you are finished with the first journal come and get me. You can read it in here." Mom led me into the sitting area in the master bedroom. I sat down in her favorite reading chair, which was older than I was, but had been refurbished numerous times. She turned on the floor lamp next to me and handed me the throw blanket from the bed. She looked anxious, like she wasn't sure she was doing the right thing, but then she turned slowly to walk out of the room. When she reached the door, she paused, looked over at me, and said, "Daveney, I love you."

"I love you too, Mom," I replied, feeling overwhelmed and excited at the same time. What was this secret my beloved grandma and grandpa had kept? As soon as she was gone, I opened the journal and found myself lost in my mother's words.

Chapter One

Senior Year of High School, 2011-2012
Greer

My earliest memory is ice-skating with my mother on a frozen pond in Madison, Wisconsin when I was seven. The winters there were beautiful, with fresh snow almost every week and plenty of opportunities to go ice-skating, which we did on numerous occasions during the three years we lived there. Our last winter in Madison, Mom bought my twin sister Darcy and me gorgeous white ice skates with pink laces. I absolutely adored mine. Darcy never even tried hers on. She rarely went skating with us because she hated the cold. Our younger brother Will was too young to go, which meant my mom and I got to spend great one-on-one time together. She had grown up ice-skating in the Northeast, and I inherited her passion.

Darcy's dislike for skating and my love for it was only one of many differences between us. We pretty much had opposite personalities. I was day and she was night, but we also looked very different, and that bothered me. The last time we went ice-skating in Madison, I asked Mom, "If Darcy and I are twins, then why does she have red hair and green eyes and I have blonde hair and blue eyes?"

Mom stopped and knelt down to my eye level, looked at me for a moment, and replied, "It's because you're fraternal twins, not identical." Sensing I had no idea what that meant, she continued, "You both grew in my tummy at the same time, and that's what makes you twins, but you look different because..." She paused for another moment and looked away, searching for the right answer.

"Why do we look different, Mommy?" I inquired again, the way a precocious second grader often does.

Mom hesitated and then looked back at me and said, "Because you look like me, and Darcy looks more like your father's side of the family." It was true; I did look and act more like our incredible mother, but even when we were children, there was something striking about Darcy. People would stop our mother in stores and tell her that we looked like dolls come to life. Mom would thank them and always remind us afterwards that real beauty came from within. She modeled that for us every day in her actions.

I wanted to ask Mom more questions about why Darcy and I were so different, but she changed the subject, saying, "Do you see that little girl over there with her father? They've been watching us skate for a while now."

"Why aren't they skating?" I asked naively.

"I think they don't have skates, sweetheart. Should we see if the little girl would like to borrow Darcy's?" Mom asked with a smile.

We skated, hand in hand, slowly over to the father and daughter, who watched us closely. They were both dressed warmly, but I could tell their clothes were well used. The little girl was about my age, and I could see a little of her short, dark brown hair coming out from under her cap and just over her scarf. Her deep brown eyes and rosy cheeks showed she was a cute little girl, and I thought that if we went to the same school, we might be friends. Her father, on the other hand, was kind of scary looking. He was tall and foreboding, with a scarf wrapped around most of his face, only revealing his dark brown eyes staring back at us.

"Hello," Mom said with a warm smile, as she briefly looked at the man and then down at his daughter. "We have an extra pair of skates that we'd be happy to let you borrow. You can skate with us, if it's alright with your father."

"Can I? Please!" the little girl begged her father. He simply nodded, and our mother said that we would go get the skates from our car and come right back. When we returned a few minutes later, the little girl's father was off sitting on a bench watching us, and the little girl was still standing in the exact same spot. My mother helped her put on the skates, which fit perfectly. We then skated for about an hour. The little girl said her name was Kiley, but whenever Mom asked her a question, she only responded yes or no, always looking at her father, who never took his eyes off of us. Kiley looked at my mother with awe, but didn't once speak to me; instead she just glared at me.

"It's getting late, we should probably get going," Mom said, as she led us over to Kiley's father, who began to walk toward us when he saw us approaching.

"Thank you for letting me borrow your extra pair of skates." Kiley smiled at my mother, and began to fumble with the laces to take them off.

"You're welcome, Kiley. Please, you should keep them," Mom said, to everyone's surprise.

"Really? Can I?" Kiley looked at her father, uncertain what he would say.

Kiley's father never took his eyes off of my mom as he spoke through his scarf, which was still covering most of his face. "That is very generous of you." His voice was warm and alluring, and it made me wonder what he looked like; however, when he spoke, my mother froze in place. I could see from the squint in his eyes that he was smiling at her. In a split second, Mom grabbed my hand and screeched, "We have to go, now!" Before I knew it we were across the entire length of the pond and trudging up the hill to our car with our skates still on, something we had never done before. Mom practically dragged me the whole way, clinging to my hand for dear life.

"Mommy, what's wrong?" I asked once we were in the car. I could tell that she was very upset, but I couldn't figure out why.

"Everything's fine, Greer. It's getting late, and your father will be worried about us if we don't get home soon." Mom tried to act normal, to no avail. I knew Kiley's father had upset her, although I didn't understand how or why, but even at seven, I knew when to stop asking questions.

A few days later, we abruptly moved to Orlando. It was really fun to live so close to Disney World, and Darcy liked the warmer weather. We lived there for about a year. When a fire partially destroyed our house, we then moved to Phoenix. It was a nice enough place, but around the third anniversary of our arrival there, we moved yet again, to Casper, Wyoming.

Casper was our home for five great years. I couldn't believe how much I liked it. It was even more beautiful than Madison. I loved the snow, and would spend as much time outdoors as my mother would allow. Darcy continued to despise the cold weather, but she enjoyed Wyoming the four months a year it was over seventy degrees. Other than then, she stayed indoors a lot, mainly at the large local library, where she took a part-time job when she was fifteen. She loved to read, and would devour any new books she could get her hands on. Other than reading, there was not much in Casper to maintain Darcy's attention or allow her to get into trouble, much to the liking of our parents. Darcy was always a bit of a rebel, finding ways to push boundaries wherever possible. If our parents said something was black or white, she could find the shades of gray. Casper was the perfect place for her to spend the end of our junior high years and majority of high school, which can be a difficult time for a teenage girl. These are the years when a girl begins to shape who she is, or is shaped by those around her. Darcy definitely shaped herself, never allowing herself to be influenced by someone else. She knew her own mind and would make her own choices, no matter what the outcome.

Darcy, Will, and I were all shocked when our parents announced we were suddenly moving to Plano, Texas, a northern suburb of Dallas, two weeks into Darcy's and my senior year of high school. I could tell it was hard for our parents to take us away from a place we had grown to love, but they assured us it was for the best. I never quite understood why they were so vague about our moves. Darcy was not afraid to voice her objections and demand further explanation, to no gain. The week we moved to Texas, I had never seen her more angry with our parents.

Darcy

To say that I was upset with my parents upon hearing of our sudden departure for Texas would be an understatement. I was furious with them, mainly because I knew they were not telling us the whole truth. For some reason, I had always been able to tell when someone was lying, and every time we moved, our parents would not tell us the full story on why we were leaving so quickly. It was the only time they were ever deceitful with us, and it frustrated me for more reasons than I could understand.

Over the years, Greer, Will, and I had become accustomed to

making new friends, and our move to the Lone Star State was no different. Ella Mason was a sweet and insanely smart girl we met on the first day at our new school. Although destined to be valedictorian, she wasn't obnoxious about how smart she was. Instead, she was extremely kind and really quite funny, once you got to know her. Ms. Abrams, the Advanced English teacher, asked Ella to show Greer and me to the office so we could get registered for classes. Ella had grown up in Plano and seemed to know pretty much everyone at our senior high school, even though there were over twelve hundred enrolled in our grade alone.

"Make sure they sign you up for all of the advanced science and math you need, as well as AP English and Government. In regards to electives, drama, choir, and dance are good choices, but stay away from speech," Ella said as she walked us to the main office. I noticed that her shoulder length brown hair was perfectly combed and thought that, while she seemed a bit bookish, she had a nice air about her.

"Why's that?" I asked as we took in our surroundings. Plano High School was definitely the largest school we had ever attended, and it only consisted of juniors and seniors. I could tell Greer was a bit intimidated by how big it was. I acted like the size didn't bother me at all, when all I really wanted was to be back in Casper.

"The teacher's kind of weird. Not in a pervy way, just in that he's really intense and a little too passionate about speech, especially debate. He's also notorious for playing favorites," Ella whispered as we reached the office. She left us there after introducing us to the assistant principal, Mrs. Johnson, who helped us with the tedious task of arranging our new class schedules.

Within a few weeks, we were settling into the rhythm of our new life in Plano and had begun to make friends. I became friends with one girl, Mallory Jenkins, who appeared to dislike Greer from the moment she laid eyes on her. I could tell the feeling was mutual, as Greer tried to avoid her as much as possible. Mallory was a fair-haired beauty and fair-weather friend if there ever was one. She was extremely popular and headed up a pretty mean-spirited clique. They picked on people, used people, and pretty much were all-around jerks. Her clan was mostly made up of clones of herself, and she kept them on a tight leash.

Greer had become good friends with Ella and her close friends Mia, Rebecca, Katie, and Sloan. She and I ended up in most of the same AP classes with them. They had all been friends since elementary school and were pretty nice.

To Greer's surprise, I floated between Mallory's group and Ella's group pretty seamlessly. Greer knew I had an uncanny ability to spot liars and fakes as soon as I met them, so it baffled her, at the time, why I would ever become friends with Mallory. I knew she thought I wanted to put some distance between her and me. That wasn't the case at all. I realized I had to become friends with Mallory in order to protect Greer when, on the third day at our new school, I overheard their conversation in the bathroom. I could tell she had Greer in her sights when I heard her snidely ask, "You're Darcy's twin sister?"

"Yes," Greer replied cautiously as she continued to wash her hands. I waited in the stall, knowing they were unaware of my presence.

"Hmm, you look nothing alike," she sneered as she looked her up and down and then abruptly walked out of the bathroom. It was true; Greer and I hardly even looked like we were related. We had grown to the same height (5'9") and possessed the same thin build as our mother, but Greer still looked more like her, having received her finer, long blonde locks and her bright blue eyes. I still had my thick red hair from childhood, which I wore in long layers to my mid-back, and green eyes.

I knew Mallory was trying to mess with Greer's head and I wanted to know why, so I decided to become friends with her, which was rather easy to do. I really only had to speak with her every so often, and she considered me one of her converts. I knew she thought it was only a matter of time before I'd be following her around like her little minions, but I had other plans.

Before long, we had all settled into our new lives in Plano. The weather was very nice, and the people (for the most part) were even nicer. It seemed like a good place to finish high school, assuming we didn't have another abrupt move. Our younger brother Will had adjusted to life as a sophomore, having already made friends through soccer. Our father enjoyed his new job as the director of a non-profit that helped homeless families in the Dallas/Ft. Worth area. It didn't pay a lot, none of my father's non-profit jobs had, but that did not really seem to affect us. We had always lived a modest upper-middle class existence. Our father's grandparents had been extremely wealthy, and had left him with what I believed to be a comfortable trust fund, but that was never really discussed.

We never knew how much money we had; our parents always taught us economy, especially through their own purchasing choices, but we also never went without anything we needed or really wanted. On our seventeenth birthday, our parents surprised Greer and me with a two year old, bright red Volkswagen Beetle. It was in great condition and had low mileage. It was a good car for us to share.

Our father loved his work; he was passionate about helping others, as was our mother. She had never worked outside the house, but took great pride in taking care of her three children and creating a home where we all felt safe, loved, and a bit overprotected. She volunteered wherever possible, and had always been very involved with our schools' parent organizations. Once I had complained about how often she was at our junior high in Casper, accusing her of always checking up on us, to which Mom replied, "It's my responsibility to make sure you're in a safe environment, and the best way for me to do that is to know firsthand the people you're around." This resulted in an immediate eye roll, as my thirteen year old self stomped off. Our mother's ability to keep close tabs on us had worked well when we were younger, but as seventeen year old seniors, it had become more difficult for her to keep a tight rein on us, especially me. While our mother knew all about Ella and her crew, she knew nothing of Mallory and hers.

However, I wasn't the only one in my family to keep a particular friend a secret from our parents. I noticed Greer had failed to mention to our mom a friend she had made in physics. Liam Alexander was the first guy to speak to Greer at our new school; the rest just stared at her or drooled over her. He sat behind her in class, and offered to let her borrow his book during our first week. I took a seat across the room, and couldn't help but smile when I saw the way she blushed when Liam spoke to her. I hadn't seen her act that way towards a boy since her middle school crush Derek had first spoken to her. I wasn't surprised when I heard a few weeks later that Liam and a couple of his friends had begun sitting with her, Ella, Mia, and Sloan at lunch, but I also knew that would put Greer even more in Mallory's sights, since she had dated Liam briefly the previous year.

Chapter Two

Greer

I was trying to keep my crush on Liam Alexander to myself, mainly because I knew he would never be interested in me. He was handsome, in a classic sort of way. He had dark hair, and sky blue eyes, which were a little hard not to stare at or get lost in. He was tall, around 6'3", and had an athletic build. He was the senior captain of the varsity soccer team, something I found out from Ella, Mia, and Sloan at lunch during my second week at our new school.

"So you met Liam, huh?" Sloan asked, with a smile.

"He's so handsome!" Mia chimed in.

"And nice," Ella said, glancing towards where Liam sat with two of his friends just a few lunch tables away. I did my best not to look, but found it difficult, as he sat right where I could see him and he could see me. At least once every lunch period since I had arrived, our eyes had met and we had exchanged smiles. Every time it happened, my heart went aflutter.

"And single, but look out for his crazy, mean ex." Sloan laughed, but there was some seriousness in her voice.

"What do you mean?" I asked, trying not to show too much interest.

"Last year, he kinda went out with Mallory Jenkins, but broke up with her after about a month," Ella said, with a quick glance across the cafeteria in the direction of Mallory and her crew. From what I gathered about Mallory, I guessed that had probably not gone over so well with her.

Seeing Mallory across the room, I was glad Darcy was in a different lunch period, where she sat with Katie and Rebecca. The less she was around Mallory the better, I thought. Darcy had always possessed an intuition for what people were really like, which was why I was so surprised when she became friends with Mallory, who clearly was not a nice person. Darcy was never really friends with any of the mean girls we had come across over the years. Instead, on occasion, she found herself holding her own against them. Darcy was not someone to ever be crossed or to allow someone she loved to be crossed. If someone made her really mad, then look out—she could and had completely obliterated people before. It seemed to come naturally for her. I had seen it firsthand, and to be quite honest, it scared me.

Luckily, Darcy hung out with Mallory only occasionally, and Mallory pretty much ignored me during that first month, when I sat with Ella and company at lunch. That, however, changed in late September, when Liam asked if he and his friends could join us at our table.

We all just stared at them for a moment. I was in complete shock that they wanted to sit with us, and found myself unable to speak.

"Sure," Ella said, and gave me a quick smile as she gestured to the chair next to me. Liam sat down along with his friends. Mia and Sloan scooted in a little closer to Ella to give Elliot and Nathan and their large trays of food plenty of room.

"Thanks," Liam replied, as he briefly smiled at me and then turned his attention to the plate of spinach leaves Mia was eating. In return, she spent the rest of the lunch period explaining the benefits of veganism. After that, I was fairly certain they would not join us again for lunch, but then the next day, and every day for the rest of the week, they asked to sit with us, until it just became the new norm. The guys, especially Liam, were funny and charming and a welcome addition to our table. Our new lunchmates, however, did not escape Mallory's notice, as she constantly glared at me from across the cafeteria. I tried to ignore her.

A couple of weeks after Liam and his friends had begun to sit with us, the school was abuzz about Homecoming. I had not said anything about it, because I believed Liam just wanted to be friends and I didn't want to embarrass myself by fawning over a boy. I did my best to not show anything but a strictly platonic interest in him. My friends, however, were certain Liam liked me, which I thought was ridiculous, and much to my great embarrassment, they tried to help things along anyways.

At one particularly agonizing lunch, Sloan directly asked Liam who he was taking to Homecoming. Liam replied that he had an out-of-town soccer tournament that weekend, and that, unfortunately, he had promised his parents that he would not date during soccer season, since he was trying to get recruited to play in college the following year. As he told Sloan this, I could feel his eyes glance my way; I could not bring myself to look at him, as I knew my cheeks were flushed and that I would not be able to play it cool, no matter how much I tried. After that conversation, my friends were more convinced than ever that he liked me, but I just couldn't allow myself to believe it.

Ella's crew and Darcy and I ended up going to the Homecoming game in a large group, and skipping out on the dance in lieu of a girls' movie night and slumber party at Darcy's and my house.

The fall passed quickly, and Liam and I became closer friends, talking and joking in the classes we shared and at lunch every day. Before I knew it, winter break was upon us. The weather felt nothing like the winters I was used to. Darcy and I hung out with our friends a lot over the break, including Elliot, who I noticed was spending a lot more time in one-on-one conversations with Ella. Liam was gone the entire break on a trip with his parents, and I was anxious to see him when we returned to school in January.

The first day back proved to be exciting, when another set of twins enrolled at our senior high. I had heard all morning about the brother and sister, Lorcan and Kieran Smith, who had apparently moved from Los Angeles.

"Why would anyone move from L.A. to Plano?" Sloan wondered aloud at lunch.

"I hear they are so stylish," Mia replied excitedly. Mia was the budding fashionista in our group.

"I heard the girl's hot!" Nathan blubbered, his mouth stuffed full with a cheeseburger. Obviously, Mia's lecture on his first day at our table had fallen on deaf ears.

"I heard the guy's not so bad himself," laughed Sloan, as she motioned for Nathan to wipe the corners of his mouth, which were covered in mustard and ketchup. Embarrassed, Nathan quickly did so.

Oddly enough, no one in our group had seen them yet, but that all changed in a matter of minutes. About halfway into our fifty minute lunch period, we saw Mallory stand to greet our new classmates. I knew immediately that was a bad sign—these poor new kids, already being sucked into Mallory's web.

The cafeteria stopped in its tracks when Kieran walked in. Everyone at our table froze when we were able to see her. Nathan had heard wrong; she wasn't hot. She was one of the most beautiful girls I had ever seen in person. She looked like she had just stepped out of a fashion magazine, just as Mia had been told.

Kieran was tall and thin, with beautiful long brunette hair. She was so graceful in the way that she walked, it looked like she was dancing. However, an odd feeling struck me the moment I first saw her. I felt like I knew her from somewhere, but it was not a face someone would forget. I tried to shake the feeling off, but it didn't seem to want to go away.

"Wow, she's gorgeous!" exclaimed Ella, the first to speak at our table. Elliot and Nathan sat with their mouths hanging open. I observed Liam closely as he looked up, watched Kieran briefly, and then turned and caught me staring at him, to which he smiled.

My eyes were still locked on Liam's when Sloan, Mia, and Ella, in unison, exclaimed, "Ohhh myyy!" I looked over to see that Lorcan had just walked in and joined his sister at Mallory's table. The cafeteria rumbled with chatter, all no doubt discussing the exciting new additions to our senior class.

Lorcan was extremely handsome, with the same dark hair as his sister. He was tall, athletic-looking, and very stylish. He appeared smooth and confident in the way he held himself.

I was still staring at him and his sister, trying to figure out why she seemed so familiar, when I felt the intense gaze of someone else upon me. I glanced back over to Liam and looked right into his piercing blue eyes. "Looks like someone caught your attention," Liam said, half-laughing, half-serious.

"I could say the same of you," I retorted, feeling myself blush slightly.

"No, he's not really my type," Liam joked, and flashed a sweet crooked smile while cutting his eyes downward and then back up at me. I knew then I was in a full on blush.

Before I could come up with a clever response, Mia started choking on her spinach salad. Ella handed her water and Sloan gently slapped her back. Within a few seconds, we realized it was not a 'gone down the wrong pipe' kind of choking. It was the real deal, and as Mia stood and grabbed her throat furiously, she was barely able to make a sound. Liam jumped up, said he knew the Heimlich maneuver, and began moving around the table towards Mia. Before he could get there, all of a sudden, I saw Lorcan behind Mia, with his arms around her waist, performing perfect upward squeeze thrusts into her abdomen. After two, the spinach was dislodged, and Mia was coughing. Our AP English teacher, Ms. Abrams, who had seen what was happening from across the cafeteria, finally reached our table. She offered to escort Mia to the nurse's office to be checked out.

"Thank you," Mia whispered to Lorcan, as she was slowly led away by Ms. Abrams. Lorcan gave her what had to be the most dazzling smile I had ever seen. If Mia didn't feel faint from the choking, then his smile would certainly do the trick, I thought to myself. Lorcan then looked right at me. After a moment, I forced myself to tear my gaze away from his intoxicating green eyes. That was when I realized the entire cafeteria was staring at us. Everyone at our table was still standing. We slowly began to sit back down, as the rest of the cafeteria resumed their conversations. No one had said anything to Lorcan. Everyone but me just stared at him, and it soon became awkward.

Finally, I looked back up at him and said, "That was amazing. You followed perfect protocol for the Heimlich." It was certainly not my best first line ever.

"Thank you. I was happy to help," Lorcan replied, with a slightly lower wattage smile, but with a tilt of his head that made his green eyes sparkle in the cafeteria fluorescent lighting. Sloan and Ella were open-mouth gawking at him. It was kind of funny and embarrassing at the same time.

"Would you like to join us?" I asked, trying to be polite, but also trying to keep Mallory's claws out of him. All the boys at our table (especially Liam) shot me a look that said, "You've got to be kidding me," while the girls looked especially hopeful he would say yes.

"Thank you for the kind offer, but I should probably rejoin my sister and her friends. Maybe I'll see you later," Lorcan replied kindly, before he shot what I thought was a rather piercing look at Liam, who had moved noticeably closer to me. As Lorcan walked towards Mallory's table, I noticed she looked triumphantly back in our direction.

"That was amazing!" Sloan stated loudly and probably before Lorcan was out of earshot.

"Perhaps, I am Mr. Wonderful," Nathan said mockingly. Sloan softly punched him in the shoulder as we all watched Lorcan walk back to his table.

"I don't see why he had to rush over; Liam could have handled it," Elliot said, as he slapped Liam on the left shoulder.

Liam smiled but didn't say anything. Our lunch soon came to an end, and we all headed off to AP English. Little did we know, our eventful lunch was just the beginning.

"I heard poor Mia almost choked to death on her spinach salad!" Rebecca stated, slamming her books down on her desk next to me.

"I heard the new hottie, Lorcan, had to give her mouth to mouth resuscitation!" exclaimed Katie, breathless as she sat down to the left of Rebecca.

"Mia wishes. Heck, we all wish," Ella said with a laugh, as she shot me a look. I blushed and was actually glad Liam and his friends were sitting across the room and could not hear our conversation, although I did notice him look over whenever someone laughed, which was pretty often.

Ella was about to tell Katie and Rebecca the whole story of what happened when Mallory walked in with Lorcan and Kieran.

"They're in our class!" shrieked Katie, loud enough for everyone to hear. Katie was a lot of things, but subtle was not one of them. She had also not seen them until then, but had heard what they looked like and knew in an instant who they were.

"You would think the Duke and Duchess of Cambridge had arrived," Darcy said with a smirk as she slid sideways into her seat in front of me, so she could more easily talk to us. Ella laughed and Katie rolled her eyes in a funny way. We watched as Mallory introduced Lorcan and Kieran to Ms. Abrams. Mallory wasn't in our class, thankfully, but she was apparently showing the new students where they needed to go. Uncharacteristically considerate, I thought, or perhaps, more likely, very strategic. There was no doubt in my mind that our new classmates were going to be a hit at our school, and just as Mallory had tried to rope Darcy into her little clique, I could see her doing the exact same thing with Lorcan and Kieran.

As Mallory left the classroom, she gave Darcy a quick smile, and Darcy responded with a slight nod. She shot me a glare that could have leveled a three-story building. I knew she didn't like me, but her attitude towards me was becoming a bit ridiculous.

A couple of students were absent, including poor Mia, so, aside from a few empty desks at the front of the class, there was one empty seat in front of Darcy and one empty seat next to Liam. I wondered which seats Lorcan and Kieran would choose. I thought Lorcan would want to make some guy friends, and choose to sit near Liam and his buddies, and Kieran would want to make some more girl friends and sit next to us. Everyone held their breath as Ms. Abrams gave them their copies of the novel we had read over break and asked them to find a seat. Kieran and Lorcan gave each other a quick look and then, to my surprise and the thrill of every girl sitting around me (barring Darcy), Lorcan sat down in front of her. Unable to comprehend the slight breach of teenage etiquette, I knew the guys were thrilled as well to have Kieran sit near them.

"Great," I said gruffly under my breath. I refused to look over at Liam to see his reaction to Kieran taking the seat next to him. How perfect, I thought, to have the gorgeous, stylish, and probably extremely charming new girl batting her eyes at Liam all class period.

"I'm sorry, I can sit somewhere else if you prefer," Lorcan said as he began to stand. Every girl around me (except Darcy, who laughed under her breath) shot me a look like I had better fix the situation at once, or else I would find myself friendless in under a minute.

"No, no, no, no, no," I replied quickly. "I was just talking to myself. I just realized I haven't read as much of the book as I'd hoped to by today." I grimaced at my pathetic lie and immediately felt guilty. I had already read the entire book, since it had been one of the two assigned as homework over the break. Darcy smirked, fully aware I was not telling the truth. Lorcan smiled at me as he sat back down, and I had a feeling he knew I was lying as well.

"Hi, I'm Katherine," Katie said breathlessly, leaning over Rebecca as if she wasn't there. The rest of my friends and I chuckled, because Katie never used her full first name, except when she was trying to impress someone.

"And I'm Rebecca," Rebecca said, as she blocked Lorcan's view of Katie. I tried not to laugh as Katie poked Rebecca really hard in the left shoulder. Rebecca smiled through the pain.

Ella spoke up to introduce the non-crazy part of our cohort. "I'm Ella, and this is Darcy and…"

"Greer," Lorcan said, looking past Darcy and directly into my eyes, with the same dazzling smile from before.

"Alright class, let's get started," Ms. Abrams said, signaling for conversations to end. Darcy quickly glanced at me and gave me a smile that made me desperately want to know what she was thinking.

Ms. Abrams was, by far, my favorite teacher. She was friendly and helpful, but she had high expectations, and she didn't let her students fail for a lack of trying. She seemed to be more what I thought a college professor would be like. She ran every class as an open discussion, never lecturing, expecting everyone to participate, and she could tell in less than thirty seconds of someone opening their mouth if they were prepared for class or not. After witnessing one instance, in which it was obvious a student called upon had not read a page for that class period, I knew I would always be prepared for her class.

As Ms. Abrams got the class's attention, we all picked up one of the novels we were assigned to re-read over the break. Most of us had read Jane Austen's *Pride and Prejudice* our sophomore year of high school. We were surprised that Ms. Abrams wanted us to read it again, but she explained that she thought a couple of years of maturity might help us understand it a little bit better.

"Today, we are going to start with our favorite passages. Who would like to share theirs?" Ms. Abrams asked earnestly. She frequently began class that way, and oftentimes the passage chosen would dominate class discussion. If no one volunteered, then she would choose someone. It was best to have a passage and strong defense of its importance prepared for every class period.

There was silence, as no one wanted to volunteer their thoughts. Not a good sign, I thought.

"Pardon me, Ms. Abrams," Kieran spoke ever so delicately, as she raised her hand for permission to speak further.

"Yes, Kieran?" Ms. Abrams said inquisitively.

"What chapters were assigned for today?" Kieran asked with a little smile. She had to know all eyes were on her, and she appeared to love every second of it.

"Oh, sorry dear, for not telling you before. The class was to have read the entire book over the break," Ms. Abrams said, not looking surprised when Kieran spoke again.

"If it's alright with you, Ms. Abrams, I would like to offer my favorite passage." Kieran basked in the class' attention like a sunbather soaks up the sun.

"If you'd like to offer your thoughts on the novel, that would be wonderful, and most unexpected for a new student. However, please be aware that you must provide a defense of any arguments you make, and you need to stand up," Ms. Abrams said, I thought rather kindly, as an opportunity for Kieran to change her mind.

Kieran smiled confidently and rose to her feet. "My favorite passage is in chapter forty-eight, the section which contains the letter from Mr. Collins to Mr. Bennett, regarding Mr. Bennett's youngest daughter Lydia's situation."

Lorcan let out a very subtle laugh under his breath, which no one except myself and perhaps Darcy seemed to notice, as everyone else was busy trying to find the passage Kieran had referenced.

"That's an interesting choice," Ms. Abrams said. I could tell from her use of the word "interesting" that she did not believe it to be the most important passage from the book, but she appeared curious of Kieran's defense argument. "Please read the passage aloud to refresh our memories."

Kieran stood and read with great composure. Her voice, in speaking, sounded better than even the most elegant voice singing. The entire class appeared under her spell, seeming to want to applaud her even before she defended her passage selection.

"Thank you for your fine reading, Kieran. Now, would you please share with the class why you view this to be the most interesting passage from this great work of literature?" Ms. Abrams asked, appearing surprised and delighted by the enthusiasm with which Kieran read.

"Well, I believe it's the most interesting passage because in his letter to Mr. Bennett, Mr. Collins tells the truth about what others think of the Bennetts' situation. He doesn't attempt to sugarcoat anything. People often try to encourage others, in even the worst situations, such as that one, even though that really doesn't do any good in the end. Jane Austen should be applauded for making Mr. Collins, and Lady Catherine, for that matter, so honest in their statements, even if she did make the former seem a bit ridiculous." When Kieran finished speaking she sat down, as if she believed no one could possibly disagree with her argument.

"I'm confused," Elliot confessed unabashedly, even though most of the room laughed out loud.

"Well, then perhaps we should recap the context. Who would like to volunteer?" Ms. Abrams asked, looking directly at Darcy, who appeared to mentally be anywhere but English class.

"Darcy, perhaps you could recap the situation for Elliot and anyone else who did not finish reading the novel?" Ms. Abrams gave Elliot a knowing look. He blushed and looked down at his desk.

Darcy rose and replied with such poise that I had never been more in awe of her. "Lydia, the Bennetts' youngest daughter, ran off with the con-artist Mr. Wickham while she was staying with Colonel Forster and his wife in Brighton. This was a great scandal, which would ruin Lydia and her entire family, especially her four older unmarried sisters, if she and Mr. Wickham did not marry immediately. Mr. Collins, the 'ridiculous' cousin, who was also Mr. Bennett's heir and the pastor on the estate of Lady Catherine, wrote to Mr. Bennett to offer his sympathies, but also to pretty much insult him and his family in every way possible. In the letter, Mr. Collins seemed especially pleased to not be more closely associated with the scandal by not having married Elizabeth, Mr. Bennett's second eldest daughter and the heroine of the novel. The truth was, as we all know, Elizabeth flatly refused to marry him in chapter nineteen." If Kieran had commanded the room before with her pretty reading and flimsy argument, then my sister, in her confidant voice and precise recap, astonished us all, even Ms. Abrams.

That was the first time Darcy had spoken at length, in any of our classes, since beginning at our new school. She often gave short, one sentence, but intelligent answers to questions when directly asked, but she never volunteered to answer any question. She was simply too modest to display the brilliant mind I knew was in her head.

"Well done, Miss Hagen," said Ms. Abrams in a very pleased tone. Ms. Abrams always used surnames when she was particularly happy with a student's answer or comment in class. Everyone else also appeared impressed with Darcy, even more so than with Kieran. I glanced over and saw that Kieran had begun to pout.

"I'm still confused," Elliot continued, to my amazement. Everyone laughed and even Ms. Abrams managed a small chuckle. Elliot was a very nice guy, but much more athletic than academic. Not that you couldn't be both; Liam was the perfect example of how to balance sports and books. Elliot just didn't have the same interest in studying, and it was my guess that he was pressured to take advanced classes because it was what his parents wanted.

"Where'd she lose you?" Nathan asked with a laugh. Elliot turned red again and then glanced over at Ella, who gave him a sweet smile.

It was just a moment that I was sure no one else saw, but one I found to be endearing, and I was glad to see they had not noticed I had seen.

Ms. Abrams went on to explain Darcy's recap with a little more context, highlighting the whole first part of the book. After she was finished, Elliot and a few others appeared relieved and back up to speed with the discussion.

"Now that we are all on the same page, would anyone like to share any agreements or disagreements with Kieran's argument?" Ms. Abrams asked. She looked more than ready for the class discussion to move more deeply into the material. I raised my hand, unsure of what was about to come out of my mouth.

"Yes, Miss Hagen?" Ms. Abrams replied cheerfully. I had made high As on all my assignments so far and she was usually pleased with my verbal contributions in class, so she had begun to always address me formally. Darcy had teased that I had become the teacher's pet.

I rose slowly and began to figure out what I wanted to say. "I respectfully disagree with Kieran's assessment of the importance of Mr. Collins's letter to Mr. Bennett regarding Lydia's situation. I don't believe that Miss Austen, one of the most enlightened women of her time, would want anyone to take from that passage what Kieran has argued. I feel it is much more likely Miss Austen was attempting to show, in this passage, the hurt pride that Mr. Collins felt in being rejected by Elizabeth Bennett and the superiority, or I guess you could say prejudice, he and Lady Catherine felt against the Bennett family as a whole. Unfortunately, I think that people often think the terms "pride" and "prejudice" only refer to the feelings that Mr. Darcy and Elizabeth felt towards each other at times, whereas the truth is that these same emotions can be seen throughout the novel in many of the characters, as I believe they were shown here in Mr. Collins."

I quickly sat down, more nervous than I had ever been in class. Everyone was silent for what felt like an eternity. I looked quickly up at Darcy, who turned back to me and uncharacteristically gave me a smile of approval. I immediately felt better. I then glanced at Lorcan, who turned and flashed me a disarming smile. I blushed and quickly looked down. After a minute, I checked to see if Liam was also looking, but found him staring at his book. I guess I had not impressed him.

"Thank you, Miss Hagen, for your insightful comments. Kieran, would you like to offer any more of a defense for your argument?" Ms. Abrams asked with a wide smile.

Kieran stared at me with pure hatred. She stood up, curved her mouth into a devilish smile, and, never taking her eyes off of me, replied, "No, I think we should leave the discussion with Miss Hagen's argument, however naïve it might be." Lorcan shot her a silencing look, and Kieran immediately sat down, appearing very satisfied with herself.

After Kieran's snide comment, there was a small murmur throughout the classroom, but Ms. Abrams quickly guided the class to a discussion of another passage Ella had suggested from the readings. Class soon came to an end, and as I was gathering my books, I noticed that Kieran had cornered Liam. His friends were trying to edge their way into the conversation, but she only had eyes for him. I tried to ignore it and the feeling that I knew her from somewhere. Lorcan approached me and saw the direction in which I was staring.

"Please forgive my sister; she doesn't take defeat well," Lorcan said. My friends listened in on our conversation, although they pretended to talk to each other.

"I was surprised Ms. Abrams let her get away with her little remark," Darcy inserted, rather annoyed.

"I can see you're a very loyal sister, an admirable trait," Lorcan said, giving her a warm smile.

It was killing me, this sinking feeling of familiarity that I had as I looked back over at Kieran, and it seriously annoyed me that she was so obviously flirting with Liam.

"Where are you from?" I blurted out.

"Los Angeles," he replied, returning his gaze to me.

"Is that where you were born? How long did you live there? Have you lived anywhere else?" I asked in rapid succession, as all of the questions I wanted answered came flooding out.

"You certainly are inquisitive," Kieran said, as she, unfortunately, joined our conversation. Darcy gave her a warning look, to which Kieran just smiled. It had been a long time since I had seen Darcy so protective of me.

"What did you think of today's class discussion, Darcy? Surely you're not as naïve as your sister? Even if Jane Austen's intentions were to be interpreted as Greer suggested, surely you can see my side of the argument?" Kieran asked boldly. Lorcan appeared annoyed with his sister, but curious to hear Darcy's response. I could not help but think this was some sort of test, and I could sense that Darcy felt the same way.

"I suppose it's possible that some people lack the ability to encourage others in tough situations, but I believe it is much more likely that those people choose to think of their own interests, and find satisfaction in others' moments of despair. People like that are deplorable, even if their pretty faces suggest otherwise," Darcy replied, with a fierce look that made Kieran's dark brown eyes widen.

Kieran's face contorted into such anger, I thought she was going to lunge for Darcy's throat, but in a split second, she composed herself, and all she said in return was, "How disappointing."

Darcy turned to me and said, "Let's go," and we left for our next class. The remaining three periods were a blur. I was anxious to talk to Darcy after school about what had happened in English.

Chapter Three

Darcy

As I waited after school for Greer by the big fountain out front, I flipped through my copy of *Pride and Prejudice*. I was drawn to the section Kieran Smith had discussed in class. From the moment she referred to Greer as naïve, I knew I didn't like her, but what bothered me more was the unshakeable feeling that I knew her and her brother. It made no sense—I had never met them before, but there was no mistake in my mind and in my heart that I had some sort of connection to them. It was also obvious, to me at least, that they had taken a very real interest in Greer, but I didn't know why. Lorcan's attraction to Greer was undeniable, although I knew it would be to her, and Kieran's instant loathing of her made Mallory's look like child's play. Kieran would be the one I would have to protect Greer from, that I was certain of. I pondered over all of this as Greer approached, catching me off guard.

"Hey," Greer said, as she looked over my shoulder at the book I was holding. I knew she wanted to talk, but I had too much going on in my head and was in no mood.

"Are you ready?" I replied sharply. I quickly put away my book, and threw my backpack over my shoulder.

"Sure," Greer said quickly, and I knew she had taken the hint.

She followed behind me, dodging cars hastily fleeing the parking lot, until we reached our car. It was my day to drive. We usually rotated turns, but instead, I tossed her the keys and headed for the passenger side without saying a word. She knew something was bothering me, and I knew she would try to get to the bottom of it, but she also knew me well enough to let it go for the time being.

As we pulled through the alley and into the garage, I saw that no one else was home yet, and decided to head straight to my room so I could be by myself and think. Before Greer had the ignition turned off, I was out of the car and headed for the door to the house. I bounded up the stairs and was in my room in a matter of seconds.

I threw my backpack on the floor and myself on my bed. I don't know how long I laid there, trying to process everything that was going through my mind. First, I knew that Kieran and Lorcan Smith were up to something, and that Greer seemed to be at the center of it. My intuitive side would not let me believe anything else. Second, I could not escape the feeling that I knew Kieran and Lorcan Smith from somewhere, and that really worried me. Their familiarity was eerie and simply inexplicable; at least, I thought it was, until I realized who just might be able to help me make sense of it—my parents. Over the years, they had warned us, especially Greer and me, that if we ever met someone that seemed to take a sudden interest in us without a good explanation, or if we ever had a feeling that we knew someone we had just met but couldn't explain why, we should let them know at once. Kieran and Lorcan Smith fit both of those categories, but I knew I could not tell Mom and Dad. Whenever they gave us that lecture over the years, I always knew there was more to it than them just trying to protect us. I believed they were hiding something from us, but what that was, I could never figure out.

In that moment, I knew what I had to do. I could hear Mom and Will downstairs, and knew I had to act quickly. I made my way through the bathroom that adjoined my room to Greer's, and knocked on the door.

"Yes?" Greer answered. I opened the door and found her sitting in her favorite old reading chair with a book in her hand.

"Mom and Will just got home and Dad will be home soon," I said quickly, as Greer looked over at her clock. She seemed surprised that it was already 5:30 p.m. "Do not mention the new kids Lorcan and Kieran to any of them," I said as nicely as I could while still making a command.

"I don't understand," she replied, appearing genuinely confused as to why I would want to hide what happened today, or the fact that we had two new kids at our school.

"Greer, please, just do this for me," I said emphatically. I never asked anything of her, so I knew she would reluctantly agree, but I also knew I would have to eventually explain why I wanted to keep the Smiths a secret.

We could hear Mom and Will laughing as they came up the stairs. "Okay, but you have to explain this to me later," Greer whispered, and I grimaced. "It's my condition," she finished with a smile. I nodded quickly, as our mother knocked on the door.

Mom appeared genuinely surprised and happy to see the two of us in Greer's room as she entered.

"Hi sweethearts!" she said, as she walked towards me and gave me a big hug. Our mother was a big hugger. She believed in showing affection, even to the point of embarrassment, and never shied away from demonstrating her deep love for all of us. I typically half-hugged her back, as I was not usually one for displays of affection.

"How was your day?" Mom asked, as she gently swept my long bangs out of my eyes.

"Fine," I replied tersely and looked down. Mom sighed slightly.

She knew there was no use trying to get any more information out of me. She smiled at me anyways and then moved towards Greer. Greer stood to give her a big hug in return.

"And how was your day?" Mom said, as she leaned back and looked right into her eyes.

I narrowed my eyes at Greer to make sure she knew I expected her to keep her promise. After an awkward second, she uncharacteristically replied that her day was simply good, and then she sat back down in her chair. Our mom looked puzzled, as Greer usually retold her entire day within five minutes of seeing her; well, everything except anything about Liam. She still kept her friendship with him a secret from our parents, which made me think there was some hope of her keeping our secret about the Smiths.

"Anything interesting happen?" Mom inquired, sensing something was off.

"No, it was just a normal, boring day in high school," I replied quickly in Greer's place. Mom looked briefly over at me and then back at Greer, waiting for her to speak.

"Yeah, just a normal, boring day. Nothing unusual or interesting at all," Greer said, rather unconvincingly. I rolled my eyes slightly where she could see, but Mom couldn't. Mom appeared to want to ask more questions, but just then, Will came barreling through the open door.

"What's up?" he said, as he fell onto Greer's bed.

"Ughh! Get your filthy self off my bed! Gross!" Greer yelled. He had just come from junior varsity soccer practice and smelled of sweat and dirt.

"Calm down," Will said, laughing as he got up quickly and pretended to dust off her comforter. Mom and I tried not to laugh, while Greer still appeared annoyed.

"Go and take a quick shower. Your father will be home in a few minutes. He's bringing home dinner," Mom said with a smile to Will. As soon as she said the word "dinner," he was out the door and headed for his room. He was never one to miss a meal, and to be honest, I don't know where the food went. He could eat everything in our house and he would still be all muscle. Will had gone through a big growth spurt during the previous summer, and he had shot up to over six feet tall. He had been lifting weights a lot and had filled out, looking more like an eighteen year old than his true age of fifteen, although he certainly acted his own age. Will had our father's dark hair and his bright blue eyes and looked more like him every day.

"Greer, I saw that you emptied the dishwasher. Darcy, you still need to take out the trash," Mom said as she walked towards the bedroom door. "Come downstairs and let's get everything ready for dinner," Mom requested sweetly, and left the room.

As soon as she was out of earshot, I whisper-yelled at Greer, "You're the worst liar I've ever seen!" Whisper-yelling was a talent in our family, at least among Greer, Will, and I. Our parents didn't like it; they thought it was the same as yelling. They said it didn't matter what the volume was, it was about the tone of voice used.

"I'll take that as a compliment!" Greer replied condescendingly.

"Just please don't say anything," I said seriously as we heard our dad come in the house and greet our mom.

Greer nodded and said, "Let's go help Mom. I'm starving and I don't want Will to eat everything before we get there!" We both laughed as we left her room.

We had reached the top of the stairs when Greer suddenly grabbed my arm to stop me from going any further. I gave her a questioning look. She gestured for me to look over the balcony into the kitchen where our parents were. Our father had wrapped our mother up in his arms and gave her a sweet kiss. It was a tender moment that we knew would end as soon as we were in sight. They weren't ones to have a lot of PDA. They kept that part of their lives just between them, which, in truth, was where it belonged.

"Great, Dad's home!" Will said, as he raced passed us and barreled down the stairs, his hair still dripping from his record-setting shower. What he meant was that he was glad dinner was ready.

Mom and Dad heard Will coming down the stairs and stopped kissing, smiled lovingly at each other, and started getting plates out for dinner. Greer and I followed Will down the stairs.

"What's for dinner?" Will asked eagerly, as he started sniffing in one of the bags he opened.

"Fajitas, and hello to you too," Dad replied with a laugh.

"Sorry, hi Dad." Will smiled and gave Dad a manly side hug.

"Hi Dad," Greer said as we entered the kitchen.

"Hi sweetheart," Dad replied and wrapped her up in a big hug. He looked over at me as I walked towards them. Greer moved away to help Mom get the drinks ready, while Dad gave me the same hug he had given Greer. I returned his hug and said hello.

"Hi darling," Dad said to me. Ever since I could remember, he called Greer sweetheart and me darling. They were our own little endearments, and even though it was a bit cheesy, I thought they were sweet. Now that our brother was getting older, he loathed Dad's term of endearment for him, which was "Big Guy." Dad used it sparingly, but when he did, Will always groaned, and the rest of us had a good laugh.

After moving to Texas, our whole family had become addicted to Mexican food, and fajitas were our favorite. As we sat down to dinner, Greer and I shared an order, as did our parents, while Will had his own, and he wolfed down almost the entire bag of chips before we had even said the blessing. He was still crunching a chip as we crossed ourselves to begin our prayer. Greer kicked him under the table, and he held the chip perfectly still in his mouth until the end of the prayer, when he finished it and frowned at her.

"Don't you know it's rude to kick someone?" Will said, as he grabbed the last chip from the bowl. Whenever we got takeout, which was about twice a week, our mother always put everything on proper dishes. She refused to serve from the takeout containers, which I found amusing.

"Don't you know it's rude to eat before the prayer and to hog all of the chips?" Greer retorted, as she tilted the bowl so he could see it was completely empty.

"I can't help it. I'm starving!" Will replied defensively with a sly smile.

"You're always starving, which is why Mom has to go to the grocery store every other day!" Greer stated sharply.

"Enough," Mom said sweetly, silencing Will and Greer.

"It's fine, I got an extra bag of chips this time," Dad said, as he got up and grabbed it from the kitchen island and emptied it into a bowl. Will began to reach for one, to which my father laughed and told him, "I think you have reached your chip quota for the night."

Will moved his hand back to his own plate. Mom looked over at him and smiled. "I made some brownies for dessert." Brownies were Will and Dad's favorite, and after she spoke, they both smiled.

"So, how was everyone's day?" Dad inquired, as he appeared to notice Mom's gaze drift towards Greer and me.

"Darcy, anything exciting happen at school today?" Dad asked as he took a drink of his lemonade.

"No, not really. Pretty much the usual stuff," I replied casually as I grabbed a few more chips.

"Greer, how about you? Anything interesting about your day?" Dad continued, hoping to get more information from her. Mom looked as if she were hoping the same thing.

"Ugh, it was, ugh, a pretty normal, ugh, day," she replied, ever so eloquently, trying to put food in her mouth as quickly as possible so she would not have to say anything else. She really was a terrible liar. Everyone at the table looked at her like she was either crazy or hiding something.

"Okay, what happened today, Greer, that you are trying to keep from us?" Mom's tone could not hide her anxiety.

I looked at her anxiously. I didn't want to lie to our parents, but I desperately wanted her to keep our secret.

"What did Darcy do?" Will asked, laughing. All of a sudden Greer got a look on her face that told me I was not going to like what she was about to say.

"It was English class," Greer began, slowly formulating her words as I glared at her, and our parents encouraged her to continue. "Darcy was called upon by Ms. Abrams, and gave an eloquent and precise summary of the passage we were discussing. Everyone was really impressed," she said, knowing I would not be happy, but she had at least kept our secret.

"That's wonderful." Mom was visibly relieved.

"Great job!" Dad said, also happy it was nothing bad. Will rolled his eyes and I continued to glare over at her, but she knew it was just for show.

"It wasn't a big deal; it was just a summary," I said, trying to downplay my contribution in class.

"I had a good day, if anyone's interested?" Will chimed in, ready to turn the attention towards himself. Little did he know, Greer and I were happy to let him have the spotlight. The rest of dinner was spent talking about Will's classes and friends, Dad's new project at work, and Mom's volunteer work at the hospital.

After dinner, I took out the trash, Greer swept the kitchen and dining room floors, and Will rinsed the dishes and loaded the dishwasher, complaining the entire time. Mom finished up some laundry and, after returning a few work-related emails, Dad settled in to watch some Dallas Stars hockey. Dad wasn't a huge sports junkie, but he did enjoy watching some games when he had a chance. Will was furiously finishing the dishes, his chore for the day, so he could join him.

Our parents had grown up on the East Coast. Dad was born and raised in Boston. Mom was born in Philadelphia and moved with her parents to Boston when she was in high school. They each talked about their childhoods some, Mom much more than Dad, but I always found it odd they never really talked about how they met and fell in love. Every once in a while we would get small bits of information. We knew they met in high school when Mom first moved to Boston, and were friends for a few years before they started dating sometime during college. They were married right after their college graduation, and Greer and I were born nine months later.

When I asked Mom once why Dad never talked about growing up or his parents, she said that he had a happy childhood and was very close to his parents, but that it was hard for him to talk about them because they died in an accident soon after he and Mom were married. I knew that Dad's paternal grandfather was still alive at the time, the one from which he received his trust fund, but he, apparently, died soon after. Both Dad and Mom were only children, and nothing was ever said about any other extended family, other than my mom's parents.

Mom's parents were great, but, unfortunately, we did not see them very often. They had moved to their beach house in North Carolina after my grandfather retired, when we were still in junior high. Whenever we saw them, which was only every few years, we met them at some destination, like Washington, D.C., which was where we had seen them the last time, when Greer and I had just turned fifteen. We never went to their house and they never came to ours, not even at Christmas. In spite of this, I knew my grandparents loved my parents and us dearly. My mom and grandma always cried so hard when they first saw each other and when it was time to say goodbye. My mother was always sad for a few days after they left, and I often wondered why we didn't see them more.

"I'm done!" Will yelled to Mom, as he hopped onto the sofa to watch the game.

"Did you wipe down the counters?" Mom asked.

"Mom, it's in the third period with three minutes left and they're tied!" Will pleaded for her to let him watch the end of the game.

"Arianna, can he do it after the game is over?" Dad asked in his most charming voice on Will's behalf.

Mom smiled at Dad as she continued to fold towels, "Yes, but if he forgets, you get to do it."

"Of course," Dad smiled and gave her a wink.

After the game was over, Will, Greer, and I all headed upstairs to finish (or, in Will's case, start) our homework. Around ten, I went downstairs to get some water, and when I entered the kitchen, I overheard my parents whispering to one another in the family room. I didn't mean to eavesdrop, but as soon as I heard my name, I couldn't help it.

"I think Greer and Darcy are keeping something from us," Mom said nervously.

"Arianna, they're teenage girls, I'm sure they keep lots of things from us." Dad tried to reassure Mom, which did not work.

"No, there's something wrong; I can feel it. Do you think that..."

Dad interrupted her. "No, I don't think so. We were very careful about the move, very strategic about the place we chose."

"I know, I just feel like something's wrong, more than before." Mom seemed really worried.

"We have to trust the girls. We have told them what to watch out for without revealing too much. We have to trust that they will listen to us and do what we have asked," Dad replied, so confident we would do the right thing that it put a knot in my stomach.

"I know you're right, but I can't help wanting to protect my girls," Mom cried, as Dad wrapped her up in a hug.

"Our girls," he whispered, to which she smiled and buried her head in his chest.

I turned quietly and went back up the stairs and straight into Greer's room without even knocking. She was in her reading chair again, this time working on her physics homework.

I sat down on her bed, more convinced than ever that Mom and Dad were hiding something from us. I was determined to find out what it was.

Greer just looked at me as I silently stared at the floor. I couldn't decide if I was going to tell her about the conversation I had just overheard. I felt like I really couldn't until it all made more sense to me. There was no reason to make her worry needlessly.

Finally, she spoke first, asking, "Why do you want to keep Lorcan and Kieran a secret from Mom and Dad?"

"They know we're hiding something. I don't feel comfortable not telling them about my day and keeping secrets. That's not who I am," Greer continued.

"What are we hiding? The fact that there are two new students at our school? Mom and Dad can't know everyone at our school. We don't even know everyone at our school," I said, trying to reason my way out of any guilt.

"Mom and Dad told us that if we ever met someone that we didn't know but we felt like we did know them somehow, then we should tell them right away," Greer replied quickly.

"You feel that way too?" I asked in disbelief.

Greer seemed surprised by my response, and she became visibly nervous. "Really, it's just Kieran, but I kind of get a strange vibe from Lorcan."

"Yeah, you need to watch out for him." I laughed, trying to lessen my own growing anxiety.

"What do you mean?" Greer, not surprisingly, seemed taken aback by my implication.

"Don't act like you don't know what I am talking about!" I laughed harder.

"That's ridiculous," Greer said seriously.

"Is it?" I asked, raising my eyebrows at her.

She shook off my insinuation and tried to get back to her point. "So, if you feel like you know them somehow, and I feel that way as well, then I think we should definitely tell Mom and Dad."

"I think when Mom and Dad said that, they were talking about adults, not kids our own age. It was when we were little and they were teaching us about strangers," I said, trying to reassure her that we weren't doing anything wrong, although I couldn't be certain.

"But, they've often reminded us of that, especially whenever we've moved to a new place," Greer replied.

I positioned myself on the end of Greer's bed next to her and asked, "Greer, haven't you ever felt like Mom and Dad are hiding something from us?"

She didn't answer, but her eyes told me that perhaps she did.

"There's something going on here. It's like we have this big puzzle, and a lot of the pieces are missing. I want to figure out what's going on, and I have this strange feeling that Lorcan and Kieran might be connected somehow," I said as I grabbed her hand. She knew I was serious and that this meant a lot to me, because I rarely showed affection towards anyone.

"I think Mom and Dad are just trying to protect us," Greer answered, trying to defend them.

"I'm sure they are, but from what? They can't protect us forever. We're not little kids anymore," I retorted impatiently.

"I know, I just don't like keeping secrets." Greer looked down at her hands, the guilt showing on her face.

"Really? I don't think you've ever mentioned Liam to them. Besides, now there might be a little love triangle between you, your athletic lunch buddy, and the mysterious new guy, who everyone's drooling over," I replied with a smile as she blushed.

"I don't know what you're talking about. Liam and I are just friends and I have barely even spoken to Lorcan," Greer replied defensively.

"Okay, whatever. Just think about this—what if we do tell Mom and Dad about the new kids and then we had to up and move again suddenly for some lame reason? You'd never know how your love triangle might turn out," I teased. I knew I hit a soft spot, as Greer certainly didn't want to move again.

"Okay, I won't say anything to Mom and Dad about Lorcan and Kieran for now, but if something strange happens, then I reserve the right to change my mind." Greer said, to my great relief.

Chapter Four

Greer

I kept my promise and didn't say anything to our parents about Lorcan and Kieran, even though I constantly felt guilty about keeping them a secret. By the end of their first week, Lorcan and Kieran's class schedules had been completely re-arranged, and Lorcan was in every one of the same classes Darcy and I shared, excluding choir. He was also in my speech class. Kieran was now in government and English with us, and she was also in Darcy's psychology class and had been switched to Darcy's lunch period.

School soon resumed its normal pace after winter break, except most of the guys now drooled over Kieran and the girls swooned if Lorcan even breathed in their direction. We finished *Pride and Prejudice* in English by the end of the first week back. Kieran had kept her opinions to herself, for the most part, and didn't speak to Darcy or me in the classes we shared. Lorcan still sat in close proximity to us in English and our other classes, but not right next to us as he had that first day. I had noticed that Darcy had moved to seats much closer to mine in all of the classes we shared, which was fine with me, except for in physics. Liam sat right behind me, and I didn't want Darcy to overhear our conversations.

Lorcan still sat with Mallory's clique at lunch, and I hadn't thought to ask Darcy whom Kieran sat with during their lunch period. To be honest, Kieran had kind of fallen off my radar, since it had become clear that Liam was not all that interested in her. Whenever she tried to talk to him in English, he gave her kind, but brief, answers. I often found him looking towards my side of the classroom, which always created a fluttering sensation in my stomach. I was beginning to think that he might actually like me when a strange turn of events occurred. Apparently, it was group project time at our high school, as three teachers between Darcy and I announced major assignments that would be due at the end of the spring semester.

I never minded group project work, as long as the students were allowed to pick their own partners. Unfortunately, our teachers preferred the model of assigning partners, except Ms. Abrams, of course. In English, we were asked to pick a partner and select a novel that neither of us had read. We were to pick a supporting character and discuss his or her impact on the main character, and how the story would be different if the author had not created the character.

As soon as the assignment was made, people started pairing up. Quickly, Katie and Rebecca and Ella and Mia moved closer to one another to use free class time to discuss the assignment. I looked around, trying to figure out whom I wanted to work with before all of the good partners were gone; I saw Lorcan look up at me and smile. How was it possible that he did not have a partner yet? Like everyone, I had noticed the first day how incredibly good-looking Lorcan was, but as time passed, he became this force that I encountered daily. His charming and somewhat mischievous smile and his intoxicating eyes made him hard not to stare at. I had done my best to remain composed around him, but almost every other girl melted in his presence—with the exception of Darcy, of course.

Lorcan was seated one row over and near the front of the room.

As he rose to come towards me, Darcy turned around and demanded, "We're going to work together."

I was very surprised, as she had never wanted to work on a project with me before, and over the years there had been plenty of opportunities. "Really?" I replied, not even trying to hide my shock. I glanced back over to Lorcan and saw him returning to his seat. He was far enough away that I was sure he didn't hear Darcy ask to work with me, but I guess from our nonverbals, he figured out we were going to be partners. I looked back at Darcy and nodded, and we began to discuss the assignment. I felt a little disappointed to not get the chance to get to know Lorcan a little better. My disappointment wouldn't last long.

Later that day in my speech class, we began a section on refutational speaking, aka debate-style speaking, that apparently was going to last the whole semester. Our speech teacher, Mr. Ellsworth, was much more authoritarian than Ms. Abrams, so it did not surprise me that we were assigned partners. No more than one set of partners could debate a particular topic, so once we met with our partners, we had to decide on a topic quickly, as they would be approved on a first come, first serve basis.

Ella was right when she warned Darcy and me about Mr. Ellsworth. He was very intense, and he took the art of public speaking very seriously—especially debate. Given how long we were going to spend on the subject, I knew that by the end of the semester, I would know every nuance of debate style speaking. "There is no greater skill than being able to form an articulate, persuasive argument," he would often remind us. Aside from being very commanding, he was tall and not bad looking, but he rarely smiled, which made him appear gruff.

"Greer and Lorcan, you will work together," Mr. Ellsworth said, as he gave Lorcan and I this strange, brooding look.

"That was weird," I whispered softly to myself, as I looked up at Lorcan, who sat diagonally to my front left. Lorcan gave me a quizzical look and then his usual disarming smile. This may be trouble, I thought to myself as I smiled back at him.

Lorcan gathered his books and moved towards me, pulling up the empty desk beside me that had been left vacant by my neighbor, who had been assigned a partner across the room.

A million things flooded my mind on what I should say. The couple of times I had spoken to Lorcan, I had come across less than eloquent. Now I was going to work on an assignment with him for an entire semester, so I had to get my act together. Just be calm, I thought, and act like it is no big deal. Why was it a big deal? There was no doubt that he was really good looking and charming and had pretty much every girl in school crushing on him, but what did I know about him? I knew much more about Liam—what a great guy he was, how he volunteered in the community with his family, how he worked at a camp for special needs kids in the summers, in addition to life guarding. It made sense that I would have developed some feelings for Liam, but not for Lorcan. Everything that made my stomach flutter for him was superficial, something my parents taught my siblings and me not to be.

As Lorcan sat down and gave me his best smile, I decided that I would not swoon. I would keep my wits about me and act like my normal self, and that if there were any further feelings to be developed for him, they would be based on his character, not his charm.

"Hi, I just realized that we have never been properly introduced. I am Lorcan Smith," he said, to which I nodded in return. He continued, "I, of course, already know your name." And I know your name, as does everyone, I thought to myself, as I tried to figure out how to best break through the charming facade he was hiding behind.

I decided I would start with just talking about the assignment, and then as we worked more together, I would try to uncover more information about him. I smiled at him and said, "We should probably pick a topic before all of the good ones are taken. What are you interested in debating?"

"Please, ladies first: I would love to hear your thoughts regarding a topic," he replied, oozing charm. If I weren't careful, I knew I would find myself swimming in it, or worse, drowning. Sitting close to him, I could see that he was, by far, the most handsome guy I had ever seen in person. Liam was extremely good-looking, I thought, but there was not a flaw on Lorcan's face. He was perfectly shaven and had no hint of acne, which, for teenage boys, was some great feat. His hair was a perfect mess, which was the latest trend, and his bright green eyes, in contrast with his tanned skin, made him something to behold.

I listed off some various topics I thought Mr. Ellsworth might approve. "Those are all very interesting topics that would be worthy of a debate." Lorcan smiled, but I got the feeling he already had a topic in mind.

"What suggestions do you have?" I inquired.

"I thought perhaps we might debate the latest advancements in medical research," he said. He cut his eyes up at me with a smile that I was sure usually got him whatever he wanted.

Remain calm and breathe, he is just a boy, I thought to myself. I tried to hide my heart racing as I replied coolly, "That's interesting as well, but a little vague—did you have a specific area of medical research in mind?"

"I thought we might debate performance enhancing drugs," Lorcan said in a hopeful tone.

"Oh, that is definitely a debate-worthy topic, but don't you think it might be a bit overdone?" I was genuinely surprised Lorcan had picked such an unoriginal topic.

"I think our debate would be unique if we talk about mental performance enhancing drugs—but if we want this topic, we had better get it approved before someone else gets it," Lorcan stated, gesturing to the long line starting to form at Mr. Ellsworth's desk.

"Okay, let's go see if the topic has been taken," I said, as we both rose and maneuvered our way over backpacks on the floor and eschewed desks to stand in line. At one point, I began to trip over a backpack; Lorcan grabbed my arm to keep me upright. I could tell from the force in which he grabbed me that he was very strong.

"Thanks," I said, as I touched my arm where he had grabbed me.

"I am sorry if I hurt you, I was just trying to keep you from falling," Lorcan replied defensively.

"I'm not hurt." I smiled, although I was certain I would have a bruise the next day. "Thanks for your help," I continued, trying to soften the edge that Lorcan had suddenly developed. As we walked the rest of the way to Mr. Ellsworth's desk, Lorcan kept his hand on the small of my back, and I felt my heart race again.

We remained silent in line, listening to those in front of us ask permission to debate a particular topic and then tell our teacher who would argue which side. So far, no one had requested our topic.

It was our turn. As we moved towards Mr. Ellsworth's desk, I noticed how messy it was, with papers that appeared to be in no particular order and all over the place. For someone who kept his appearance pretty neat, I was surprised that he was kind of a slob, which was made more evident by three candy bar wrappers and his half-eaten ham and cheese sandwich from lunch still sitting on his desk.

I wrinkled my nose, trying not to breathe in the noxious smell from the sandwich; Lorcan glanced my way and tried to stifle a laugh. I was slightly embarrassed, so I raised my head and moved forward to speak to Mr. Ellsworth.

"Aw, Greer and Lorcan," Mr. Ellsworth said with a peculiar expression. "And what topic have you chosen?" he continued, looking at Lorcan.

"We would like to debate the use of mental performance enhancing drugs," I said, crossing my arms over my chest. It was the only way I could brace myself; the smell from the sandwich was becoming overwhelming, no doubt intensified by how warm it was in the room. Winters in Texas, we had found, were highly unpredictable: one week was warm and the next would be cold. The week the Smiths had arrived, the highs were in the seventies. Some people joked that they were so hot that they had literally raised the temperature with their arrival.

The school had been reluctant to turn on the air conditioning, so, by the end of the week, the classrooms were getting a little too warm.

"That is a fascinating topic, and I am sure you two will make it a very interesting debate," Mr. Ellsworth replied rather oddly, like he was zoned out of the conversation for a moment.

"So our topic is approved?" I asked, ready to go back to my seat.

"Yes," he said, looking back at me, "I need to know who will debate which side."

I glanced quickly at Lorcan, as we had not discussed that. He gestured for me to pick which side I wanted.

Without further hesitation, I stated, "I will be against it and Lorcan will be for it."

"Alright, you may return to your seats." Mr. Ellsworth smiled as he wrote our information down and waved us away.

I noticed several people stare and whisper as Lorcan placed his hand under my elbow, guiding me as we walked back to our desks. I felt a little nervous and was anxious to sit down.

"Are you alright?" Lorcan asked when we returned to our seats.

"Yes, it's just a little warm in here." I gave Lorcan a small smile as I began to fan myself. I was starting to sweat, and I wasn't sure if it was from the temperature in the classroom or from being in such close proximity to Lorcan.

A few minutes later, with what had to be his most mischievous smile, Mr. Ellsworth stated, "Alright, class, it is almost time to go. Everyone has had their debate topics approved. Now, to make things more interesting for the assignment, I want you and your partner to switch sides for your debate topic." There was a collective sigh in the room as we processed what he had just said, and then the bell rang. "Put your desks back where they belong!" Mr. Ellsworth yelled over the students hastily gathering their backpacks, ready for the school day to be over.

As I slowly collected my things, I thought about Mr. Ellsworth's twist. I was all for challenging projects, but the new caveat in this assignment was a bit ridiculous. I would have to argue for something I did not agree with. Why did I have to be the one stuck in speech? Darcy could have done this in her sleep.

Lorcan had already packed up his things and was standing near my desk. "Oh, I'm sorry, you don't have to wait on me," I replied, embarrassed. I realized everyone had already left the room, including our teacher.

"I don't mind. I thought we might walk out together and discuss our assignment some more." Lorcan smiled and picked up my backpack.

We walked down the empty hall and were discussing the assignment when, suddenly, Darcy rounded the corner, appearing very anxious.

"Where have you been?" Darcy yelled, visibly irritated as she glared at me and then at Lorcan.

"I was just talking to Lorcan about our speech assignment," I answered, more than a little annoyed at her tone.

"Mom's here at school," Darcy continued with a vexed look.

"What's she doing here?" I reached for my backpack, which Lorcan was already holding out for me.

Before Darcy could answer, Lorcan interrupted, "I just realized I'm running late and should go find my sister. I'll see you tomorrow." Then he was gone.

"That was weird," I replied, turning back to Darcy. "What's Mom doing here?" I asked her again.

"Apparently, she's volunteering for something—the PTA, the Choir Parents Association, or the How Can I Most Effectively Embarrass and/or Annoy My Teenage Daughter League, I don't know. All I know is that she is here, and she cannot know about Lorcan and Kieran, and here you are traipsing down the hall with him!" Darcy shrieked, grabbing my arm and leading me towards the library.

"Lorcan and I are debate partners, and we were just discussing the assignment," I replied, annoyed but also stifling a laugh. "Besides, I still don't think we should keep them a secret from Mom and Dad."

"Did you notice how quickly Lorcan took off when our mom was mentioned? It didn't appear meeting her was at the top of his to-do list," Darcy retorted as we made our way down the hall.

"I am sure he just needed to be somewhere, like he said. I don't know why you think everyone has some hidden agenda or malicious intent." I spoke with an edge of anger in my voice.

Darcy stopped, looked straight into my eyes and said, "And I don't know why you have to be so naïve as to think that people don't have agendas." She saw the hurt in my eyes from being called naïve. It was what Kieran had said about me the first day we had met her and it had stung, but Darcy saying it was a hundred times worse. "Let's go. Mom's waiting." Darcy kept walking towards the library. I followed behind her, saying nothing else.

When we entered the library, I saw several women gathered around talking. Our Mom looked up with a relieved smile when she saw Darcy and I walk in. She excused herself from her conversation and came over to us.

"Good, Darcy found you," Mom said as she gave me a hug. "What took you so long?"

"I was just talking to a classmate about our speech assignment," I replied, glad that I could be vague without lying. Darcy shot me a warning look to not reveal too much information. "What are you doing here?" I used the most normal voice I could muster as I tried to change the subject.

"I'm attending a PTA meeting," Mom said. Darcy laughed a little, but then her eyes turned serious as she looked intently out the library window into the hallway. I glanced up and saw Kieran standing just on the other side, staring at us with an intense look of both fascination and what, I thought, had to be hatred.

Mom started to look in the same direction as Darcy and me, when Darcy quickly said, "Well, that's great, Mom." Mom appeared confused at Darcy's encouragement, and even more so by the big hug that Darcy then gave her, which turned Mom's back toward the window.

I looked back to see Lorcan grab Kieran by the arm and pull her away from the window and down the hall.

"I think I left something I need." I excused myself quickly, so I could go find out what was going on. "I'll be right back." Darcy then asked Mom to introduce her to some of the other parents.

I left quickly through the double glass doors into the hallway, following in the direction Lorcan and Kieran had gone. I could hear two people whispering as I slowly peeked around the corner.

"What were you thinking? You know this is totally against the rules. You could have just ruined everything!" Lorcan whispered angrily, grabbing Kieran by the arm.

"I just wanted to see her!" Kieran shot back, through what I thought might be tears. "Please don't tell Father, you know how angry he can get," Kieran begged.

"I won't, if you promise to stick to the plan and not do anything so idiotic again," Lorcan replied, still very angry himself. If their father's anger was anything compared to Lorcan's, then that would definitely be something to fear, I thought to myself.

"I promise," Kieran conceded, lowering her head.

I didn't breathe, anxious to hear what they might say next. Lorcan suddenly looked in my direction, and I pulled myself back around the corner, pressing firmly against the wall. I expected, any second, he would find me there—but nothing happened. After a couple of minutes, I peeled myself off of the wall and slowly peeked around the corner to find them gone.

I made my way slowly back to the library, trying to process what I had just heard. Darcy and I soon excused ourselves and headed home. We remained silent the entire car ride home, both lost in our own thoughts.

After dinner, I went into Darcy's room to discuss what had happened earlier in the day. She was sitting on her bed, reading.

Darcy's room was striking. When we moved to Plano and she decided how she wanted to decorate, she had chosen a blue comforter and accent pillows, with a beautiful chocolate brown color weaved through in a whimsical pattern. It went perfectly with her dark wood twin sleigh bed and the new chocolate brown reading chair that I had yet to see her sit in. To complete the look, she had found some vintage sepia photographs of famous parks from around the world which she framed and hung.

I've heard that bedrooms, more than any other room, often reflect a person's personality, and with Darcy and me, I truly believe that was the case. Darcy's room was dark and mysterious, yet alluring.

"I want to talk to you about what happened today." I sat down in her reading chair, placing the throw pillow on my lap so I could play with the decoration on it. Darcy slowly closed her book, put it on her nightstand, and looked up at me.

"Yes, I think we do need to talk about it." Darcy's face revealed nothing.

"Where to start? It was all so crazy." I laughed.

"Let's start with why you and Lorcan are debate partners?" Darcy asked bluntly.

"Mr. Ellsworth assigned us to work together. Why does it bother you so much, anyways?" I countered.

"Greer, Lorcan is up to something, he and Kieran both, and somehow it involves us. I don't trust them and neither should you," Darcy said, more serious than I had ever seen her. "I don't think it's a coincidence that the same day you are assigned a project with Lorcan, I am assigned one with Kieran."

"Really, you have to work with Kieran? Poor you!" I replied, genuinely feeling sorry for Darcy. "But, if you think they're up to something, then we really should tell Mom and Dad."

"No, not yet. We have to figure out what's going on first. There is a secret that is being kept from us. I can feel it." Darcy held her right fist to the center of her chest.

I then told Darcy about the conversation I had overheard between Lorcan and Kieran earlier that day.

"What do you think?" I asked, anxious for her to say something.

"I think we need to be very careful around everyone, if we're going to find out what's really going on." Darcy gestured for me to sit beside her.

"What do you think it could be?" Darcy could tell I was very worried by my tone of voice, and as I sat beside her, she placed both of her hands on mine.

"I don't know, Greer, but I do know that it's something big," Darcy replied calmly. I knew that she was serious; in addition to being able to sense when someone was lying or keeping a secret, she could also sense the impact that the lie or secret might have on those who were directly involved. Darcy was rarely wrong, and I was very worried.

We spent the next hour formulating a plan on how to subtly get more information out of Kieran and Lorcan without appearing to know that they were up to something.

"Kieran will be easy. I just have to play on her vanity. Lorcan will be much more difficult to get information out of, so you will need to be very careful, Greer." Darcy appeared very concerned; she wasn't alone, but I tried to hide it as best I could.

"I'll be careful," I said, as I rose to go back to my room. When I reached the bathroom door, I turned to say goodnight.

"Greer, I'm sorry about what I said earlier. You're not naïve. You just have a pure heart and only want to see the best in people. That's a good trait, trust me." Darcy flashed an apologetic smile.

"Thank you Darcy," I replied, sincerely moved by her remorse and kind words. "Goodnight."

"Goodnight," Darcy said, as I shut the door behind me.

Chapter Five

Darcy

The following week, Greer and I were only able to gather some generic background information on Kieran and Lorcan. Lorcan proved to be as difficult as we thought, but Greer and I were relieved that he showed no sign of knowing she had overheard his and Kieran's conversation. I was surprised that Kieran had not offered much information either, but after hearing how scared she was of Lorcan and her father, I should have guessed she would keep her promise to be more careful around us.

That Friday, as I made my way to English class, I saw Greer and Lorcan walking together to class. The hall was crowded, so I snuck in a few steps behind them and listened in on their conversation.

"I have some ideas about our debate, and I wanted to see if we could work on the assignment after school today?" Lorcan said, walking right next to Greer. I had to strain to hear them.

"Darcy and I already have plans after school," Greer replied honestly. I was relieved that we did, in fact, have plans, because if they had met later in the day, we would not have had any time to prepare beforehand.

"What?" Lorcan exclaimed abruptly. I could tell he did not completely believe her.

"It's Katie's birthday, and a bunch of us are staying the night at her house tonight," she replied a bit defensively. I could tell that she didn't like that he thought she wouldn't have plans on a Friday night.

Lorcan could tell from her tone that she was bothered by his, so he quickly changed it and said, "Oh, well perhaps we could meet on Sunday afternoon?"

"Don't tell him about Sundays!" I thought to myself, willing her to hear me, but she replied quickly with, "I'm sorry, but I spend Sundays with my family."

"Really, what do you do together?" he asked, appearing genuinely interested.

Greer appeared caught off guard by his question, and without thinking said, "We always go to church and then to lunch, and we take turns choosing what we do in the afternoon."

He stopped walking, turned to look at her with bewildered eyes, and replied, "That sounds nice." His abrupt stop made me have to move over to the other side of the hall, where I almost ran right into Liam, who was standing at his locker. He watched Greer and Lorcan as they paused in the hallway for a moment before continuing on to class.

"Sorry," I said to Liam, as he slowly turned his gaze from Lorcan and Greer over to me.

"No problem," he replied, with a forced smile. I could tell that he was not happy about seeing them together.

I felt kind of bad for Liam—he really was a nice guy, and he had no clue that Greer liked him, like she had no clue that he liked her. I started to try and catch up with Lorcan and Greer before they made it to class, as I was already out of earshot, when Liam called out to me.

"Wait! I wanted to ask your advice on something," Liam said with a bit of hesitation in his voice.

As I turned back around, I already knew what he wanted to ask me. With a small smile, I replied, "You want to know if I think Greer will go out with you?"

Liam appeared genuinely surprised by my blunt and accurate prediction. "Yeah, actually, that's exactly what I want to know. I kind of get the feeling she just wants to be friends, and maybe she wouldn't be interested in anything more than that."

"Yes, she would," I said, with a laugh that seemed to inspire new hope in Liam that he did, in fact, have a shot with my sister.

"Really?" Liam asked as he began to smile.

"Trust me—but I do think you should act quickly. There appears to be someone else who might be interested in her as well," I said, my face turning more serious.

Liam frowned. "Yes, I know exactly who you're talking about."

"Then don't waste any time. Oh, and keep what you decide to do on your date a secret. Greer loves surprises," I replied with a smile, and turned to walk to class.

"Thanks!" Liam yelled out. Not turning around, I threw him a wave as I continued on to class.

When I entered English class, I saw that Greer was already sitting at her desk and that Lorcan was whispering with Katie, who could not contain her smile. As I passed by them, I heard him ask her if she would invite Kieran to her birthday party, and tell her how much it would mean to him. I knew there was no way she would say no to him. I made my way to my desk, and as I sat down, Ms. Abrams stepped to the front of the room. Class was about to begin, so everyone, including a very happy Katie and a smug looking Lorcan, quickly took their seats.

The entire class period, Katie was flushed; when she was called upon, she could not put a coherent sentence together. She also shrugged off every whisper from Rebecca trying to get her to talk.

Her mind was obviously somewhere else, and it took little effort to guess where.

As soon as class was over, Rebecca was giving Katie the third degree, refusing to be denied the information she wanted.

"What?" Rebecca exclaimed loudly. Ella and Mia rushed over to join the conversation. Greer and I would have joined them as well, but Ms. Abrams came over to talk to us about our group project. We tried to end the conversation as quickly as possible without being rude.

Greer and I looked across the room to see Liam, Nathan, and Elliot walking towards the door. Liam smiled in Greer's direction. She blushed and shot a small smile back. I surveyed the room to see who was left, and I saw Lorcan and Kieran standing by her desk, engaged in a serious conversation. He did most of the talking, and she quietly listened, even though she appeared to be fuming. She did not seem to like that she was going to have to go to Katie's party, but it appeared she was going to follow her orders.

"Oh my, I have kept you way too long. You girls need to get to your next class. If you are late, please tell your teacher to speak with me," Ms. Abrams said, as she looked up at the clock. We had four minutes to get to our next class, which was on the other side of the building.

We had a test in calculus, and I had a guest speaker in psychology. Kieran looked sullen and pouty the whole time the psychologist spoke to our class. After the final bell rang and our teacher thanked our guest speaker, I packed up my things and headed for the door to go find Greer. I walked quickly down two halls, over to where she would be leaving speech class with Lorcan. As I rounded the corner, I saw Lorcan standing way too close to my blushing sister, and I heard him say, with an enigmatic smile, "I hope you have fun tonight."

"I'm sure we will," Greer replied with a small smile in return.

"Greer," I shouted, as I rushed up to her without even acknowledging Lorcan, "we need to go, now."

I briefly glanced at Lorcan, and saw his annoyance that their conversation was cut short. Greer could see it too, and, in an attempt to lessen his frustration, she very sweetly told him to have a nice weekend.

"You too. I look forward to Monday," he replied, back to his normal self, and then turned and walked away.

"Really, you can be so rude. I think he knows you don't like him," Greer whispered to me.

"I don't care. Anyways, he would know if I was lying and pretended to like him," I said as I grabbed her arm and pulled her down the hall.

"How do you know that, and where are we going in such a hurry?" Greer asked, put out by my aggressiveness. Suddenly, she stopped and asked worriedly, "Is Mom here again?"

I laughed. "No, we just need to run home really fast before we go to Katie's. I forgot something."

"That's what all the rude behavior and mystery is about?" Greer replied, clearly annoyed.

"Let's just go," I said, as I led the way out of the building and to our car, trying to avoid the Friday afternoon hustle in the parking lot.

I turned on the radio once we were in the car, my signal to Greer that I didn't want to talk. I wasn't ready to tell her about the new addition to Katie's party.

Once we were home, I ran inside to get my overnight bag, and Greer went in to say hello to Mom and Will in the kitchen. When I came downstairs with my bag, Mom was unloading the dishwasher and Will had half of his body inside the fridge, trying to find something.

"We have nothing to eat in here!" Will exclaimed as he shut the door.

"You mean we have nothing you want to eat," Greer said with a laugh, as I sat down at the bar next to her. Will shot me a sarcastic look and headed towards the pantry.

"What are you girls doing tonight at Katie's?" Mom asked, as she stacked plates on the counter.

Will stuck his head out of the pantry and said in a cheesy, girly voice, "They're gonna do each other's hair and text boys all night."

"How old are you?" Greer asked, throwing a dishtowel across the room, which didn't come anywhere close to reaching him. Mom and I stifled a laugh at their exchange.

"I believe he stopped mentally maturing at the age of seven." I smirked, as I reached for something in my bag.

"Ha, ha! Very funny!" Will said, exiting the pantry with his arms filled with bread, peanut butter, and wheat crackers.

"Really, William, you'll ruin your appetite for dinner." Mom sighed, while Greer and I just laughed.

"No, I'll be hungry, don't worry. Are we still ordering pizza?" Will asked with his most persuasive smile. It made him look just like our father, and worked like a charm on our mother.

"Yes," Mom replied.

"We'll need to order one or two more," Will said, as he slathered a heap of peanut butter on a slice of bread. "I have a friend coming over from soccer."

"You have a friend?" I joked, feigning surprise.

"You're really on a roll today," Will replied sarcastically. "Yes, in fact, I heard he sits with G at lunch." "G" was the nickname Will used for Greer most of the time, unless he was mad at her about something or worried; then he called her by her full first name. It was the same with me, whom he called "Darce," with the "ce" sounding like an "s."

We all looked at Greer. I was a little surprised Will was friends with either Liam, Nathan, or Elliot, who all played on the varsity soccer team.

"I thought you sat with girls at lunch?" Mom asked, putting on her questioning face and moving closer to where Greer was sitting.

"I do, but a few guys sit with us as well. It's no big deal," she said truthfully, since she didn't really think Liam was interested in her. "Who do you know from my lunch table, and why's he coming over here?" Greer asked Will, trying to shift the conversation away from herself.

"Liam Alexander," Will said, with his mouth stuffed full of peanut butter. I couldn't help but laugh slightly as Greer turned as white as a sheet.

"How exactly do you know him?" Greer asked, trying to compose herself so she didn't give away that she was completely freaking out. I, of course, knew better.

"We've been scrimmaging with the varsity soccer team this past week, and he and I have become friends. He's been helping me learn some of the varsity soccer drills." Will was unhappy that Greer was so calm about him knowing Liam. He had hoped to get a rise out of her.

"But why's he coming over here?" she asked again, this time a little more impatiently. We all noted the distress in her voice.

"Because I asked if he wanted to." Will smiled. "Does it bother you that he's coming over? Do you like him or something?" Will asked, dragging out his last sentence. I unsuccessfully hid another small laugh as Greer blushed.

"You do!" Will exclaimed.

"I do not! We're just friends!" Greer said defensively, and hopped off her barstool. Will and I laughed at her little moment of drama.

"Okay," Will replied, but he didn't believe her in the least little bit.

Greer looked over at me as I mouthed to her, "Don't worry about it."

"Well, I look forward to meeting him if he is a friend of yours and Greer's. What time should we expect him?" Mom asked Will as she smiled at Greer.

"Any minute now. He said he had to run an errand after school, and then he would head on over. Apparently his parents and sister are out of town," Will said, rinsing his plate. It was amazing how fast he could eat. In the short time we had been talking, he had eaten a peanut butter sandwich and several crackers also loaded with peanut butter.

Greer looked at me, and I knew she wanted to insist we leave right away. I wanted to wait and see if Liam would take my advice and ask Greer out, or, at the very least, see their first interaction since he learned he had a chance with her.

"So, what are you girls going to do tonight at Katie's—no comments from you this time." Mom pointed to Will, who had his mouth open to say something.

"We're probably going to have dinner and watch movies and just hang out," I replied quickly.

"Are you going anywhere?" Mom began her third degree.

"No," Greer replied.

"Are Katie's parents going to be there?" Mom continued.

"Yes," Greer answered.

"I met her mother at PTA. She's very nice. Who all is staying the night?" Mom's anxiety was lessening.

"Well, Katie, Rebecca, Mia, Sloan, Ella, Darcy, and me," Greer said truthfully, since she didn't know that Kieran had also been invited. Mom nodded, which suggested she was okay with the guest list, as she looked through her purse for something.

"We should probably get…" Greer was about to say "going," when the doorbell rang and she froze.

"He's here!" Will said, emphasizing both words and laughing as he looked over at Greer.

"Don't embarrass your sister, and go answer the door," Mom directed Will, as she handed Greer some cash from her purse. Will sauntered out of the kitchen towards the front of the house.

"This is for the both of you, just in case, but if you go anywhere, you need to text me and tell me where you're going, and again when you get back to Katie's. Do you both understand?" She looked at Greer and then meaningfully at me.

"Yes," we both said in unison. We could hear talking from the hallway, and as we waited for them to enter the kitchen, Greer ran her fingers through her hair.

Will led Liam into the kitchen. He seemed pleasantly surprised to see Greer and me there.

"Mom, this is Liam," Will said, moving out of the way so Liam could make his way into the kitchen. Mom walked over and they shook hands across the island.

"Nice to meet you, Mrs. Hagen," Liam said genuinely.

"Pleasure to meet you." Mom smiled back at him graciously. "I believe you know my daughters as well." Mom gestured over towards Greer and me standing by the bar.

"Yes, we have several classes together," Liam replied as he raised his hand to say hi to us.

Greer softly whispered, "Hi," and I gave him a small smile and nod.

"And lunch together," Will chuckled. I shot him a fierce look and he stopped laughing.

"Yes, Greer and I sit together at lunch," Liam said, staring straight at her. How she could not know he liked her was beyond me—it was so evident in the way he looked at her.

"With several of our friends," Greer chimed in. No wonder he didn't think she liked him; she always tried to make it seem like they were just friends, because she feared he would not return her feelings.

"And you know Will through soccer?" Mom asked, changing the subject.

Liam looked back at Mom and replied politely, "Yes ma'am, the junior varsity and varsity teams have been practicing together the past week. Your son has a lot of talent."

"Tell them something they don't know." Will pretended to brush off his shoulder.

Greer and I rolled our eyes. "He also has a lot of ego," I said quickly. We all laughed, except Will, who shot me a mock frown.

"An appropriate amount of confidence can be a good thing in varsity sports, especially for the team's leaders, which Will should learn before becoming junior captain next year," Liam said with a smile.

"What?" Will said, completely shocked, as Mom and Greer sighed in surprise. He knew that he would play on varsity next year, but there were already so many talented athletes that would be on the team—he had never really thought he might become one of the team's leaders, especially since he was still relatively new to the school.

"That's wonderful, sweetheart!" Mom said, going over to give Will a hug.

"Are you sure?" Will said to Liam, releasing himself from our mother's quick hug.

"The coach has had his eye on you since you moved here. He thinks you're very talented, and likes the way you've already earned the respect of your teammates. He asked me to give you some pointers from my experience as junior and senior captain." Liam was still smiling. He took real enjoyment in seeing Will so happy. He and Greer would be perfect together, I thought to myself.

"That's awesome!" Will walked over and shook hands with Liam.

Greer and I walked towards Will and Liam who were now standing beside each other.

"Congratulations," Greer said as she gave Will a side hug. I moved towards him and Greer scooted over towards Liam.

"Way to go, kid," I told Will. As he and Mom began to chat, I pretended to listen to their conversation, when really I was listening to Greer and Liam's.

"It's really nice of you to help my brother," Greer said, smiling at Liam.

"It's no big deal, it'll help me stay on top of my game for next year," Liam said, cutting his eyes over at her with a charming smile.

"What are you guys going to do tonight?" Greer asked.

"Probably just hang out here for a while. My parents don't like for me to have people over when they're out of town," Liam replied. There was a slight pause in their conversation, and I thought maybe he would take that opportunity to ask her out; for some reason, he didn't. The pause started to get awkward so I decided to step in.

"We should get going," I said, smiling at Greer and then giving Liam an encouraging look.

"Have fun at your sleepover," Will said in his mocking girl voice, but then, in a more serious tone, "give Katie my cell number if she needs someone to text all night."

"In your dreams!" Greer laughed, as she and then I gave Mom a hug bye.

"You girls be careful, and remember what I said." Mom gave us an anxious look. She hated for us to not be under her roof at night. She preferred for us to host sleepovers, but knew she had to let us go do normal teenage things.

"We will, and tell Dad we said hi. We'll be back in the morning by ten," Greer said.

"Have fun," Liam said, never taking his eyes off of Greer.

When we were almost to Katie's, I turned off the radio and said very seriously, "Okay, so I have something to tell you."

"Alright?" Greer replied, a little nervously.

"We're going to have one more person at the sleepover tonight," I said, with a wicked little smile.

"Who?" Greer asked curiously.

"Kieran." I turned and looked Greer right in the eyes.

"What?" Greer was completely dumbfounded. "How'd that happen?"

"You told Lorcan about Katie's party, and he asked Katie if she would invite Kieran," I replied, turning my eyes back to the road.

"So that's what he was talking to Katie about at the beginning of English class, and what he was talking to Kieran about at the end of class. Kieran did not appear all that happy," Greer replied, as she tried to process everything.

After a moment, Greer continued, "Well, this should be an interesting night."

"Very interesting," I said with a laugh as we pulled up to Katie's house, the last to arrive.

Chapter Six

Greer

"This can't be her house," I whispered to Darcy, as we walked up the beautifully paved front walkway. Her house was a mini-chateau, with landscaping that would rival Versailles—and that was just the front of the house.

"This is the address she gave me, and everyone's cars are here," Darcy said, admiring the rose bushes.

Darcy rang the doorbell, and we waited in silence, taking in the grandeur of it all. I half expected a butler to answer the door; instead, I was surprised when it was opened by Katie's older brother Edmund, a sophomore at Southern Methodist University. We had never met him, but we had heard enough from our friends to know him by his description. First of all, he was very tall and had blonde hair and blue eyes like Katie. Secondly, he was really good looking, just like our friends had said. He wore a pair of jeans and a polo shirt, untucked, with topsiders. He was perfectly shaven, and his hair was a bit tousled, like he had just run his fingers through it. He was just Darcy's type, I thought to myself and smiled.

"You must be Darcy and Greer," Edmund said kindly. "Come in. I'm Edmund, Katie's brother." Edmund opened the door wider so we could make our way into the grand two-story foyer, where everything appeared to be made of marble and decorated in a classic

French style. Someone in Katie's family was definitely a Francophile.

Darcy smiled at Edmund and said, "Nice to meet you."

"You too," Edmund replied sweetly, entranced by Darcy's captivating smile and her sparkling green eyes.

"Did you stop by to wish Katie a happy birthday?" I asked, still taking in our ornate surroundings.

"Yeah; I wanted to surprise her, but I didn't realize she was having a girls only party. I'll leave after dinner," Edmund said kindly, finally tearing his eyes off of Darcy.

"Oh, but we don't mind having him here. I've tried to talk him into staying, but he won't listen to me," Katie said, walking up and giving him a side hug. I could tell their relationship had grown past the typical teenage bickering stage to one of respect and love. "He's a pretty awesome big brother. See what he gave me?" Katie held up a beautiful silver cross necklace. It would match well, I thought, with the small silver hoop earrings Darcy and I bought her.

"It's very pretty," I said, as I leaned in to get a better look. Darcy smiled and agreed.

"I'll take your bags up to Katie's room," Edmund interrupted, embarrassed at his sister showing off his gift.

"Thanks." Darcy handed him her Vera Bradley overnight bag. He reached for mine and turned to go up the stairs. I noticed Darcy watch him for a minute, as Katie began to chatter.

"Welcome to our home," Katie said, extending her arms out grandly.

"It's beautiful," I said honestly, and Darcy smiled in agreement.

"It's a little over the top, if you ask me," Katie whispered behind her hand, "but that's my mom for you." We had not met her mother yet, but our own mother had liked her when they met, so I was sure she was nice.

"Is it new?" Darcy asked, smiling at Katie's honesty.

"Yeah, we moved in a couple of months ago," Katie replied, her face turning a bit sad. "I really loved our old house. We had so many great memories there, but my Mom really wanted to build a grand, French style home. So, voila!"

"Mission accomplished." Darcy smiled, as she took in the grand stairwell.

"It was her big project to help her get over Edmund going off to college. Dad's terrified of what her next project will be, when I leave and they have an empty nest." Katie laughed again. Darcy and I joined her.

"Darling, have your other friends arrived?" I heard a woman with a beautiful light French accent ask. Katie's mother was exactly what I thought Katie would look like in twenty-five years. She was tall and thin, with long blonde hair swept up on top of her head, highlighting her bright blue eyes. She was beautiful; looking at her, I was surprised I had not noticed before how pretty Katie was.

"Yes, Mom, this is Darcy and Greer." Katie gestured towards us.

"So nice to meet you! Katie has told me all about you, and you're both just as beautiful as she described," Katie's mom said with a warm smile, walking over to us and giving Darcy and me each a hug and kiss on both of our cheeks. Very European, I thought, and the house began to make a lot more sense to me.

"Nice to meet you, too, Mrs. Dobry. Your home is beautiful," Darcy replied genuinely.

"Thank you, sweetheart. We're very happy with how it turned out." Mrs. Dobry smiled, and then led the way through the house to where we could hear several girls chattering.

"I didn't know your mom was French?" I whispered to Katie as we followed behind Darcy and Mrs. Dobry who were chatting.

"Oh yes, very French," Katie said with a slight laugh.

"She seems great," I smiled.

"She is. She just has a big personality," Katie whispered, as we reached what had to be the family room. It was a grand two-story room with intricate woodwork throughout. There were two luxurious leather sofas facing each other near the fireplace, and lots of other beautiful and expensive looking furniture placed perfectly around the room. Across the room, where it connected to the kitchen, was a large bar area, where all of our friends were hanging out.

"Greer, Darcy!" Ella exclaimed as we walked towards them. Everyone paused their conversations and said hello. I surveyed the bar area and saw everyone, except Kieran. Maybe she changed her mind and didn't come after all, I hoped.

"There is lots of food!" Mrs. Dobry said in her cute French accent, and began to place various snacks on the bar. Everyone went straight for the chips and dips, bypassing the gorgeous vegetable and cheese spread nearby. Darcy and I hung back a little.

"I guess Kieran decided not to show," I whispered.

"No, she's here somewhere," Darcy replied quietly, raising her head to look around.

"How do you know that? No one's even mentioned her." I searched the room again and saw no trace of her.

"Do you see the Louis Vuitton purse sitting on the table over there? It's hers." Darcy motioned to a bag I was surprised I had not noticed. "Remember, you need to be very careful in what you say and do around her. The goal is to figure out her and Lorcan's agenda, not for them to find out more information about us," Darcy whispered, turning her head to look straight into my eyes.

"Kieran, there you are," Katie said loudly enough for everyone to hear, as Kieran entered the room from a hallway we had not yet been down. Right away, I noticed she was overdressed. While we all still had on the more casual clothes we had worn earlier that day to school (mostly jeans and nice tops), she had changed into a form-fitting dress. There was no doubt she looked gorgeous, but she also looked like she should be headed to a club, not a high school slumber party.

"I got lost trying to find the bathroom," Kieran replied with a sharp look at Darcy and me, as she grabbed a carrot off of the vegetable tray. Darcy snickered a little, and looked down at the floor. "I just love your home, Mrs. Dobry," Kieran continued, sitting down on an empty barstool and carefully straightening out her dress.

"Thank you," Mrs. Dobry replied happily. I could tell she was very proud of her new home.

Mia and Sloan moved closer to Kieran, and began to nibble from the vegetable tray as well. They asked her about her dress, commenting on how beautiful it was. Kieran responded with her usual vanity, discussing the designer and how it had been custom made. She continued with a long monologue about her wardrobe and who her favorite and least favorite designers were. Mia and Sloan were eager to listen.

I walked over to Katie, under the cover of wishing her a happy birthday again, but really, I wanted to talk to her about her conversation with Lorcan.

"Happy birthday, again!" I said, and Katie turned to me and smiled. Ella and Rebecca went over to talk to Darcy; I had my chance, so I tried to be subtle. "So, I saw you talking to Lorcan earlier today in class?" Not very subtle, I thought. I would have to try harder.

Katie smiled dreamily while pouring some drinks for everyone, and replied with a slight squeal, "Yeah, he wished me a happy birthday and told me how pretty I looked!"

"That's great!" I tried to be as positive as I could, although I knew

Lorcan, while telling the truth, was not probably all that sincere in his motives. "What else did he say?" I asked. Katie did not disappoint.

She stopped pouring drinks and stared right at me to signify the importance of her story. She whispered, "Well, he asked what I was doing for my birthday. I told him about the slumber party and then he seemed sad. He said his sister used to attend slumber parties in L.A., but that she had such a hard time with their move, and didn't really have any nice friends like us. Then he asked if I would invite her."

"Really?" I tried to say in a sympathetic tone, to encourage her to go on.

"I said I'd be happy to. He was really excited! I have never seen him smile so big, and man, he is so handsome when he smiles—but like he could ever not be handsome, right? He said it would mean so much to him, and that he would have to find a way to thank me. I look forward to finding out what that means!" Katie said excitedly. She quickly realized that she did not mean to say that last sentence out loud, and blushed as she cut her eyes down and then back up at me.

"Did Lorcan say anything else?" I asked, trying not to make it seem like a big deal.

"My, you sure are interested in my brother's conversations," Kieran said, slithering into our private discussion.

I blushed, wondering how much she had overheard. I glanced over at Darcy, who looked back at me with concern. I looked straight at Kieran and quickly responded, "I'm interested in Katie's conversation, not Lorcan's."

"Really? Well, in this case, is there a difference?" Kieran snickered as she picked up a glass of Diet Coke. She took a drink and smiled sarcastically as she lowered the glass from her lips.

I was trying to figure out what to say when Darcy appeared, and said defensively, "You give him too much credit. Like Greer would be interested in him."

"My brother deserves all of the credit he receives, and has never had a problem with girls," Kieran said, still smiling, but now looking at Katie.

Katie was painfully unaware of what we were really talking about, but she blushed, thinking we were referring to her liking Lorcan. Still, she remained silent and listened.

"It must run in the family. I don't typically have any problems getting what or who I want." Kieran said snidely.

Darcy laughed. "Oh, and do you have a particular target in mind right now?"

"A few, but at the top of my list is Liam Alexander," Kieran replied with her wicked smile, as she locked eyes with me. There was something so familiar about her brown eyes. That thought, however, quickly passed, as what she had said registered. I fumed, but knew I should say nothing; saying something would just escalate the conversation, which was exactly what she wanted.

Darcy, however, did not have a problem with escalation. She was ticked off by Kieran's comment, and said very seriously, "Liam has better taste than that."

"Dinner is served," Mrs. Dobry said, thankfully interrupting us.

"We'll see." Kieran gave Darcy a wicked smile before walking towards the dining room. I tried to ignore what she had said, and followed Darcy into the grand dining room.

On a wall length buffet table, we found a spread fit for hungry teenagers. Katie loved Mexican food (as I was convinced every Texan did), so there was some of everything: fixings for fajitas, soft and hard shell tacos, enchiladas, burritos, and nachos. As we entered the room, everyone gasped at the sight—we knew we could not eat this much food in three days.

"If Will could only see this," I quietly said to Darcy with a laugh, still trying to get over Kieran's comment. She smiled and nodded in agreement, and then we got in line behind the others to serve our food.

We all sat around a long rectangular dining table, with Mrs. Dobry at one end and Edmund at the other. We sat four to each side, with Katie beside her mother; next to her were Rebecca, Mia, and then Kieran sitting next to Edmund. Ella sat across from Katie, and next to her were Sloan, me, and Darcy, who sat across from Kieran and next to Edmund. We were the last to take our seats, but I thought the seating arrangement couldn't have been planned better.

After everyone sat down at the table, Mrs. Dobry asked Edmund to say a blessing. He said a short but sweet prayer that acknowledged our presence and the significance of the day. He was very eloquent, I thought, and I couldn't help but peek up near the end of his prayer, to see Kieran squirming a little. She acted as if she had never prayed a day in her life.

"Will your husband not be joining us for dinner?" Kieran asked Mrs. Dobry bluntly, as we began to eat. In an instant, I saw Katie's eyes begin to tear, Edmund stiffen his back, and the rest of our friends begin to look very uncomfortable.

"No, he's working late tonight," Mrs. Dobry responded tersely. Her tone alone should have ended the conversation, but Kieran was curious.

"Oh, what does he do?" Kieran said, completely unfazed by how uncomfortable everyone had become.

"He's a doctor," Edmund replied quickly.

"What kind?" Kieran continued. Her lack of consideration was astounding.

"He does medical research," Edmund said, obviously hoping the conversation would end, but Kieran developed a fascinated look.

"What does he work on?" Everyone began to look around at each other.

"He works on developing drugs to fight various diseases, which is obviously more important than my eighteenth birthday," Katie said quietly, but still loud enough for us all to hear. Everyone was silent, and I could see that Edmund was fuming. Katie's mother reached out and placed her hand on top of her daughter's.

Feeling the tension in the room, I quickly said to Mrs. Dobry, "Everything is so delicious!"

"Thank you dear," Mrs. Dobry replied sweetly, obviously glad for the change of subject.

"Katie, I forgot to mention earlier that our brother Will said to wish you a happy birthday. Apparently, he has quite a crush on you!" Darcy said, as our friends erupted in laughter and began to pick on Katie for being a cougar.

Katie quickly wiped her eyes and began to blush. Edmund smiled appreciatively at Darcy, and for the brief moment they locked eyes, I saw something in Darcy's face that I had never seen before. She was interested in him. The only problem was that Kieran saw it too, and her mouth quickly twisted into a plotting smile.

Everyone else was still picking on Katie, when Kieran stated, "I didn't realize you two had a younger brother."

We didn't respond right away, because we didn't want to give out too much information about our family, but everyone was looking at us. Mia chimed in, saying, "Oh yes, and he is quite the hottie for a sophomore, isn't he Katie?"

"Seriously, he's too young, I could never go out with him!" Katie replied, although I sensed some hesitation in her voice.

"I don't think he looks very young!" Rebecca laughed, elbowing Katie slightly. Katie's face was so red she almost looked sunburned.

"Well, he does have a tendency to act kind of young, so you better give him a few years to mature," Darcy said with a small laugh, hoping to end the conversation she had started.

"What do your parents do?" Kieran asked Darcy and me, as soon as the table was quiet. Darcy looked at me for a moment, and I knew exactly what she was thinking. Kieran knew her best shot to get any information from us was to ask it in front of everyone else. If she asked us one-on-one, we could easily deflect her questions, but to do so in front of everyone would make us look either strange or rude.

We were going to try and keep the information to a minimum. "Our father runs a non-profit, and our mother stays at home," Darcy said quickly.

Kieran snickered and gave Darcy a meaningful look. "What's your mother like?" Kieran continued, as she took a slow bite of her food. She was trying to act as natural as possible, but she had to control everything she said and did. It was apparent, at least to Darcy and me, that it was hard for her; perhaps this was something we could use to our advantage.

Darcy and I didn't respond, partly because we were chewing our food, and partly because we did not care to reveal anything regarding our saintly mother to this strange new girl who so clearly had an agenda.

"Their mom is so sweet," Ella replied for us, although we wished our silence had created an opportunity for another conversation to start.

"Yes, I liked their mother instantly when I met her," Mrs. Dobry chimed in.

"Don't forget to mention how gorgeous she is! And their dad, too! They are like the cutest parent couple ever!" Katie said sweetly, trying to hide the pain that she felt.

"Alright, I am sure everyone is getting bored with all this talk about our family. I think we should keep our attention on the birthday girl here, and we should start with a toast," Darcy said quickly, as she raised her glass of Coke.

Everyone, except Kieran, smiled, and then we all raised our glasses to toast Katie. Darcy ignored Kieran's glare, as she turned towards Katie and said, "To Katie on her eighteenth birthday, and the beginning of her wonderful, adult life."

"Here, here!" everyone said in unison, raising our glasses higher.

"I couldn't have said it better myself," Edmund whispered over to Darcy, to which she smiled sweetly in return.

Everyone stopped chattering for a moment as Katie, who was blushing, stood up and said, "Thank you," to Darcy, and then to everyone, "I am so glad that all of you are here to share this special day with me. I am lucky to have such good friends." She sat back down, and everyone smiled and began to chatter again happily, except for Kieran, who appeared irritated.

As dinner ended, everyone began to help Mrs. Dobry get ready for the birthday cake. Before long, the table was cleared, and fresh dessert plates and forks were placed and ready for use. Edmund helped Mrs. Dobry bring out a large three tier chocolate cake that had the shape of the Eiffel Tower on one side. It was so gorgeous, I couldn't imagine us cutting into it. The cake was alit with eighteen candles that looked like lights on the tower. Mrs. Dobry and Edmund began to sing "Happy Birthday" to Katie in French, while the rest of us sang in English. When we were finished, Katie closed her eyes for a brief moment, smiled and opened them, and, with a great force, blew out all of the candles in one breath. We clapped, but we soon all noticed a loud clapping and cheering from the kitchen doorway.

A man in his late forties, with light brown hair, blue eyes, and a smile that I quickly recognized as Edmund's, stepped forward.

"Daddy!" Katie said, smiling her biggest smile of the night and racing over to give him a hug. "You made it!" Katie said happily. I saw a look of relief on Mrs. Dobry and Edmund's faces as Dr. Dobry embraced Katie.

"I'm so sorry I'm late, peanut. It took longer than I expected to pick up your present." Dr. Dobry smiled.

"Oh, and what might that be?" Katie asked hopefully.

"Yes, what might that be?" Mrs. Dobry asked with a curious tone.

Dr. Dobry pulled out an envelope from inside his coat pocket and smiled.

"What is it?" Katie asked as he handed it to her.

"Open it and see," Dr. Dobry smiled encouragingly.

Katie quickly opened it and gasped. "It's airline tickets to Paris!" Everyone cheered. Katie quickly raised her hand for everyone to quiet down, as she had more to say. "And there are four of them!" she said excitedly, as she looked at her mother and then back at her father. Her mother began to tear up and quickly dabbed her eyes with her napkin.

"Yes, it's about time we took a family vacation; I thought we would start in Paris and travel Europe for three weeks this summer," Dr. Dobry said, smiling. Mrs. Dobry quickly rose and walked over to her husband, joining Katie in hugging him. Edmund also got up, and went over and shook his father's hand. It was a sweet moment, and we were all so happy for Katie.

As everyone was chatting about Katie's fantastic birthday gift, I thought I would excuse myself to find the bathroom. With bad directions from Rebecca, I finally found one, after walking into two closets and an office. There was a bathroom adjacent to the office, so I decided to use it; I could not wait to find another one.

The home office obviously belonged to Dr. Dobry, as it was filled with medical journals and books. It was decorated with beautiful dark wood picture-frame paneling on the walls, an ornate ceiling, and a gorgeous marble fireplace that I envisioned only being used a couple of times during mild Texas winters.

Quickly using the bathroom and washing my hands, I started to head back to the others, when something on Dr. Dobry's beautiful mahogany desk caught my eye. It was a proposal from a company named Smith Industries. I briefly saw the cover letter, which discussed their proposed merger with Dr. Dobry's research lab. What struck me was the signature of the CEO and President, Drake Smith. It looked just like Lorcan's writing, which I had seen in class. I wondered if Drake could be Lorcan and Kieran's father.

I realized I was taking too long and found my way back to the others, who had now finished their cake and were helping Mrs. Dobry clear the table.

"You girls go have fun; I will take care of all of these dishes," Mrs. Dobry said sweetly.

"I will help you, Mom," Edmund said considerately.

"No, darling; if you're going back to school tonight, you should go ahead and get going. I don't want you driving too late," Mrs. Dobry said. She was obviously unaware how late most college students stayed out during the weekend, but Edmund did not strike me as your typical college student.

Edmund gave his mother a hug and shook his father's hand, who had begun to help with the dishes. He then came over to give Katie a hug and wish her a happy birthday one more time.

"Thanks so much for coming tonight!" Katie said happily.

"I wouldn't have missed it!" Edmund replied kindly. "It was nice to meet some of your new friends," Edmund said, glancing at me and then staring a bit longer in Darcy's direction.

"It was certainly nice to meet you as well," Kieran said, vainly assuming he had meant her.

"Thank you," Edmund said, reluctantly taking his eyes off of Darcy and looking over at Kieran.

"I'm very interested in visiting colleges in the area. Perhaps you could give me a personal tour of yours sometime," Kieran said with a flirtatious smile, placing her hand on Edmund's arm. Edmund looked down briefly, and I noticed that everyone in the room was watching their conversation, especially Darcy.

"Katie, maybe all of your friends might want a tour sometime?" Edmund said, glancing back in Darcy's direction.

"Yes, we should do that!" Katie replied excitedly.

"Well, I guess I'll take time with you however I can get it." Kieran laughed, but she was obviously unhappy that her flirting had failed miserably.

Edmund then said his goodbyes to us and was gone. We spent the rest of the night watching movies, eating way too much food, and falling asleep in the media room. I woke up the next morning with a crick in my neck, as I had slept in one of the leather theater style chairs. I noticed Darcy had not fared much better, having slept on the floor. Everyone was scattered around the room, except for Kieran, who Katie found asleep in her bed.

Darcy and I had managed to stay away from Kieran most of the night. She sat by Mia and Sloan and dominated the conversation with them, when she was not complaining about something to Katie.

Overall, it had been a good night. After a grand breakfast prepared by Mrs. Dobry, we headed home and were there by 10 a.m., just as we promised.

Chapter Seven

Darcy

The rest of our weekend was pretty normal. At dinner on Saturday night, we heard all about Liam's visit with Will and our parents while we had been at Katie's sleepover.

"I really like him. He seems like such a nice young man." Mom smiled at Greer, as she passed the potatoes to Will.

"Yes, and he's very funny." Dad laughed, no doubt thinking of something Liam had said that he had found amusing.

"He sure loved all of the pictures of you growing up that we showed him," Will said, with a devilish smile directed towards Greer.

"What pictures?!" she exclaimed in horror. Will laughed; he loved getting a rise out of Greer or me whenever he got a chance. As I was more prone to retaliate than Greer, she was more often his target.

"Will, don't tease your sister. We didn't show him any pictures," Mom reassured her.

"What did you guys do?" I asked curiously, giving Will a small smirk.

"We just watched some hockey and hung out," he replied more seriously.

"He certainly knows a lot about hockey," Dad smiled. Dad's favorite teams growing up had been the Red Sox and the Boston Bruins. When Will had shown an interest in soccer at an early age and then proved to have a natural talent, Dad learned everything he could about the sport.

"You should plan on him hanging out here more, especially since we are training together now. That won't be a problem, will it Greer?" Will asked, hopeful for a dramatic response.

"Why would it be?" she replied, trying to act as normal as possible. Will frowned in defeat.

After dinner, our parents were picking out a movie to watch in the family room while Will, Greer, and I cleaned the kitchen together. I brought the dishes in from the dining room, while Greer rinsed them, and Will loaded the dishwasher.

"Sorry if I gave you too hard of a time about Liam, G," Will said sheepishly.

She appeared honestly surprised he felt bad and replied, "It's really not a big deal."

"But you do like him?" Will asked seriously.

"Why does it matter if I do or not?" she questioned.

"Well, I think he likes you," Will continued.

"What makes you say that? Did he say something about me?" she asked quickly. I lingered in the doorway, listening as they talked.

"The only thing he asked was if you ever talked about some guy named Lorcan. I told him that I had never heard of him, and he seemed relieved," Will said, trying to interpret the surprised look on her face. "Who is this Lorcan guy anyways?"

"No one, just some new guy at our school. Not even worth talking about," I said, a little too sternly, as I walked closer to them.

"Really? Then why did Liam bother to ask about him?" Will replied.

"Listen, you just need to drop it," I said. I realized that now that Will knew about Lorcan, we were going to have to try and convince him that he was not worth mentioning, or bribe him to keep quiet. It appeared too late for the former, so we were going to have to find a bribe that would work.

"This is very interesting. Is G in a love triangle?" Will said with a laugh.

"You listen to me, William. You won't say one word about Lorcan to anyone, especially to Mom and Dad; for that matter, you're going to leave Greer alone about Liam. More than likely he likes her, but you're going to stop teasing her about him." I was right in Will's face, with my finger about a half an inch from his nose.

"Okay, geez Darcy. I didn't know it was such a sensitive subject. When did you become Greer's great defender anyways?" Will said, backing off a little. "But, if you want me to keep this Lorcan a secret, you'll have to offer something in return."

Greer stood there, watching the exchange between Will and me. I was hoping our parents didn't hear us, as the whole situation would require way too much explaining.

"What do you want?" I said, glaring at Will.

"Relax, I will let you off easy: how about you guys let me pick our family outings for a month, and you two clean my room for two weeks?" Will smiled. Greer and I laughed; we refused to even go in Will's room because it was always such a mess, not to mention it had a strange odor.

"You can choose the family outings, but you can forget about the maid service," I said.

"Okay, how about one week?" Will tried to counter, but the look on his face told us he knew it was hopeless. We just stared at him, silently. "Alright, I'll just pick the family outings."

"And you won't say a word about Lorcan," I said, looking straight into his eyes.

He knew I was serious, and without any jokes, he responded, "Not a word."

We finished cleaning the kitchen in silence, and Will went to watch a movie with our parents. Greer and I excused ourselves to work on some homework.

Greer and I had not had a chance to chat about what happened at Katie's sleepover. We had dropped off Sloan, who lived just a couple of blocks from us, and then we spent most of the day with our parents, doing stuff around the house. I went to speak to her, but I found her fast asleep.

I went back to my room, knowing I wouldn't have a chance to talk to her about everything until Sunday night. The next day would be busy with church, lunch, and our family outing, which Will had decided would be a hiking excursion at Sister Grove Park, a trail thirty minutes northeast of where we lived.

The hike turned out not to be as bad as I thought it would be, even if we did spend all afternoon there. After we got home and all cleaned up, we had dinner, and then each of us kids went off to work on homework. After Mom and Dad came by to say goodnight at a little past ten, I passed through the shared bathroom and knocked on the door that led to Greer's room.

"Come in," she replied, knowing it would be me. "Some weekend," she said from her reading chair.

"Yes, it was," I replied as I took a seat on her bed.

"Well, I think tomorrow could provide us with some interesting information," Greer said enthusiastically.

"What do you mean?" I asked, although I was pretty sure I already knew what she was going to say.

"I am meeting Lorcan after school to work on our speech assignment." Greer smiled.

"Yes, I know," I said with a small laugh.

"What? How do you know?" Greer replied with raised eyebrows and slight irritation in her voice.

"I was listening in on your conversation as you walked to English on Friday," I said, still smiling.

"Alright, stalker!" There was a lightness to her tone, which made me believe she was glad I had been close by.

I laughed again and told her my plan. "Okay, we'll tell Mom that we're both working on projects after school, and I will find a corner of the library to camp out, where I can keep an eye on you both. If I'm going to be your stalker, then I plan to do a thorough job of it."

We discussed how to try to extract information from Lorcan.

"Are you ready for this?" I asked.

"Yes, I'm sure I can do it. Besides, it's time we got some answers," Greer said, in a tone that I knew meant she wanted to know the truth as much as I did.

The next morning, we told Mom we had to stay late at school, studying.

"That's fine, just be home in time for dinner." We assured her we would, and then we were off for our big day.

Greer

I was determined to get answers from Lorcan, and that was all I could think of most of the morning. I barely spoke to anyone until lunch, except for an occasional hello. Liam had smiled and said hi to me in physics, but we had not talked more than that.

"What did you do the rest of the weekend?" Ella asked me near the end of lunch.

"Just family stuff," I responded, practicing vague answers, which I planned on using with Lorcan.

"Some of us are going to hang out after school today at my house, if you and Darcy want to come?" Ella offered kindly.

"I'm sorry, but I have to work on my speech assignment after school today," I said. I realized I should have been more vague, as what I said caught our friends' attention, and the rest of our lunch table looked over in my direction.

"With Lorcan?" Mia asked curiously.

"Of course with Lorcan! He's her partner!" Sloan replied excitedly. "Lucky girl!"

"Oh, he's so handsome and dreamy!" Nathan said in a high-pitched voice. He and Will could be good friends, I thought. All the girls at our table rolled their eyes, while Elliot stifled a laugh. Liam just looked down at the remainder of his lunch, and appeared bothered.

"Leave her alone," Ella said sternly. Nathan shot me an apologetic look; he was a nice guy, but he was always trying to be funny and make people laugh—sometimes he needed to pick his moments a little better.

The bell rang, signaling lunch was over, and we all began to quickly gather up our things. Liam turned to me and whispered, "Can I talk to you after school? Do you think you will still be around at five?" His eyes were sweet but serious, and I could not wait to know what he wanted to talk to me about away from all of our friends.

"Yes, I should still be in the library," I said slowly, trying to hide some of my enthusiasm.

"Okay, I'll meet you there." Liam smiled, and we all made our way out of the cafeteria.

The rest of the day was a blur, as my thoughts bounced between the excitement of my meetings with Lorcan and Liam. When I tried to figure out which meeting I was more excited about, I couldn't tell, and that began to worry me.

After speech class, Lorcan and I walked to the library together, stopping by my locker to grab some things I needed. I noticed that as we walked, lots of people stared in our direction, and some even whispered. I blew off the stares and tried to focus on my mission.

"How was your weekend?" Lorcan asked kindly, cutting his eyes over at me as we made our way into the library.

"Good," I said quickly in response, and then countered, "what did you do this weekend?" I noticed Darcy was already sitting in a back corner table.

Lorcan appeared surprised at the quick turn in conversation, no doubt used to girls getting lost in his green eyes and gorgeous smile. He simply replied, "I helped my dad on a work project."

I picked out a table where we could not see Darcy, but I was almost certain she could see us. As Lorcan pulled out a chair for me, I hastily followed up with another question before he could ask me one. "What does your father do?"

I could tell Lorcan was somewhat guarded in discussing his family, but he smiled graciously and replied, "He is the CEO of a mid-size company."

"What kind of company?" I asked as nonchalantly as possible, while I unpacked the materials we needed to work on our speech assignment.

"It's a private medical research company he inherited from his grandfather." Lorcan searched my eyes quickly before he said, "But, you seem to already know that?"

How in the world did he know that I thought his father might be the CEO of Smith Industries? His intuition made me uneasy, and reminded me a lot of Darcy's. I continued to be careful with not just my words, but also with my facial expressions, just like Darcy had practiced with me the night before. Perhaps she knew Lorcan shared her gift. If so, she hadn't mentioned it, but she had worked with me on how to monitor myself to not give away too much information. I was amazed at how good she was at it, and I realized that, in most instances, she only revealed the emotions and information she wanted.

"What makes you say that?" I replied, trying to make my face expressionless, which was no easy task. I had to consciously work to not allow my eyes or mouth to move, and it seemed like forever, waiting for Lorcan's response.

He just stared at me and began to smile. "I just thought maybe Katie's dad had mentioned my father the other night at the sleepover."

"No." I shook my head slightly and reached for a book.

Lorcan picked up the book, and when he placed it in my hand, he did not let go. We locked eyes. All of a sudden, I felt really warm in the library, where I usually felt slightly cool. "Oh, my mistake," Lorcan said, still holding the book while he interrogated my eyes. I revealed nothing.

Lorcan never stopped smiling, but finally let go of the book. I decided to shift the conversation to our assignment. We were allowed to know two of each other's main arguments, but one had to be kept secret, and I was for following the rules. When I mentioned the two arguments I had come up with in favor of using mental performance enhancing drugs, Lorcan chuckled softly.

"Excuse me?" I replied, slightly angry, knowing full well I had lost my emotionless mask.

Lorcan smiled playfully and said, "Don't be upset. I just think there are stronger arguments than those, and I don't want to win too easily."

"Oh, you're not going to win. I may not like at all that I have to argue in favor of this, but I can still win this debate," I replied confidently. I noticed that people in the library had started to stare. I had raised my voice above the approved hushed whisper.

"Well, well," Lorcan replied happily. "I didn't know you had such a competitive side! I like it!"

I blushed, partly embarrassed because I lost control of the emotions I so wanted to keep in check, and partly because I knew my competitive nature was one of my biggest faults, and I did not like it.

Trying to recompose myself, I looked up and saw Mallory and Kieran enter the library and walk towards our table. I quickly re-masked my face to one of no emotion, and waited for what I thought would be an interesting exchange. Kieran and Mallory rarely disappointed.

"Hello, brother," Kieran said condescendingly to Lorcan, looking over to me.

"Hi, Lorcan," Mallory said admiringly. She continued to stare at him; it was obvious he was the current object of her affection.

"Hello, ladies." Lorcan smiled, but I had a feeling he was upset at the interruption. He shot Kieran a warning look. She certainly didn't have the control Lorcan possessed in monitoring her emotions. She tried, but was often unsuccessful.

"What are you working on?" Mallory asked, smiling at Lorcan before giving me a hateful look.

"Our speech assignment," I replied with my best smile. Mallory promptly rolled her eyes and looked back over at Lorcan.

"What are you two doing in here?" Lorcan gave me an approving smile, and then looked more seriously at his sister.

"We're just looking for someone. Oh, and I think we just found her," Kieran replied, as she scanned the library and saw Darcy sitting in the back corner.

"Then you should go and talk to her. We need more time to work on our assignment," Lorcan said, in a slightly demanding tone. I realized that was the way he had to be to get Kieran to do anything, as she often did what she wanted.

Mallory smiled one last time, rather desperately, at Lorcan, before she and Kieran walked towards Darcy's table. Neither of them looked in my direction again. I didn't like that they were going to talk to Darcy, even though I had no doubt she was fully capable of handling them.

Lorcan and I continued to discuss the basics of the assignment, and I refused to be baited again into revealing my competitive side. Within a few minutes, I saw Darcy leaving quickly with Kieran and Mallory. I was concerned because I saw she had her backpack; I thought she surely would not leave me alone with Lorcan, as much as she distrusted him. As she passed by a few tables away, I saw her give me a worried look and then Kieran passed by me with a wicked little smile.

Lorcan saw the concerned look on my face and asked, "Is everything okay?"

"Darcy's leaving and she has the keys to our car," I replied honestly.

"Oh, I didn't realize she was here," Lorcan replied. I knew he was lying.

"I'm sure she'll be back. We're almost finished here anyways," I said, looking at my watch and realizing that it was already 4:50. I was supposed to meet Liam in ten minutes.

"Well, if she doesn't come back, I can give you a ride home," Lorcan said, a little too sweetly, as he reached for my hand. I didn't have time to react, so I just left his hand there for a moment, trying to figure out what to do next.

"That's so kind of you, but I have some other studying I'd like to do. I'm sure Darcy will be back," I replied confidently, as I gently slid my hand out from under his.

"I'd be happy to move to another table, just until Darcy returns. I'd feel terrible if you got stuck here," Lorcan said, a bit too dramatically for my taste. I was certain almost any other girl would have already melted in his arms.

"Really, it's okay. You're so kind to worry, but I'll be fine." I looked around and realized we were the only two students left in the library, even though it didn't close until six.

"Okay, but I am going to give you my cell number, and if you need me, all you have to do is call." Lorcan grabbed my cell from the table and added his contact information.

"Thank you," I replied, as he handed me back my phone. It was almost five, and I knew Liam would arrive any minute.

Lorcan looked at me strangely for a moment, as he rose and packed up his things. He said goodbye and left. I was alone in the library, except for the eighty year old librarian's assistant, who was dozing off at her desk.

I was trying to work on some other homework when I heard a noise from the back corner, where Darcy had been sitting. I thought no other students were left, but maybe I was wrong. I ignored the strange noise for a minute, but I couldn't concentrate, so I slowly got up and began to walk over towards where the sound was coming from. I acted as if I were looking for something, thinking I would find a student tucked away studying. As I rounded the corner, I saw the table where Darcy had been sitting. There was no one there, but there was a sheet of paper held down partially by a book on the edge of the table. A fan directly above the table was causing the paper to flap up and down. I was relieved, realizing I had probably not heard the sound before because Lorcan and I were talking.

I walked towards it, to shove it under the book entirely, when a word on the paper caught my attention. It was my last name. I moved it out from under the book so I could see it; it was a photocopy of a New England newspaper article, dated a few months before my birth. The headline read "TRAGEDY STRIKES WEALTHY HAGEN FAMILY," but before I could read any more, I heard someone approaching.

"G?" I heard a familiar voice say. I jumped and turned around to see Will, who laughed when he realized he had scared me. I quickly folded the piece of paper and held it tightly in my hand.

"What are you doing here?" I asked impatiently.

"I needed a book, so Mom brought me," Will replied, still laughing.

"Mom's here?" I asked anxiously.

"Yeah, she's outside talking to Darce. I think she's going to go on home, and I am going to ride back with you guys." Will was trying to understand why I was so worried.

"Was anyone else with Darcy when she came out?" I asked, my mind racing.

"It was just her and some girl named Mallory. What's going on? Does this have something to do with the mysterious Lorcan?" Will whispered. It was evident he was becoming impatient with me.

Just then we heard someone else enter the library, and I raised my pointer finger to my mouth to shush Will. He stood still, and I began to peek around a bookshelf to see who it was, when the intruder rounded the corner and ran right into me.

I screamed and Will laughed. I looked up to see it was Liam; he gently held my forearms, which I had raised in defense as we collided.

"Are you okay?" Liam asked, very concerned. He looked me straight in the eyes, and I felt myself blush, something that often happened in his presence.

"She's okay, she just startles easy," Will replied, laughing.

Liam continued to look at me, and I reassured him, "I'm fine. You just surprised me, that's all."

"What are you guys doing in the back corner of the library?" Liam asked, as he slowly let go of me and backed up slightly.

"What *are* we doing back here, G?" Will asked amusingly, dragging out his words.

"Weren't you looking for a book?" I said, a bit annoyed. I glared at him.

Reading my nonverbals, Will knew he should leave it alone, so he responded to my great satisfaction, "Yes, I was, and I think I'll see if I can find it now." He scurried off to another part of the library.

"Are you sure you're okay?" Liam asked sweetly again.

"Yes, I'm fine, I promise," I said. I realized that I had dropped the copy of the newspaper article I was holding when Liam and I ran into each other. I looked down quickly and saw it had fallen just under the bookshelf. Liam saw the direction I was looking and reached down as I did to pick it up. Please do not let him see what it says, I thought.

Without opening it, he handed it to me and asked considerately, "Did you drop this?"

"Yes, thank you." I smiled and placed it in my back pocket. I remained silent, as I remembered that Liam had said he wanted to talk to me about something. I was excited about what the subject might be, so I wanted to make sure I gave him an opportunity to speak. I smiled up at him and pushed some loose strands of hair behind my right ear.

He smiled in a way that made me think whatever he wanted to talk about was going to be good. "Thanks for waiting for me," he said, gesturing for us to sit down at the table nearby. We walked the short distance, and for the second time in one day, a guy pulled out a chair for me.

We sat down and I said, "Thank you," and then I waited for him to continue.

"How did working on your project go?" Liam asked curiously.

"Fine," I quickly responded, preferring not to talk about Lorcan.

Liam looked at me, a bit bewildered, and said bluntly, "Lorcan doesn't seem to have the same effect on you as the rest of the girls in school, although it's certainly not for his lack of trying."

I laughed slightly and said, "I guess the same could be said about you and Kieran."

"Yes, she is a bit persistent." Liam blushed for the first time in my presence. I couldn't believe it, but it made him more handsome.

We remained silent for a moment, as it became clear that Liam was trying to figure out what he wanted to say next. I gave him a small, encouraging smile, and he cut his eyes down at his hands clasped together on the table. He was obviously nervous, but for what reason, I couldn't understand.

He looked back up at me and said, "Greer, would you like to go out with me on Saturday night?"

I was shocked. A million things had run through my mind, but I had not anticipated him actually asking me out on a date. This was going to be my first date! I realized I was taking too long to respond; Liam began to look more nervous, partly because of my delayed response and partly because I was so shocked my face wasn't displaying any emotion.

"Yes," I replied, giving Liam my best smile. He smiled in return, appearing happy and relieved.

Before either one of us could say anything else, Will came around the corner. "Sorry to interrupt, but Julius Caesar's mother, at the front desk, said she is closing the library early."

I ignored his old age quip about the poor librarian's assistant and, while trying to keep my smile to a reasonable wattage, asked, "Did you get the book you needed?"

Will looked at me, then at Liam, and then back at me, trying to figure out what had just happened. "Yeah, and Darce texted and said she is waiting outside for us."

"We should probably get going," Liam said, as he stood up from his chair. We walked over to where I had been sitting with Lorcan earlier, and I quickly packed up my things. Liam and Will waited and then we all walked out of the library and down the hall to the front doors. The school was eerily quiet, and, as we were about to exit, I thought I heard whispering. I quickly turned around, squinted my eyes, and thought I saw someone move swiftly back behind a corner.

"Is something wrong?" Liam asked, holding the door open for me.

"No, I just thought I heard something. It's nothing," I replied, as we walked out into the late afternoon sun.

We said our goodbyes to Liam when we reached our car. Darcy and Will looked at me a little quizzically when Liam asked if he could call me that night. I told him he could, and I quickly entered my cell number into his phone.

Once we were in the car, Will asked, "So why is Liam going to call you, G?"

"I don't want to talk about it right now. We'll talk about it later," I said, turning on the radio. I didn't want to talk about it yet because I was still processing our conversation, and because I realized I had to get permission to go on a date with Liam from my parents, which, even though they had met him and liked him, was not guaranteed. I knew I would need to talk to Darcy about everything that happened, and get her advice on how to best approach our overprotective parents for permission to go on my first date.

Chapter Eight

Darcy

After dinner, Greer and I excused ourselves under the pretense we were going to work on our English project.

"You mean I have to clean the kitchen by myself?" Will moaned as we walked up the stairs.

"No, your father and I will help you," Mom said, and smiled at Dad.

Greer and I continued up the stairs and could still hear Will grumbling as we walked into Greer's bedroom. I sat in her favorite reading chair, which was quite comfortable, and Greer sat on the end of her bed. She checked her phone, which I had heard vibrate during dinner. She had not checked it then because of our strict rule against electronic devices at the dinner table. I could tell she was anxious to tell me about her afternoon. From the smile on Greer's face as she quickly shot off a text, I knew it was Liam, and that he had finally gotten the courage to ask her out. I was glad, because I knew she liked him, plus I wanted to make sure Lorcan had some real competition.

When Greer looked my way, I smiled and asked, "So?"

"Where to start!" she replied excitedly, placing her phone on her nightstand.

"Why don't you start with what happened with Liam, and then we'll talk about Lorcan." I replied, hoping she would sense from the tone of my voice that I wanted her to get to the point quickly.

"Okay." Greer smiled and I knew she had caught on. "He had asked me at lunch to wait for him after school. I told him we could meet in the library, and luckily Lorcan had left just in time. Liam showed up after Will had come in, and while Will was looking for a book, Liam asked me out on a date for this Saturday night!" she squealed. Greer wasn't one to go on like a typical teenage girl, but in that moment, I was genuinely happy for her, so I found it more amusing than annoying.

"Well, Liam finally worked up the courage to ask you out, good for him," I said with a laugh.

"What do you mean? Why would he need courage to ask me out?" she asked, puzzled at my remark.

"Oh Greer, you don't give yourself enough credit. You're one of the prettiest girls in school and you don't even know it! That's why Mallory can't stand you, and probably Kieran too," I replied, sincerely surprised at her naïveté.

Greer's mouth hung open; she could not believe what I had just said. "You have got to be kidding me!" she said with a laugh. "You've always been the pretty one."

"For some reason, you've always believed that. Look in the mirror," I replied. I knew she had thought I was prettier because of the comments she had always heard about my red hair and green eyes. That was why I wore it pulled back most of time and rarely wore makeup. She, however, had never really thought of herself as some great beauty, which was completely ridiculous.

Greer looked across the room at the mirror on the wall and stared for a moment as I spoke again, my voice still very serious. "You look so much like Mom." I wondered why that made me so sad.

"You think so?" she asked, turning back to face me.

"Yes, I do," I replied, and looked down at my clasped hands. There was silence for a moment as she seemed to search for something to say.

"Enough about this; what else did Liam say?" I said quickly, trying to get the conversation to move forward. I couldn't dwell on my inexplicable feelings, not now, at least.

"Nothing, that was all we had time to discuss, but I need to get permission from Mom and Dad to go," Greer said in a worried tone.

"Oh, they'll give you permission. Don't worry about that. They met him. They liked him. It'll be fine. After we're done talking, you just need to go ask them if you can go. They're not going to say no," I responded, with enough confidence for the both of us.

"You really think so?" she questioned. I knew she was thinking of how Mom and Dad could be really overprotective. It was true; our parents were happy the dating issue had never really come up, as neither Greer nor I had ever wanted to go out with a boy on a one-on-one date before, but I knew they would let her go out with him. No boy would ever be good enough for Greer or me in their eyes, but he was about as good as they would get. I knew they would see that.

"Yes, now tell me what happened with Lorcan?" I asked and leaned forward.

Greer hesitated, and I had a feeling she wanted to keep talking about her date with Liam: what she should wear, where she thought they would go, etc. I selfishly wanted to focus on our mission.

"What did you find out?" I asked again, impatience creeping into my tone.

"Well, I did just as you suggested and turned everything back around on him. I asked him lots of questions and remained very vague in my own answers," Greer replied happily.

"Good," I replied, and gestured for her to go on.

"Unfortunately, I didn't find out a lot before Kieran and Mallory interrupted us. We talked a lot about the assignment, and he gave me a hard time about my persuasive points. I slipped a little there and showed a bit of my competitive side, to his amusement," Greer replied, with a regretful look.

"That's no big deal; it makes you seem like you were being yourself, plus it tells us something about him," I said with a smile.

"Really, what's that?" she asked curiously.

"He likes finding your weak spots. Let's just be careful to not let him use them to his advantage. What else happened?" I asked eagerly. I could tell Greer was puzzled by what I had said. The truth was that I had a way of understanding people's motives very easily. It was a trait Greer did not possess.

She continued, "Well, I did confirm that Lorcan and Kieran's father is the CEO of Smith Industries, a mid-size private medical research company that has entered into a partnership with Dr. Dobry's labs."

"What?" I asked as I leaned towards Greer. "Why didn't you tell me about this before?" I continued, trying to muffle the anger in my voice. This was disturbing to me in a way I couldn't explain, and when something really bothered me, anger was the first emotion to emerge.

Greer quickly told me about the papers she had seen at the Dobrys, and then told me what Lorcan had said about his father in the library.

I knew she had honestly forgotten to mention it to me, and I wasn't going to punish her for that. In a fairly normal voice, I replied, "Well, we've made some progress." I leaned back and relaxed a bit.

"What happened with you leaving so abruptly?" Greer asked.

"Oh, Kieran and Mallory stopped by and 'happened' to mention that they had seen our Mom and Will pulling into the parking lot from a classroom window. So, I headed out to find a way to stop Mom from coming inside and meeting Lorcan and Kieran," I said with a smile.

"Didn't Kieran and Mallory leave the same time you did?" Greer asked.

"Kieran said she had forgotten something in her locker, so she headed upstairs, but Mallory came outside and met Mom and Will."

"What did Mom think of Mallory? And how did you convince Mom to leave?" Greer asked with a look of awe.

"Well, Mallory just said hi and that was about it, so there really wasn't that much of an impression to be made. I just told Mom that you were still in the library, I would bring you and Will home, and that she could go start working on dinner if she wanted. That was really it; it wasn't so hard," I replied with my same smile as before.

Greer reached over to grab something from her nightstand, but suddenly stopped and pulled out a piece of paper from her back pocket.

"What's that?" I asked, leaning forward again.

Greer explained how she found it and that she had only read the headline when Will showed up.

"You say you found this on the table where I was sitting?" I moved next to her on the bed so I could see the paper better.

"Yes, it had to have been the table where you were sitting," she replied confidently.

"There was nothing on that table when I left. Did you get a look at the book the piece of paper was under?" I asked, as I began to examine the paper more closely.

"No, I didn't see the title, but I do know that it was a large, thick, black book, like a research journal," she replied. At least she remembered that much, I thought, as I held the mysterious paper in my hand.

"And you haven't read it?" I asked, looking up at her. She shook her head no. "Well, let's see what it says," I whispered as I began to unfold it.

TRAGEDY STRIKES WEALTHY HAGEN FAMILY

A fire late last night at the Boston based headquarters of Hagen International Research Labs claimed the lives of the founder and CEO Charles Hagen's only son James and his wife Alexis. James Hagen worked alongside his father at the lab, and had been instrumental in recent break-through drug testing to reverse the effects of early onset Alzheimer's. His mother, former socialite and current recluse Jocelyn Fitzpatrick Hagen, allegedly suffers from the illness.

James and Alexis, married for twenty-five years, had been instrumental in Boston philanthropic society, serving on many boards for worthy causes, including the Hagen Foundation, which provides full college scholarships to underprivileged students in the Boston area. The couple was also known for their volunteer work, including person-ally working in soup kitchens throughout the year, and their frequent visits to local orphanages they generously supported.

It is unknown at this time what started the fire or why Mr. Hagen and his wife were at the lab at such a late hour. Investigators said it would take weeks to determine the cause of the fire, although a source did speculate they believed it was the result of arson.

The Hagen family has declined comment at this time, requesting privacy during their mourning. James and Alexis Hagen are survived by their son David and his wife Arianna, who are expecting their first child; his parents, Dr. Charles and Jocelyn Hagen; his sister ███████████ and her husband ████████████, along with their son ████████████; and her sister Jacqueline and her husband Edward Oliver, and their daughters Patricia and Cassandra.

The family will hold a private funeral Mass and burial on Saturday, February 23rd. In lieu of flowers, the family kindly requests that donations be made in James and Alexis' names to the Hagen Foundation or the Boston Children's Home.

After I finished reading the newspaper clip aloud, we just stared at the piece of paper for a moment, trying to process what we had discovered. The article I held in my hand told us more about our extended family than we had ever learned from our father. A million questions ran through my mind.

Greer was the first to speak. "How did this copy of an old newspaper article about our family from a Boston-based paper end up in our high school library, right where I could find it?"

"You're sure you saw no one else go over to where I had been sitting?" I asked, tearing my eyes away from the paper for the first time to look up at Greer.

"You were the only one over there until Mallory and Kieran went over to talk to you," she said, slowly articulating Kieran's name. I realized that when the three of us exited the library, Kieran was several steps behind Mallory and me. I told Greer that Kieran had not caught up to us until the hallway, and then she said she had to get something from her locker. I had assumed it was an excuse to not meet our mom, whom Greer had overheard Lorcan forbid her to go near.

"Well, then we have our answer. It had to have been Kieran who placed this article there," I said, looking back at the paper.

"But why? And why are the names marked out?" Greer asked, pointing to them.

"Both are good questions. I didn't even know that Dad had any aunts or cousins, but it's strange that his father's sister's family is blacked out," I replied, reading over that section of the article again.

"Kieran is playing some sort of game with us," Greer retorted, with a tone that told me she really did not like her. Greer normally liked everyone, but I was glad she felt that way about Kieran, even though I believed Kieran's behavior was masking something that I planned to find out.

"Her and Lorcan both," I said, looking back up at her.

"I know he's up to something, but he's not as bad as she is," Greer said. It made me nervous that she was defending him.

"You need to concentrate on liking Liam and not Lorcan. Don't confuse your feelings in anyway, do you understand?" I replied seriously, and continued, "You may have to spend time with Lorcan to find out more information, and you have to keep a clear head."

"I don't like Lorcan like that, but I can see that there is a good side to him, unlike his sister," Greer said defensively.

"Maybe, but that's yet to be determined." I looked at her closely. "Are you going to have a problem spending more time with him?"

"No," Greer replied quickly.

"Good, because we need answers now more than ever." I looked back at the newspaper article.

"What if…" Greer began.

"Don't even think about it!" I cut her off.

"I don't see why…" she began again.

"No, absolutely not!" I said forcefully. I placed my hands on her feet, as Greer sat with her knees pulled in towards her chest.

"They'll have to know sooner or later," Greer said, trying to match my stare.

"Then it'll have to be later. I guarantee you, if we tell Mom and Dad right now, we'll get no answers and our things will be packed before we get home from school tomorrow—which would mean no date with your dear Liam," I said emphatically. Greer lowered her head slightly and sighed. She knew I was right.

"Okay, but I really hate all of this, just so you know." Greer stared at her fidgeting hands.

"I know, Greer, it's not in your DNA to keep secrets from our parents." I moved further back on the bed and leaned against the wall.

"And it's in yours?" Greer asked. That was when I realized she was becoming teary-eyed. She quickly wiped at her face, trying to get rid of any evidence that she was about to cry.

"Let's just say it comes easier for me." I gave her a half-smile in an effort to make her feel better. She gave me a half smile back, and we remained silent for several minutes, deep in our own thoughts, until we heard a knock on Greer's bedroom door.

I whispered, "Act normal!" as I folded the copy of the newspaper article and slid it under my leg.

"Come in," Greer said, wiping her eyes again and trying to look as normal as possible.

Mom entered the room. She smiled at the sight of us sitting on Greer's bed, obviously in each other's confidence. Mom was an only child, and I knew that she had always wished for siblings, especially a sister.

"Am I interrupting?" Mom whispered, still holding on to the door handle, waiting for the okay to come in further.

"It's fine," Greer said, trying to wipe her eyes again without her noticing. Of course, that was hopeless.

"What's wrong?" Mom said in the kindest, gentlest voice, quickly shutting the door and moving towards us.

I spoke up, knowing Greer wouldn't have a clue what to say. I admired that she was so good and honest, but in this moment she had to be more reserved. "Greer's really excited, because Liam Alexander asked her out for Saturday night, but she's worried that you and Dad won't give her permission to go." Greer looked at me, and I could tell she was surprised I had come up with a cover so quickly. I gave her a reassuring smile.

"Oh, sweetheart! Why would you worry about that?" Mom asked, still smiling as she sat down beside Greer on the bed.

"Because I know how crazy protective Dad is," Greer replied quietly. I could tell she was still unsure if she was going to get to go on her date with Liam, although she seemed to take Mom's response as a good sign.

"Well, for the record, I'm every bit as protective of you children as your father. In most cases, I think we would have a million questions before allowing any of you out the door on a date, but lucky for you, most of our questions have already been addressed." Mom was still smiling.

Greer and I looked at her, completely puzzled. "What do you mean?" Greer said, anxious for her to go on.

"We got to spend a lot of time with Liam the other night when he was visiting with your brother. We learned a lot about him and his family. He seems like a very nice young man," Mom said, never losing her beautiful, sweet smile.

"So she can go?" I asked, before Greer had the chance.

"Well, we told him the other night when he asked permission to take you out that it was fine with us. Of course, we made him tell us his plans for the evening, and I said I would like to speak with his mother beforehand," Mom replied with a small laugh.

"Are you serious?" Greer said, with a combination of elation and embarrassment. I could see her point on both counts. First of all, who asks for permission from parents anymore to take their almost eighteen year old daughter out on a date? I knew our parents loved that, and I had to admit I thought it was pretty genius of him. Secondly, I was not surprised at all that our parents made Liam tell them everything they were going to do on the date, and I wouldn't be shocked if he had to write out a play-by-play for our dad. Finally, I thought it was pretty funny that Mom wanted to meet his mom before Greer and Liam went out. I laughed slightly, knowing that had to severely embarrass Greer, given that they were just going on one date, not getting married.

"Yes, I am meeting his mother for coffee tomorrow morning. She seemed lovely when I spoke with her on the phone on Sunday evening."

Greer sat there in a state of shock and appeared grateful when I spoke up, "I am surprised that Will was able to keep all of this a secret."

"Oh, he doesn't know," Mom laughed.

"How's that possible?" Greer asked. She still appeared surprised.

"He left the room in search of something, and Liam used that opportunity to ask us if he could take you out. I think he was slightly nervous and wanted to have as little of an audience as possible," Mom replied happily.

"So, what are they going to do on their date?" I asked, looking over at Greer and smiling.

"No, that's a surprise. We promised Liam we wouldn't tell you. You'll be happy we kept our promise."

"I hate surprises!" Greer groaned. I smiled, happy that Liam had taken my suggestion.

"You'll like this one." Mom said. We all glanced up towards the door; someone had just started gently knocking on it.

"Come in," Mom said happily. Dad entered, with Will looking sheepish behind him. Dad looked at us, the three Hagen women, and I could tell he was nervous that he had just interrupted some serious girl talk.

"What's going on in here?" Dad said, a bit relieved when he saw the smile on Mom's face.

"Liam asked Greer out today," Mom replied sweetly.

"Oh, did he now?" Dad laughed.

"I told you he liked you! So that is what you two were talking about in the library!" Will said in an unexpectedly excited tone. "Are you going to let her go out with him? He's really a great guy!"

Mom and Dad looked at each other for a moment, and then Dad finally spoke, "Yes, she can go." Greer literally jumped off her bed and wrapped her arms around his neck.

"Thank you!" Greer said, first to him and then to Mom, as she sat back down on the bed. I laughed out loud; I was sure that no one had to work so hard to go on a first date, although technically Liam was the one who did all of the work. He and Greer were a good match, I thought to myself.

We all talked for a few more minutes before Mom realized it was getting close to ten, which meant we should all be heading to our own rooms for the night. Will said goodnight to all of us, fist bumping Greer and me, and hugging Mom and Dad before leaving Greer's room.

I was expected to leave next, and that was when I realized I could not stand up without exposing the piece of paper under my leg. I could tell Greer was getting anxious as she realized the same thing. "I need to talk to Greer another minute about our assignment, and then I will go straight to my room, I promise," I said calmly, with my most convincing smile.

"Okay, but don't take too long, you both need your rest," Mom said, cupping her hand under Greer's chin and then walking over and doing the same to me.

Greer and I made no effort to get up from the bed, so Dad bent over and kissed each of us on the head and said, "Goodnight, sweet dreams," before leaving the room.

As she was about to leave, Mom turned and said, "If you girls don't have any plans after school tomorrow, I thought we might do a little shopping."

"That sounds good; Greer will need a new outfit for her date," I said, smiling at Mom and then at Greer.

"Alright, goodnight my darlings," Mom smiled and shut the door behind her.

"Goodnight," Greer and I said in unison.

I immediately pulled the piece of paper out from under my leg and walked over to Greer's bookshelf. I grabbed an old hardback copy of *Alice in Wonderland*, opened it to a random page in the middle, and placed the folded up news article inside. I replaced the book and turned to Greer. "Leave that there," I said seriously. "I will think of a plan for what we need to do next. We need to proceed very carefully."

Greer nodded in agreement, and I walked back towards her bed and sat down right next to her.

"Greer, I'm sorry that you have to be involved in this. I know it makes you uncomfortable keeping secrets. I wouldn't ask you to help unless I felt it was important. There's something going on here, and I will discover what it is," I said confidently.

"But if Mom and Dad are keeping a secret, then you know they are doing it for a good reason. What if your discovery changes everything?" I knew Greer did not have a good feeling about the whole situation; the truth was, neither did I, but that just made me more determined to find out what was going on.

"That's a chance I have to take. Lorcan and Kieran are obviously playing at something, and there is no stopping them now," I replied. Greer gave me a small smile, but I could tell she was still worried.

"I had better get to my room before Mom comes back in here," I said, heading for the door. When I reached it, I turned to Greer and said, "I really am happy about your date with Liam. He seems like a nice guy."

"Now we just need to find you a nice guy," Greer said with a broad smile. I immediately thought of Edmund and the weird feeling I got in my stomach when we met.

There was a pause in the conversation for a moment, and I saw Greer staring at me as if she were reading my mind. I laughed and said, "Let's not overwhelm Mom and Dad right now. One teenage daughter dating is probably enough for them."

Greer laughed and said goodnight. I gave her a slight wave and walked out through her bedroom door and into the hall, so our parents would know I had left her room for the night.

Chapter Nine

Greer

I woke up late, having forgotten to set the alarm on my phone, and scrambled into the bathroom; thankfully, Darcy had already vacated, no doubt having finished her fifteen minute morning regimen much earlier. I took the world's fastest shower (for me, at least), hastily dried my hair, and brushed it into a ponytail. I brushed my teeth, put on enough makeup to make me look presentable, and grabbed the first clean fitted t-shirt and pair of jeans I could find. I looked at the clock and realized Darcy would be downstairs waiting for me. I threw my things in my school bag, and looked up at the copy of *Alice in Wonderland* that sat undisturbed on my bookshelf. For a brief moment, I wondered what the day might have in store for me, and I ran out my bedroom door and down the stairs.

When I arrived in the kitchen, Darcy, having already finished her breakfast, was waiting for me at the bar. Will was sitting at the table, wolfing down his remaining pancakes, which I was sure were the last two of about ten. As I stopped at the bar, I said to Darcy, "Sorry, I'm running a little late this morning."

"There you are! I'm sorry, I thought you were already up, or else I would have woken you." Mom smiled and handed me my lunch.

I smiled and said, "Thanks," in my still out-of-breath voice.

"Do you have time for breakfast?" Mom asked.

"No, we need to go or we'll be late," Darcy replied for me.

"I'll just grab some Pop-Tarts from the pantry." I walked across the kitchen quickly, grabbed what I was looking for, and headed towards the garage door, where Darcy was already waiting.

"Bye Mom, bye Will!" I turned and yelled.

"Bye!" Will yelled, his mouth stuffed full with his last pancake.

"Wait!" Mom exclaimed, rushing over to us. "Let's meet at the mall right after you get out of school, at the front entrance of Nordstrom."

"Sounds good." I gave her a quick hug.

"We'll see you there." Darcy smiled and also gave her a quick hug. Then we were gone, out the door, in the car, and on the way to school. Darcy drove, even though it was my day. I didn't care. I took a quick look in the vanity mirror, frustrated at my super casual appearance. My hair was straight and pulled back, instead of down with the big wavy curls I typically wore, and my makeup was quite minimal (I wasn't even wearing eyeliner).

"You look fine," Darcy said, sensing I was feeling a little insecure.

"Of all the days to wake up late!" I grumbled to myself, although I knew she could hear me. I roughly closed the visor, shoved it back into place, and broke off a piece of my Pop-Tart to eat.

"A little change is good," Darcy replied sweetly, and a bit out of character.

"So, what's the plan for today? What do you want me to do?" I asked, ready to shift the subject away from me.

"I want you to keep your guard up around Lorcan and Kieran as much as possible, but we do have to make sure they know you have a date with Liam," Darcy said, formulating her plan.

"I don't think Lorcan will care, but Kieran will not be happy! Anyways, how will that help us?" I questioned, taking another bite of my breakfast.

"Well, their responses will reveal something. I can't really explain it. I just need to be there, so I can see their reactions. Trust me," Darcy replied, with a rather wry smile.

"Okay, it seems simple enough. They'll find out sooner or later; news travels fast in our school," I said. I was squirming at the thought that my date with Liam would be the talk of our friends and acquaintances for the next day or so. High school was as bad as the tabloid press. Gossip became news, and there was nowhere to escape until the next big story.

We were some of the last to arrive at school without actually being late. Darcy and I hurried off to first period. History class was a blur; I hadn't even noticed Lorcan and Kieran weren't there. The bell ringing startled me out of my daze. All during class I had been excited for physics class, where I would see Liam.

"Anxious much?" Darcy laughed as she saw me jump.

"Let's go." I shot her a mock frown as I gathered up my things, and we headed for our lockers. We had not had time to drop off our books from earlier, so I happily unloaded my heavy book bag, keeping just what I needed for my next two classes.

Darcy whispered, "Did you notice two missing students this morning?"

"No," I replied in the same hushed voice. Darcy frowned. I knew she was just as anxious as me, but for a different reason. She wanted answers.

We remained silent as we left our lockers and walked the short distance to class. When I walked in, I immediately saw Liam sitting in his usual desk, with my desk in front of him, empty and waiting for me. He looked up at me and smiled the warmest, most inviting smile. I actually felt my heart jump, and I stopped in my tracks. My stomach was rumbling, and I couldn't tell if it was from my hastily half-eaten breakfast in the car, or if I actually had butterflies. I could feel Darcy looking at me, no doubt smiling, as she passed by. I slowly began to move towards my desk, not able to take my eyes off of Liam, as he watched me walk towards him.

"Hi," he said sweetly, as I dropped my bag on the floor by my desk. I sat down and turned sideways in my chair so I could see him better. He leaned forward and, for a moment, I actually thought he was trying to smell my hair—in a sweet way, not a creepy one.

Finally, I said hi back, and then there was silence for a brief moment. I looked down at my hands, unsure what to say next.

"How was your night?" Liam asked kindly.

"Good, and yours?"

"Good," he replied, as if he was waiting for me to say something else.

I hesitated, but then I smiled; I knew what he was waiting on. "I mentioned our date to my parents."

"Yes?" Liam quickly cut his eyes down and then back up at me. I realized then that he either really liked me or he was an expert flirt, because the butterflies in my stomach were doing somersaults.

"So, you asked their permission?" I teased.

Liam's smile broadened, "Yes, I thought it was the best approach."

"Why's that?" I asked curiously.

"Because, if you had used your parents as an excuse to say no when I asked you out, then I would have had that base covered."

"And what if I had used some other excuse?" I asserted, in my pathetic attempt to flirt. Apparently it worked, as Liam appeared flustered for a moment.

"I would have thought of something," he declared, regaining his composure.

"I'm sure you would have." I smiled, locking my eyes right on his.

Class was about to begin, so I slowly turned around to face forward. I felt Liam lean in; his mouth was right beside my left ear.

"You look really nice today," he whispered, before leaning back in his chair. I didn't dare turn around. All of the tiny hairs on my forearms were standing straight up, as though a shot of electricity had jolted through my body. I had never felt anything like it before.

For class, our teacher worked through some new material, so Liam and I didn't have another chance to speak. I looked over at Darcy a couple of times, who was sitting just two rows over. She smiled encouragingly.

After class, Liam and I resumed our conversation as we walked towards my locker. Darcy had gone ahead to our next class. I had everything I needed for choir as well, but took the opportunity to spend a few more minutes with Liam.

"So, what are we doing on Saturday night?" After I spoke, I tried out what I thought was my most persuasive smile, which was where I kept my mouth closed and just curved my lips slightly upwards. I had rarely used it on purpose.

"Your parents didn't tell you?" Liam teased, knowing full well they had not.

"No, but surely you won't keep me in suspense?" I added, slowly batting my eyelashes. I felt silly, and probably looked like an idiot.

Liam paused for a moment and appeared to catch his breath, and then responded, "Nope, nice try, you'll have to wait and see."

"Alright, I've got the rest of the week to get it out of you," I laughed, mockingly punching him in his arm.

"Go ahead, but I warn you, I am a sealed vault. Plus, you'll be happy I kept it a secret."

We said goodbye after Liam walked me to choir. I couldn't wait to see him at lunch. Since Liam had asked me out, I had finally allowed myself to realize just how much I liked him. I had denied it before, because I was trying to protect myself.

I didn't get a chance to talk to Darcy during class, as we had begun rehearsing for our big final spring concert, and our teacher was quite determined to keep us focused.

I left my next class in the foreign languages hall, anxious to get to lunch. I wasn't paying attention to where I was going, and I ran right into Lorcan. The force of our collision was so strong, it knocked me off balance, and I dropped the two books I was carrying.

"I'm so sorry," I said, looking up, surprised to see it was him. I immediately bent down to pick up my books.

"Please let me help you; it was my fault," Lorcan insisted, reaching for my books. As we got up at the same time, I was holding one book, and Lorcan the other. I reached for it, but he just held it for a moment, looking into my eyes. It was a move he apparently used for effect. His bright green eyes sparkled in the awful, flickering fluorescent hallway lights. He was gorgeous, there was no doubt, and his eyes were hypnotizing. There was something so alluring about him; I couldn't put my finger on it, but it was almost overpowering.

"I thought you weren't here today," I mentioned quickly, taking my book from him and breaking away from his gaze. I had to remember what Darcy said, and not confuse my feelings for him and Liam.

"You noticed; I'm flattered." Lorcan smiled, and for a moment, I actually thought he was trying to flirt with me.

I began to walk briskly towards my locker to drop off my books, and I thought how it would be a good time to tell him about my date with Liam. Darcy had specifically requested to witness his reaction, so I knew I had to wait and tried to think of something to say. The best I could come up with was, "I think everyone notices whether you and your sister are here or not."

Lorcan smiled again, keeping pace with me. "I'm not sure about that, but it's nice to know you did."

I blushed at his comment, which appeared to make him happy. We were then at my locker, and I realized Lorcan wasn't going anywhere. He was planning to walk me to lunch. I was anxious, because I didn't want Liam to see us together and get upset. Hopefully, I thought, Liam would be a little late to lunch like normal, because he had to walk from his class on the other side of school grounds. If I hurried, I could already be sitting at our table when he came in, so I quickly shut my locker and began to walk hastily towards the cafeteria.

"Where's the fire?" Lorcan laughed through his words, as he once again kept up with my stride with ease.

"Where were you this morning?" I asked pointedly, looking over at him and then straight ahead, to watch out for all of our fellow classmates I was maneuvering around.

"It bothered you that I was gone?" Lorcan responded, partly asking a question and partly sounding a bit vain.

"No," I replied, a little too bluntly.

"Well." He blanched at my comment and slowed his pace.

"I'm sorry, I didn't mean to be rude." I felt guilty at my abruptness, and stopped in the middle of the hall and tried to look Lorcan in the eye. He just stared at the ground, so I gently reached up and placed my hand on his forearm to show him I meant my apology.

He looked up, gave me a small smile, and we resumed walking towards the cafeteria. After a moment, he unexpectedly said, "Kieran and I had to help our father with something in his lab this morning."

"Oh," I replied, unsure what to say next. I just kept walking, looking straight ahead. He seemed surprised I didn't question him further, and I felt his gaze upon me as we walked.

"You seem different today." Lorcan smiled at me strangely.

"What do you mean?"

"Your hair, makeup, even the way you're dressed," he replied, gesturing towards my casual outfit.

I suddenly felt self-conscious and blushed. "Oh yeah, I woke up late this morning and was rushed." I thought it was odd he noticed with such specificity what was different about me. Most guys would not.

"You always look beautiful, but you should definitely wear the color red more; it's striking on you," Lorcan replied, stroking my upper arm with the back of his hand. I got chills from his touch; suddenly, I felt very confused. I realized we were now at the entrance of the cafeteria, and I could feel people staring at us.

"I should get to my table," I said, sensing I needed to move away from him as soon as possible. In that moment, he had some unusually strong effect on me that I could not explain, and I hoped would lessen with some distance. Luckily, as I walked towards my table, I felt my confusion begin to decrease.

As I made my way around tables, I tried to focus my thoughts. I looked up and saw Liam was already sitting at our table, staring at me as I approached. My heart froze when I realized he had most likely seen Lorcan and I walk in together and him touching my arm. Suddenly, I felt a little sick.

When I reached our lunch table, I wasn't sure what to say. Luckily, Liam spoke first, sweetly saying, "Hello."

I smiled at him as our eyes locked, and I responded with a simple, "Hi." I was relieved to see that he wasn't mad.

We were the first ones at our table, having both brought our lunch. "You got here really fast today." I tried to act as normal as possible.

Liam smiled what had to be one of his most flirtatious smiles at me while cutting his head to one side, and replied, "Did I?"

If I thought Lorcan had any power over me earlier, I was clearly mistaken, because I was completely taken in by Liam in that very moment.

"What's happened to you?" I blurted out, surprised at my directness.

"What do you mean?" He laughed.

"You have become so flirty with me lately," I said, more bluntly than I intended.

"Is that a problem?" Liam asked in a concerned tone.

"No, not at all! It's just different. I'm not quite used to it." I laughed, as I thought to myself how easily I could get used to it.

"I have a hard time believing guys don't flirt with you," Liam said, glancing in the direction of Lorcan's table across the cafeteria. Lorcan was already sitting down, also the first of his table to arrive, and as Liam and I looked in his direction, Lorcan glanced our way and gave us a small smile. I quickly turned my head away.

Liam laughed slightly and looked back at me, waiting for my response. "He's just friendly, that's all," I said, trying to downplay Lorcan's actions towards me.

"He's friendly to you because he likes you." Liam emphasized the word 'you' both times.

"We were assigned to work together in speech, so we talk some when we are working on our project. That's really about it." I tried my best to be convincing.

Liam wasn't buying it and laughed, saying, "That may be it for you, but trust me, that's not all it is for him. He has had his eye on you since his first day here. I've been watching."

"You've been watching?" My heart began to race a little.

"Very closely," Liam admitted, leaning in towards me.

"Uhh, umm," Ella uttered, standing across the table from us with

Mia and Sloan slightly behind her. They were all staring at Liam and me with huge smiles on their faces. Liam and I immediately straightened up in our chairs, and I am sure my face became the color of my shirt. They quickly sat down and began chatting amongst themselves. I smiled, a bit embarrassed, and Ella gave me her best "I told you so" look.

Liam leaned over as soon as our friends weren't looking and whispered, "We'll finish this conversation later." I nodded in agreement, and then we resumed our usual lunch routine—with the exception of a few stolen smiles, which I was certain did not go unnoticed by anyone at our table.

After lunch, we all made our way to English. I walked with Ella, who patiently waited to talk to me until Liam was out of earshot. I whispered that Liam had asked me out. She was thrilled. Liam walked a few paces behind with Elliot and Nathan. I glanced back a couple of times to find him looking at me, and when our eyes met, we both smiled.

Soon we were in Ms. Abrams class, and I noticed Darcy was already at her desk. I gave her an "I have some information for you" look, to which she nodded. Ella and Mia came in and starting talking, and were soon joined by Katie and Rebecca. I sat down behind Darcy and was about to tell her everything that had happened that morning, when Kieran and Lorcan walked in. Their arrival grabbed everyone's attention, and the room went quiet for a moment. I glanced over to Liam, who looked back at me and smiled. Students in the class slowly resumed their conversations in more hushed tones, as Kieran and Lorcan sat down at their respective desks.

Suddenly, the room got quiet again and everyone's attention turned to either Liam or me, as Katie yelled out in excitement, "Greer's going out with Liam?!"

Darcy

Greer blushed ten shades of red after Katie's announcement. It was the moment I was waiting for, because I wanted to see Lorcan's reaction to the news. Greer looked at Liam, who looked over at her with a big smile. He was just fine with everyone knowing and, really, why wouldn't he be—Greer was a great girl, not to mention gorgeous. I looked briefly at Kieran, who gave Greer the most hateful, venomous look I had ever seen. I glanced back at Greer, and was pleased to see that she didn't hide her slight eye-roll as she also saw Kieran's reaction. I looked over at Lorcan. His reaction was intriguing. He wasn't smiling, but he wasn't frowning. He had an almost expressionless blank stare on his face, looking right at Greer. Greer saw it too, and I could tell she became uncomfortable, as she quickly looked away.

"Interesting," I whispered, leaning back in my chair and turning my head slightly towards Greer, so only she could hear me.

Class began, and while there was a very heated debate over the inspiration of Edgar Allen Poe's poems, I only half paid attention. When class ended, Katie, Rebecca, Ella, and Mia quickly descended on Greer and me.

"It's so awesome that you're going out with Liam!" Katie exclaimed, with her voice a little lower.

"He just asked me out for Saturday," Greer said, trying to downplay it a little.

"Saturday?" Rebecca repeated and then continued, "My parents said I could have a party on Saturday, and I was hoping all of you would come!"

"A party!" Katie screeched, back to her megaphone level.

"Maybe you and Liam can stop by," Ella suggested at a normal volume.

"Maybe, I'll ask him," Greer replied, as we all made our way out of class. Kieran and Lorcan had already left. They must have left as soon as the bell rang, I thought, glancing over to Greer, who seemed to be thinking the same thing.

Greer and Liam smiled briefly at each other as they went in separate directions after class. Greer and I stopped by our lockers before heading to calculus. "Be very careful in speech today," I whispered.

"What do you mean?" Greer asked nervously.

"Don't reveal too much about your feelings for Liam or anything about your date on Saturday," I continued seriously.

"Well, I don't know anything about what we're doing on our date, so that should be easy."

"Good, the less Lorcan knows the better, but you have to make sure he doesn't know just how much you like Liam." I didn't have time to explain why this was so important.

"I don't even know how much I like him," Greer confided honestly.

"I know you don't, but I do," I said with a smile.

Greer laughed a little and then we were off to calculus. We were busy the whole class period; all of our teachers were making their last hurrahs, presenting new material before our senioritis fully kicked in and we were incapable of learning anything new.

Greer

Darcy and I parted ways after calculus, and I headed nervously off to speech class.

Lorcan entered class late and didn't look at me the entire period, which I found kind of unnerving. I had witnessed his temper with his sister, and knew for certain he was not someone I wanted mad at me.

After what had to be the longest lecture on the importance of debate style speaking, class was finally over. I packed up my bag, and as I stood up, I noticed Lorcan standing right beside my desk. Startled by his close proximity, I jumped a little and said, "Oh, hi."

"Did I scare you?" Lorcan asked devilishly, leaning in a little closer.

"No, I just wasn't expecting you to be standing there," I responded, straightening up. I wouldn't allow him to scare me—or confuse me, for that matter.

"Good, because I certainly wouldn't want to do that." He reached for my bag.

"What are you doing?" I asked defensively, placing my hand on it.

"I thought I would walk you out, and it's the gentlemanly thing to do to carry a lady's heavy bag for her, don't you think?" He smiled the mischievous smile I had grown accustomed to in the short time I had known him, although it didn't lessen its effect.

"That's very nice, but I can carry my own bag, thank you." I batted my eyelashes at him the way I had at Liam. I wasn't trying to flirt; I was just trying to avoid having to explain to Liam why some other guy (especially this guy) was carrying my bag for me. I realized then that I had become very loyal to Liam, even though we had yet to go on our first date.

Apparently, my eyelashes had some strange effect on guys, because Lorcan smiled his broadest and most becoming smile and gently whispered, "As you wish."

We walked towards the door, and he asked nonchalantly, "Are you going to Rebecca's party Saturday night?"

"I don't know," I answered truthfully.

"Because of your date with Liam?" His words became bitter.

I knew I had to be careful with what I said, just like Darcy warned, so I tried to remain vague. "I'm not sure what my plans are yet."

When we reached the door, I was extremely relieved to see Darcy waiting for me. She spoke first, saying hello to Lorcan.

"Hello Darcy," Lorcan replied with a smile. I could tell he was upset that our conversation was about to be cut short.

"We need to get going if we are going to meet Mom," Darcy said to me tersely.

'Yeah, we should probably go." I smiled apologetically at Lorcan.

"Maybe I'll see you both at Rebecca's on Saturday," Lorcan said, before we could say goodbye.

"I'm sure we'll see you before then," I replied, a bit confused. It was only Tuesday, and there was still a lot of time until the weekend. Darcy looked at him curiously as we waited for his response.

"No, Kieran and I will be gone the rest of the week. We have to help our father with some important family affairs on the East Coast." Lorcan stared meaningfully at Darcy.

"Where on the East Coast?" Darcy asked directly.

Lorcan paused for a moment, but then a small smile curved his mouth, as he answered, "Boston."

Darcy's face showed no response, but I could tell by her eyes that she was thinking a thousand different things. I thought it best we leave then or we would actually be late meeting our mother, so I said, "I hope you and your family have a safe trip, Lorcan."

"Thank you and I hope to see you Saturday," Lorcan replied, and then turned and walked in the opposite direction of the way Darcy and I were headed.

"What do you think?" I whispered as we walked quickly towards the front exit.

"I don't know," Darcy snapped.

"Alright, but you should try to at least fake a better mood when we see Mom in a few minutes," I suggested, to which she responded with a roll of her eyes.

We met up with Mom twenty minutes later and spent a great couple of hours shopping. Darcy acted normal, for the most part, only appearing deep in thought a few times. Afterwards, we grabbed takeout Chinese and headed home to meet Will and Dad.

The rest of the week was pretty normal, except for my friends hounding me about my upcoming date with Liam and if we were going to Rebecca's party.

Darcy had become somewhat quiet, and I didn't bother to ask her any further questions about Lorcan or Kieran and what we should do next. I knew she would talk when she was ready.

Liam and I continued to flirt at lunch and in class. He still refused to tell me where we were going on Saturday night, and I had not brought up Rebecca's party. The truth was that I wasn't sure if I wanted to go. He hadn't mentioned it either, which made me think it probably didn't matter to him either. We also had not talked anymore about Lorcan. His and Kieran's absences had created a strangely more peaceful environment, for me at least. Little did I know, that would all change on Saturday.

Chapter Ten

Greer

On Saturday morning, I woke up early and sat straight up in bed. I was anxious about my date, and knew that if I did not calm my nerves, I would be completely sick by 6:30 p.m., when Liam and I agreed he would pick me up.

I threw my robe on over my favorite pajamas and headed downstairs to get something to drink. As I entered the kitchen, I found Dad sitting at the bar drinking a cup of coffee and reading the newspaper. The house was quiet so I whispered, "Good morning," as I went over and gave him a hug.

"Good morning, sweetheart." Dad appeared surprised and happy to see me already awake. "Have trouble sleeping?" He smiled.

"No, I slept okay. I just woke up early for some reason." I smiled back at him.

"Hmm," Dad laughed and gestured for me to sit down next to him.

"You know, it is completely normal to be nervous when you are going on a date with someone you like, especially your first date," Dad said kindly. I nodded, waiting for him to continue into a lecture on the high standards I should have for my date. Instead, he completely surprised me and began to talk about when he and Mom first started dating.

"When Liam asked your mother and me if he could take you out, he told us that you and he had become friends over the past few months. He said he had no interest in dating anyone his senior year of high school, but the more he got to know you, the more he liked you. When I asked him what he liked most about you, he said, without hesitation, that it was definitely your heart. He said that he could tell, since becoming friends, that you had a pure heart, and, as young as he is, he knew that was hard to find." Dad gave me a proud look.

I tried to break the silence with a cheesy joke, "Oh, he doesn't know me all that well."

"Oh, I think he knows you pretty well. When Liam said that about you, I knew exactly what he meant. That's the way I felt about your mother. She and I had become good friends in high school, but I didn't get the courage or chance to ask her out until we were in college. She was so beautiful and amazing—just like you. What Liam likes most about you is what I liked most about her." He smiled at me. He had no idea how much what he had just said meant to me.

"I was surprised you told him he could ask me out, since you always told Darcy and me we couldn't date until we were thirty five," I joked, in my attempt to fight back tears.

"Well, to most guys I would have said no, but Liam seems different. I believe Liam is one of the good guys, and that is exactly what I want for my girls." Dad smiled again.

I nodded in agreement, and then thought I would take the opportunity to ask some questions about when he and Mom were just friends, since he had brought the subject up. "How old were you when you and Mom met?" I asked subtly.

He got up to pour some more coffee and hesitated a moment, but then replied, "We met when we were sixteen."

"Were you juniors then?" I followed up smoothly.

"Yes." He remained standing at the bar across from me, with a bit of a far-off look in his eyes.

"Did you meet her right after her family moved to Boston?" I continued slowly.

"Yes."

"What was she like then?" I asked curiously. The thought of my parents in high school amused me.

"Intoxicating," he said with a sigh, followed by a small laugh.

"Hardly!" I heard Mom say as she rounded the corner and entered the kitchen with a smile on her face. She walked over and gave me a kiss on the head and then moved towards Dad, who enveloped her in a big hug.

"You're still intoxicating," Dad said sweetly. I just watched them and what I knew had to be a real, true, forever kind of love, the kind of love I hoped for someday.

I smiled and laughed just slightly. The sound of my laugh brought them out of their own little world. "Why are you up so early? Surely not to grill your father on what we were like in high school?" Mom smiled. She had let go of Dad and walked over towards the refrigerator to get out some of the necessary ingredients for her world-famous homemade blueberry muffins. They were so delicious, we had all long ago demanded they become a Saturday morning tradition.

"I like hearing about when you and Dad were young," I replied, watching her begin to melt some butter.

"It's not like we are ancient now," Dad laughed.

I blushed at the thought I had offended them and replied quickly, "No, of course not, that's not what I meant." The truth was that they were definitely younger than most of my friends' parents, having gotten married the summer after they graduated from college. Nine months later, Darcy and I arrived—or, more accurately, I arrived, and then Darcy.

"We know that, sweetie, he's just teasing you." Mom smiled, mixing together an egg, some milk, and a small amount of vanilla.

"Yes, sweetheart, I was just teasing. You seem on edge today, is everything okay? Are you just nervous about your date?" Dad asked, looking more serious as Mom stopped her mixing and also looked at me with concern.

"I'm fine. Of course, I am a little nervous. That's normal, right?" I replied candidly.

"Absolutely, but you're going to have a wonderful time tonight. You have no reason to be nervous. You just need to be yourself," Mom replied in her most reassuring voice. It was amazing how she could comfort me so easily. I'm not even sure it was what she said, but how she said it.

Suddenly, Dad cleared his throat and appeared a little nervous. "Since everyone else is still asleep, perhaps we should take this opportunity to discuss some things you might need to know about boys and girls."

"Dad!" I gasped, mortified at the thought of my father wanting to discuss any issue about boys and girls with me.

Mom laughed as she continued with her baking, adding the melted butter to the eggs, milk, and vanilla and stirring slowly. "David, you know I had that talk with the girls a long time ago. I don't think there is anything else we should discuss now."

I was sinking on my barstool as Dad spoke again, his voice slightly embarrassed, "Oh, I'm not talking about that!"

Mom and I laughed in relief. "Then what are you talking about, honey?" Mom asked sweetly. She had begun to mix in some flour, sugar, baking powder, and salt to her liquid mixture.

"I am talking about how important it is that she always make sure that Liam, or any other boy she is around, always treats her with respect," Dad said seriously, looking right at me.

"Of course, Dad," I replied, still so relieved that was all he wanted to talk about.

"No, this is important, Greer. We met Liam, we liked him and we have a good feeling about him, but if he shows any sign of disrespect towards you, you should not put up with it for a minute. That means if he doesn't treat you like a lady at all times, and especially if he doesn't respect boundaries you have." Dad looked at Mom for reinforcement.

She obliged, stopped her stirring and walked towards the bar. "Yes, of course, your father's right. This is a big deal, your first date with a young man. He does seem like a very nice boy and I really liked his mother when I met her the other day. But sometimes people are not always what they seem, and you have to be careful not to believe what you want to about someone." Mom paused for a moment with a far-off look, as if she wasn't talking about me anymore. Dad glanced up at her and gave an encouraging smile as she continued, "Let people reveal who they are in their own way. If Liam is the great guy we all think he is, he will continue to be so; if not, you will soon find out and we trust that you won't put up with anything less than what you deserve."

I was a bit speechless at this very serious and somewhat cryptic conversation. I muttered, "Of course," hoping it would all end. Mom and Dad looked at each other for a moment and I was afraid the conversation was going to continue, but thankfully, I heard the sound of size eleven footsteps bounding down the stairs.

"Are the muffins ready?" Will asked, springing into the kitchen. I had never been so happy to see him in my life. "I thought I smelled them."

"No, Mom is just about to put them in the oven," I laughed.

"They'll be ready in about thirty minutes," Mom added.

"Aw, man! What can I eat until then? I'm starving!" Will hopped on the barstool next to me and grabbed his stomach.

We all laughed, as Dad slid the bowl of fruit that Mom normally kept on the bar down in his direction. "Try to leave some for the rest of us. And good morning to you as well," Dad said, half-seriously.

Will replied, embarrassed, "Oh, sorry, good morning everybody."

Mom smiled briefly at Will and slowly folded fresh blueberries into her muffin mixture. They were almost ready to go into the oven. Dad resumed reading his paper, although I noticed when he picked up the *Dallas Morning News*, there was a copy of the *Boston Herald* underneath. I didn't bring any attention to it, but thought it would be worth mentioning to Darcy later, along with the strange look Mom had given me.

"So, tonight's the big night!" Will chuckled, in between bites of a banana.

"Yes, I have a date with Liam tonight," I replied, but saying the words aloud made the butterflies in my stomach start to go crazy. I reached for an apple, unsure if I was going to eat it, so instead I just played with the stem.

"I'm sure you guys will have fun at the..." Will stopped abruptly as Mom and Dad both shot him a warning look. "Oh, yeah, I forgot it's a surprise!" he laughed.

"This is really ridiculous! Why is he keeping what we're doing a secret?" I moaned. I really did hate surprises, especially if I knew one was waiting for me. I thought that people (myself included) would always build up the surprise to be so much more than it actually was, and then be disappointed. I had consciously made myself downplay my date with Liam all week, so there would be no unrealistic expectations. The truth was that I was thrilled just to be going on my first date with a guy I really liked. That was more than enough. Anything we did on the date would just be a bonus, for me at least.

Darcy

"Oh Greer, trust me, it's better it's a secret," I said through my yawn as I entered the kitchen. "Good morning everybody," I said sleepily, sitting on the only remaining barstool. I was tired because I had spent half the night doing research online about our family history. It would take every acting skill I possessed to not let any of them, even Greer, know what I had uncovered.

Will gave me a nod, gulping down what looked like his second banana. Mom smiled and said, "Hello, sweetie," as she placed muffins in the oven. Greer gave me her best sarcastic smile.

"It looks like everyone is up early this morning. So, what's on the agenda for today?" Dad put down his paper and smiled at us, sitting in a line across from him. We all just stared at him. "Aside from the obvious, of course."

"I thought I might go to Rebecca's party," Will said in an unsure, yet hopeful tone.

"You mean crash Rebecca's party," Greer snickered.

"I thought as long as I went with Darcy, it would be okay," Will replied. I didn't respond to his request; I was more focused on my own thoughts.

"I don't think a sophomore should go to a party with seniors, even if his sister is there," Mom said, squelching Will's plans for the night. Dad nodded in agreement, but gave Will an understanding look. Will knew enough about our parents to realize he should begin to make alternative plans.

"So, are you going to the party, Darcy?" Dad asked.

"Probably," I answered, a tad unsure.

"I assume her parents will be there," Dad said seriously, "and there will be no alcohol."

"Yes and yes," I sighed.

"How many people are they expecting?" Mom asked.

"I'm not sure; not a ton, she just invited a lot of our friends from the senior class. But don't worry, I know what to do; if there is anything going on that shouldn't be, I will leave immediately and come home, I promise," I said, ready for the questioning to be over.

Satisfied, Mom and Dad started to talk about what they needed to do respectively for the day, including some yard work for Dad and Will (who groaned at the sound of it), and a little bit of cleaning for Mom and us girls.

"I think I might try a gym nearby that has been completely renovated. They have some yoga classes that I heard are really good. Would you girls be interested in joining me?" Mom asked hopefully. "The class is at ten, and I thought we might grab some lunch afterwards."

"Sure," Greer answered quickly. She probably welcomed the idea of some distractions, so she didn't get too nervous about her date with Liam.

"Yeah, that sounds good," I agreed.

After a leisurely breakfast, Greer and I took care of our minor cleaning tasks for the day, and headed upstairs to straighten our rooms and do a little reading before heading the gym. Dad and Will planned to begin the yard work when we left, so Will plopped himself down in front of the television to watch ESPN until then.

A little before ten we left for the gym, taking Mom's Suburban. The gym was only a couple of miles from our house, so we were there in a matter of minutes. It was nice, clean and modern looking. We registered as guests and made our way to the studio for the yoga class. It was a large studio with a wall full of mirrors. I had never liked rooms like that. The peppy and tiny yoga instructor welcomed us to the class and showed us the loaner yoga mats the gym provided. We got all set up in the back of the room. Ten minutes later, I was in my first downward facing dog.

"Wow, those planks were crazy!" Greer said with a laugh an hour later as we left the gym.

"Yes, those were really hard, but I liked the class. What did you think, Darcy?" Mom asked as we made our way to the Suburban.

"I liked it," I replied quickly, glancing at our Mom, but I had something troubling on my mind. When Mom wasn't looking, I grabbed Greer's arm and cut my eyes back to the far right of the parking lot, where we could make out someone standing just behind the driver's door of a flashy black sports car. I squinted my eyes against the sun to get a better look. The young woman turned suddenly, whipping her mass of dark hair as she entered her car and peeled out of the parking lot.

"Some people really should be more careful," Mom said, looking in the direction of the fleeing black car. Greer and I exchanged a look, and she knew immediately what I was thinking.

I was still looking in the direction the car had gone when I heard Mom say, in a very cheerful voice, "Hi there, Liam!" Liam? I looked up and saw him, and then looked over to Greer as I imagined her going into panic mode. She slowly turned her head and saw Liam a few paces in front of us and rapidly approaching. I knew she was nervous, as she began to tug at her workout apparel. She was wearing a form-fitting pair of black yoga pants with a coordinating black and red halter workout top. She had bought them by mistake on the clearance rack at Target a few months earlier, thinking they were jammies, and had never bothered to take them back. Her outfit was definitely more form-fitting than anything she typically wore. As Liam approached, Greer hid it well, but I could tell she wanted to crawl under a rock; she was probably wishing she was wearing a t-shirt and shorts like me, and fretting over the fact that she didn't have any makeup on.

"Hello, Mrs. Hagen!" Liam said, excited to see us there. Greer had not made eye contact with him yet, instead looking over at me for reassurance. I smiled at her, and she forced herself to look in his direction. He was smiling from ear to ear as he continued, "Hi Darcy, hi Greer." He had lingered for a moment when he spoke Greer's name, and it did not escape any of our notice.

Mom and I exchanged a look and took a few steps away towards our vehicle parked nearby, leaving Liam and Greer a moment to talk alone.

Greer

"I didn't know you belonged to this gym," I said coyly, trying not to touch my workout clothing, which I was totally uncomfortable wearing in front of him.

"My family just joined, so I thought I'd come check it out." Liam smiled and winked, "Plus, I needed a distraction." He never took his eyes off of my face.

I laughed, "Same here."

He smiled and said, "I'm looking forward to tonight."

"Me too," I was unable to hide my enthusiasm, to his great enjoyment. "But, I should probably get going." I looked over at Mom and Darcy, waiting in the Suburban.

"Sure, I'll pick you up at 6:30," he replied, and I knew he wouldn't be a second late.

"6:30." I smiled and turned to walk towards Mom's SUV, trying to contain my utter bliss. I looked over my left shoulder to see that Liam had begun to walk towards the gym, but suddenly he looked over his shoulder at me and flashed his dazzling smile. I smiled back and then turned and walked faster towards the Suburban.

I climbed back into the front passenger seat, as Darcy had reclaimed her seat behind Mom. As soon as I had snapped my seatbelt, I sighed and could not hide my huge smile. Mom and Darcy laughed, and, even though I was embarrassed, so did I.

"I think he likes you very much," Mom said, backing up.

"You think?" Darcy laughed.

Suddenly, it dawned on me that Liam had said his family had just joined the gym and that Mom had said she had recently heard that it was a nice place. I turned to Mom and asked, "How exactly did you hear about this gym again?"

Mom smiled. "Oh, Liam's mother told me about it the other day."

"Did she say that they had joined?" I inquired further.

"No, but she said they were probably going to join," Mom replied, waiting for traffic to clear so she could turn out of the parking lot onto the road.

"Do you think maybe you could have mentioned that before? I didn't exactly bring my A game this morning." I gestured to my face and hair.

Darcy laughed at my comment. Mom just smiled and said, "I honestly didn't even think about the possibility of Liam being here this morning. Besides, you look beautiful."

Mom finally got a break in traffic, and she turned right onto the road. She had reached the speed limit when a car turned out right in front of us. Mom had to slam on the brakes, and she instantly threw her right arm out across in front of me, the typical protective Mom driver move. All of our seatbelts tightened. Luckily, there was no one behind us, or else we would have been creamed.

I looked up at the car that was zooming away, and gasped when I saw it was the same black sports car from the gym parking lot. Darcy leaned over to her right, looked out the front window, and saw the car as well. We immediately looked at each other and knew it was no coincidence.

"Goodness, are you girls alright?" Mom asked, catching her breath and reaccelerating to the speed limit. She hadn't noticed it was the same car as earlier, thankfully.

"I'm fine," Darcy muttered.

"Me too," I said reassuringly.

"Thank goodness." Mom tried to compose herself. "How about we run home and change and see if your father and Will would like to join us for lunch?"

"That sounds good," I replied quickly; Darcy remained silent. I had forgotten about our plan to eat out, and welcomed the chance to change clothes.

In a few minutes, we were home. Dad and Will were finishing up their yard work. They both took fast showers while we changed from our workout gear, leaving me no time to talk to Darcy about what happened with our friendly Autobahn enthusiast. I put on a little makeup along with my jean capris, a fitted white t-shirt, and flip-flops. Texas was still having a much warmer than usual January; it was sixty-seven and sunny. As I left my room, I grabbed the Boston Red Sox baseball cap my grandparents had given me a few years prior and threw it on my head.

On the way to lunch, we decided to go to a nearby deli we all loved. As we got out of the SUV, I couldn't believe my eyes. I saw a flashy black sports car, just like the one from earlier, parked in front of a jewelry store a few buildings down from the deli. I nudged Darcy, who looked over and saw it instantly. She shot me a knowing look, as we remained silent.

Will asked if he could run down to the sporting goods store to look at some new soccer shoes. "I won't be gone long, back by the time our food arrives. You can just order my usual," he bargained.

Darcy and I looked at each other warily; the sporting goods store was right next to the jewelry story. "I'll go with him," I announced quickly.

"Me too," Darcy chimed in.

"I'm not eight, I don't need an escort. I'll be right back," Will replied, puzzled at our sudden interest in sporting equipment.

"Maybe we should all go," Mom suggested to Dad.

"Why don't you and I stay and order food for everyone? They'll be back in a few minutes," Dad said persuasively.

"Alright, ten minutes. Everyone want their usual?" Mom conceded as Dad put his arm around her.

"Yes," Darcy, Will, and I said in unison and then laughed.

As Mom and Dad entered the deli, Will, Darcy, and I walked down to the sporting goods store. "Why did you want to come with me?" Will asked directly.

"I thought I would look at some new workout apparel," I replied, half-telling the truth. Darcy remained silent, as we were passing the black sports car that sat empty in front of the jewelry store.

"Wow, now that's a legit ride!" Will said, noticing Darcy and I staring at the car and then at him, puzzled. Will sighed and continued, "It's a Jaguar XKR with twenty inch Kalimnos-style wheels. It costs like a hundred grand." Will rolled his eyes at us as we remained silent, and we all entered the sporting goods store.

I scanned the store and saw a father and his young son looking at youth footballs, a middle-aged man trying a new golf club, and an older man inspecting some fishing poles. Will went over to the soccer section, while I scanned the women's workout apparel. Darcy went to look at running shoes.

I was skimming through the clothes finding nothing any less revealing than my outfit from earlier, when I heard Will talking to a girl. I looked over and saw Darcy was still standing in the shoe section, so I gestured for her to come over. As she approached, she could also hear Will and the girl. We remained silent as we walked over towards them. We were just a few feet away, and I saw Will smiling his biggest, most enamored smile and the backside of a tall, thin, long-haired brunette. She looked just like the girl driving the Jaguar, and then I realized she looked just like Kieran!

As I thought her name, Darcy spoke it just loud enough to make her turn and face us. "Hello Darcy, Greer." Kieran's words were like venom, especially when she said my name.

"Oh, you know my sisters?" Will asked, apparently still hoping she was closer to his age than ours.

"Yes, I do." Kieran flashed him her brilliant smile.

"We need to go," Darcy said impatiently to Will. Will hesitated, obviously still wanting to talk to his potential new crush. "Now," Darcy demanded.

"I should go, as well. It was so nice to meet you, Will." Kieran smiled and touched his forearm.

"You too," Will fumbled over his words. "I hope to see you again!"

"Oh, you will," Kieran replied, flashing Darcy and me a wicked smile and taking a moment to stare at my hat. She quickly exited the store.

Will stood there with his mouth hanging open. "Come on, let's go," I ordered, pushing Will towards the door.

"How come you never mentioned her?" Will asked, still a little in awe of his encounter with Kieran. We could hear her peeling out of the parking lot.

Darcy grabbed Will by the arm and stopped him in his tracks. "Oww! Watch those claws!" Will pulled his arm back instinctively.

"We didn't mention her because she is Lorcan's sister, and you are not supposed to ever mention Lorcan, remember? That goes for Kieran as well," Darcy raged. I knew her anger wasn't really directed at Will, but the effect was the same.

"Okay! Geez Darcy, you can be really scary. I got it, I won't mention her name to anyone, I promise!" Will replied as he backed away.

Darcy didn't say anything else until we were almost to the deli, when she stopped us and said, "Everyone act normal." Will looked at me, and I nodded for him to follow orders, which he did surprisingly well.

When we entered the deli and sat down with our parents, the food had just arrived. We enjoyed a nice lunch as a family, but Kieran's appearance at the gym, almost causing an accident, and obviously stalking Will made Darcy and me quite uneasy. Unfortunately, we would not have time to talk everything through until much later in the day, as our parents suggested we all see a matinee after lunch. If I wanted to have a day full of distractions to keep me from getting anxious about my date with Liam, I certainly accomplished it.

Chapter Eleven

Darcy

We were home from the movies by 4:30 p.m., leaving Greer two hours until Liam arrived to pick her up. Once home, I went straight to my room to process everything that had happened. I didn't pay much attention to what everyone else was doing as I headed upstairs. After a while of frustratingly rummaging through the journal I was keeping about what we had discovered, I heard a low rumbling from the bathroom. I knew immediately Greer was giving herself a pedicure with the kit Will had given us for Christmas the year before. It was basically a bucket for water that vibrated when you plugged it into the wall, but it did the job. I decided now would be a good time to warn Greer, before Mom undoubtedly came up to check on her.

"Come in," Greer said, in a tone that revealed she knew it was me.

I entered, shut the door behind me, made a face at the loud rumble of the pedicure machine, and propped myself against the bathroom wall. "We don't have much time," I whispered, just loud enough that she could hear me over the noise. "I'm sure Mom's going to check on you."

"Okay, let's talk fast then," Greer replied, turning off the machine so we could hear each other better.

I could tell the distraught look on my face alarmed her. "Greer, promise me you will be very careful tonight."

"Of course. You know Liam, he's a nice guy; everything will be fine." Greer was a little defensive, and I knew she had no idea what I was really worried about.

I replied quickly, "I'm not worried about him. I'm worried about Kieran, or Lorcan for that matter, crashing your date. You saw Kieran today. She loathes you, and I think she's capable of just about anything. That's why I suggested to Liam to make your date a surprise. The only people that know are me, Mom, Dad, and Will. He was going to tell his parents right before he left. I figured that if fewer people knew, then your date was less likely to be crashed. After Kieran's performance today, I think I was right."

Greer was completely taken aback by what I said. After a moment of processing, she replied, "I'll keep a lookout for anything weird," and then continued with a small laugh, "especially flashy black Jaguars trying to run me down." I didn't look amused, although I thought it was kind of funny.

"Are you going to Rebecca's party?" Greer asked, trying to change the subject.

"Yes, and I can't decide if you should come or not."

"Liam didn't mention the party, so I'm not sure if he even wants to go," Greer said, taking her feet out of the water to dry them off.

"You will have time at the end of your date, and I'm sure that if you want to stop by the party he would be fine with it. It would be his chance to show you off as his girlfriend," I said, with my first smile since entering the bathroom.

Greer stopped what she was doing and gaped at me for a moment before saying, "I don't think one date will classify me as his girlfriend."

I laughed and gave her a "trust me" look.

Greer laughed, but I could tell she was nervous. After a moment, she asked, "Well, what do you think, should we come to the party?"

"I don't want your date to be ruined in any way, and who knows what Kieran and Lorcan might do if you come to the party," I replied with genuine concern.

"If Kieran wants to ruin my date with Liam, I doubt she will leave it to chance that we might come to the party and she will get her opportunity. In that case, she would probably make some sort of appearance much earlier in the night," Greer said matter of factly. I nodded in agreement, and she continued, "How about this—if we have time to stop by before my curfew, then we will, if not, then we won't."

"I guess that sounds okay." I attempted a smile, but I was still wrestling with what I thought was the best thing to do.

Just then we heard an expected knock on Greer's bedroom door. "Come in," Greer stated.

Mom entered excitedly and asked sweetly, "I'm not interrupting any private girl talk, am I?"

"No, you're fine, Mom," I said with a laugh, as Greer and I exited the bathroom.

"Is there anything I can do to help?" Mom asked hopefully.

"I'm just going to paint my toenails, and after they dry I'll take my shower. You can help with my makeup later, if you want?" Greer replied, knowing that would make her happy.

"Sure," Mom replied. "Do you want some help with that polish?"

Greer certainly was not going to win any awards for toe-nail painting, as Mom well knew. Greer happily handed over the polish to her much more capable hands.

Mom sat down on the floor in front of Greer, as she placed her right foot up on the edge of her chair and hugged her knee to her chest. I took a seat on Greer's bed and just watched.

"This is such a pretty color red; it perfectly matches your dress," Mom commented as she began to paint Greer's toes.

Greer and I could tell she was feeling very sentimental. Greer shot me a quick "Go with me on this one" look, and I nodded slightly and waited for what she was about to do.

"Dad was telling me earlier about when you two first met," Greer said, and I sat up a little on the bed, paying closer attention.

"Yes?" Mom replied, a bit reserved.

"I was hoping you would tell me more about how you started dating. He said you were friends first?" Greer continued.

Mom paused for a moment from her professional style polishing, but then slowly began, "Yes, my family had just moved to Newton, a suburb of Boston. My father had accepted the head of pediatrics position at Mass General. I met your father and his…" Mom paused for a moment, and I could see the anxiety creep up on her face. She wasn't sure how to continue, but Greer and I were eager for her to go on. She had just told us more in two sentences about her family's move to Boston than we had pretty much heard in our entire lifetime.

"Yes?" Greer asked cautiously. Greer was doing an amazing job, much better than I would have ever anticipated.

"Friends," she said, more sure of her word choice, and continued, "I met your father on my first day of school there." She acted as if that was all she was going to say, and she gestured for Greer's other foot.

"What year were you in high school?" I asked nonchalantly.

Mom smiled at me, and I could tell from her face that she would answer our questions as long as they were ones that she wanted to answer. Mom replied, "We were juniors."

"Dad said that you became friends in high school, but that you didn't date until college—something about how he didn't get the courage or chance to ask you out until then," Greer asked, trying to act as if we were not probing her for information we really wanted.

"Yes," Mom laughed slightly. "Your father and I hung around with the same group of friends in high school. We had lunch and several classes together."

"That sounds a bit familiar," Greer joked, no doubt thinking of Liam and our group of friends.

"Yes, it is a little similar, I guess. I had never really given much thought to your father as anything more than a good friend. He was the nicest guy I knew, but he was a very serious student athlete and had…" she paused again, carefully searching for what to say next.

"A girlfriend?" Greer questioned.

"No, your father had not dated much when I first met him. He had other duties that kept him busy," she said, satisfied with her vague answer.

I was not, so I asked, "Were they family duties?"

"Yes," Mom replied curtly, and she gave me a puzzled look. It was obvious that line of questioning was a dead end.

"Since it took Dad so long to ask you out, did you date anyone else in high school?" I continued, unaware that would be the question that would end our conversation.

"There, all done," Mom said, as she finished painting Greer's left pinky toe and acted as if she had not even heard my last question. "I should go check and see what plans your brother has made for tonight. Let me know when you are ready for help with your makeup, if you still want it?"

"Okay, thanks," Greer replied. I tried to read Mom's face, but all I could detect was anxiety.

"Okay, see you in a bit," Mom replied and was out the door, closing it swiftly behind her.

Greer and I just stared at each other for a moment before she said, "Looks like you hit a nerve."

"Definitely," I said as I stood up. "I'll come back when Mom does."

"Let's try not to push her too much with the questioning. We don't want her to get suspicious, remember?" Greer suggested as I walked towards her bedroom door.

I whipped around and gave her a smile. "Don't worry, I have some other ideas on how to get the information we want."

"Darcy," Greer said, emphasizing the last syllable in my name.

"Don't worry, it'll be fine. Just keep getting ready." Then I was gone.

I went straight to my room and grabbed my journal to add all of the information Mom had just told us. The pieces of the puzzle still didn't make sense, but at least we had some more information. After about an hour of pouring over my notes, I went to my dresser and grabbed my most treasured piece of jewelry from my jewelry box, a silver Tiffany bracelet my parents had given me for our sixteenth birthday. I figured Greer would wear the matching earrings they had given her. I was going to offer the bracelet to Greer to wear on her date.

I heard Mom's light footsteps headed towards Greer's room. I slipped the bracelet in my pocket and bolted for my door.

Mom knocked on Greer's door and I made my way towards her.

"Come in," Greer uttered nervously. Mom entered with me on her heels. Greer was staring at her clock, which said it was 5:45 p.m.—forty-five minutes until Liam arrived.

Always prepared, Mom handed Greer a plate of wheat crackers and a glass of water and said, "Eat and drink."

Greer obeyed her command and sat down in her chair to nibble on a cracker as Mom took over, looking through her makeup bag.

"I think you should look as natural as possible. A little lightness on the eyes, perhaps subtle eyeliner, some color on the cheeks, a little bit of color for the lips, and then a minimal amount of mascara—goodness knows those gorgeous lashes don't need much. What do you think, girls?"

"I agree, she doesn't need much," I replied, and flashed Greer a reassuring smile.

"Greer, does that sound okay?" Mom asked, looking right at her.

"Yeah," she replied simply.

"Okay, then eat another cracker and let's get started," Mom said excitedly.

Greer gulped down another cracker and darted into the bathroom. After she washed her hands, Mom passed her the face moisturizer and foundation. I watched from the bedroom as Greer applied her second coating of moisturizer and then her foundation, using just the right amount. She turned for Mom to inspect, who nodded in approval. Greer turned and propped herself up on the bathroom vanity, as I had done earlier, so Mom could more easily apply her makeup.

Greer looked over at me. I was lost in the moment, watching my sister and our mother. Greer was so much like her, but I wasn't, and I didn't understand why. I just knew that our parents were hiding something and that, for some reason, I thought it would explain why I was different. I didn't know how it related to Kieran and Lorcan, but I was determined find out.

A short time later, Greer's makeup was done. She hadn't even turned around to see it yet when I exclaimed, "Perfect!"

Mom smiled and agreed, "Yes, I do think it's just right."

Greer turned and saw her reflection. Her makeup had never looked better, and she knew it.

"It does look so natural, I can't believe it! Thank you!" she replied happily.

"Good, now you need to get those rollers out of your hair and get dressed. You have twenty minutes until he gets here. I'm going to get my camera ready," Mom said, heading towards the door.

"No cameras!" Greer yelled, no doubt mortified at the thought of having to awkwardly stand with Liam in front of the fireplace and take pictures.

Mom turned and was about to protest when I spoke up, "Maybe you can just take a picture of Greer? It might be a bit much to take one of them together. Besides, I'm sure you'll be able to take as many pictures as you want when prom rolls around, and don't forget about graduation!"

Mom perked up and replied, "Okay, just a picture of Greer after she's ready." She was then out the door.

"Thank you!" Greer said, and turned to hastily take the cool rollers out of her hair. Her hair fell perfectly into place as she headed for her closet to take a look at her dress, which was hanging on the door.

"Are you sure this is what I should wear?" she asked me.

"Absolutely!" I replied, standing beside her. I had found the dress when we were shopping with Mom earlier in the week. It was a simple, form-fitting, red cotton dress with small spaghetti straps and an A-line skirt. Greer thought it showed too much of her shoulders and collarbone, so Mom found this beautiful charcoal grey cropped sweater to wear over it. It was perfect. Greer was planning to wear her black ballet flats, but I had offered up my new charcoal grey ones that would coordinate perfectly with her sweater.

"I'll go get the shoes while you're getting dressed," I said, and hurried out the door. I was genuinely excited for Greer; as I made my way to my room, I suddenly began to think of Edmund and how I certainly wouldn't mind going out with him. I laughed at myself as I allowed myself to daydream for a moment while I waited for Greer to change into her dress. I soon cleared my head and knocked on Greer's door once again.

As I entered, she was putting on her sterling silver Tiffany stud earrings. "You can wear this if you want," I said, trying (to no avail) to avoid eye contact with her as I held the bracelet open in my palm.

"Are you sure?" she replied, her eyes starting to water.

"Don't cry! You'll ruin your makeup and he'll be here in like five minutes!" I scolded. "Besides, the bracelet will match your outfit great, and I have wanted to borrow your earrings. Now you'll owe me," I said with a smile.

Greer quickly dabbed her eyes and took the bracelet. She finished putting herself together and took a look in the mirror.

"You look great!" I said, handing her a clutch I had just packed. "Everything you need is in there." She inspected it and found her driver's license, house key, phone, forty dollars cash, a credit card, a vanity mirror, lipstick, and mace. When she saw the mace, she looked up quizzically at me.

"You never know," I replied, laughing. "As they say, it's better to be safe than sorry."

"I'm sure this will be really helpful with any flashy black Jaguars that might try to run me down," Greer replied sarcastically.

"That's really not funny," I said seriously.

"It kind of is," she joked.

Just then, Mom entered through Greer's half open bedroom door, happily holding her camera.

"Just in time. You had better get your picture now. Liam should be here any minute, and I doubt he will be late," I laughed.

"Oh, he's already here." Mom smiled.

"What?" Greer shrieked.

"Relax; maybe I should put some Pepto in next to the mace." I smiled at Mom. Mom stared at us for a moment, then realizing that I had given Greer the mace, she gave me a proud look.

"I didn't hear the doorbell," Greer said, as Mom positioned her in front of her desk.

"Oh, Will was waiting by the door when Liam arrived, so he didn't get a chance to ring it," Mom replied, taking a picture of Greer with her most mortified look ever.

"Okay, this time try to smile," Mom asked kindly.

"Where's Liam now?" Greer questioned anxiously.

"I'll tell you after you smile for one picture," Mom bargained. Greer quickly plastered on her fakest happy smile.

"That will do, I guess. He's with your father in his office. Your father wanted to talk to him before you go out tonight," Mom replied, looking like what she had just said was completely normal.

"He already asked for permission to take me out, which is beyond what any normal guy would do. What else could Daddy possibly want to talk to him about? How long has he been in there?" Greer's embarrassment was quite amusing.

"About five minutes."

Greer stormed for her bedroom door, grabbing her handbag from me. She hurried down the stairs and rounded the corner to the front entryway to find Liam and Dad exiting his office. I was right on her heels, not about to miss one moment. Liam looked a little peaked, but when he saw Greer, the color quickly came back to his face, and he gave her a sweet smile.

"There she is," Dad said, smiling. At least he was happy with his conversation with Liam. Liam looked back at him and appeared a little nervous. I could tell Greer was anxious to get out the door; I had to admit, the whole situation was a little like a country and western song about a dating teenage daughter. I had no doubt that if our father had owned a gun, he would have been cleaning it at that very moment.

Our entire family was standing in the entryway as Liam nervously handed Greer a beautiful bouquet of tulips. He remained silent.

"Thank you," Greer said, as she smelled them quickly and handed them to our mother. "We should probably get going," Greer said, gesturing towards the door.

Liam smiled and opened the door for Greer as she turned to say goodbye to our family. Everyone was waving except for me. I just smiled, thoroughly amused.

"Have a good time," Mom said. I could tell from the crack in her voice she was about to cry. Our sweet, sentimental mother would always see us as two-year olds running around the house, not young women who were old enough to date.

"Be home by curfew and not a second later," Dad said seriously. I saw, out of the corner of my eye, Mom gently nudge him in the ribs. "And have a good time," Dad continued, a little hesitantly.

We stood there watching as they walked to Liam's SUV. My mind wandered off again, and watching Greer leave with Liam, I thought of Edmund and when I might see him again.

Chapter Twelve

Greer

Liam and I remained silent as we walked down the path in front of my house to his black FJ Cruiser. It was sparkling in the evening sun, obviously freshly washed. Liam opened the door for me and I climbed in. The inside was immaculate. I smiled, thinking of the effort Liam had made so far for our date. He walked quickly around and hopped up into the driver's seat. As he turned the ignition, I said, "Sorry about all of that," gesturing towards my house and my parents who, to my horror, were still standing at the front door waving.

"They're nice, but your dad can be a little scary. I understand where he's coming from though," Liam replied, smiling at me before slowly beginning to drive down my street.

My heart raced and I was silent for a moment. "So, are you gonna finally tell me where we're going?" I asked curiously.

"Yes," Liam smiled sweetly, cutting his eyes over at me, "we're going to dinner." I could tell from the plotting look in his eyes that everything would be revealed when he wanted it to be, so I settled in for a night full of surprises.

"Did you have a good workout today?" I asked, as we turned out of my subdivision. Plano was a large enough suburb of Dallas that there was no telling where we might be going to eat just by the direction we went.

Liam was hesitant for a moment, and I thought I detected a troubled look on his face as he said slowly, "Yeah, it was okay." I just stared at him, trying to interpret his meaning. He must have felt my scrutiny, because he looked over at me, and with a smile continued, "Seeing you was definitely the highlight."

I blushed happily, but I couldn't help but feel there was more he was not saying. We drove in silence for a few minutes, passing several restaurants I considered possible contenders, before I bravely broached the subject most pressing on my mind. "So," I started slowly, "what did my dad have to say?"

Liam momentarily lost the color in his face. I couldn't help but laugh out loud and ask, "Was it that bad?"

"I never knew someone so nice could be so…intimidating," Liam started to laugh, in what I believed was an attempt to lessen his own anxiety.

"I'm so sorry," I replied rather unconvincingly. 'What did he say?"

"You know, I'm not even really sure, it's kind of a blur now," Liam replied, his voice still filled with laughter.

"That's probably a good thing." I stared out the window, thinking of my sweet and seriously overprotective parents and how I wouldn't want them any other way.

"I do know that the gist of what he said was about how I was to respect you at all times and if I ever did anything to hurt you, I'd have to answer to him," Liam said, with a little more seriousness in his voice.

"Yeah, earlier today my dad had a talk with me about boys and respect. It was highly awkward, but I guess it could have been worse," I stated, matching Liam's more serious tone.

"Well, I'm relieved I'm not alone in this." Liam shot me a sweet smile that made his whole face light up.

"No, you're definitely not alone," I replied coyly, looking at my hands and fidgeting with my handbag before looking back up at him.

He smiled more as he caught my meaning, and we turned into a parking lot. It was a shopping area that I knew well. It had several clothing stores that Darcy and I frequented; I was trying to guess which of the restaurants we were going to when we pulled up in front of a quaint little 'hole in the wall' style Mexican food restaurant we had discovered right after we moved. We had eaten there after a couple of shopping trips and loved it.

"Aw, Sabroso," I said, smiling at Liam.

"Wait there," he commanded as I began to reach for my door handle.

I waited and couldn't believe my eyes; as Liam walked around his SUV and opened the door and reached for my hand to help me out, I looked at him quizzically.

"I'm not doing anything to tick your dad off. I intend for you to report that I was a perfect gentlemen all evening." Liam beamed as he took my hand to help me out.

"Thank you," I replied, certain I was going to explode from the spark I felt when he touched my hand. To my great thrill, he didn't let go of it as we walked towards the restaurant.

"I hope you like Mexican food." Liam's face revealed that he knew that I loved Mexican food and in particular this restaurant.

"Darcy," I whispered.

"Pardon me?" Liam acted confused.

"Did Darcy tell you I like this restaurant?" I asked, as he held open the door for me and we entered the charming little place. It was beginning to fill up for the Saturday night dinner rush, and it was sure to be at least a twenty minute wait.

Liam smiled a bit mischievously in return, and raised his shoulders like he had no idea what I was talking about. I gave him a fake scowl and poked him in the ribs. He pretended it hurt and we both laughed.

As we waited for the hostess to return to her station, Liam wrapped an arm around my waist and finally answered my question. "I did a little research to find out some of the things you like." I blushed; thankfully, the hostess soon arrived back at her post and we approached her, his arm still around me.

"A reservation under Alexander." Liam smiled and cut his eyes back down at me.

After quickly glancing at her list, the hostess smiled and said, "Please come this way." Liam gestured for me to follow her, as he walked behind me. We ended up in a back, private corner of the restaurant. There were only two other tables nearby; if we spoke quietly, no one would hear any of our conversation with the mariachi music playing.

The hostess placed the menus beside the only two place settings on the table for four. She told us our waitress would be right with us, and Liam and I thanked her as she walked away. Liam pulled out my chair for me and I quickly sat down. With his help, I slowly pulled the chair closer to the table. He then went around and sat across from me.

As he walked around the table, it was the first time I really noticed what he was wearing. He was dressed similar to what my brother would wear to Sunday Mass. His blue, button-down, long sleeved collared shirt and flat-front khaki pants were both neatly pressed. He wore a bright white undershirt that just barely peeked out from under the neck opening, and matching brown belt and dress shoes. He looked so handsome it made my knees go a little weak, which made me glad I was already sitting down.

"So, when did Darcy tell you about this place? When she told you to keep what we're doing tonight a surprise?" I asked with a knowing smile.

"Oh, she told you about that, huh?" Liam smiled and picked up his menu, pretending to read it while avoiding answering my question.

I picked up mine as well and smiled as I began to look at it and simply responded, "Yeah, she did." We both couldn't help but laugh.

"Greer!" I was startled to hear someone ecstatically yelling my name.

Liam and I looked up. To our shock, we saw Mia approaching, wearing an apron and holding a notepad and pen.

"Mia?" I said aloud, not quite able to believe that she was there, let alone going to be our waitress.

"Hi guys! I can't believe you came here for your date! And I get to wait on you! How cool is this?" Mia was so excited I thought she was about to explode. Liam and I just stared at each other in disbelief.

"Looks like someone requested the romantic table in the back," Mia said, using her elbow to gesture towards Liam as she gave him a wink. I tried to stifle a laugh and Liam remained composed, but I could tell he was either embarrassed or annoyed. "What can I get you guys to drink?" Mia looked over at me with the grin of a Cheshire cat.

"Water, would be great, thanks Mia." I smiled and looked over at Liam.

"Make that two, please," Liam asked kindly.

"Be right back." Mia dashed away. Liam and I stared at each other for a moment and then we simultaneously burst into laughter.

"I had no idea that she worked here!" I said, trying to compose myself.

"Obviously, me neither. As serious a vegan as she is, I can't believe she does!" Liam laughed. The low lights of the restaurant made his normally bright blue eyes appear darker, more mysterious, and completely alluring.

"What's good here?" Liam asked, returning his gaze to his menu.

"Let's see—Darcy and I split the fajitas once, and I've also had the enchilada combo. They were both awesome. You haven't eaten here before?" I looked back up at him and then in the direction Mia had gone, hoping she wouldn't return just yet.

Liam followed my gaze and then we locked eyes again. "No," he said simply. Then, right on cue, I heard Mia returning, bringing two large glasses of ice water with lemon wedges hanging off of the sides.

"Here you go!" Mia placed the drinks in front of each of us; for a moment, my glass wobbled and I was afraid it was about to spill all over the place. I quickly grabbed it and stabilized it. I wasn't even sure how I was fast enough to do it, and I noticed Liam and Mia staring at me in a bit of disbelief.

"Wow, someone has some cat-like reflexes," Liam stated, with an amazed look.

"Sorry about that, Greer!" Mia was mortified; if the drink had actually spilled on me, she would have been inconsolable. For her sake and ours, I was glad I was able to stop it.

I tried to reassure Mia, "It's really no big deal."

Sensing the awkwardness and the need for a subject change, Liam suggested we order. "Would you be interested in sharing the combo fajitas?" Liam asked me, as Mia fumbled for her pen and paper. She seemed more nervous since her return with our drinks than she had been when we first saw her just a few minutes prior.

"Yeah, that'd be great," I said, closing my menu and moving it towards the edge of the table near Mia. She quickly wrote down our order, grabbed our menus, and darted off in silence.

Liam and I looked at each other, puzzled by Mia's sudden change in demeanor. I knew she hadn't been working here very long, as she had never mentioned it. She didn't seem embarrassed when we first saw her, so I knew that wasn't it, plus, why would she be embarrassed? Lots of our friends had part time jobs in clothing stores or restaurants, it wasn't a big deal.

"So, do you want to know where we are going after this?" Liam asked, bringing my attention solely back to him and our date.

"Yes," I replied without hesitation.

"Maybe I should make you wait, I don't want to ruin the best part of our date," Liam teased.

"No fair, you can't tease me like that! Besides, I don't even like surprises," I said with a flirtatious huff, and crossed my arms across my chest.

"Darcy said you love surprises!" Liam retorted, stunned at my revelation.

I laughed. "Well, I guess that really shouldn't surprise anyone!"

Liam joined me in laughing, "Well, at least you not knowing probably made you think about our date a lot more this week."

I smiled more seriously and replied, "I'm sure I would have thought about this date every bit as much, even if I had known what we were doing, but since it has been a surprise so far, let's just keep it that way. It only seems right."

"Alright, whatever you say." Liam smiled and then paused for a moment, appearing to try and find the words he wanted to say next. He just about floored me with, "I know this is not subtle and suave, but I'm absolutely crazy about you."

I could feel the heat rising in my face, and I found myself speechless. The only thing I could think to say in response was, "Thank you."

Lucky for me, Liam smiled at my awkward response to his confession. "You have no idea the effect you have on me, do you?"

I blushed and smiled as I looked at my hands and then back up at him. I was totally speechless.

"That's what's so great about you," Liam said, leaning in towards me. "You're completely unaware of your charm."

"Okay?" I laughed. "So I'm charming and I don't know it?"

"Exactly! You completely have me under your spell, and you haven't even tried at all. To be honest, it scares me. If you tried even a little, I would be an absolute goner."

I laughed again, partly at the thought that I could really hold that much power over anyone, and partly because I couldn't believe that Liam Alexander was telling me he was crazy about me. I had to be dreaming.

Mia returned with our order before we could say anything else. She seemed even more nervous than before and was sweating as she placed the food on the table.

"Are you alright, Mia? You look like you're sick," I asked, genuinely concerned for my friend. Liam looked worried as well.

"Uhh, I'm fine. Everything's fine. Here you go," Mia said, as she gestured towards the food in front of us. She hesitated for a moment and darted away before either Liam or I could say anything further.

"That's weird. I hope she's okay," I said to Liam, as an uneasy feeling crept into the pit of my stomach. I felt as if someone was watching us. I quickly looked around and saw no one else nearby.

"I'm sure she's fine. You don't think her conscience is bothering her about serving us all of this?" Liam said, gesturing to the table full of anything but vegan food.

I couldn't help but laugh as Liam continued, "Come on, let's eat. We have a schedule to keep."

The food was delicious. I was surprised that Mia didn't come to check on us even once, although I did see her nervously peeking around the corner a couple of times, which I didn't mention to Liam.

Throughout dinner, we talked about our favorite types of music, subjects in school, where we hoped to attend college (as neither of us had made up our minds yet), and what we thought we would major in.

Around 7:30, Liam glanced at his watch, and I could tell that he was getting anxious to leave. Mia must have noticed as well, because she came over with our check. Liam glanced at it quickly and then placed some cash in the folder.

"I'll be right back with your change," Mia said, looking like she was about to cry. I was really worried about her.

"No, please keep the change," Liam said to Mia. He turned to me and asked, "Are you ready?"

I nodded yes, and Mia glanced at how much cash Liam had put in the folder. She immediately protested, and on the verge of tears said, "No, it's too much."

Liam looked at her and said, "No, really, it's fine, please take it."

"Are you alright, Mia?" I asked and gestured with my head for Liam to go on ahead without me. He understood, and headed towards the front of the restaurant.

"What's going on, Mia? You were so excited to see us and then your whole attitude changed. Are you okay?" I asked, kind of worried about Mia's mental health at that moment.

"I'm alright. Are you alright? Do you feel alright?" Mia asked, searching my face for any trace that I might be in any way unwell.

"Yeah, I'm totally fine. Why would you be worried about that?" I replied. I could tell there was something Mia was not saying.

"I just want you to be alright and safe," Mia responded cryptically.

"Please don't worry, everything's fine, but I should get going. I don't really want to leave you like this, are you sure you're okay?"

"Yes," Mia said insistently, as she grabbed a hold of my arm and squeezed tightly, "just promise you'll be careful."

"I promise." I stared into her worried eyes and began to walk away.

I glanced back at Mia as I hurried towards the front of the restaurant. She had sat down in my seat and had a blank stare on her face. I was really worried about her, but something about the way she was acting also made me nervous. My instincts told me Liam and I should get out of there as soon as possible.

When I reached Liam he saw the scared look on my face, took my hand and ushered us out the door. As soon as we were outside, he quickly led us to the passenger side of his SUV, where he turned and faced me, tenderly placing his hands on top of my shoulders. "What happened? What's going on with Mia? Are you okay?" he asked, his words came rapidly.

"I don't know what's wrong with her; she kept asking if I was okay and telling me to be careful," I said, telling the truth.

"Why would she say that?" Liam asked, genuinely puzzled.

"I have no idea, but I do know that I'd really like to get out of here," I said, placing my forearms on his.

"Of course, let's go." Liam opened my door and, after I was safely inside, he shut it behind me. He practically ran around the front of the SUV and hopped up into the driver's seat. Within a matter of seconds, we were leaving the parking lot, both of us completely silent, no doubt trying to figure out what had just happened.

Finally, I broke the silence and said, "Okay, so I think you should tell me where we're going now."

Liam looked at me with alarm. Our carefree, surprised-filled date had been overshadowed by our strange encounter with Mia, whose insistence on my safety had begun to mess with my head a bit.

"Sure; I was planning for us to go to the Jackopierce concert at the House of Blues tonight, but if you don't want to go, that's fine. We can do whatever you want." Liam's concern for me was absolutely endearing, and I immediately began to feel better.

"That sounds perfect. I'd love to go to the concert with you." I smiled reassuringly at him. I had heard that Jackopierce was coming to Dallas and I had wanted to get tickets, but they had sold out pretty quickly.

Liam appeared relieved and smiled at me as he entered onto the toll road to take us closer towards downtown Dallas. Suddenly, I felt my phone vibrating in my bag, so I peeked in to see who was calling. It was Darcy. I knew I had better answer it, so I sweetly said to Liam, "I'm so sorry, but this is my sister calling. I'm sure she wouldn't call unless it was something important. Do you mind?"

Liam laughed, "No problem, go ahead."

Before I could even say hello, Darcy was yelling in the phone, "Are you alright?"

"Why does everyone keep asking me that?" I replied, a bit fussy.

"Well, are you?" she demanded.

"Yes!" I whisper-yelled.

I could hear Darcy sigh and she paused for a moment before continuing to speak, "Mia texted me and said she had seen you and Liam at dinner, and that she was worried about you. She said I should check on you and that she would tell me more at Rebecca's party when she gets there around 10:30."

"Well, I'd like to be there for that. Hold on for a minute," I told Darcy. Turning to Liam, I said, "Would you mind if we stopped by Rebecca's party after the concert? I think Mia is going to be there, and I would like to check on her."

Liam smiled and replied, "No problem."

I placed the phone back to my ear and said, "We'll be there."

"That's a good idea. Greer, you need to be really careful. Something's going on; I don't know what it is, but something isn't right—I can feel it." Darcy's words made me shiver.

"I know, I agree with you," I replied. "I'll text you when we're on our way."

"Okay—be careful, but try to have fun," Darcy said, trying to be a little more upbeat.

"I will. Bye."

"Bye."

I pressed end call and placed my phone back in my handbag.

"So, if you don't mind me asking, what's going on?" Liam asked with a concerned look.

"The truth is, I'm not sure, but I intend to find out when we see Mia at Rebecca's party later." I smiled reassuringly at him. "Enough about this craziness, I want to know how you managed to get tickets to this sold out show."

Liam smiled and said slyly, "It's all about who you know."

"And who exactly do you know?" I said, raising one eyebrow at him with the most charming smile I could muster.

He stared at me for a moment longer than he should have, given the rate of speed at which he was driving. He quickly turned his head back to the road and said emphatically, "You can't do that!"

"Do what?" I laughed.

"You know, give me a look like that!" he said, keeping his eyes on the road with both hands gripping the steering wheel.

"Why? Is it working?" I said, leaning in a little with the same look as before.

He wouldn't even look at me, but he knew what I was doing. After a moment of intense silence, he replied slowly, "Yes, a look like that would be much more effective than any form of torture for getting information out of me."

I was surprised by what he said, and sat back in my seat. "My look is like a form of torture?" I asked, confused.

Liam burst out laughing, "No! Just the opposite, in fact!"

I smiled, relieved a bit, and continued, "I would like to know how you got the tickets."

"The truth is, my cousin works at the House of Blues as a bartender in the summers when he comes home from college. The manager really likes him because he works really hard. So, when I heard you mention the Jackopierce concert a while back, I asked my cousin to see what he could do about getting a couple of tickets."

I was trying desperately to remember when I had mentioned the concert and realized that I had talked to Ella at lunch about it two months earlier.

"You knew you were going to ask me out two months ago?" I asked, shocked.

"Yes," he replied sweetly.

We both remained silent the final few minutes before we reached the venue. I was so excited. My parents had introduced Darcy and me to Jackopierce's music a few years earlier. They had seen them in concert on Cape Cod when they were in college and thought we would enjoy their music as well. They were right.

The show was set to start at 8:00 and it was already 7:50. I silently hoped parking wouldn't be an issue, and it wasn't. Apparently, along with the tickets, Liam's cousin got him VIP parking; we pulled right up front, and a valet took the keys from Liam.

We headed straight inside, where the manager greeted us and showed us to our front row balcony seats, just to the left of the stage. They were, without a doubt, some of the best seats in the house. I couldn't believe it. I smiled at Liam as he took my hand in his. I squeezed it as the announcer introduced Jackopierce and I held my breath, knowing no matter what craziness might happen later, I was in a moment I'd never forget.

Chapter Thirteen

Greer

The incredible concert came to an end, and as the lights came up and people started to leave, Liam asked, "So, how'd you like it?"

"It was awesome," I replied quickly. "What'd you think?"

"I think their music is even better live," Liam replied, gesturing us towards the aisle.

"I totally agree." I walked slowly through the narrow row of seats.

"I'm so glad you liked it. I thought it'd be worth the wait," Liam replied playfully.

I stopped suddenly and spun around on my heel. "What do you mean, worth the wait? Were you waiting to ask me out so this concert would be our first date?" I asked, staring Liam right in the eyes.

"Yeah, I wanted our first date to be special," Liam replied sincerely.

"If you'd taken me to a fast food restaurant and to the dollar movie, this still would have been a date I wouldn't have forgotten," I said quickly, and then blushed at my directness.

Liam placed the side of his right index finger under my chin, raising my head up ever so slightly, and whispered, "I'll remember that for next time." For a brief moment, I thought he was going to kiss me right there, in front of all the people still trying to leave, but he said, "We should get going." He smiled and I blushed again.

As we made our way down the stairs, I asked, "Would you mind if we stopped by a ladies' room before we go?"

"Sure," Liam replied sweetly. We made our way to the main floor and headed towards the restrooms. We could see there was a long line for both, but especially for the women's.

"Wait here, I'll see if you can use the employees' restroom." Liam headed towards the bar to talk to the manager.

"You don't have to go to all that trouble," I said, even though I was certain he could not hear me over the noise of the crowd. I waited, and in a few minutes, Liam came back.

"It's no problem," he said, happy with his success. "Follow me," he continued, taking my hand.

It was a good thing he had found an alternative, because the ladies' room line had not moved an inch. We made our way through the crowd and towards the bar. Just beside it, there was an entrance to a back storage room, where I was to find the employees' restroom.

"Would you like for me to help you find it?" Liam asked.

"No, I'll be fine, thanks," I replied confidently.

"Okay, I'll wait here. The manager said it's through this door, take a right, then a left, and then another right, and you will see it," he said, his blue eyes sparkling in the low lights of the bar.

"I'll be back in a few minutes," I said, knowing I would want to rush back as soon as possible. Liam reluctantly let go of my hand.

I went through the swinging door and found myself in a poorly lit, large storage room that looked more like a warehouse. There were boxes stacked everywhere that seemed to form aisles, which explained the directions Liam had given. I took the first right and was trying to remember which way to go, when I heard a noise behind me. I turned around and saw no one was there; I turned back around, taking the next left and then another left, frantically searching for the restroom, which was nowhere in sight. I walked forward quickly and took a right. It had to be somewhere, I thought.

Suddenly, I got a chill and I stopped in my tracks. I was lost in the crazy warehouse storage room, and I was not alone. I slowly reached for the mace inside my handbag and hid it inside the palm of my right hand, ready to fire if necessary. I turned, and, to my relief, saw no one. I turned back around, crept forward, and took another right. I walked more quickly when I saw a light ahead and what appeared to be a door. I was almost running when I saw a sign that said Employees' Restroom. I ran inside and locked the door behind me.

When I was ready to leave, I realized I was so turned around, I had no idea how to get back out to Liam. I slowly unlocked the door and gripped the mace inside my hand. I was scared stiff, but I could also feel my adrenaline pumping. I felt kind of like a spy on a mission. If Darcy could see me, I laughed to myself. As soon as I left the restroom, I took an immediate right and headed towards another light. Light was good, I thought, I liked well-lit places. Then, I heard sounds of footsteps that I knew I was not imagining. I stopped again and was thinking to myself…

"This place is an absolute maze," a man's voice that sounded like lavender came from behind me.

I turned around slowly, trying to decide if I should show him my mace or not. I was so scared that my body made the decision for me; my hand shot up, and I found myself pointing the mace right at the mysterious man, lurking in a shadow not four feet from me.

"Don't come any closer," I demanded. "I have mace and I will use it if provoked."

"I assure you, dear, I have no intention of provoking you," the man replied, remaining where he was. I could tell by the tone of his voice he was amused by my can of mace.

"Who are you? Do you work here?" I asked, standing as confidently as I could, given how terrified I was.

The man laughed, "No, I don't work here."

"Then what are you doing back here?" I asked insistently.

"The same as you, dear: looking for a restroom," he replied calmly, as if he was absolutely certain I would not dare mace him.

I needed to get to Liam as soon as possible. The chill I had gotten earlier had definitely returned when I saw this man, whoever he was. I spoke bluntly, "Well, you've found what you're looking for. Excuse me."

I stepped back in the direction I had been walking and was about to bolt, when the man took two quick steps forward and was standing in the light. I audibly gasped from the shock of seeing his bright green eyes and his dark hair. A quick glance at his features told me he was one of the most handsome men I had ever seen. He was probably my parents' age, which made that a little gross, but still he had an intense presence and a wickedly good-looking smile. He instantly reminded me of someone; I was racking my brain, trying to place how I could possibly know him, when he spoke again.

"Yes, I've found what I was looking for." He smiled deviously. All of the hairs on my arms stood up, and chill bumps covered my body. My mind told me to run, but my body was numb, and I couldn't tear my eyes away from him.

"Lorcan," I whispered, not realizing I was speaking aloud as I lowered my mace.

"Pardon me, dear?" He took another step closer, his face beaming.

I cut my eyes down to the floor, summoned all of my courage, and looked right back into his alluring and familiar eyes. "Are you

Drake Smith, Lorcan's father?" I asked, even though I was certain I was right. The eyes, the hair, the demeanor—it was all too similar. It was like I was looking at Lorcan, just aged twenty years or so.

The man clapped his hands together loudly, and the sound made me jump slightly. "You're very good! My son must have made quite an impression on you, for you to recognize the resemblance between us so quickly," he replied, appearing thoroughly pleased.

"We're working on a project together for a class, that's all," I shot back, thinking loyally of my waiting Liam.

"I've heard a lot about you, Greer. Although, I don't think Lorcan was quite as forthcoming as he should've been about how beautiful you are," Drake said with enthusiasm.

I flinched at his comment and his knowledge of who I was. I was also still scared. In fact, knowing who he was almost made me more scared and more convinced that Darcy was absolutely right about the Smiths. There was something going on, and the Smiths, all of them, were part of it.

I tried to remain polite and calm, even though I was thoroughly convinced that it was no coincidence that I had just met Lorcan's father. I took one step closer to Drake, to show to him that I was not intimidated (even though I was), and said, "Thank you for your compliment. It was nice to meet you, Mr. Smith, but if you'll excuse me, someone is waiting for me."

I turned to walk away; before I managed two steps, Drake said, in a playful tone, "Oh, yes, that'd be Liam, right? I had heard my son had a rival for your affections."

I glanced over my shoulder at Drake, and replied emphatically, "Your son and I are just friends, and I'm afraid I really must go." I refused to listen to anything else he might want to say. I walked quickly towards the light I had seen before.

I took a left when I came to what appeared to be a manager's office, walked a long distance, and then decided to take another left, not deviating again. I was thrilled when I saw the exit sign above a door, and realized it was the way I had entered. I ran for the door and pushed it open, bursting through it.

"Are you okay?" Liam asked, grabbing my hands. "I was about to come looking for you," he said, visibly relieved to see me.

"Next time, I'll wait in line," I said, so happy to see him.

"Let's go," he took my hand and led me through the crowd.

I kept my head down and my eyes on the floor, and allowed Liam to continue his death grip on my hand until we made it outside. When we reached the fresh night air, I stopped, breathed in deeply, and then exhaled slowly.

"Are you okay?" Liam asked again, turning towards me and wrapping his arms around me in a tight hug.

I suddenly felt safe, like nothing in the world could touch me. I whispered, "Yes, I'm just fine now."

My arms were wrapped around his neck, and I had laid my head on his chest for a moment when I heard a low chuckle. I slowly lifted my head to look over Liam's left shoulder, in the direction from which I had heard the now familiar laugh. I saw Drake, standing by the black Jaguar Kieran had been driving earlier in the day. He gave me a wicked smile and a brief wave. Liam turned to see what I was looking at, and, in an instant, Drake was in his car, peeling out of the parking lot. I knew immediately where Kieran had learned how to drive.

"Are you sure you're okay? Did something happen?" Liam asked, puzzled by my odd behavior.

I didn't know what to say to him. I wanted desperately to tell him the truth, but how could I without going into detail about everything? If I did that, Darcy and I might sound crazy. So, as much as I hated to, I kept my encounter with Drake a secret from Liam. Instead, I just told him that I got a little lost trying to find the restroom, and that it kind of freaked me out.

After Liam turned on his SUV, I noticed the clock in the dash said it was 10:20 p.m. We were going to be later than expected to Rebecca's party. Liam must have sensed what I was thinking, because he turned to me and asked, "Do you still want to go to Rebecca's?"

"Yeah, if you don't mind? I'd really like to check on Mia," I replied.

"You're a good friend." Liam smiled and reached for my hand.

I smiled in return. Liam opened the moon-roof, and I stared at the stars the whole way to Rebecca's. I must have been lost in my own thoughts. Before I knew it, twenty-five minutes had passed and we were pulling onto Rebecca's street, which was lined with cars as far as I could see.

Surprisingly, Liam found a spot close to her house and let go of my hand to parallel park. I fully woke from my own little world to realize that Liam and I had spent the entire car ride from the concert in silence, and that his hand had not left mine until that moment.

After Liam parked and turned off the car, I looked over at him, searching his face and trying to decipher his expression. He asked, "Are you sure you're alright?"

I hesitated for a moment, looking down, but then looked up quickly and said, "Yes, I'm sure. How could I not be okay when I'm with you?"

Liam smiled and reached out, gently touching the left side of my face with the tips of his fingers before cupping his hand under my chin. He leaned in and whispered, "I want nothing more than to kiss you right now, but you deserve better than for our first kiss to be in a parked car in front of a high school party."

We stared at each other for a moment, and I thought he was going to kiss me anyways. To be honest, I wouldn't have minded in the least. Finally, his willpower won over; he sat back in his seat and said, "We should go in before I change my mind."

"Okay." I smiled, and my heart nearly leapt from my chest.

Liam met me at the passenger door and closed it behind me. We walked hand in hand towards Rebecca's large house. I had never been there before and, like Katie's house, I was surprised at its grandeur. It was a large, Georgian style, two-story red brick home.

The number of people at the party also surprised me; I had thought it was supposed to be a small party for friends. It looked like half of our school had shown up. How was I ever going to find Darcy, I thought; I should have known she would find me.

Darcy

"There you are! You're late!" I barked at Greer and Liam, as I barreled through the crowd of people on the front porch. I didn't recognize a single face.

Greer just stared at me, and I could tell in an instant she had a lot to tell me, as I did her.

"Sorry Darcy, it was my fault," Liam said chivalrously.

"No, it wasn't," Greer said, refusing to let him take the blame.

I caught the intense look that passed between Greer and Liam, and I decided not to be too mad. "It doesn't matter, you're here now," I said with a small smile. "Liam, can I steal your date for just a little while?"

"Only if you promise to return her soon. I have to have her home by midnight, or I'm afraid your father will have my head." Liam smiled as he reluctantly let go of Greer's hand.

"More than likely, he would just maim you," I replied with a laugh, dragging Greer away. Greer smiled back at Liam, as Elliot and Nathan made their way towards him. I saw Liam's eyes linger on Greer as we walked away. He was completely taken in by her. I was happy she had found such a good guy to date, especially since I knew it was keeping her from becoming involved with Lorcan. I glanced over at Elliot and Nathan. Elliot gave me a huge smile and Nathan gave me a reassuring nod. Apparently they had taken care of what I had asked them to do—I just hoped it worked.

"Where are we going?" Greer asked as we went into the house. She looked around and asked, "Who are all these people?"

"We're going up to Rebecca's room; Mia is there waiting for us. And all of these people are party crashers, told about the party by... guess who?" I stopped and waited for Greer to guess correctly.

"Kieran," she replied, certain she was right.

"Yep, but neither she nor Lorcan have shown up yet. You haven't seen them at all tonight, have you?" I asked, looking at her intently.

"No, I have not seen *them*," Greer said cryptically. I was about to ask her what she meant when Mia opened the door behind me and screeched Greer's name.

I pushed Greer into Rebecca's bedroom and quickly shut the door behind me. Greer gasped as she took in the room—it was just her taste—light and airy and an explosion of pink. It had light pink walls and white furniture, with a light pink rug covering the dark hardwood floors. There were two old coordinating paintings that hung over her queen bed, which had a white and pink floral duvet. The tops of Rebecca's desk, dresser, and nightstand were meticulously organized.

"What a pretty room," Greer exclaimed.

I frowned. "Of course, you think so."

Mia laughed and Greer smiled at her with a sense of relief.

"Where's Rebecca?" Greer asked, walking over to the window. She looked out intently, and I smiled, knowing she was searching for Liam in the sea of unknown faces on the front lawn.

"She's running around, trying to keep people from destroying her house, and trying to get ahold of her parents," I replied as I moved towards Mia, who had taken a seat on the bench at the foot of Rebecca's bed.

"I thought Rebecca's parents were supposed to be here?" Greer asked, shooting me a look suggesting our parents would have a fit if they knew we were at a party without parental supervision.

"They were here, but then Rebecca's younger brother had some sort of allergic reaction to something in the food they had catered. They had to take him to the hospital. There were only about twenty kids here at the time, and Rebecca and her parents knew all of them, so they thought it was okay to leave," I replied, crossing my arms over my chest.

"Is Rebecca's little brother going to be okay?" Greer asked with concern, as she took a seat by Mia on the bench.

"They think so, but apparently it was a bad reaction, that is why both of her parents wanted to go with him," I replied soberly.

We all remained silent for a moment and then Greer asked, "Well, what happened to the party? When did all of these people get here?"

"About ten minutes after Rebecca's parents left, people started showing up and there has been a steady stream ever since," I replied. I knew the Smiths, Kieran in particular, had something to do with the out-of-control party. What bothered me was not knowing her motive behind it, but I was determined to find out what was going on, and stop her from hurting anyone I loved.

"We should help her get rid of the uninvited guests," Greer said, beginning to stand up.

I gestured for her to sit back down. "It's being taken care of." Greer knew enough about me to not question me further. If my plan worked, the uninvited guests would be gone in less than a half hour.

"Besides, Mia has some things she wants to tell you." I smiled encouragingly at Mia, who looked apologetically over at Greer.

"I know I must have seemed totally crazy at the restaurant," Mia said, looking down.

"A little," Greer whispered with a small laugh. She reached for Mia's hand, to encourage her to go on.

Mia looked up and gave her a small smile. I knew what she was about to tell Greer was extremely difficult for her, as it had been earlier, when she told me. I remained outwardly calm, but I was still fuming. Greer waited patiently as she continued, "I was so excited when I saw you and Liam. You really are such a great couple, and I was happy to see you guys on your date." Greer smiled in response and nodded for her to go on. "When I was getting your waters, someone came back to the drink station," Mia paused and Greer looked at me; I could tell that she already knew who it was before Mia continued. "It was Kieran Smith. I asked what she was doing there, and she said she was concerned about you."

Greer laughed. "She said she was concerned about me?" Greer looked over at me, and, as much as I was trying, I found it very difficult to hide the anger I felt hearing the story again.

"Kieran said that she was afraid that Liam was going to put something in your food or your drink that would…" Mia said, looking back down at her hands.

"That's ridiculous," Greer interrupted.

"I know, that's what I told her, but she insisted that I put something in your food as like an antidote. She said that her father's medical research company had recently come up with it, and that it was completely safe."

"I doubt that," Greer said, with a tone and look that said she was thoroughly repulsed at the thought of what Kieran had tried to do. I remained completely silent, and as much as I wished Kieran would dare show her face at the party, it was certainly not in her best interest to do so, and I was certain she knew that.

"I doubted it too, but she would not leave me alone about it, and said that if I was your friend, I would do it to protect you. I was so confused. I told her that I would think about it, but that she had to leave or else I was going to get into trouble. I could tell she wanted to stay and watch me do it, but she saw my manager looking at us suspiciously. That's when she threatened my family," Mia said, beginning to cry.

"That's when she seriously overplayed her hand and underestimated you, Mia," I said, coming out of my hate-filled thoughts for Kieran and sitting down on the other side of Mia for encouragement.

"I wasn't sure whether to believe her, up until she threatened me. I decided not to do what she wanted. I figured that if she would resort to threats to get her way, then she must not have the best intentions," Mia said, still crying.

"So, you didn't give me the pill?" Greer asked, relief evident in her voice.

"No, in fact, she wrapped it in a napkin and gave it to me," I said, smiling and gesturing to my handbag.

"Thank you, Mia, you're a good friend. But I don't understand— how did she threaten your family?" Greer asked, as Mia continued to sob gently.

"My dad lost his job over a year ago, and as careful as my parents have been, they have gone through their entire savings. I've been working as much as possible at the restaurant to help out," Mia said, looking down, embarrassed even though she had absolutely no reason to be. She looked up at Greer and continued, "We were so relieved a week ago, after my dad had a really great interview with a company that has recently opened up a Dallas office. I hadn't seen him that excited in months. He was interviewed by the CEO himself, and he thought the company would be a great fit, because it was so family friendly. My dad said he answered more questions about our family and the area than about his qualifications. He knew those were illegal questions to ask during an interview, but he didn't care. He was so excited—he thought it was the perfect job for him." Mia stared at Greer, waiting for her to put the pieces of the puzzle together.

"I'm so sorry, but am I missing something?" Greer asked, looking over at me and then back at Mia.

"She threatened that if I didn't do what she wanted, she would make sure my father didn't get the job he had just interviewed for," Mia said, starting to cry again.

"But, how could...?" Greer began to ask, and then I could see from the shocked look on her face that all of it suddenly made sense to her. Mia's dad had found a great opportunity to work at Smith Industries, owned by none other than Drake Smith, Kieran and Lorcan's father.

"Smith Industries," was all Greer said, looking at me in disbelief. I nodded, confirming her suspicions, and Mia continued to softly cry.

"Oh Mia, I'm so sorry!" Greer replied. I could tell she was unsure what else to say to the person who had just risked her family's livelihood to protect her from Kieran's dangerous game. Mia had proven herself to be a true friend, and I would not forget how she had helped my sister.

"Mia, don't worry. I'll have a talk with Kieran, and thanks to this pill you gave me, I'm sure I will convince her it is not in her best interest to try and stop your father from getting that job," I said, certain I could make it happen.

"And I will speak with Lorcan too. Please, try not to worry," Greer pleaded with Mia, placing her hand on her shoulder in an effort to comfort her.

"The thing I feel the worst about is that I considered doing it. I tried to convince myself that maybe she was telling the truth, and that I'd be helping you, which made me doubt Liam, who I've known since we were little kids. I know he'd never do anything like what Kieran was suggesting!" Mia said, with sadness and anger in her voice. Greer reached over and gave her a hug. Then, all of sudden, we heard what sounded like a stampede in the front yard.

I laughed and turned to Mia, "I guess our little plan worked!" Mia dried her eyes, and we all made our way to the front window, where we saw a major exodus of kids fleeing Rebecca's house.

"What's going on? What plan?" Greer asked, puzzled.

"Come on, let's go see!" I said excitedly, leading us out of Rebecca's room and down the stairs. It was quiet in the house, as even most of the people Rebecca had invited were gone. We found Rebecca standing in the living room, staring at the mess people had left. There were plastic cups everywhere and the house smelled of cheap beer, but luckily it looked like nothing had been broken or too badly damaged.

I saw a huge smile on Liam's face as I turned around. "It looks like your plan worked, Darcy!" Liam said, walking into the living room with Nathan and Elliot flanking his sides. He and Greer exchanged flirtatious smiles. Sloan, Ella, and Katie came in from the kitchen, and we all surveyed the house.

"We don't have much time to get this house in order before some of us have to leave to make curfew," Ella said. She quickly told everyone what their job was, and we all got to work immediately. Within thirty minutes, the ten of us had the house back to normal. Rebecca was Febreezing the last piece of furniture when Greer told her we had to get home.

"Thanks so much for your help!" Rebecca said, giving Greer an appreciative hug and then one to me.

"I hope your brother is better soon," Greer replied.

"Thank you, I'm sure he will be, although I've never seen him have such a bad allergic reaction before," Rebecca said, obviously worried.

"We'll call you tomorrow to find out how he's doing," Greer said, and then we went to say goodbye to everyone else.

I overheard Greer tell Liam, "I can ride home with Darcy if you want to stay here for a little while longer." I knew she secretly hoped he would say no, and I was certain he would.

"Like I would ever agree to that!" Liam smiled sweetly as he wrapped his arm around her waist, and they headed towards the front door.

They waved and said goodbye to everyone and we all said goodbye back.

"I'll see you at home," I said, smiling at Greer. I was happy because I knew she was safe, for now.

Greer

Soon we were out the door and in Liam's SUV, headed the short distance to my house.

"Well, that was interesting," I said, still processing everything that had occurred at Rebecca's.

"Yeah, it was." Liam laughed.

"I'm curious to know what the plan was that got everyone to leave in such a hurry. It was as if the cops showed up or something," I joked.

Liam laughed at my intuitive comment and replied, "Well, the people at the party thought they were on their way."

"Why would they think that?" I asked curiously.

"Well, your sister found two old CB radios in a hall closet, and she told Nathan and Elliot her plan before we got there. Nathan and I set one up in the living room, and told everyone it was a police scanner and that we wanted to see if it worked. Elliot's dad is a reserve deputy sheriff and they have a real police scanner at their house—which looks nothing like a CB radio, by the way." Liam was laughing so hard, I thought he wasn't going to be able to continue. I couldn't help but laugh as well, as he tried to finish what he was saying. "Elliot has grown up listening to the scanner, and knows what they are supposed to sound like; he went into Rebecca's parents' room, and used the other CB radio and pretended to be the dispatch and various officers reporting in. It was rather convincing, although Nathan and I had to try and keep from laughing the entire time. Elliot continued on for about five minutes, but then he mentioned a complaint of a noise disturbance, using the code numbers and everything, and said Rebecca's address. As soon as he said that, we started telling everyone that the cops were on their way, and they all took off. It was hilarious!"

I laughed. "Leave it to Darcy."

We pulled up in front of my house, and I could see that several of the lights were still on; no doubt my parents were waiting up for Darcy and me. Liam walked me to the front door and I turned to him. All I could think about was whether or not he was going to kiss me when I said, "Liam, I really had a great time tonight."

He softly stroked the left side of my face and hair, and whispered,

"Me too."

I closed my eyes, waiting, thinking it was the moment. I could feel him leaning in, and then he kissed me gently on the left cheek. I opened my eyes as I felt the distance between our faces increasing. He smiled at me, intertwining his fingers in mine, and asked, "I know you spend Sundays with your family, but would it be alright if I call you tomorrow night?"

"Yes!" I replied, a bit too loudly. He and I laughed, and he pulled me closer and gave me a tender, but all-encompassing hug. I fit perfectly in his embrace.

Liam slowly and reluctantly released me. I moved towards the front door as I reached for the key in my handbag. He watched as I opened the door and stepped inside. "Goodnight," I said softly with a smile.

"Goodnight," he replied, never taking his eyes off of me.

I slowly closed the door and leaned up against it, feeling like I could scream from excitement. Although many strange things had happened throughout the course of the evening, it was the most incredible first date I could have ever imagined. I sighed, thinking about the rush I got every time Liam touched my hand or my face. What was this new feeling I was experiencing? Could it be that I was falling in love? I was lost in my thoughts for a few moments, until I heard the sound of delicate footsteps quickly coming my way. I braced myself for the seriously edited version of my date I was about to tell my mother.

Chapter Fourteen

Greer

Lucky for me, in my brief conversation with my mother, I was able to focus on all of the positives of the night and omit all of the craziness. Darcy arrived home within a few minutes, and after seeing both of her daughters home safely, Mom excused herself to bed.

Once Darcy and I were in my room, I told her all the details of my date, not leaving anything out, except maybe how many times I had hoped Liam would kiss me. Darcy didn't even try to conceal her shock when I told her about my dark, warehouse-like, storage room run-in with none other than Drake Smith. She made me repeat the story a second time, and then asked a series of follow-up questions, probing me for anything else I could possibly remember. My encounter with Drake seemed to disturb Darcy more than my almost-drugging by his seriously deranged daughter.

I asked Darcy what she thought about him showing up, and she responded simply, "I don't know." I knew she was lying, even though she stared me straight in the eyes. She had a blank expression, which scared me, because I knew she was masking whatever emotion she was truly feeling. It was her way of trying to protect me. Darcy told me she was tired, and went to her room. I went to bed and tried to sleep, hoping to dream about Liam. Instead, I found myself waking from a nightmare I couldn't exactly remember, but I knew included

Drake, Kieran, and Lorcan.

Our Sunday morning was fairly normal, aside from the fact that Mom wasn't feeling well. Her sudden and atypical headache freed us from our family activity that afternoon, a rock-climbing excursion at the gym we were thinking about joining. Our brother, whose genius idea that activity was, was obviously disappointed, but Dad told him that he and a friend from soccer could go on without us. I spent the afternoon reading, and Darcy locked herself away in her room.

I waited anxiously all afternoon for Liam to call that evening, and exactly at 8:00 p.m., my cell phone rang. We talked for a good hour and a half about everything and about nothing. Near the end of our conversation, Liam asked me something so quickly that I had no idea what he had just said; my heart jumped for a moment, thinking he had asked me to prom, which was still three months away. I asked him to please repeat himself, and he did, sweetly saying, "Would you like to go with me to the Spring Sports Banquet?"

I had known about the banquet, which was in mid-March, as my brother and parents were planning to attend. It was a big deal, especially for graduating seniors like Liam. I knew his parents would attend as well, which made me a little anxious.

I paused for a moment in my nervousness, but then replied happily, "Of course, I'd love to go."

Liam sighed in relief, and I smiled to myself. We talked for a few more minutes and then he wished me sweet dreams. I hoped his wish would come true, but it didn't. Instead, I dreamed of Drake, Kieran, and Lorcan and, again, woke up terrified.

Monday morning came and I was up early and ready for school. I was the first of my siblings downstairs, where I found Mom in the kitchen making lunches.

"Hi," I said happily, taking my spot at the bar as I placed my phone on the counter and my bag on the floor.

I could tell Mom was distracted from her quick glance at me and half-smile as she said, "Morning."

I was worried that Mom was on to the fact that Darcy and I were keeping a secret from her. I decided, despite my better judgment, to ask, "Mom, is everything okay?"

She looked up quickly at me, alarmed that I had noticed the obvious. She avoided my question for the moment, by replying in a slightly more normal tone, "What do you mean, sweetheart?"

"You just seem like something is bothering you," I replied honestly, watching her face and hoping she would give something away.

Instead, she looked down at the sandwich she was making and replied softly, "Everything's fine, please don't worry." I knew not to believe her, even if I had not seen her quickly dab the corners of her eyes with the back of her fingers. Something was bothering her in a big way, and it was obvious she wasn't going to just open up and tell me what it was because I asked nicely. I would have to try an alternative route.

I waited a few minutes, pretending to look through a home goods magazine that was lying on the bar, and then slowly got up and walked towards my father's office, where I was sure to find him.

I knocked softly and opened the door slightly, peeking my head around the door to find my dad sitting at his desk, staring at his laptop. When he saw me, he smiled and closed the screen so I couldn't see what he'd been looking at. "Good morning, sweetheart," Dad said, surprised but happy to see me.

"Good morning, Daddy." I entered the office and sat down across from his desk in one of the armchairs.

"You're up bright and early this morning. Anxious for school?" Dad smiled rather knowingly, I thought.

"Yeah, you know I like school," I replied.

"Yes, I know," Dad said, leaving the discussion at that.

"Dad, I am a little concerned…" I paused, hoping I was making the right choice in talking to him about Mom.

Dad began to look anxious and asked quickly, "Greer, what are you concerned about?"

"Mom," I replied quickly, not wanting him to question anything else—especially not Liam, or the Smiths, who I was fairly certain he and Mom knew nothing about.

Dad looked a little relieved, but not much. He asked, "Why are you worried about your mother?"

"She just seems like something's bothering her."

"I'm sure your mother is fine. Maybe it's hitting her that you are turning eighteen next month and will be graduating soon?" Dad replied rather convincingly, although I believed there was still something more to it than that. Just then, we heard Mom call everyone to breakfast.

"We should get going; I'm starving, and I don't want your brother to eat half of everything before we even get there." Dad smiled as he stood up and walked towards the door.

"Okay, I'm just gonna use the restroom and then I'll be right there," I said, walking towards the half-bathroom adjacent to Dad's office.

"Alright, I'll tell your mother you're on your way," Dad said, walking out the door and leaving it half-open.

I reached for the pocket door to the bathroom, and then, when I was sure Dad was gone, I quickly walked over to his computer and lifted the screen of the laptop, to see what he had been looking at when I came in. I knew I shouldn't snoop, but I had to see what he was hiding and if it offered any new information.

When I saw the website he was looking at, I took a step back in surprise. It was the homepage for Hagen Pharmaceuticals. I didn't even know such a company existed. I quickly glanced at some of the subsidiaries, and my surprise turned to shock when I saw that one of them was Smith Industries. I wondered if Dad had a chance to see that as well. Could he know Drake Smith? I returned back to the exact page he was on and closed the screen just as it was before. I hurried to the kitchen, acting as normal as possible, although I was freaking out on the inside.

Darcy

When I arrived at the kitchen table, everyone was already there and serving the pancakes and fruit my mom had prepared. When I sat down, we all said our usual prayer and began to eat. Will and Dad talked about sports throughout most of breakfast, while I noticed Greer and Mom both seemed withdrawn and deep in their own thoughts.

At the end of breakfast, Will mentioned the sports banquet; I saw Greer's eyes light up, and her countenance changed from a mixture of confusion and anxiety to more of her normal, happy self when she announced that she would be attending the banquet with Liam. That news wasn't surprising to me, but I was interested in what she had been so worried about moments before. I knew she would tell me on the way to school—she wasn't the one good at keeping secrets, that was my department. Everyone smiled and said that was great, except Mom, who quickly turned to me and said, "I think you should come with us as well."

"Why?" I asked bluntly. I loved my brother, but spending a Saturday evening praising a bunch of jocks wasn't my idea of fun.

"Because I think it would be good if you supported your brother. He'll be attending your and Greer's choir concert at the end of the year," Mom said, in a way that demonstrated she was not making a request.

"I am?" Will asked, sounding a little surprised and a tad annoyed.

"Yes, you are," Mom replied swiftly. Greer shot me a look that said I should let it go, and I did.

"Alright," I said quietly, finishing my last bite.

We all remained quiet, and I saw Greer and Dad exchange a look that I was sure to find out the meaning of on our way to school.

"Mom, Darcy and I may be a little late getting home today," Greer said as I was rinsing my plate.

Mom stopped loading the dishwasher and replied anxiously, "Why, who are you going to be with?"

"I just need some things from the school library. We won't be very late; definitely home in time for dinner, I promise," Greer said, touching the side of her arm to try and make her feel better. I wondered if she noticed that Greer didn't really answer her question.

I gave Greer a slightly impressed look, and Mom replied, "Okay, just text me when you're on your way home, and don't be late!"

"We won't be, I promise!" Greer hugged her and grabbed her lunch from the counter and her bag from the floor. I did the same, as did Will. Greer and I headed for the garage, giving Dad a hug and saying goodbye to Will. Dad was about to leave to take Will to school, and Greer and I were about to pull out of the garage. I had every intention of finding out exactly what Greer knew, even though I wasn't quite ready to share my own speculations—I knew Greer wasn't ready for it. Then Greer realized she had left her phone in the house.

Greer

I noticed Will was sitting in the passenger seat of Dad's Grand Cherokee, messing with his own phone, as I ran inside to grab mine off of the bar. My parents didn't hear me as I came in. Walking towards the kitchen, I heard my Dad say, "Everything's going to be alright, Arianna, but you have got to try and act a little more yourself. The children are starting to notice."

"He's nearby, David. I know it. The girls are almost eighteen, legal adults. What if he's just biding his time until then?" Mom's voice shook. Who were they talking about, and how did it involve Darcy and me? I wanted to listen more, but I knew I had to get my phone and get to school, or else we would be late.

"Hey," I yelled, to signal to my parents I was back in the house. "I forgot my phone." I rounded the corner to grab it off the bar, and saw my parents standing at the kitchen sink, trying to figure out if I had heard any of their conversation. I smiled at them and said happily, "See you later," and ran for the door to the garage. I interpreted my dad's sigh of relief to mean that he thought I hadn't heard anything.

When I was in the car and Darcy and I were safely down the street, I told her about what had happened with Mom and Dad before breakfast, and then what I had overheard when I went back in to get my phone. I asked her what she thought, to induce her out of her silence. Her simple response of "I don't know," was starting to get old. Maybe she didn't know, but I wanted her to at least speculate. I knew it wasn't the right time for that fight, so I told her about my plan, saying, "I want to confront Lorcan today in the library after school, and I want you to do the same with Kieran. I'm tired of playing games. They should know that we know something is going on, and maybe the truth will just come out." I wondered if she was going to protest.

To my surprise, Darcy smiled and said, "I agree. Besides, it will be kind of fun to confront Kieran. Do you really think you can handle Lorcan all by yourself?"

"I plan to start out being nice, and then move into being mean if need be," I replied, confident of what I had to do.

"You can be mean?" Darcy asked sarcastically.

"Unfortunately, everyone can be mean if they want to be. I hope I don't have to go that route, but I assume that is what you plan to do with Kieran?" I replied, knowing what we were going to do was not going to be easy.

"Not quite," Darcy smirked. I didn't ask any further questions, as I truly didn't want to know.

Overall, it was a good day at school. All of my friends, except Mia, asked about my date with Liam, and I happily gave the highlights. Everyone wanted to know if he had kissed me, and they thought it was sweet when I said he hadn't.

Liam was extra attentive in class and at lunch, and the smiling glances he gave me were definitely the best part of my day. In physics that morning, he had whispered in my ear, "You look beautiful today." I shivered when his breath tickled my neck. I smiled back at him, and he chuckled at my visible response to his closeness.

Liam and I walked to English together close enough to hold hands, but we didn't. When we entered the room, Liam lingered for a moment, and then he hesitantly went over to his usual seat. I sat down and noticed Lorcan as he walked in. I returned his smile and he took that as an invitation to come over and speak to me. I didn't look over at Liam, but I could sense he was watching us.

"Hi Greer," Lorcan said, slightly less charismatic than normal. He sat down in the chair in front of me and turned to face me, his back towards Liam.

"Hi," I replied, trying not to act like I was surprised that he had taken that desk. I immediately began to wonder if he was going to return to his own seat, or stay in front of me the whole class period. I wanted to look over at Liam so I could see his expression. I knew he was looking at us. I could feel his blue eyes on me, but I knew I couldn't look away yet. I had to remember what I needed to do. I would explain it all to Liam later, and hopefully he would understand.

Before Lorcan could say anything, I got right to the point, asking, "We need to make some more progress on our speech assignment, and I have a lot of other things going on. I was hoping we could meet this afternoon and work on it?"

Lorcan thought for a moment, as if he were going over his schedule in his head, and then said in his most alluring voice, "That should be fine. Would you like to work in the library again or should we work at my house?"

I considered it for a moment, what information I could get from Lorcan in his own home. Perhaps he would tell me everything I wanted to know, but perhaps I could get that in the library as well. I wanted to know more about Lorcan and his family, but I had no desire to be alone in their home with them. I had to remember what Kieran tried to get Mia to do. I replied, with a slight bat of my eyes, "I think the library would be best."

Just then, Darcy came in and walked quickly towards us. She looked over at Liam, which I still couldn't bring myself to do, and then bent down and whispered to Lorcan, "I think you'd better return to your normal seat, before Greer's boyfriend loses it."

Lorcan laughed and looked back at me. I nodded in agreement with Darcy. Lorcan got up and walked slowly back to his seat, flashing a self-satisfied smile towards Liam. I finally made myself look over at Liam, who I saw was engaged in a fierce staring competition with Lorcan. I'd never seen Liam look that way; he was obviously upset, I just hoped not with me. "I have good reasons for doing this," I wanted to scream, but when Liam looked back at me, I could tell that he didn't understand. I felt awful.

Ms. Abrams had us break into groups of five and talk about our favorite book from when we were children. We were to make lists of the common attributes they possessed. I worked with Ella, Mia, Katie, and Rebecca. Darcy went over and worked with Lorcan and three students that sat near him. I glanced over, hoping Liam would see that I was not in a group with Lorcan, but he didn't look up. Kieran pulled her desk closer to Liam, as she, Elliot, Nathan, and one other student were going to work with him. My blood began to boil; she was no doubt trying her best to flirt with him. Would he ignore her flirting like normal, I wondered, if he thought I had been flirting with Lorcan right in front of him?

We started working on the assignment, and I didn't get to pay as much attention as I wanted to Liam and his group. I could hear Kieran's shrill laugh every once in a while, and I imagined her placing her hand on Liam's arm. Mia must have read my mind. or was still shaken up by what Kieran had tried to convince her to do, because she watched Kieran as closely as I did, trying not to be noticed. Mia had followed Darcy's instructions perfectly, not saying a word to anyone about what had happened with Kieran at the restaurant. I had no doubt of Mia's friendship and loyalty.

Luckily, class went by quickly. I rushed to gather my things so I could wait for Liam. I saw Liam making his way towards the door, and I walked quickly to the front of my row to meet him. I was stopped by Lorcan, who, knowing exactly what he was doing, said loud enough for anyone passing by to hear, "I look forward to hanging out after school."

I looked at Liam's face as he walked by, and I could see the hurt in his eyes. I flashed Lorcan a look that said I would deal with him later, to which he only seemed more amused. I walked quickly after Liam, catching up to him in the hall.

"Liam, wait, please," I said, trying not to sound as desperate as I felt. I was so afraid Liam would think me disloyal, and that couldn't be further from the truth.

Liam slowed down, but didn't turn around to face me. I caught up and positioned myself in front of him. When I saw the blank look on his face, I pulled him over to an empty set of lockers nearby.

"So, you're hanging out with Lorcan this afternoon?" Liam asked before I could even open my mouth. I couldn't tell by his tone of voice if he was more angry or hurt.

"Liam, it's not what you think. I know what he said sounded bad. We're not hanging out together. We're just meeting in the library to work on our speech assignment," I said. I wanted to tell him more, but knew I couldn't in the short time between classes.

Liam looked a little relieved, but said in a slightly jealous tone, "I saw the look you gave him in class."

I quickly thought through my conversation with Lorcan, and realized that I had batted my eyes at him—that must have been the look to which Liam was referring. "I promise you, I have absolutely zero interest in Lorcan Smith," I said, emphatically.

"Well, then you'd be the only girl in school who feels that way," Liam replied, looking down.

"Well, I'm not like other girls," I retorted, hoping he would believe me.

Liam looked back at me and smiled, "No, you're definitely not. But you do have to be careful about giving looks like that. They're pretty powerful, and I don't want Lorcan thinking he can go asking my girlfriend out."

I laughed, although my heart was racing. "Your girlfriend?" I questioned teasingly.

Liam softly touched the left side of my face with the back of his bent fingers, and I closed my eyes. It was, without a doubt, my new favorite thing in the whole world. "Yes, my girlfriend," Liam said with a small laugh.

The three minute warning bell rang, which snapped me out of my daze. "We had better go," I said, reluctant to remove myself from the little world Liam and I had created right there in our high school hallway.

"Alright, but please do watch out for those looks; you have no idea the effect they have on us mere mortals," Liam said, a bit more seriously.

I smiled and said, "I promise. They will be reserved only for my boyfriend."

Liam's face brightened and I knew I was forgiven. "I'll call you tonight," he said, and then backed away and headed in the opposite direction I had to go to get to calculus.

I turned to run to class, and I saw Kieran leaning up against a wall just down the hall. She had her arms folded across her chest and an awful little smirk on her face. I had no doubt she was watching Liam and me the entire time we were talking, and probably overheard some of our conversation.

I walked past her, never taking my eyes off hers. I gave her a little smirk to match her own, and then I laughed just a little. She seemed surprised and obviously wanted to say something, but she kept quiet and just watched me as I rounded the corner slowly. Once she was out of my line of sight, I hauled it to class, just making it into the room as the bell rang. Darcy looked at me strangely as I sat down beside her, and I just shook my head—I would tell her later.

Darcy

After calculus, Greer and I walked to our lockers and she asked me, "When are you going to talk to Kieran?"

"I'm going to catch her right after school. Because of the rain, they're doing study hall in the cafeteria instead of tennis practice. Are you going to confront Lorcan in the library?" I asked, putting books away and grabbing the ones I would need for my homework.

"Yes," Greer said hesitantly. I could tell she was nervous; confrontation was not her strong suit, but I knew she was tired of all of the secrets. She was ready for the truth to come out, as was I.

"You know, you don't have to do this. We can do some more investigating first," I said. I didn't want her to be too uncomfortable, even though I desperately wanted her to get some information out of Lorcan. I wanted to know if my suspicions were correct.

"No, we need to do this now. It's the right time," Greer replied with confidence. I was impressed with the strength Greer was showing. I began to think she might be ready for me to tell her what I was thinking, but I would make that decision once we gathered more information.

"Okay, text me when you're done, and I'll meet you at the car," I said, giving her my most encouraging smile.

"Okay." Greer smiled back.

I closed my locker, looked right at her, and said, "Greer, you're stronger than you know. You can do this."

"Thanks. I suppose I don't need to wish you luck. I actually kind of feel sorry for Kieran," Greer said honestly.

I laughed and whispered, "Only you would feel sorry for the person who tried to drug you."

The truth was that I was looking forward to my little chat with Kieran after school. I had a feeling it would be quite informative and just a tad enjoyable, for me at least.

Chapter Fifteen

Greer

Lorcan's green eyes brightened as I entered speech class. I gave him a guarded look, which he seemed to notice. I thought all class period about what I was going to say to him. When class was over, I procrastinated and told him that I had to stop by the ladies' room, and that I'd meet him in the library. I tried to act as normal as possible. After a few minutes in the bathroom, I composed myself and headed towards the library, braced for whatever I was about to find out.

As I entered the library, I noticed there were only a few female students, sitting together at a table near the doors. They were whispering and didn't notice my arrival. I searched for Lorcan but didn't find him, until I walked around a corner and headed towards the back. I was unsettled when I saw him sitting at the same table Darcy had chosen the last time we were all there.

I tried to act as normal as possible, arranging a smile on my face, as I approached him. He stood up and gave me his best smile, which would have knocked most girls off their feet, because he was so "hot," as my friends would say. Luckily, I felt like I had built up an immunity, at least somewhat, to his looks and charm. All I had to do was think about Liam, and my mind cleared and I was focused.

"There you are!" I tried to sound happy to see him, as well as bring attention to the fact he had chosen an out of the way table.

"I thought we could use some privacy," Lorcan replied with an intense stare. He moved some of his papers over so I could sit next to him, but I sat down directly across from him. He smiled through his surprise, although I could tell he was used to getting what he wanted.

"Let's go ahead and get started," I suggested. We did need to make more progress on our speech assignment, but I also wanted to get that over with, so we could move on to why I really wanted to meet— to find out what he, his psycho sister, and their creepy father were up to, and how it involved my family.

"Sure." Lorcan smiled. We spent about thirty minutes discussing the items we needed to agree on for the assignment. To my surprise, Lorcan was very amenable and deferred to me on pretty much everything.

While I checked over my list to make sure I had missed nothing, Lorcan leaned over the table and whispered, "I love how organized you are, but I'm afraid that it made our little meeting here go much faster than I would have liked."

"Well, lucky for you, I have something else I want to talk to you about," I replied, putting down the piece of paper I was holding and clasping my hands together, in an effort to keep them from shaking. I just hoped that I could keep my voice from shaking as well.

"Really? That's great, because I certainly wasn't ready to say good-bye yet." Lorcan smiled. He had no idea what I was about to do; for a moment, I thought I was crazy, but barreled ahead anyways. I was tired of the secrets Darcy and I were keeping, and of the mysterious actions of the Smiths. It had to end.

"Why did you and your family move here?" I asked bluntly, and with a little edge in my voice that did not escape his notice.

He smiled and replied simply, "Because my father opened a new office for his company."

"Is that the only reason?" I asked pointedly, not moving in the slightest bit.

"What other reason could there be?" Lorcan asked, sitting up a little in his chair.

"Why Dallas? There are lots of other cities to choose from." I tried to control my tone.

"What's this all about, Greer? Why so many questions about my father's company?" Lorcan asked, his face turning much more serious. He leaned in a little closer to me.

"I want to know what your family is up to—why Kieran was stalking my family the other day and then threatened Mia if she didn't put who-only-knows-what kind of pill in my food, and why that same night I met your father in, of all places, a shadowy storage room of a concert venue." I don't know who was more stunned at my bluntness—Lorcan or me.

Lorcan's face was stone cold as he slowly moved back in his seat. He stared at his hands and I could see the anger build in his face. I wasn't sure what I was going to do if he unleashed it on me. I had a feeling his wrath could rival Darcy's. I waited for him to say something. After a moment, when he had composed himself somewhat, all he managed was, "I see."

That was certainly not going to do, I thought, so I reached out and touched his hand and said, "Lorcan, I need answers, and you're the only one I trust to give them to me. Please, help me understand what's going on."

Lorcan breathed in and then exhaled slowly. I believed that he wanted to tell me everything, but for some reason he couldn't; whether it was his loyalty to his family or his embarrassment over their actions, I wasn't sure. He looked up at me with the most sincere look I had ever seen from him, and said, "Greer, I'm sorry if at any point you have been scared. I never wanted that. I'm sorry, but I need to go, now."

"Lorcan, wait please," I said as he started to throw all of his things in his bag. "I think you care enough about me, at least as a friend, to tell me more."

Lorcan rose from his chair, and I stood to meet him as he walked past me. I grabbed his arm, knowing that I wouldn't be able to hold him for long. "Please," I begged, one last time.

Lorcan paused and looked at my hand; locking me in with a look that said more than words ever could, he shocked me by saying, "Greer, you must know that I care much more than a friend would." Then he was gone. I sat back down in my chair, trying to process what he had said and the information he had refused to give me. After a few minutes, I reached for my phone and texted Darcy to let her know that I was ready to go.

I met Darcy five minutes later at our car. I was numb from my pointless discussion with Lorcan. When I saw Darcy, she was smiling, and I knew she had accomplished what she wanted. At least one of us had, I thought.

Darcy

As Greer approached, I saw the distressed look on her face and asked immediately, "What's wrong?"

"I'll tell you in the car," she replied, defeated.

We got in quickly, and I turned to her and said, "Spill it."

She told me everything that happened with Lorcan in the library; to her surprise, I laughed.

"Why are you laughing?" she asked, not trying to hide her annoyance in the slightest.

"Because you think he didn't tell us anything, when what he said and didn't say actually told us a ton!" I smiled to myself as I looked out across the nearly empty parking lot.

"I'm sorry, but I'm not following you," she said, still annoyed but obviously curious.

"From what Lorcan said and the information I got from Kieran, we now know a few more things to help piece everything together: (1) Lorcan likes you—we weren't sure before if that was just a part of the plan, or if it was real; (2) he didn't know about Kieran going rogue the other day, which tells us she has her own agenda; (3) he wasn't surprised about his father's mysterious meeting with you the other night; and (4) he's the least dangerous of the three of them, and will probably do what he can to protect you," I replied, satisfied for now with the progress we had made.

"But, none of that tells us why they have an agenda that involves us in the first place," she replied, still processing everything I had just said. I knew I couldn't keep much more from Greer—she deserved more answers, and I had to share at least some of my speculations.

"Don't you see? Our families have some sort of connection. Smith Industries is a subsidiary of Hagen Pharmaceuticals, out of Boston. Even though we have never heard of it, it doesn't mean that it wasn't our family's company at some point. Plus, we also have some extended family we have never heard about. Remember the mysterious press clipping?" I countered. "What if..."

Greer finished my sentence for me. "The Smiths are our extended family?" She visibly shuttered at the idea.

"It's okay, Greer; if we're related, I'm sure Lorcan doesn't know, or else he wouldn't have allowed himself to like you." I tried to comfort her, to no avail.

"Gross!" she yelled. I had to laugh. "I wasn't thinking about that. I was thinking how I couldn't stand the thought of being related to Kieran or Drake. That would be absolutely awful!"

"You weren't thinking about Lorcan, even a little?" I asked playfully. I was trying to keep Greer's focus on that aspect of my theory, in order to keep her from asking any other questions I couldn't or wasn't ready to answer. The truth was that I had some other suspicions I wasn't quite ready to vocalize, mainly because I hoped I was wrong.

"No. Besides, it'd make more sense that they'd all know if we're related; if that were the case, then what might be seen as Lorcan flirting was probably just him being nice. When he said he cared more than just a friend, it was because he knew we were family. That'd make a lot more sense." Greer said quickly. I could tell by the look in her eyes she hoped she was right, if in fact we were related to the Smiths, which my gut told me we were.

"Maybe you're right," I replied, as I turned the car on.

"But let's say that we are related to them. That would mean that Mom and Dad obviously know them, and have been trying to keep us away from them, since they never told us about any extended family. They probably have a good reason for that, don't you think?" Greer asked as I cut across the parking lot.

"Maybe," I replied seriously.

"What happened with Kieran?"

I laughed a little too mischievously. "Well, Mia's dad's job is safe, and she admitted that she worked alone on the incident at the restaurant."

"How'd you get all of that from her?" Greer asked, half-impressed and half-concerned with what methods I might have resorted to.

I kept driving, and said with a smile, "I have my ways." The truth was that I didn't have to do very much. Kieran talked a big game, but I knew from the moment I confronted her that she'd gone out on her own with the plot to drug Greer, and that she didn't want to face Lorcan's wrath. Too bad for her, she would face it anyways, now that Greer had told him.

"That's what concerns me," Greer said with a small but serious laugh. "Were you able to find out any more useful information from her?"

"It took me a while to locate her, but I finally found her lurking outside of the library right after school. I think she was trying to see you and Lorcan, but you must have been in the back. We didn't get to talk very long before Lorcan came rushing out of the library. As soon as she saw him, a look of absolute terror came over her face. He grabbed her arm and they took off without saying another word. That's when I headed out to the car to wait for you," I said, matter-of-factly.

Greer

"Why didn't you come inside to meet me?" I asked, thinking it was an odd thing to be concerned about, considering everything else that was going on.

"Because, sometimes, people need time to process things. I did after my short-lived conversation with Kieran, and I figured you would too, after talking with Lorcan." We were getting closer to home and I knew we should let Mom know we were on our way, so I quickly sent her a text.

"What are you doing?"

"I'm letting Mom know we'll be home soon," I replied with a sharp edge in my voice.

"Why are you so fussy? This was a great day!" Darcy flashed a smile and her green eyes sparkled.

I stared at her for a moment and said, "I don't know why you think it was so great. We still don't know why the Smiths are doing what they are doing."

"At this rate, we'll know soon. Kieran's about to crack. If I can just get her alone one more time, then I think I can get all of the information we need from her," Darcy smiled confidently. I hoped she was right, because I didn't think Lorcan was going to tell me anything else; the truth was that I kind of dreaded seeing him again after our awkward conversation.

Luckily for me, but not for our mission, Lorcan and Kieran were not at school the next day. Darcy didn't seem too surprised, but when a week passed and they had not returned, I could tell she was getting antsy.

Our other friends noticed Lorcan and Kieran's unexplained absences, and it became a topic of conversation at lunch and in class. I listened but said nothing; I could tell Liam paid extra attention whenever Lorcan's name was brought up.

A week turned into five, and there was still no trace of them. Most people thought they had moved away, and I hoped that was the case. Darcy had Mia ask her dad lots of questions about his new workplace, Smith Industries. She reported back to us that all seemed normal, but the CEO had returned to the main headquarters in Boston for a while, to take care of some matters there.

As the time passed, I felt like our lives had returned to a normal, much less dramatic pace. I admit, I was doing a lot better with the Smiths' gone, even though I would occasionally think of Lorcan and the last words we had exchanged. Darcy, on the other hand, was not alright. She had thought she was so close to getting the information she wanted, and then it all slipped away. She was frustrated, and isolated herself somewhat from the rest of us.

In the meantime, Liam and I went on several more dates, including one to a drive-in movie, one to an art museum, and one to a hockey game. I had no doubt that I was falling hard for him. He was kind, considerate, funny, smart, a complete gentleman, and incredibly handsome. We had a great time together, and I was thrilled when he told me that he was staying in Dallas to go to college. He had a received a soccer scholarship from Southern Methodist University. When I told him that was where I had decided to go as well, he grabbed me up in his arms and twirled me around, right in front of my favorite Monet. I laughed as he slowly lowered me to the floor, and then I just stared at him as he softly brushed the hair out of my face with his fingers. That was the moment I knew I was in love with him—just before he kissed me for the first time. There were no words to describe our first kiss. I just knew that it was amazing, and I was glad he was partially holding me up, because I felt my knees give way a little in the middle of it.

It was soon the middle of March, and Darcy had not decided where she was going to school yet. She became irritated whenever our parents asked. We had both applied to a few schools. I was also accepted at Notre Dame and Saint Louis University, but my parents were thrilled when I decided to stay close to our new home and chose SMU.

Darcy had been accepted at UCLA, SMU, and, much to everyone's surprise, Boston College. Our parents didn't know that she had applied there. Most parents would have been thrilled that their child had been accepted and was considering going to their alma mater, but not ours. When the acceptance packet arrived the day of the Spring Sports Banquet, Will came in with the mail and yelled to

Darcy that she had received something from BC. We were all in the kitchen, and our mother froze in her tracks and looked right at our father.

"Darcy, why are you getting mail from Boston College?" Dad asked calmly, but seriously.

Darcy was sitting at the bar flipping through a magazine, and, without even looking up, she said, "They're probably sending me either my acceptance or rejection letter."

Will and I looked at each other and then looked at Mom to see what her reaction was going to be. To our amazement, she remained calm, walked over to Will, and held out her hand for the letter. She then walked over to Darcy and placed the letter on top of the magazine, and said in a casual tone, "Well, let's see what they have to say."

Darcy looked up at our mom, and, to my surprise, a guilty look flashed across her face. She took the envelope and slowly opened it. She read over it briefly and then handed it to Mom. Mom looked at it, and with as much composure as she could muster, she smiled and said, "Congratulations," before she sat the letter down, turned, and walked out of the room. I looked over at Dad and his concerned look said enough. He soon followed after her.

When they were safely out of the room, Will and I walked over to Darcy. "Man Darce, I knew you were crazy, I just didn't know how much!" Will said, mock-punching Darcy in the upper arm. Darcy gave him a sarcastic frown, but said nothing.

"When did you apply to BC?" I asked, hoping she would respond to me.

"A while back," she replied, looking at the letter again.

"You know Mom and Dad will never pay for you to go there. They don't want any of us to go there," Will said a little more seriously, sitting down next to her at the bar.

"And don't you think that's odd? That our parents, both of whom graduated from there, don't want us to even consider it? That they've never even taken us to Boston for a visit? That they hardly ever talk about their lives before we all came along, and never talk about any of our extended family, except Grandpa and Grandma D, who we only see like every three years?" Darcy barked at Will, the anger and frustration evident in her voice.

"I don't know, I never thought about it." Will backed away from Darcy.

"Well, I think about it all the time," Darcy said, grabbing the acceptance letter and storming up to her room.

"What's her deal?" Will asked when he knew she was out of earshot, rolling his eyes.

"She just has a lot on her mind," I replied, knowing that the longer Kieran and Lorcan were away, the more irritable she had become. She was so close to getting the information she wanted from Kieran, and then they were gone, and who knew if they were coming back.

"Well, she'd better get it together before the banquet tonight," Will replied seriously. He was terrified of being embarrassed in front of his friends, and if anyone could do the job, it was Darcy. With the mood she was in, we both knew she was highly unpredictable.

I nodded to Will in agreement and headed up the stairs to talk to Darcy. Had I really thought about what I was doing, I probably wouldn't have gone, but she was my sister, and I had to try and help her.

Darcy

I heard a knock on my door, but I didn't respond. I just continued to lie on my bed, in the dark, with a pillow over my face. The knock came again, with a little more force. I didn't have the will to tell Greer to go away; when she gently cracked open the door and whispered, "Darcy, can I come in?"

"What are you doing?" Greer asked, walking into my room and shutting the door.

I slowly rose to an upright position. "I was just thinking. I think better when it is dark."

"Okay," Greer replied, as she turned on the lamp and moved towards my chair to sit down.

Greer smiled and took a seat, pulling the pillow out from behind her and holding it to her chest. She began to play with the embroidery as she spoke softly. "Why didn't you tell me you applied to BC?"

"Because you'd have told me not to waste my time," I replied, positioning my head against the wall and looking up at the ceiling.

"Do you really want to go there?" she asked. I could tell she was trying to tread carefully and not set off my unpredictable temper.

"Maybe?" I said, still not looking at her.

Greer sighed, and I could tell she was holding back something. I looked over at her and said, "Just say what you want to say."

She breathed in and began, "I don't think you really care about going there at all. I think you just applied to irk Mom and Dad, and see if somehow it would provide you with some more information regarding their past." I just stared at her, waiting for her to finish. "You've become obsessed with the idea that Mom and Dad are hiding some big secret from their past, and that somehow the Smiths are involved."

"They *are* hiding something, and the Smiths *are* involved," I said calmly, even though I wanted to scream it at her.

"Okay, let's say they are hiding something huge, a life-changing secret. You know Mom and Dad—they love us, they'd do anything for us, anything to protect us. If they're hiding something, they're doing it for a good reason. Why can't you believe that? Why can't you leave it alone?" she pleaded.

"You don't understand. You can't understand. Whatever it is Mom and Dad are hiding has to do with us; it has to do with me." I sighed and quickly wiped my left eye, to get rid of the evidence that I was about to cry.

Greer moved towards me and sat next to me on the bed. "What do you mean it has to do with you? What do you know that you've not told me?"

"Haven't you noticed the similarities between Kieran and me?" I asked, looking directly at her.

"That's ridiculous, what similarities?" she scoffed.

"We have similar mannerisms—our tempers, the way we walk, our dark personalities," I replied, looking down at my hands.

Greer shook her head no and said vehemently, "You're nothing alike."

"We also look alike," I replied, looking up at her.

"What? No, you don't!" Greer laughed. She wanted to think I was joking, but I had never been more serious.

"I don't just resemble Kieran; Lorcan and I have similarities as well."

"This is crazy! What in the world are you talking about?" Greer's laugh started to fade.

"Our eyes," I whispered, as I stared at her.

Greer gasped. She looked away and said nothing. I gave her a moment to process everything. She had spent enough time with Lorcan, and she had met his father; they both had the same bright green eyes—my green eyes.

"So, we are related to them. They must be cousins of some sort,"

Greer said, and I could tell she was troubled at the thought.

"Maybe," I said quietly, as I got up and walked over to my desk. I began to open the drawer, but then changed my mind. I had shared enough with Greer today. I wasn't ready to tell her anything else. I turned back to her and said, "We'd better start getting ready for the banquet. You know how Will gets if we're late to anything of his."

"Yeah, he gets almost as fussy as you have been lately," Greer said, trying to make me laugh. I just smirked and rolled my eyes.

"Can you try and rein that in a bit? It's kind of putting everyone on edge," Greer said with a small smile. "Also, do you think you could lay off this Boston College thing? Unless it's your dream school, don't push Mom and Dad too much on it. Give them a little break? I'm sure they have their reasons for not wanting us to go there."

"Alright," I said, and gave her a smile that affirmed I would.

Greer paused for a moment at my bedroom door. Just before she opened it, she turned and said, "Is there anything else you're not telling me?"

I looked straight at her and replied, "No."

She said nothing as she left my room for hers. I knew she knew I was lying, but even though I had more information, I knew she wasn't ready for it—not yet.

Chapter Sixteen

Greer

Darcy was on her best behavior at the sports banquet. I noticed, from where I sat with Liam and his parents, that she even spoke with a few people other than our parents and Will. When Will received the Outstanding Junior Varsity Male Athlete Award, she clapped and smiled. Our parents beamed, and Liam laughed as I almost jumped out of my seat in excitement and surprise.

The varsity soccer coach, when handing out the award alongside the JV coach, said how excited he was about Will joining the varsity soccer team the following year, and that he expected to see great things from him, just as he had seen from his graduating star athlete, Liam. It wasn't a surprise when Liam received the Outstanding Varsity Male Athlete Award, and neither was the fact that he received a standing ovation from all of his teammates. When Liam's name was called, they all stood up and cheered. It was easy to see that he wasn't just loved by me.

Liam's parents were very nice, as was his younger sister, Lily. She was a little nervous about being around a lot of older boys, as most high school freshmen girls would be. She had dark hair and blue eyes like her brother and was quite pretty, but she looked very young. She hadn't blossomed at the rate Darcy and I had by the time we were her age. I had no doubt that when she did, she would be striking, and then Liam, who I could tell was quite protective of his shy little sister, would have to be even more so.

My parents also appeared to have a good time. My mother looked more relaxed than I had seen her in a while, which surprised me, given the bombshell college news Darcy had dropped earlier in the day. Nevertheless, Mom smiled and chatted with the other parents nearby. She beamed with pride over her only son on his special night.

After the banquet, our two families went out for dessert, and it was fun to see everyone interacting so well. Will and Liam joked around, and Darcy and I got Lily talking about her hobbies, which included playing the piano and painting. Liam had told me she was amazing at both, and Lily blushed when I mentioned his boasting. Her shyness and modesty made her completely endearing.

After dessert, Liam drove me home, where we parked in front of my house. He sweetly kissed me, then grabbed both of my hands and looked right into my eyes, and asked sweetly, "Greer Anne Hagen, will you go to prom with me?"

My sudden burst of laughter surprised him, and I realized he wasn't sure of my answer. I quickly composed myself and replied, "Of course I will!" I cupped my hands around his face and kissed him softly on the lips, and then leaned back and smiled.

Overall, I would say it was a very good night. I'd been so nervous about meeting Liam's parents and sister, but it all went well; the night was free from any drama, which was the way I liked it. I'd have been content if only life could have stayed that way, but I should have known it wouldn't last much longer.

The following Monday, rumors began to float around school that Kieran and Lorcan were back. I hadn't seen them, and neither had Darcy. I noticed Liam appeared a little on edge at lunch, and I wondered if he had also heard the rumors.

No one seemed more anxious than Mallory. She had been beside herself for several weeks, after the sudden departure of her closest friend Kieran and her love interest Lorcan. A week after they left, Ella had asked Mallory about them, and to everyone's shock, Mallory actually broke down crying. She'd discarded most of her other friends for them, and then they'd abandoned her. She was devastated, and I kind of felt sorry for her. She had sat alone at lunch for almost a week before one of her old friends joined her, and then a few others. She'd just begun to regroup and get back to her normal level of annoyance when the news of their possible return put her more than a little on edge. That was the one thing we had in common.

Thankfully, the rumor just turned out to be that—a rumor. We never saw them, and soon people stopped talking about them. I still had a bad feeling that we had not seen the last of the Smiths. However, one major benefit of their departure was that Mallory had been so focused on regaining some of her old friends, she had forgotten about her hatred for me, and barely even looked my way anymore.

In mid-April, with three weeks left until prom and five weeks until graduation, everyone I knew was starting to get a bit antsy and ready for the end of the school year. We all had senioritis, but most of us had made two big decisions: (1) who we were going to prom with, and (2) where we were going to college. Ella and Elliot were going to prom together, as were Rebecca and Nathan. Katie, Mia, and Sloan were all going in a group with three of Liam's friends from the golf team. They all knew each other and thought it would be fun, even though no one was assigned a particular date, which I found amusing and they found a bit confusing. I had heard Mallory was going with the captain of the football team, which was no big surprise. Darcy had been invited by three different guys, but decided to tag along with Katie's group. Much to her chagrin, they added one more guy (a pretty cute one at that) from the lacrosse team, to make the numbers even.

We were also happy to hear that all of our friends were staying in state for college. Rebecca was going to Texas Christian University, Sloan was going to UT Austin, Mia was going to Texas Tech University, and Katie and Ella had chosen SMU, like Liam and myself. We had heard Mallory was going to Texas A&M University. Darcy had still not made up her mind, but by the time prom rolled around, she was leaning towards UCLA. She had taken my advice and given up on torturing our parents with her plans to attend Boston College. Maybe the guilt had really gotten to her, or she realized that her plan to try and find out more information wasn't working.

Darcy also had begun to act better. I knew she was still frustrated about Lorcan and Kieran's sudden departure, but I could tell that she was actually a little excited about graduation, even though she tried to hide it. Mom was also in better spirits, less stressed in the absence of the Smiths. I inherited my intuition from my mom, and I believed she could somehow feel their absence as much as I did. Even though Mom was less stressed, she was still emotional. Everything was happening at once. In a short amount of time, we turned eighteen, were going to our senior prom, and graduating from high school—all monumental landmarks in the life of a teenager.

Darcy and I had asked that our eighteenth birthday be a low-key family affair. Our parents obliged us, and we had a small party with just the five of us at home, with Mom's famous lasagna and a delicious chocolate cake for each of us to blow out our candles. Mom and Dad did surprise us with the announcement that we were taking a family trip to Europe over the summer, which was a joint birthday/graduation gift. The airline tickets we unwrapped showed us leaving mid-July and returning two weeks later, just in time to get ready for college. We were all so excited.

Two weeks after our birthday, prom night finally arrived. Mom helped Darcy and me both with our makeup. We had gone that morning and had our hair done, and Mom threw in mani/pedis. It was a relaxing morning and the most fun the three of us had together in a long time.

When 6:00 p.m. arrived, I waited anxiously upstairs in my bedroom to hear the doorbell. When it rang at 6:05 p.m., I peeked out my front bedroom window and saw a limo parked, with all of our friends disembarking and converging on our front lawn. Mom had ordered them all out so she could take pictures of the group. I heard Darcy walking down the hall, and even though I knew Liam wasn't there yet, I decided to go downstairs and see my friends.

Before I went outside to meet them, I stared out the window for a minute to take the moment in. They were all outside chatting and laughing. The boys all looked similar, but handsome, in their tuxedos. The girls, on the other hand, were a sea of color, and all so gorgeous. Mia was wearing a short silver dress with a high neck and no back. Her dark hair was swept off of her face and her makeup was a bit dramatic, but looked great. Sloan was wearing a long, formfitting, beaded black gown. She wore her light brown hair down in big waves, and giant sparkly earrings. Rebecca was wearing a purple, empire-waist, flowing strapless gown, with her jet black hair pulled up and loose curls framing her face. She definitely looked the most comfortable of us all. Katie, who was being chatted up by Will, was wearing a light pink, strapless ball gown and looked the most like a princess from a fairytale, with her blonde hair swept up into a twist. She wore very natural looking makeup, and gorgeous diamond jewelry that I had every reason to believe was real and borrowed from her mother. Conservative valedictorian Ella surprised me the most, with her daring, floor-length, hot pink halter dress. I laughed, noticing that Elliot could not take his eyes off of her.

Darcy looked even more beautiful than when I saw her try on her prom dress at the boutique a few weeks earlier. She wore her gorgeous red hair pulled up on one side with a stunning sapphire clip (a family heirloom we didn't know we had until Mom presented it to Darcy as she was getting dressed), with the rest in long waves over her strapless, navy blue, formfitting floor-length gown. I laughed as I watched every guy on our front lawn do a double-take when she stepped out the front door. Will chuckled, Mom looked like she was about to cry, and Dad stood there with a classic, "Don't look at my daughter that way," expression on his face as he surveyed the boys.

I looked again for Liam and realized he was more than ten minutes late. I told myself not to worry, but he had always been exactly on time (if not early) for every other date, so I couldn't help but be a little disconcerted. I decided to go out and see my friends, and hoped that he would arrive soon. I stepped out the door and, much to my surprise, I heard a low whistle. I looked over to the left and saw that Liam had arrived in a sporty little antique convertible. He didn't even look at anyone else on my front lawn as he bee-lined straight for me. His blue eyes sparkled, and I could hear some of the other girls say, "Aw," as he approached me and presented me with a single red rose and my wrist corsage.

"You look so beautiful," he whispered, as he slipped the corsage on my wrist.

"Thank you." I blushed what I was certain was the same color as my red dress. I had been hesitant to buy such a dramatic color for my prom dress, but when I tried it on, Mom and Darcy insisted it was the dress for me; I had to admit, I really did love it. The dress was formfitting on top, with two medium sized straps. It had an A-line, floor-length skirt and was very flattering, but still comfortable. My hair was pulled up, with some loose curls framing my face. I still wasn't confident in the red lipstick I was wearing, but it did look just right with the dress. Like the sapphire clip for Darcy, Mom had presented me with gorgeous pearl and diamond earrings to wear. The pearls in the center were medium sized, but they were encircled by two small layers of diamonds. They were the most gorgeous earrings I'd ever seen. When she gave them to me to wear for the night, I started to believe that Mom had a jewelry stash Darcy and I knew nothing about.

I looked up and noticed everyone was staring at us, so I whispered to Liam that we should probably join the rest of the group. Liam smiled and proudly held my hand as he guided me down the stairs of my porch and onto the path into my front yard. As soon as we joined the group, everyone started talking at once to each other. The girls bombarded me.

"You look so gorgeous," Katie said sweetly.

"Did you see Liam's face when he saw you?" Sloan sighed.

"It was like something out of a movie," Rebecca laughed.

"Well, you know prom night is one of the entertainment industry's favorite events to include in teen genre movies," Ella said with a laugh.

"Yeah, I love those types of movies," Mia chimed in.

"Let's just hope it's that kind, and not one of the ones with a psycho killer stalking the gorgeous group of girls," I heard Will say, as he tried to ease in next to Katie. We all stared at him for a moment, and I noticed Mom was shaking her head in slight disapproval. He looked at her and, gave his most innocent look and raised his hands and shoulders, and exclaimed, "What'd I say?"

We all laughed, and Darcy rolled her eyes. He got a little embarrassed, but soon recovered. He was trying his hardest to keep Katie engaged in a conversation, but she was staring at her phone. All of a sudden, she smiled and said, "Mrs. Hagen, I hope it's okay, but my parents are on their way here. They wanted to see our whole group and get some pictures."

"That's no problem dear," Mom said, holding her camera. "We'll just wait until they get here to get you all situated for pictures."

The boys walked over to see when we were leaving for dinner. They were hungry, of course.

"It'll just be a few more minutes. I have some cookies that can hold you over, if you'd like?" Mom suggested. They all smiled, and Mom sent Will to retrieve them.

"So Liam, your dad actually let you drive the 'Vette, huh?" Elliot said, slapping him on the shoulder.

"Yeah, that was why I was late getting here. He was going over the ground rules for the tenth time," he said, as we all listened. He then turned to me and said, "Sorry about that."

I shook my head and replied, "No problem." Will returned with the cookies, and the boys all took a few.

"It's a sharp looking car. How long has your father had it?" my dad asked as he, Liam, my mother, and I all separated from the group and walked towards the sporty little car.

"For as long as I can remember, sir. We have worked on it together for a few years now," Liam replied proudly.

It was a beautiful charcoal grey color, with red leather interior, and a white soft top, which I selfishly hoped Liam would put up before we left for dinner.

"What type of car is it?" I asked, not caring that I was ignorant when it came to most cars, especially antique ones.

"It's a 1958 Chevrolet Corvette," my father said, stroking the red leather passenger seat.

"Do you know much about old cars, sir?" Liam asked hopefully.

"I know a lot about this type of car. My father owned a 1960 version, and we worked on it together while I was in high school and college," my dad replied nostalgically. My mother walked over to him and placed her arms around his waist. He pulled her closer to him. I looked over at Darcy to see if she was looking our way, and I saw she was observing us closely.

"That sounds familiar," Liam replied, appearing happy to have something so meaningful in common.

"We had a lot of good times in that car, didn't we?" Dad said, looking at Mom and smiling.

"Yes, we sure did," Mom said back to my father, and then turned to us. "We left our wedding reception in that car."

I remained silent, waiting to see if they would reveal anything else useful about their past. They so rarely said anything about their lives before they had us, and this was the first I had ever heard of my grandfather owning an antique sports car. Even with Kieran and Lorcan's departure, I was still in investigator mode; when something fell into my lap, I wasn't going to ignore it, so I watched my parents carefully. I could tell by the look on his face that talking about his past was hard for my dad, even though he tried to mask the pain with a smile. My mom was empathetic, and kept a tight hold on him as she also watched him carefully.

"Where's the car now, sir?" Liam asked innocently.

My father paused for a moment, but then said, without breaking his gaze on the car, "It was destroyed in a fire a long time ago."

I gasped, wondering if it was the same fire that killed my grandparents. Mom stared at me, trying to figure out if I knew more than she thought I should about what happened, but I quickly composed myself.

"That's awful, sir," Liam replied, looking down at the ground, regretful for asking that particular question.

"Yes, it was awful," my dad replied solemnly. We were all silent for a moment, none of us sure what to say next, when we saw a Lexus SUV pull up behind Liam's dad's Corvette. As soon as it stopped, Mrs. Dobry popped out of the passenger side with her camera in hand. Dr. Dobry exited the driver's side, and I was pleasantly surprised to see Edmund emerge from the backseat.

Darcy

"Fleur, so wonderful to see you!" my mother exclaimed, as she and Mrs. Dobry embraced.

"Hello, Arianna. Thank you for allowing us to come over and take pictures. I was so excited, I just made the boys come with me," Mrs. Dobry replied, in her light French accent.

Edmund and Dr. Dobry introduced themselves to Liam and my dad. Katie squealed as soon as she saw her family arrive. She would have run to them if her four-inch heels would have allowed, but instead she walked as quickly as she could. I noticed Will was right behind her, while her 'assigned' date was hanging back, talking to his friends. Greer looked over at me and smiled when she saw that I'd been watching Edmund. I quickly looked away and tried to understand why my heart was racing.

"We should take some pictures, so these kids can get to dinner and their dance," Dad said.

"Yes, let's get them all together in front of the house," my mom said, escorting everyone over to the rest of the group.

It only took about five minutes to get us all grouped together the way my mom and Katie's mom liked, but it felt like forever. All of the assigned dates became a little confusing to the moms, and to us as well. I tried to hide my laughter. After the group shot with everyone, the moms wanted group shots of just the girls, then just the boys, and finally, to get one good shot of each of the couples. Liam and Greer went first and had come over to stand by me when we saw Edmund approach us.

Edmund and I smiled at each other, but after about twenty seconds of silence, Greer thankfully piped up, saying, "It was so nice of you to come and see us in all our glory."

Edmund just smiled in return. "Did your mom make you come?" I asked him, realizing we were standing very close to one another.

"No, I wanted to come," Edmund smiled at me; I actually felt I was at a slight loss for words. No one had ever had that kind of effect on me before. I had to think of something to say—I refused to be one of those girls who would lose all sense over a good-looking guy, but it didn't mean I couldn't flirt.

"I'm sure Katie appreciates having such a devoted brother," I replied, cutting my eyes down to the ground and back up at him, a signature Hagen flirtatious look.

"I do," Katie said, popping up on the other side of her brother and wrapping her arm around his. Will had followed her over to us, and his puppy dog routine was getting a little sad, or a bit stalkerish—although she appeared to have no problem with it. Liam, Will, and Edmund began to chat, and Katie pulled Greer and me off to the side. "I'm not the only reason Edmund wanted to come over here," Katie said, giving me a targeted smile.

Greer smiled and asked, "Oh? What's the other reason?"

Katie looked right at me and whispered, "You!"

I laughed, "That's ridiculous." We all looked over at Edmund and saw he was staring right at me. When he saw us watching him, he quickly looked away with a small smile.

"Well, I think we need to give them a chance to talk," Greer whispered to Katie. She nodded in response with a big smile, and began to walk towards Will.

"This is not necessary," I protested in a whisper-yell.

Greer hooked her arm around mine, and we began to walk over towards Liam and Edmund. Katie had already dragged a very accommodating Will over to another part of the yard. When Greer and I approached, Liam and Edmund stopped talking.

Greer

"Liam, can I speak with you for a minute?" I asked, taking him by the hand. "Edmund, would you look after my sister for a moment?" I asked innocently. Darcy looked at me in protest but didn't resist in any other way, which told me she really didn't mind. Her resistance so far had been for show. If Darcy didn't want to do something, she didn't do it.

I pulled Liam just far enough away that I could still hear what was said between Edmund and Darcy. I whispered, "Just talk to me, I want to try and overhear what they're saying."

"Why?" Liam asked curiously.

"Because, I think he likes her," I said as I watched them closely.

"Oh, okay." Liam appeared amused.

"Just talk to me about anything. Tell me about your day." I didn't take my eyes off of Edmund and Darcy who were just beginning to speak. It was adorable how nervous they were around each other.

"You look really beautiful," Edmund said to Darcy sweetly.

"Thanks." Darcy blushed. She actually blushed. I couldn't believe it; that is when I knew she really was interested in him.

Liam began as I had asked, "I had breakfast with my parents and then I took our dog for a run…"

"Your date might get a little jealous, with me over here talking to you. Which one is he?" Edmund asked, looking over at the last couple taking their individual pictures and the group congregated near them.

"I'm not exactly sure." Darcy smiled.

Edmund laughed. "What do you mean?"

"…I came home and took a shower and then later I played some games on the Wii with Lily…" I looked up at Liam and smiled because I thought that was adorable, but then cut my gaze back to Darcy and Edmund. I couldn't believe I was able to pay attention to both conversations.

"I thought I was signing up to go with a large group, not a date. I was kind of assigned one. I didn't pay much attention when we were taking pictures. They all kind of look alike to me." Darcy continued to laugh a little as she spoke.

"Wow, that's a little awkward," Edmund gave a sympathetic laugh, although I thought he appeared relieved.

"Tell me about it," Darcy smiled in return.

"…Then I had lunch with my dad," Liam said, stroking my upper arm. "I watched some television and then took a nap…"

"I was sure one of these guys was your boyfriend," Edmund stated, not so subtly.

Darcy laughed even harder. "No, not a chance."

"…Then my dad gave me the first five lectures on what to and what not to do with his car…" Liam said, laughing. I smiled, still not looking at him.

"…I went out to pick up your flowers…" Liam's tone got a little more serious, but I still didn't look at him.

"So, you're not dating anyone?" Edmund asked hopefully.

"No, I'm not dating anyone," Darcy replied, with a small encouraging smile.

"…Unfortunately, I ran into someone…" Liam said, as I listened more intently to him, but still tried to hear what Darcy said next.

"…I wasn't sure if I should tell you…" Liam's tone got very serious. I looked up at him and wondered who he could have possibly run into. I looked back at Darcy and Edmund. There was a brief pause in their conversation, and they both looked down at the ground. Edmund had his hands in his pockets and was rocking back on his heels.

"Then maybe we could go out sometime, if you'd like?" Edmund asked sweetly. By the way he looked at Darcy, I could tell he was completely enamored with her.

"That'd be nice," she replied in a sweet tone. I could tell she really meant it, she wasn't just placating him. From the look in her eyes, she was very interested in him, and I knew she was going to go out with him.

"You can tell me anything," I said quickly, glancing up at Liam. I was very pleased with how Edmund and Darcy's conversation was going.

"…Leaving the flower shop, I ran into Lorcan Smith," Liam said, not trying to hide his annoyance.

My head turned quickly back to him and I lost all track of what else was going on around me.

"What?" I said, a bit more loudly than I intended.

Liam pulled me closer as he could see I was upset. "I knew I shouldn't have said anything. At least not until later." He wrapped me in a hug.

I pulled back because I had to know more, but I looked around and saw that everyone was staring at us because of my loud outburst. I quickly laughed, and whispered to Liam, "Just go with it." After a brief moment, he laughed as well, and I could feel that people weren't staring as much anymore. The last thing I wanted to do was draw any negative attention to us, and I didn't want my parents asking any questions. I decided to wait to tell Darcy until I knew more. I knew I could get the whole story from Liam in the car on the way to dinner. Then I would make up my mind if it was something Darcy had to know right away, or if it could wait until after prom. Maybe Lorcan was just in town briefly, maybe he wasn't staying, I frantically thought. Maybe he would be gone soon, I hoped.

"Alright, I think we're finished," my mom said, looking to Mrs. Dobry, who nodded in agreement. The guys thanked my mom for the cookies, and then they and the rest of our friends started to enter the limo in a girl-boy order. Liam and I walked towards my parents and the Dobrys and Will (who I had noticed looked very annoyed when Katie's date came and got her so they could get into the limo). I could sense that Darcy and Edmund were right behind us. When we all reached my parents, I saw that my mom and Mrs. Dobry also noticed how closely Darcy and Edmund were standing. They looked at each other and smiled.

Our dad came over to us, and pulled Darcy and I towards him into a hug. "Now, I expect you girls to be very careful. No alcohol whatsoever, do you understand?" Dad said seriously.

"Yes," we replied in unison.

"And I expect you home by midnight," Dad said, trying to be serious.

"What?" I replied, not trying to hide my shock. Most of our friends were given a curfew-free night for prom.

"Alright, 12:30," Dad said with a sigh.

"Don't listen to him; you can use your best judgment, but I expect texts, so we won't worry," Mom said, reaching to hug Darcy and then me.

"Of course," I told her.

Darcy looked back over at Edmund and said goodbye. He smiled as she walked over to the limo and got in. Apparently, her date had not waited for her. Liam and I waved as we walked over to his father's Corvette. He opened the door for me, and I somehow managed to get my entire dress into the small passenger seat. Liam raised the convertible top, and I anxiously waited—I had to know more about his run-in with Lorcan, but I wasn't sure how I would explain to him why I wanted to know.

"Thank you," I said, relieved to not have wind-blown hair for prom.

"No problem," Liam replied, and walked around to his side as he finished securing the top. He got in and we waved to my parents, Will, and the Dobrys. My mom and Mrs. Dobry were busy snapping pictures. I laughed; they kind of looked like the paparazzi.

The limo took off and we followed behind it. When we were safely down the street, I turned to Liam and said, "Now, what exactly happened when you ran into Lorcan Smith?"

Chapter Seventeen

Greer

Liam didn't look at me at first, and remained silent for a moment. It was obvious this was not the conversation he wanted to have, but he should've thought of that before he brought it up. Finally, after what seemed like several minutes (which in actuality was probably only a few seconds), Liam spoke. The tone of his voice told me he wasn't happy. "I was leaving the flower shop, walking to my SUV, and I recognized Lorcan's Land Rover parked right next to me. I thought, or hoped, it wasn't really him, just an SUV that looked like his, but I looked through the front windshield, and I saw him. He was just sitting there, and he gave me this weird smile."

"What happened next? Did he speak to you? Is the rest of his family back?" I asked in rapid succession.

Liam looked at me with trepidation and a slight bit of anger. "Why does it matter to you that he's back?"

"I can't explain it," I said honestly.

"Try," Liam replied seriously.

I wanted to explain it all to Liam, but where would I start and how could he possibly understand, when I didn't understand most of it myself? I thought for a long moment and was about to try and begin, when Liam asked what I thought was a ridiculous question, but I could tell from the look on his face that he needed to ask it. "Do you have feelings for him?"

"What? No, absolutely not!" I said, raising my voice more than I ever had with him before.

Liam appeared relieved, but still concerned. "Then why do you care so much if he and his family are back?"

"Liam, do you trust me?" I asked, hoping he would go along with what I was about to ask.

He looked over at me and smiled hesitantly. "Yes."

"All I can tell you is that somehow his family is connected to mine. I don't know how, but there's something there, and Darcy and I've been trying to figure it out." I was surprised I had told him that much, but at least it didn't sound too crazy, I hoped.

"You think your families are related somehow?" Liam repeated. He appeared surprised, but not shocked.

"Maybe, we're not sure—but you cannot tell anyone about this, especially my parents!" I said emphatically, as I placed my hand on his arm.

"Alright, but you have to let me help you," Liam demanded, looking straight into my eyes. He only tore them away to watch the road.

"Liam, I'm not sure I can do that."

"Well, if you want my silence, then you are going to have to, or no deal. I don't trust Kieran, and I especially don't trust Lorcan. This isn't the first time I ran into him like that. He was also parked outside the same flower shop the day of our first date. He gave me the same creepy smile then, but I blew it off. Now I know he is up to something."

I realized then that was why Liam had acted so strangely on our first date, when I had asked about his day. He had been thinking of his encounter with Lorcan. "Liam, it would be easier if you let Darcy and me handle this," I pleaded on deaf ears.

"No way, I want in. You're my girlfriend. I love you, and I will protect you," Liam replied seriously.

I sighed. What could I say to that? Sensing his victory, I noticed Liam was smiling.

"Don't get smug. I'll let you help, but you have to do exactly what I say, do you understand?" I said, pointing my finger at him.

"Yes, ma'am." Liam's smile had grown even wider.

Darcy was not going to be happy about this, I thought to myself. "So, what else happened with Lorcan?" I asked Liam, as I realized we were getting closer to the exit for the restaurant.

"Nothing. He just gave me that weird smile, and then I got in my SUV and left," Liam replied, watching the traffic start to get heavier on the toll road.

"Hmm," I said, just loud enough for Liam to hear me. He kept his eyes on the road, as traffic had become bumper to bumper, and we appeared to be coming to a rather abrupt stop. The limo was, I believed, a couple of vehicles ahead, but we couldn't see it because of a massive delivery truck directly in front of us. Liam appeared a little nervous. The car behind us just stopped short of rear-ending us, as we quickly came to a complete stop.

"Where did all of this traffic come from? This is crazy!" I said, looking around at all of the vehicles that seemed to loom over us in the small antique Corvette.

"I know; there must be some sort of accident ahead. That's the only reason I can think of that traffic would be this bad," Liam replied, with a tinge of concern in his voice.

"I hope everyone's okay," I responded. I offered up a quick prayer, something my mother had always taught us to do when we saw an ambulance or an accident.

I didn't really feel like talking about Lorcan anymore; apparently, neither did Liam. He placed the car in park, since we were at a complete standstill and there was no evidence we would be moving anytime soon. He sat back in his seat, looked over at me, and said, "You do know you're absolutely breathtaking tonight, don't you?"

I blushed and looked down at my handbag and then back up at him, and smiled as I replied, "Thanks. You're not so bad yourself."

"It amazes me that you've no idea how incredible you are, but I think that's probably a good thing for me," Liam said with a laugh, gripping his hands around the steering wheel and looking forward.

"What do you mean?" I asked curiously. Liam cut his eyes back over at me.

"Well, if you did realize how amazing you are, then you would also realize you could go out with anyone you want, and then I'd be left completely heartbroken." Liam smiled, but I could tell he actually feared that.

I placed my right hand on Liam's right arm and leaned in towards him. With my most reassuring smile, I said, "Liam, you're the nicest guy I've ever known, and I'd be crazy to ever want to go out with anyone but you!"

Liam smiled and leaned in to kiss me. I didn't even care that my red lipstick was about to be a huge mess—but then I heard my name being yelled from outside the car. Liam and I quickly looked up and saw Darcy standing, diagonally a few car lengths away from us, surveying the vehicles, as she yelled, "Greer! Greer!" She was visibly shaken; her hair was a bit messy, and it looked like her dress had been ripped. I gasped at the sight of her, and began to make my way out of the tiny Corvette. She saw me and started maneuvering around cars, practically running to me. Liam and I quickly emerged from the car, and as Darcy got closer, I could tell something was terribly wrong. She threw her arms around me.

Darcy

"I'm so glad you're okay," I cried as I held Greer tightly.

"What do you mean? Are you okay? What's going on? What happened to you?" Greer asked quickly, pulling back and surveying my dress.

"I'm okay, but we were in a massive accident up ahead. We're all okay. There are a few cuts and bruises, but there were some other people ahead of us that caused the collision, and we're not sure how they are. I had to come back and see if you were okay. I was afraid it was a chain reaction and…" I stopped speaking and pulled her back into a hug.

"We're fine. Are you sure you're okay?" Greer asked, leaning slightly back from me and looking me up and down, inspecting me more closely for any injuries.

"Has anyone called an ambulance?" Liam asked, reaching for his phone. Just then, we heard sirens coming up from behind us, and looked to see a police car leading the way for an ambulance and a fire truck.

"We're going to be stuck here for a while; I want to go up and make sure all of our friends are alright. Liam, you should stay with the car in case you need to move it. I'll be back soon," Greer said quickly. I knew Liam would not like Greer leaving him there, but he understood we had to go and check on our friends.

"Don't be gone long, and you should call your parents and let them know you're both okay," Liam replied thoughtfully.

"Okay. Call yours too," Greer said, waving to him as we started darting through the highway parking lot, running in the direction from which I had come. Once we were around the huge delivery truck parked right in front of the Corvette, we could see the massive pile-up just a few cars ahead. My limo was one of the last involved in the crash, thankfully, but it was obvious that the front end was totaled, and my friends and I would be seeking alternative transportation for the night. Everyone, including the driver, had emerged from the limo unharmed, even though we were all disheveled. We had been thrown around during the impact. Ella was trying to comfort Mia and Sloan, who were both crying. Elliot was trying to take care of Ella. Katie and Rebecca were glued to each other's sides, and all of the other guys were just standing around and appeared to be in shock.

"Where's Nathan?" Greer asked Ella as we approached.

"He went to check on the others further up," she said, gesturing towards several cars that were mangled together, along with another limo. I could tell from the wreckage ahead that there were probably serious injuries, and I instantly knew why Ella had spoken so vaguely.

In the time since we had reached our friends, three ambulances had arrived, and I could hear a helicopter above us. Greer was trembling from the sights and sounds of it all. It was all so surreal. We were a bunch of high school seniors on our way to prom—then a tragic accident happened, and everything that truly mattered really came to light.

"Nathan, are you okay man?" Elliot yelled as Nathan came barreling towards us. He was missing his tux jacket, and one of his sleeves from his shirt was also gone. He was covered in blood, and Mia and Sloan cried harder when they saw him. Rebecca rushed to his side to make sure he was okay. I didn't know until that moment just how much she liked him.

Nathan had been running towards us, and was completely pale. He looked around at all of us, and we all in turn stared at him, terrified of what he was about to tell us. His words were broken, as he tried to fight back his tears, "It's awful, just awful. The other limo was full of kids from our school. Mallory Jenkins and her crew." He stopped as we all gasped, and I felt Greer tighten her grip on me. I looked at Greer and her look said she knew something else—that someone else was in that limo. I immediately thought of Lorcan and Kieran. I gave Greer a questioning look as Ella began to speak.

"Are they okay?" Ella asked quickly. We all looked at Nathan, holding our breath until he spoke.

"Some of them are hurt pretty bad. Kieran Smith was completely unconscious, and she's the one being care-flighted. She had a whole team working on her. Her brother Lorcan was pretty banged up and, from the looks of it, has a broken right arm, but was there beside her the whole time, begging her to hang on." Nathan paused to wipe the tears from his eyes, and Rebecca held him tighter. "Mallory was also pretty bad off. Her left arm was cut pretty badly and was bleeding like crazy. I used my sleeve to stop the bleeding until a medic could get to her."

"Aw, man," Elliot said, placing his hand on Nathan's shoulder.

"That's awful," Ella said quietly.

I took a step back and I tried to process everything. Kieran and Lorcan were back, and they were hurt. I couldn't explain the way I was feeling, so many emotions flooded me.

Before anyone else could say anything, Mia screamed, "Katie!" We all looked over in horror, and saw Katie lying on the pavement, shaking violently with her eyes rolled back in her head.

"She's having a seizure!" Rebecca yelled, running towards her.

"Someone get a medic! Now!" I hollered as Greer and I ran to our friend.

"She needs something to bite on," Rebecca yelled.

Greer quickly emptied the contents of her small clutch handbag, and we eased it into her mouth. Greer held the purse steady with both hands, and I grabbed Katie's arms to keep her from hurting herself. Rebecca, being a true friend to Katie, pushed everyone back and told them to look away; Katie wouldn't want anyone to see her like that. Everyone did as she commanded.

Elliot and Nathan soon arrived with a medical team to help Katie. They took over and soon Katie's seizure ended. They told us they were taking her to the hospital to be checked out, and that all of us should go and be checked out more thoroughly as well. Greer and I volunteered to go with Katie, and much to my surprise, Rebecca, Katie's closest friend, didn't disagree. It was clear she, Ella, and Elliot were taking charge of getting all of our friends out of there and to the hospital. The medic had told us everyone from the accident was being routed to Presby Dallas. Greer asked Nathan to run down and tell Liam that she was going with Katie, and to meet us at the hospital as soon as he could.

I helped Greer quickly gather all of her things from the ground and place them into the shredded remains of her handbag. As we entered the ambulance, I saw them loading Kieran into the helicopter. The team appeared to be doing CPR on her. From the shocked look on Lorcan's face as he entered the helicopter, I could see that she was worse than Nathan had said. For a brief moment, my eyes met Lorcan's, and I had to force myself not to cry. They closed the helicopter door and I looked over at Greer, who also had witnessed Kieran's departure. I could see the tears about to flow down her face, but, much to my surprise, she also composed herself and said nothing. We sat close together, trying to be as much comfort to Katie as possible.

As soon as we got to the hospital, Katie was rushed into the ER. Greer and I were asked to stay in the waiting room, and to try and contact Katie's parents. I realized that we needed to contact our own as well, something we should have done much earlier.

Greer

Darcy and I found a seat, and I called our mom. When I had reached for my phone, I realized there were three missed texts from Liam. The phone rang, and I waited, trying to figure out what to say to keep her as calm as possible.

Mom's happy voice answered the phone, saying, "Hi sweetheart, we were just talking about you guys! How's dinner?"

I tried to maintain my normal voice, to ascertain more of the situation. "Oh, who is 'we'?"

"Oh, the Dobrys. Will, your father, and I are having dinner with them." Mom said with a laugh. She was obviously having a good time, as was everyone else, from the noise I could hear in the background.

I braced myself for what I had to do. "Mom, I need you to listen to me and stay as calm as possible, okay?"

"Alright," Mom said hesitantly. I imagined she was turning her body away from everyone else at the table as she spoke to me.

"Darcy and I are okay, but there was a major accident on the toll road. Most everyone that was with us is fairly okay, except Katie had a pretty major seizure after the accident. We are at the Presby Dallas ER with her right now." I said, noticing Darcy just staring off into space.

"Okay, we're on our way," Mom said, much more calmly than I imagined she would be. I guessed once she knew Darcy and I were okay, she moved into the role of helping take care of the Dobrys, as they were certain to be terrified when she told them about Katie.

"I love you, Mom," I said before we got off the phone.

"We love you and your sister so much! We'll be there as soon as we can," Mom said. I could tell the table had gone quiet, trying to figure out what was going on.

I pushed the end call button and looked over at Darcy. She looked up at me and, in an accusatory tone, asked, "How long have you known that Kieran and Lorcan were back?"

"What are you talking about?" I replied, surprised at her sudden change in demeanor.

"When Nathan mentioned them, you didn't seem the least bit surprised they were in that limo," Darcy shot back at me. It had to be the stress that was making her this angry, I thought.

"In the car, just before the accident, Liam mentioned that he had run into Lorcan at a flower shop earlier today. That was all I knew," I replied in the calmest tone I could muster, considering I was being yelled at for no apparent reason.

Darcy looked me over and she knew I was telling the truth. She looked away, staring again at nothing. "I did have a strange feeling that they were in the limo, as soon as Nathan said Mallory was in there," I said truthfully.

"I did too," Darcy responded, a bit calmer, but still not looking at me.

We remained silent for several minutes as more ambulances began to arrive. The most severely injured, including Mallory, were taken straight back for treatment. Soon the ER waiting room was filled with those who sustained minor injuries from the accident. The rest of the girls in our group had been shuttled to the ER by one ambulance, and all of the boys had been dropped off by a nice man driving a Suburban, who had also been stuck behind the massive accident. Our group all sat together, but no one really said anything. Liam arrived next. He walked in and I could tell he was frantically searching for me. I stood up so he could see me, and he ran over.

"Greer, you've got to reply to texts!" Liam wrapped me up in his arms.

"I'm fine, you knew I was fine," I said reassuringly, as he held me tighter.

One of the guys in our group whose name I couldn't remember moved down so Liam could sit next to me; he never took his hands off of me.

"Nathan told me about Katie. How is she?" Liam asked, taking in the chaos of the waiting room. There was a mixture of people in shock, people crying, and people talking loudly on their cell phones.

"We haven't heard anything yet," I whispered, resting my head on his chest as he wrapped his arms around me. Liam had taken off his tux jacket, but he still had on his tie and vest, and I couldn't help but think he looked so handsome. I closed my eyes and must have dozed off for a few minutes. The next thing I knew, Darcy was shaking me and saying that our parents were there. I awoke startled, and tried to pull myself together as quickly as possible.

Darcy and I stood up as Mom, Dad, and Will rushed over to us. I could see that Dr. Dobry, Mrs. Dobry, and Edmund were all at registration, trying to find out information on Katie. The concern on all of their faces was heartbreaking.

"Darcy, Greer!" Mom yelled in relief as she wrapped us both in her arms. Dad and Will were right behind her. Darcy and I didn't say anything, and we just allowed our mother to hold us for a moment. After a minute, she leaned back and said, "You're both really okay?" We nodded yes and she sighed with great relief.

Our mom, being our mom, then went over to everyone else in the group and checked on each one, asking if she could contact their parents for them, or if there was anything she could do. Meanwhile,

Dad and Will each took turns giving Darcy and me hugs. The relief on their faces was also evident. I had never seen Will act so serious, in all of his life. He didn't crack one joke. Dad was talking to Liam when I saw Dr. and Mrs. Dobry were finally allowed to go back and see Katie. Apparently, Edmund was going to have wait. I told Will to go over and have him come sit with us. Darcy looked nervous as Will and Edmund approached.

As soon as Edmund was standing near us, Rebecca was on her feet, asking, "Did they tell you anything about Katie? How is she?"

"They said she's recovering from her seizure now, and that there appears to be no initial complications from it. They're going to move her to a regular room and hold her overnight for observation. My parents have gone back to see her now." Everyone was relieved, especially poor Will, who I realized had more than just a crush on sweet Katie; he really liked her.

I was talking to Liam and my dad, and Darcy was talking to Will and Edmund, when someone entering the waiting room caught my attention. I knew his face in an instant. It was Drake Smith. Darcy looked up and appeared as though she was in a trance, watching him make his way to the registration desk. He was dressed in fine wool pants and a button down shirt, and looked like he had just stepped out of a GQ ad. I quickly looked over at Mom; she was trying to comfort Mia, who was still crying. When Drake had entered the ER, Mom had looked up, like she could sense something had changed in the room; since she was sitting, she couldn't see him through all of the people, and she was not about to leave poor Mia.

I then looked over at my father, who had a clear view of Drake with his back to us as he stood at registration. I had heard the phrase before "If looks could kill," but I had never actually thought those words could really apply to a situation, until that very moment. I had never seen my father like that before. There were a combination of emotions on his face, but he mostly looked angry and worried.

Liam saw our line of sight and asked, "Do you know him?" I said nothing, refusing to give anything away before I had to. My father also remained silent, perhaps using my same strategy.

Apparently, Edmund had overheard Liam's question; he and Darcy and Will were walking over to us, and he replied, "That's Drake Smith, his company just acquired my father's research lab."

Dad appeared very agitated by what Edmund said, but a little relieved when he saw Drake leave registration and go in the same direction the Dobrys had gone, without my mother seeing him. I looked over at Darcy. Without having to say a word, we knew, without a doubt, that our parents definitely knew Drake Smith.

We finally all sat down after another hour, as the waiting room started to clear, with more patients being seen and parents coming to pick up their stranded kids. Mia, Sloan, and all of the guys from our group except Elliot, Nathan, and Liam, all had left. We were still waiting for news on Katie, and we had heard that Mallory and Kieran were both in surgery. Edmund was finally allowed to see Katie, once she had been moved into a regular room. Our group of friends and my family had moved to the closest general waiting room near where the nurse said she was. Mom had asked Will and Liam to go and get food for our group. Ella had suggested that she, Rebecca, Elliot, and Nathan all go down to the gift shop before it closed and find some things for Katie. We had all agreed to meet in the cafeteria when Will and Liam returned with the food.

Mom, Dad, Darcy, and I were left by ourselves in the waiting room. We were all silent for a moment; then, as if he had orchestrated the whole thing, in walked Drake Smith.

Chapter Eighteen

Darcy

When Drake Smith entered the waiting room, his fierce green eyes immediately locked on my mother. She inhaled deeply when she saw him, and for a brief moment, I thought she might faint. Instead, she slowly moved in front of Greer and me, pushing us with her hands so we were standing just to her right and left, a step or so behind her. Our father had already moved halfway across the room and stopped; Drake stood just inside the doorway. He stared at Drake, his face full of anger. I had never seen either of our overprotective parents behave like that before. I realized in that moment that we had seriously underestimated how dangerous Drake was.

Drake just stood there, smiling at my mother, and then he cut his eyes over to me and looked me over closely. His stare seemed to stop at the sapphire clip in my hair, and his smile grew wider. I just stared at him, as so many thoughts ran through my mind. The moment had finally come—I was going to learn the secret that our parents had hidden from us. From the smile on Drake's face, I was certain of it.

Drake finally acknowledged our father, in the same velvety voice Greer had described from the night of the Jackopierce concert. "David, long time, no see."

"Not long enough," our father replied. The anger in his voice had risen from somewhere deep inside of him, and my kind-hearted father looked more like a warrior than the peacemaker I had always known him to be.

Drake laughed wickedly in response, and looked over at our mother again. "Please go away," she said, her voice soft, but strong. When she spoke to him, his face changed for a brief moment, and I actually thought he might do what she asked; then he looked at me again and took a step towards us. Our mother stood up straighter and she instinctively threw her arms out to her sides in a protective stance, creating a small but distinct barrier between Drake and Greer and me.

"Don't take one step closer to them," our father yelled at Drake, which stopped him in his tracks.

Drake looked Dad over and smiled, saying, "You're brave for someone who hasn't taken their medicine in quite a while."

What did he mean by medicine? Greer and I exchanged a quick look. Mom stood completely still; I couldn't see her face, but she stood tall. Dad didn't say anything in response to Drake's odd comment, but Drake had not moved any closer to us. In fact, he walked over to the opposite side of the medium-sized waiting room, and began to pace. We all watched him closely as he walked back and forth slowly, with a plotting smile plastered on his face.

"I've waited so long for this moment. It wasn't how I planned, but it'll have to do," he said. He stopped and looked over at me, and then, not taking his eyes off of me, continued, "It seems remarkable really; the night I could lose one daughter, I will gain another." I gasped.

Before Drake could say anything else, Mom cried out, "No! Stop! Don't say another word!" Dad looked at her and then back at Drake, and rushed towards him, pushing him with all of his might up against the wall. There was a loud noise that sounded like thunder as they collided. Dad held Drake firmly by his upper arms, and I could see that Drake was smiling at him.

"I'm impressed. You have more strength left than I would have thought. That's very interesting," Drake replied. I was still processing what he had said about gaining a daughter when I looked over at Greer. She shook her head from side to side, and I knew what she was thinking—that this was crazy, that we were twins, we obviously shared the same parents! But she looked at me closely, with my red hair and bright green eyes, and looked back at Drake, who was still being held by our father as they spoke quietly to one another. His bright green eyes were flashing, the same as mine did when I was really angry. I could tell Greer was questioning it, but she feared that it'd mean he was her father too. I knew in my heart he wasn't.

Drake smiled and said so we could all hear, "Looks like sweet little Greer has something to ask. By the way, what a pleasure to see you again, dear; may I just say, those earrings look striking on you."

Mom turned quickly around to Greer and asked, as her voice shook, "Greer, how do you know him?"

Greer looked quickly at Dad, who was still holding Drake against the wall. He was staring at her, his eyes filled with worry and anger; he held Drake even tighter, waiting for her response. Drake only smiled as he looked at Greer, no doubt fully enjoying the game he was playing. Greer glanced over at me, and I nodded for her to answer Mom's question. She looked back at our mother, who was waiting more patiently for her answer than I would have, if I'd been in her shoes. She began slowly, "It was the night of my first date with Liam. I saw him at the Jackopierce concert."

"What else happened?" Mom asked, grabbing both of her shoulders.

"We just talked for a few minutes, that was it," Greer said, as reassuringly as she could.

"Was Liam with you?" Mom asked quickly.

"No, I'd gone off to the bathroom, and I ran into Drake when I was trying to find it," Greer said. She omitted the part that we were sure he had stalked her, but my guess was that we weren't the only ones who thought that anymore. "We didn't talk for very long, and it's the only time I've ever seen him."

"Well, not technically. I believe we met several years ago, on an icy pond." Drake flashed Greer a wicked little smile, and I realized in an instant what he meant. It was he and Kieran that day in Madison, the last time Mom and Greer went ice-skating before we moved abruptly. Greer had told me about it after it happened, and I had never forgotten the strange story.

Mom ignored his quip, and asked Greer nervously, "Nothing else happened?"

"No."

"Don't worry, Arianna, I didn't touch your precious girl. I have other plans for her," Drake said, with such a fiendish smile and laugh that it sent shudders down my spine. My father pulled Drake off of the wall and pushed him forcefully back against it. The movement made a loud noise, and everything on the wall shook as if about to fall.

I knew in that moment that our parents had been right all along to try and protect us from him. He was the reason we had moved so many times; if we'd just told our parents about Lorcan and Kieran, or Greer's encounter with Drake, they probably would have moved us again. If not, at least they could have been more prepared for this moment. I'd failed our parents by not being honest with them, as Greer had wanted to from the beginning. I felt terrible about how my selfish want to uncover the secret my parents had been hiding was causing so much pain now. I'd do whatever I needed to make things right, but first I had to brace myself, because I knew the whole truth would soon be revealed.

"I'm so sorry, Mom," Greer whispered as tears filled her eyes. Mom gently touched Greer's face and smiled softly, and I knew she was forgiven.

"Aw, that's so sweet, but I think we should get down to the matter at hand, don't you? I've been waiting eighteen years, after all!" Drake said sharply.

"Arianna, what do you want to do?" Dad yelled, not taking his eyes or hands off of Drake. My mother paused for a moment, and then she looked at Greer, and then over at me.

"Just tell me the truth," I said in a quiet, pleading voice. Mom stared at me. It devastated me that I'd caused so much pain, but there was no turning back now. Before she could respond, I asked the question I feared the most: "Is he my father?"

Mom's face never changed; she continued to stare at me, but Dad let go of Drake and moved towards us. Drake smiled his cryptic, devilish smile, remaining where he was and watching us all closely.

Dad was standing beside Mom as she finally spoke, softly saying, "Why would you ask that, Darcy?"

"Please, just tell me truth," I asked again. Mom and Dad exchanged a heartbroken look that answered my question.

Just then, Greer jumped into the conversation, and in her shock and confusion, she started yelling. "What are you people talking about? This is insane! There is no way that man is your father! We're twins—remember? If he's your father, then that would mean he's my father as well, and there's NO WAY he's my father!" Greer was pointing at Drake. She was so angry that she began to shake.

Everyone just stared at her after her sudden outburst. Drake was the first to respond, saying with a laugh, "Wow, David, yours has more fire in her than I'd have thought. I can see why my son is so enamored with her."

"I'm warning you, Drake," Dad said fiercely, turning and pointing at him. Drake raised his hands in a sarcastic apologetic stance, and laughed again.

I took our mother by her hands and said, "I know you don't want to do this, but either you can tell me, or I'm sure he will. I'd rather hear it from you." I tried to keep my devastation hidden as much as possible.

Mom touched my face and I could see the tears forming in her eyes as she spoke. "It's true, Darcy, Drake is your biological father." I showed no emotion as these horrendous words were spoken. I just continued to stare at our mother, refusing to let anyone know that this was, by far, the worst day of my life.

"But..." Greer began again to protest. "He's not my father!" she said confidently.

"No, Greer, he's not," Mom said, reaching for her.

Greer walked towards her and grabbed ahold of her right hand. She was holding me with her left.

I just kept blankly staring at our mother as Dad walked over and put his hand on her back.

"I will tell you the whole story, I promise, just not here. Let's go home, and I'll tell you there," Mom suggested gently.

Greer looked over at me to see if I would agree. I didn't speak, but nodded that I would go along with the plan. We had all begun to walk towards the exit when Drake spoke, "Remember there are two sides to every story, Darcy." I thought Dad was going to go over and pummel the smug look off of his face, and he began to move towards him.

"No, David, please, let's just go," Mom pleaded.

As the door shut behind us, I could hear Drake saying, "I'll see you all very soon." A promise I knew he'd keep. I was in his sights now, and he wasn't going anywhere.

"We need to find Will and let the others know we're leaving," I said, leading the way to the cafeteria. "We'll have to make up an excuse for why we need to go." I could tell my calmness unnerved Greer, but no one else could know what was going on.

When we reached the cafeteria, we saw that Liam and Will had just arrived with the food and were beginning to pass it out to our friends. Edmund was giving everyone an update on Katie.

Edmund stopped talking as soon as he saw us enter, and waited for us to come over before he continued, "I was just telling everyone that Katie is resting now, but that the doctor said she should be fine. She has to stay here overnight; she'll be allowed a few visitors tomorrow and, hopefully, will come home then."

"Do they know what caused the seizure?" Dad asked, trying to act as normal as he could. No one seemed to notice the distressed look on his face. If they did, I was sure they thought it was for Katie and her family's sake. Only Greer, Mom, Dad, and I knew the real truth.

"No, she'll have to see a neurologist next week and have some further tests done," Edmund replied.

Greer and I smiled. We were glad to hear that Katie was going to be okay, but we obviously had some other things on our minds. "That's great, Edmund, I'm so glad she's going to be okay," Greer said, trying to sound like her usual self.

"Yes, that's wonderful news. I'm so relieved for you and your family." Mom gave Edmund a quick hug and then continued, "It's been an exhausting night. I think my family and I should go, since we won't be able to see Katie until tomorrow. Ella, would you like us to take all of you home?"

"That's okay Mrs. Hagen, my mom is on her way," Ella replied sweetly, but appeared surprised that we were all leaving so soon.

Greer

Darcy and Edmund spoke for a moment while my parents went over to speak to Will, who I was sure was going to protest leaving. "I'm so happy Katie is doing better," Darcy said with a genuine smile.

"Thank you for everything you and your family did for her tonight. I can't tell you how much it meant to us, to me." Edmund reached for her hand and held it for several seconds.

I could not hear any more of their conversation; I felt Liam come up from behind me. He spun me around and wrapped me in a gentle hug. "Are you okay?" he whispered. He could tell something was wrong. I tried to smile, but that made him look even more concerned. He knew I was masking something.

"Yeah, I will be," I said, hoping it was the truth.

Liam pulled back and searched my face. He could tell I was hiding something, but I just smiled and placed my head back on his chest. "Can I come over?" he asked hopefully.

I stepped back and looked at him, and replied honestly, "There's nothing I want more, but I need a little time with my family first. Can I call you later tonight?"

"Yeah, that's fine, I understand," Liam said sweetly, but I could still detect the disappointment on his face.

Then my mom came over to get Darcy and me. Dad was already leading a frustrated Will out of the cafeteria. Darcy and I quickly hugged and said goodbye to all of our friends. I hugged Liam one last time, and I noticed Darcy and Edmund lingered for a moment in their hug. Even in the midst of all of the craziness, I hoped that something good would work out there.

"I'll call you later, I promise," I said to Liam as we left.

Dad and Will were holding the elevator for us when we arrived. After we were all in and just as the doors were about to close, I saw Lorcan step into the hallway and look our way. He raised his left hand slightly and mouthed what I thought were the words, "I'm sorry." The look on his face was one of pure anguish. The usually confident guy I knew looked defeated. The elevator doors closed and I looked around to see if anyone else had seen him. Will, Mom, and Dad were all looking down, but as soon as I locked eyes with Darcy, I could tell I hadn't imagined his appearance.

In the Suburban on the way home, Will continued to protest our leaving. "I just don't see why we had to leave so soon. I think it was rude." No one responded to him, which seemed to make him fume even more. We remained silent the rest of the car ride. I tried to not think of what was said in the waiting room, but I kept wondering how it could be possible that Drake could be Darcy's father but not mine, and yet we could still be twins.

When we arrived home, Mom asked us all to go into the family room. She wasn't even going to wait for us to change clothes, which I was glad about. I didn't want to put off the whole truth any longer. "Everyone, please, let's just sit down. Your father and I have some things we need to tell you," Mom said. Her voice was still strong, but I could see tears forming in her eyes.

Will's fuming seemed to evaporate as soon as he saw her like that. "Mom, is everything okay?"

"Everything will be, sweetie," Mom said. I could tell that she hoped she was right, but wasn't certain.

The three of us kids sat down on the sofa, with me in the middle, and waited for the story to begin. I knew our lives were about to change forever. Mom nodded for Dad to begin, and I could see they were going to tell it together.

"I know we have never told you very much about our past. That's because there are some family secrets we have kept, in order to protect you. It's also the reason we have moved so many times over the years. Whenever we felt like someone from our past might be getting too close to us in our new lives, we would move on. We know it has been hard, but we really have done this for your own protection." Dad sighed and paused for a moment. It appeared hard for him to continue.

Will used Dad's pause to ask a question that was also looming in my mind. "Are we moving again?" Will and I looked anxiously at Mom and Dad, while Darcy just stared at her hands.

Dad looked down at Mom, who was sitting in the chair he was standing next to. I couldn't tell anything from the look they exchanged, but was relieved and surprisingly devastated at the same time when Dad replied, "No, it's too late to leave now. Maybe if we had known earlier, but not now." I was relieved because I didn't want to move again, and really didn't see how that was going to be possible with two weeks until graduation. Plus, I was going to college in Dallas, and had no plans to change that. I was also devastated, because I realized that if we had told my parents about the Smiths much earlier, as we should have, we could have saved our family from all of the drama we were in. The truth was that I didn't want to know any of it. I wanted things to go back to the way they were.

Darcy stared at her hands as Dad continued, "We're not going to go into all of the details now, but we will honestly answer any questions you have after we tell you the main points that you need to know, now that Drake and his family have found us. First, Drake is my cousin. My father and his mother were brother and sister. We grew up together in Boston, and he and your mother and I were all friends in high school." Dad paused again and glanced down at our mother to make sure she was alright; after seeing her stoic face, he went on, "Drake's father was a really, really bad man. He was dangerous, and as Drake got older, he became more like him, much to the disappointment of our grandfather, who loved us both so much. Drake and I had a bitter and irrevocable fallout in college, which had really been brewing since the end of our senior year of high school. Drake showed up at your mother's and my wedding, claiming to want to mend our friendship. Your mother and I were hopeful that he had changed, and were pleased to see him." Dad stopped there, as the anger in his voice was building the more he spoke.

Mom reached up and touched his arm, and said, "I will tell it from here, sweetheart." Dad nodded in agreement, and she continued where he left off, "We made plans to see Drake when we returned from our honeymoon. We were happier than we ever could have imagined as we left for Hawaii." My mother paused for a moment, closed her eyes, took a deep breath, then opened her beautiful blue eyes and continued her story with a clear voice. "Three days after we arrived in Hawaii for our honeymoon, I came down with a case of food poisoning, so I had to stay in bed for the day. Your father and I had reservations to go scuba diving for that whole day. We couldn't reschedule, and your father had never been. He was really looking forward to it and had worked so hard to get certified, so I insisted that he go on without me. I had already started to feel better and thought that I would be completely recovered by the time he returned that evening. Before he left, he made sure that I had everything I needed: crackers, water, the remote for the television. He had even circled items on the room service menu that he thought I would enjoy and would be easy on my stomach. I assured him that I was okay and would enjoy the day in bed, resting and reading a good book if I felt up to it. I insisted again that he go before he missed his boat. After he left, I ordered a light breakfast from room service. When I had finished eating, I decided to take a nap. I closed all the drapes to make the room really dark, and put out the "Do Not Disturb" sign so that I could get some uninterrupted sleep. I woke up a few hours later, when I heard a key in the door. I had been sleeping soundly, and found myself in a strange haze when I heard what I truly believed to be your father's voice. The next thing I remember, I woke up again several hours later to another key in the door. Your father rushed in, and I asked him where he'd gone."

My mother's voice broke again, and I feared what she was about to say. "Your father was panicked because he saw the severely disoriented state I was in. He told me that he had been scuba diving all day, but that he had seen Drake in the hotel lobby as the elevator doors closed when he was on his way back to our room. He saw the look of horror that crossed my face and wrapped me in his arms. He immediately asked what had happened, and I told him that I wasn't sure, that I couldn't remember much, but that I had a very bad feeling. My head was throbbing and I felt like I was going to throw up. After I was sick a few times, your father held me, and as the hours passed, my mind became a little clearer. We tried to piece together what we thought had happened. We were certain that I had been drugged, most likely from my breakfast. There was also evidence that I had been..." Mom stopped there. She couldn't say the word that most accurately described what had happened to her, most likely because she was afraid of the further trauma it might cause Darcy and the rest of us to actually hear her say it.

As Will processed what Mom was telling us, his face turned to pure rage. "Why wasn't he arrested?" Will demanded. I looked over and saw that Darcy was staring at her clenched hands, no doubt trying to take in what Mom had just said.

"Your father wanted to go to the police right away, but I was traumatized and couldn't face what had happened to me. By the time I even really considered it, all of the evidence was gone," Mom replied honestly, wiping the tears from her eyes. My father placed his hand on her shoulder, and I placed my head in my hands to try and control my tears. It was in that moment that it came to me how Darcy and I could be twins, but have different fathers—I couldn't believe I hadn't thought of it earlier.

I wasn't sure where the strength came from to speak, but I began softly, saying, "You conceived both Darcy and me on your honeymoon. We are twins, but we have different fathers."

"Yes," Mom replied softly.

"This is crazy!" Will yelled as he stood up. "There's no way that's possible!"

"It is possible; extremely rare, but possible," I said, grabbing his hand and pulling him back down to the sofa, as I wiped my tears with my free hand. "Mom has a double uterus, which means she could conceive a child even if she was already pregnant. She got pregnant with me first; that's why I was born first. Then she got pregnant with Darcy a couple of days later," I blurted out.

"How do you know that?" my mother asked nervously.

"Because I'm the same way," I said, without realizing the implications it might have for my own future.

"Why didn't you tell me this?" Mom asked, as she moved closer to us and sat down on the coffee table across from me. "When did you find this out?"

"When I went for my first gynecologist visit a couple of months ago. They said it was genetic, and that someone in our family probably had the same condition," I said, slightly embarrassed. My face flushed red, and I just stared at my hands, which were clasped together.

"Darcy, did the doctor say anything to you about having this as well?" Mom asked quickly.

"No, she said that everything was completely normal," Darcy said, without reservation. My mother seemed relieved at that, but she still looked at me with some concern in her eyes. My father walked over and sat down next to my mother, and it was then that I saw the look of sadness on Darcy's face. I knew that it had hit her that these were my and Will's parents, but they weren't hers. Of course, this was her mother, but the man who had held her as a baby, been to every sporting event and choir concert, and been there to lovingly correct her when she acted inappropriately was not her biological father— although I knew that he couldn't have loved her any less than Will or me. Darcy began to cry, something I had rarely seen before.

"I know this is a lot to take in. We kept this from you because we wanted to protect you, but maybe we were wrong; maybe we shouldn't have kept this secret for so long," Mom said, looking at all of us and lingering on Darcy before she continued, saying, "I'm so sorry."

"We were the ones who were wrong. We should have told you about Lorcan, Kieran, and Drake back when they first arrived in January." I hung my head in shame. "I was being selfish; I was afraid you would make us move again, and I really liked it here."

"They've been here since January?" Dad replied, visibly upset.

"Please don't get upset with Greer. I was the one that made her promise not to say anything to you guys, and I also made Will keep quiet about what little he knew as well. If anyone is to blame, it's me," Darcy said, looking back and forth between Mom and Dad.

"Why would you keep this from us?" Mom asked her, trying to

understand.

"Because I've always known that I was different, that I didn't completely belong here. I've always felt something was missing in me. There were things about myself that I couldn't understand. I didn't know why I was so different from the rest of you, until Kieran and Lorcan showed up. You see, I've always known that you were keeping some big secret from us. I could sense it ever since I was a little girl. And when Kieran and Lorcan arrived, I immediately started seeing similarities—not just in the way we looked, but also in our personalities. I started doing some digging, and things started to make more sense," Darcy said, wiping the little moisture that remained around her eyes.

"How long have you known?" Mom asked, looking her right in the eyes.

"I knew from the first day I met Kieran and Lorcan that I had a connection to them, I just didn't know how. I thought for a while that maybe you and Dad adopted me, but I knew that I had some of your traits as well, and couldn't reconcile that with the idea of being adopted, so I started looking for other alternatives. I hadn't come up with anything concrete until I saw Drake in person in the ER tonight; in that moment, I knew he was my biological father." Darcy avoided looking at Dad. I knew she didn't want to hurt him. I couldn't help but look at him, and the pain in his eyes was so brutal that I thought I would break down crying again.

"When did you know that I was his daughter?" Darcy asked quietly.

"We knew it was a possibility as soon as I found out I was pregnant, but when you were born, it was evident immediately. Even as a baby, you had those piercing Hagen green eyes—the same as him, the same as his mother. You also have her hair color. There was no doubt in our minds, but it didn't make us love you any less," Mom replied, as she reached for Darcy's hand.

"So Kieran and Lorcan are your sister and brother, like Greer and I are, but they are also some type of cousins to Greer and me?" Will asked, trying to work everything out in his head.

"Yes," Darcy said quietly.

"But I thought Lorcan had the hots for Greer? Doesn't he know that we are all related? Seriously? That is just gross! He's as twisted as his father!" Will said, shuddering as he spoke.

"What?" Mom said, looking at me, concerned about what Will had just said.

"He doesn't like me like that!" I replied ardently, really hoping that I was right.

"Darcy?" Mom said, wanting to know what she thought.

"He has shown some interest in her," Darcy said, avoiding looking at me while I shot her a fierce look.

Dad stood up and started pacing around the family room. "This is Drake's doing!"

"That's gross!" Will said again, emphatically.

"Will, you and Greer are not blood related to Kieran and Lorcan, or Drake, for that matter; it's not gross, but it's disturbing nonetheless," Mom replied, trying to reassure us.

"What do you mean?" I asked curiously.

"Your paternal grandfather was adopted by the Hagens when they believed they wouldn't be able to have biological children; however, when he was two years old, his adoptive mother gave birth to a baby girl, who would become Drake's mother. So, while there is no blood connection, our families are still quite intertwined," Mom clarified.

I was relieved to know that, but I could tell from the way Dad was still pacing that he was very upset. "I don't like Lorcan," I said to him. "He and I are just friends, there's nothing more. I'm dating Liam, remember?"

"Greer, you don't know Drake, what he's capable of. He's planning something, and is probably using Lorcan and Kieran to help him. He's dangerous. That's why we gave up almost everything to get away from him." Dad looked right at me, trying to make me see the gravity of the situation.

"Why did he let you take me?" Darcy asked, looking at Dad. It was a question I had not thought of, but I was sure there were many questions Darcy had that I couldn't even imagine. In all of my selfishness, I hadn't once considered how she was feeling, with our family secrets coming out and her being at the heart of them.

Dad paused for a moment and looked at Mom. Mom nodded for him to answer Darcy's question, but I could tell Dad was hesitant to do so. I wasn't sure why, but it crossed my mind that he was afraid what he was about to say would cause her more pain, and I knew that was the last thing he wanted. It was written all over his face in that moment that, even though Darcy was not his biological daughter, she was still his little girl, just as much as she had ever been. He began slowly, "When our grandfather died, soon after you and Greer were born, it split the Hagen estate between Drake and me. I gave him the majority of it, if he would confidentially sign away any rights to you. He had a secret paternity test done right after you were born, to prove that he was your father. The offer was too tempting for him, there was too much money at stake, so he agreed. We never considered what he would do when you turned eighteen. That was our mistake. We were just concerned at protecting you as much as we could then, when you were still a child. I'm so sorry, darling."

We were all surprised at what Dad had said, but it was clear that Darcy was the most impacted. She had to realize what an evil, crazy person her biological father was—he had committed an unspeakable crime against our mother, and then he gave up his rights to Darcy for money. There really were no words to describe how depraved I thought he was, and I felt so terrible about keeping the fact we knew him, Kieran and Lorcan from Mom and Dad for so long. I was also counting myself lucky that I had only been scared by him in that back room at the Jackopierce concert. After what I had heard tonight, I knew he was capable of anything.

Darcy looked down for a moment and then back up at Dad, and asked softly, "How much money did you give up for me?" Mom and Dad looked at each other for a moment, trying to figure out what to say. It was obvious they weren't quite used to being so open with us, but I think Darcy needed to know how much she was worth, at least monetarily, to them and to Drake.

Dad moved towards her, sitting down on the coffee table across from her and reaching for her hands. She placed her hands in his as he spoke. "I know this all must be so incredibly difficult for you. Your mother and I have struggled with the thought of this day for years. We will tell you anything you want to know. You have that right, but please don't consider us giving up part of my inheritance for you as anything but the fact that we both loved you immensely from the first time we laid eyes on you. We knew in our hearts that we had to protect you. From the first moment I held you, you were my daughter. You will always be my daughter, and I will always do anything to protect you."

Darcy wiped away the tears from her eyes, as did Mom and I, as we watched Dad and Darcy hug. After a long moment, she leaned back and said, "Thank you. While I've always felt a little off and that I never quite fit in perfectly with our family, I've never doubted anyone's love for me, especially you." She paused for a moment and then said, "But I do have more questions I need answered, so I can make what little sense I can of this. I would like to know how much you gave up, if you don't mind?"

Dad leaned back and sighed. He never liked talking about money in front of anyone, but he had agreed to tell Darcy anything she wanted to know. After a short pause, he said, "Well, my grandfather's estate was left in its entirety to Drake and me, his sole remaining heirs. It was to be split between us evenly. After taxes and legal fees, it came out to about four hundred million." Will and I gasped, and then Will laughed for a moment before Mom shot him a look, which quickly wiped the smile off of his face. Darcy just stared at Dad, waiting for him to continue. "I offered Drake ninety percent of my part of the inheritance, if he would sign away his rights to you. He took it, but I should have known the first time he showed up in Madison, and then eventually everywhere else that we lived, that he would never leave us alone."

"So, that's why we moved so many times. He kept showing up where we lived?" Darcy asked. It all made sense to me now. I couldn't help but think of the fact that my dad just told her he gave up one hundred eighty million dollars for her—but that also meant that they had kept twenty million dollars.

"Yes. He never made direct contact with us, but one way or another we always knew he was there, and that is why we moved each time. I'm sorry we could never tell all of you the truth then. It was so hard to make all of you go through that difficult process each time, but we did what we thought we had to do," Dad replied, the exhaustion of the night starting to show on his face.

"I know you did. Thank you. I do have some more questions, but I would like to change first, if that's alright, and I would also like to ask you them in private," Darcy said, looking over at Will and me. How could we be upset with her request? We nodded in agreement.

"Okay sweetie, why don't you all go change, and then Darcy, when you're ready, we'll be down here waiting for you," Mom replied, and we all rose. Mom and Dad each took turns hugging all of us tightly before letting us head upstairs. Will had asked if he could take some food up to his room, and Mom smiled and said yes, so Will traipsed off to the kitchen first.

When Mom hugged me, she whispered in my ear, "Everything's going to be alright." I nodded in agreement, willing it to be the truth. I followed Darcy silently up the stairs. She went straight into her room, and I into mine. After I shut my door, I sat down on my bed and got my phone out of the remains of my handbag. There was someone I needed to call; I found the contact number in my phone, pressed the call button, and waited.

"Hello?" I heard the surprised voice say.

"Lorcan, we need to talk," I replied firmly.

Chapter Nineteen

Greer

My conversation with Lorcan didn't last very long; it was obvious from his tone and vagueness that Drake was nearby, and Lorcan wanted to hide that it was me on the phone. In fact, he kept calling me Hillary. I went along with it, and we planned to meet the next day at the hospital when I came to visit Katie. I wasn't sure how I was going to get away from my parents, or Liam for that matter, so I could talk to him, but I had to try. I really believed he would be honest with me regarding his family's intentions towards us. I knew there was a chance I was being naïve and underestimating what they were all capable of, but I had to try.

After I got off the phone with Lorcan, I called Liam. His voice was the last one I wanted to hear for the night. While the phone rang, I considered what I was going to tell him about what had happened. He obviously knew something was wrong, but I couldn't tell him the truth. It was still too difficult for me to believe, and I certainly couldn't tell him over the phone. The crazy *Twilight Zone* episode I was living in could only be explained in person.

"Hi sweetie," Liam said as he answered his phone; for a moment, all seemed right in my world.

We spoke briefly and I was successful in avoiding any discussion of what was bothering me, playing it off to the general craziness of the night. I told him that I was sure my family planned to go to the hospital the next morning and check on Katie. We made plans to meet there. He told me he loved me just before we got off the phone, and I knew that I wouldn't be able to keep my family secrets from him for much longer. If he was going to be with me, then he was going to need to know everything, or else our relationship would never work.

An hour after getting off the phone, I finally settled into bed, after struggling with my dress and the monumental task of undoing my hair and the multitude of bobby pins that held it perfectly in place. After I finally got all of my makeup off and brushed my teeth, I was beyond exhausted, and, to my amazement, fell right asleep.

Early the next morning, I heard a light knock on my door. I looked over at my clock and barely made out with my half-open eyes that it was 6 a.m.

"Yes?" I said, with a tired voice. I was still somewhat asleep, but I was beginning to fear something was wrong, as everything that had happened the night before flooded my mind.

"Sweetheart," I heard my mom say as she peeked around the door. "I know you probably want to go see Katie this morning, so I would really like it if we went to early Mass before going to the hospital." I knew Mom well enough to know that Mass was exactly where she needed to be. It was the only place she could clear her mind of all the craziness. The truth was that it sounded like a pretty good idea to me.

"Okay, Mom, I'll start getting ready," I replied as I slowly started to rise from my bed.

"Thank you," she said sweetly and shut the door.

I got up and heard Darcy was already in the shower, so I went to my closet to pick out what I was going to wear. As I passed my book-shelf, I grabbed my copy of *Alice in Wonderland*, where Darcy had placed the newspaper article about our grandparents. I took it out and read over it again. I stood there thinking about the whole situation until I heard a quick knock coming from my bathroom door, which meant Darcy was finished. I placed the newspaper article back in the book and the book back on the shelf and went about getting ready for church.

Darcy

After Mass, we headed straight to the hospital to check on Katie, a condition Will demanded for going to early Mass. No one had spoken about what we had all talked about the night before. I think, in some ways, we were all still trying to process it. When we got there, we ran into Edmund standing at the nurses' station.

"Hi," he said, genuinely happy to see all of us.

"Hi Edmund, how's your sister?" Dad asked, but from the smile on Edmund's face, we could all tell that Katie was most likely doing much better.

"It looks like she'll be able to come home later today," Edmund said as he and I locked eyes.

"Well, if she's going home today, we shouldn't overwhelm her with visitors this morning," Mom said quickly. I could tell it made her nervous to be back in the same place where there was a good chance Drake might be. Before she could say anything else, Mrs. Dobry stepped out into the hall from what was presumably Katie's room. When she saw my mother, she rushed down the hall to see her.

"Arianna, David, Will—and these beautiful, wonderful girls!" Mrs. Dobry said in her sweet French accent. "I cannot tell you how much I adore your Greer and Darcy for what they did for my Katherine!"

Greer blushed and I shook my head and raised my hands to suggest that we really didn't do anything extraordinary. Mrs. Dobry started talking to Mom, and Edmund was talking to Will and Dad, when I noticed Greer looking around anxiously. I instantly knew she was up to something. She whispered to Dad that she had to go find a bathroom. He said not to go far. When I said I would go with her, Dad appeared relieved and Greer annoyed.

"I can find the bathroom on my own," Greer huffed at me after we rounded the corner.

"I think we both know you're not looking for the bathroom," I snapped back at her.

"How did you…oh, never mind," she said and kept walking, but I had stopped at another nurses' station.

"Excuse me, I am looking for Kieran Smith's room? I'm her sister," I said, matter-of-factly.

The nurse looked down for a moment, and then back up at me and smiled. "She's in room 614—just down the hall and to the left."

Greer followed me down the hall, and as we approached room 614, I noticed the door was slightly open. I peeked in and saw that Kieran was asleep with a plethora of wires attached to her. Sitting beside her was Lorcan, but there was no trace of Drake. I slowly pushed the door open a little further, and it made a slight creaking noise. Lorcan looked up quickly and saw Greer and me standing there. He slowly got up and walked across the room to us. He looked like he had not slept at all the previous night. His right arm was in a sling, and he had cuts and scrapes on his face and left hand.

"You can't stay here long. My father will be back soon," Lorcan said as he came out of the room. He looked up and down both sides of the hall, but there was no one but us three.

"Don't you mean our father?" I said flatly.

"Yes, I guess I do. He's been chomping at the bit to tell you, ever since he sought out Greer at that concert," Lorcan replied. I wasn't shocked at all by his statement.

"How's Kieran?" I asked, trying to see her through the small crack in the door.

"She's stable now. She gained consciousness early this morning, which is a good sign, but she'll have a lot to do for her recovery. She had a collapsed lung, which they had to do surgery on," Lorcan replied, holding his right arm.

"I'm glad to hear she'll be okay," Greer said genuinely. Greer may not have liked Kieran at all, but she certainly didn't wish her any harm, especially since finding out she was related to me.

"Thank you, I really appreciate your kindness, but if there's something you want to talk to me about, you should do it now, before my father returns," Lorcan said anxiously as he looked at Greer.

"I want you to tell us what Drake's plan is. What's he going to do next?" Greer asked bluntly.

"I wish I knew," Lorcan replied quickly enough that I believed he was telling the truth.

"He's up to something, isn't he, bigger than just telling us about him being Darcy's father?" Greer locked her eyes right on to Lorcan's.

"I'm sure he's up to something, but I promise you I have no idea what it is. But listen, both of you—you have to be careful. Once he makes up his mind that he wants to do something, there is nothing I have ever seen that can stop him. He has no boundaries," Lorcan said, moving closer to us. "I really think you should both go now, before he sees you here," Lorcan continued, moving back towards Kieran's door.

"Thanks, and I hope Kieran is better soon," I said, turning to walk back down the hall in the way in which Greer and I had come. Lorcan suddenly grabbed Greer by her hand and pulled her close to him. He stared intently into her eyes, and I moved closer to both of them, uncertain what he was doing. I didn't think he was going to hurt her, but I was going to make sure of it.

"Greer, please remember what I said, and make sure you are never alone with my father again," Lorcan begged.

"Don't worry, I have no intention of being anywhere near your psycho father," Greer replied quickly. Lorcan snickered slightly at Greer's response. I stared at the floor, thinking about what Lorcan had just said, and how I had to find a way to protect my family from Drake.

I grabbed Greer by the hand, and we began walking down the hall. I looked back at Lorcan once and saw him watching us walk away. I glanced back one more time before we rounded the corner and saw he was gone, presumably back into Kieran's room.

"That didn't tell me as much as I had hoped," Greer whispered to me, as we made our way back to where we had left our family, Edmund, and Mrs. Dobry.

"Ugh," Greer sighed, stopping for a moment.

"What is it? Did you forget something?" I asked urgently.

"Yes, I wanted to ask Lorcan what Drake meant when he was talking to Dad about taking his 'medicine'?" Greer replied.

"Oh, that, I asked Dad about it last night," I said, starting to walk again.

"You did? What'd he say?" Greer exclaimed, catching up to me.

I slowed my pace and whispered, "During their senior year in high school, Drake and Dad were at the main Hagen Pharmaceutical lab, where their grandfather was working on a drug to combat early onset Alzheimer's, the disease his wife suffered from. There was an accident in the lab, and Dad and Drake were both exposed to some unstable chemicals. A personal physician that worked at the lab checked them out and said they were okay. After a few days, however, Dad noticed some differences in himself. He seemed to be better at everything he had once been good at. For example, he had always been good at math, but all of a sudden, he became interested in things like probabilistic metric spaces. His athletic strength and flexibility had increased as well. Drake had similar results, and when they told their grandfather, he had some further tests run on them." I stopped talking when we saw Dad and Liam round the corner and almost run right into us.

"There you two are! We were worried about you!" Dad grabbed both of us by the hands and pulled us into a hug.

"Sorry, this hospital is like a maze," I said, not exactly lying.

"Well, let's get back to the others. Your mother is getting very anxious, wondering where you went," Dad said, turning around and walking back the way they had come.

Greer

Liam smiled and grabbed me by the hand, and whispered sarcastically, "Did you get lost trying to find the bathroom again?"

"Something like that," I laughed and squeezed his hand.

"From now on, I will have to escort you there myself," Liam pulled me closer so he could walk with his arm angled down my back with his hand resting on my hip.

"That might be a good idea," I replied. I smiled up at him genuinely, happy to be staring into his blue eyes.

We soon were back at the main nurses' station. When Mom saw us, the panicked look she had been trying to hide from Mrs. Dobry and Edmund morphed into one of great relief. We all spoke for a few more minutes and then said our goodbyes. Mrs. Dobry assured us she would call us once Katie was settled in at home and up for visitors. I had no doubt Mrs. Dobry was going to keep Katie home the entire next week of school, and that she'd be catered to like a newborn. It was obvious that Katie and Edmund were their mother's whole world.

As we left the hospital, Will, of course, suggested that we get something to eat, so we all headed out to our favorite local deli. I was pleased when Dad asked Liam to join us. He declined at first, not wanting to intrude, but my mom insisted and so did I, which left him with little defense. We all had a very pleasant lunch. With Liam being there, we couldn't talk about everything from the night before, which made it a wonderfully normal event, something we all needed.

After lunch, we headed home, first dropping Liam back at the hospital so he could get his SUV. Will and Liam made plans to go over some drills later that day, which I had no problem with, as I planned to get the rest of the 'medicine' story out of either Darcy or Dad. Liam and I gave each other a quick hug with my entire family watching, and he said he would swing by and pick up Will an hour later.

We rode the rest of the way home in silence, not knowing how to adjust to our new normal. When we got home, Will ran upstairs to change, and Darcy and I followed Mom and Dad into his office.

"Girls, you cannot wander off like that. You really scared me," Mom said, pacing around the office as we sat on Dad's leather sofa and Dad sat at his desk.

"Mom, we're not children," Darcy replied, in a surprisingly unoffending tone.

Mom stopped and looked at her, saying, "You're our children, and I don't like you wandering around where you know he and his family might be."

Darcy and I remained silent for a moment, knowing that Mom, of all people, knew what Drake was capable of. For her sake, we knew we should try to not put ourselves in dangerous situations, whenever possible. After a minute, Mom stopped pacing and sat down in one of the chairs that faced Dad's desk.

"You said last night that if we have any questions about what happened a long time ago, we can ask you. Well, I have one—what did Drake mean when he was talking about you taking your medicine?" I asked, looking right at Dad.

Dad recounted the first part of the story Darcy had told me at the hospital, but then continued, "The test results that came back on us were interesting. We'd been exposed to an unstable substance that was being tested to see if it could replicate the strongest features of a person's mind and body. It was being developed in the hopes of finding a cure for early onset Alzheimer's, but it still had a long way to go. However, as I said, the results on us were interesting. It gave us greater mental capabilities and enhanced strength, but probably the most significant change was that it enhanced our personalities. Personality characteristics we possessed prior to the accident were significantly modified in a short amount of time," Dad paused, looking over at Mom to see if she wanted to continue the story. She nodded.

"Your father mentioned that he and Drake and I were all friends in high school. I met them when my family and I moved to Newton at the beginning of our junior year. Drake and your father were inseparable, as close as brothers, but they were different. Your father was much like he is now, extremely kind and generous, as well as humble. Drake, on the other hand, was boisterous, loud and a bit prone for the mischievous. We all became friends, and Drake and I began dating at the end of our junior year," Mom stopped for a minute and looked over at Dad, who was staring down at his desk. It was obvious that all of this was hard for them both to remember. He looked up and nodded for her to continue, and so she did, saying, "Everything was fine for a while, but, during our senior year, Drake began to change. There were rumors that he was cheating on me with other girls from area schools. When I confronted him about it, instead of just denying it, he became enraged. Then, after the accident at the lab, I noticed a significant change in both your father and Drake. Drake touted his increased strength and intellect, but it became clear that the negative aspects of his personality had become emphasized as well, including his vanity and ability to manipulate and lie—all traits he had inherited from his loathsome father. Your father, on the other hand, had become even more compassionate and kind." Mom stopped and smiled at Dad. It was obvious she didn't mind remembering when she began to fall in love with him.

Darcy

Greer was on the edge of her seat as Mom continued, "I finally ended things with Drake when I found out he was cheating on me with my closest friend, Allison. I was heartbroken. I had just lost the boy I loved and my best friend all in one day. I immediately turned to your father, who was kind and patient and just listened to me. He and I became even better friends, and that was when Drake asked your father to try and convince me to take him back."

Mom looked up at Dad, who had now moved from around his desk and was standing beside her. They smiled at each other, and he picked up where she left off. "Of course, I couldn't do that. Drake had become what I thought at the time was the worst version of himself— he had become his father, only smarter and stronger. Drake was furious with me when I wouldn't help him get your mother back, and accused me of being in love with her. Of course, that was true, even though I wouldn't admit that to your mother or myself until almost a year later. Soon after our high school graduation, our grandfather, sensing the trouble brewing with Drake, sent him and his father on an all-expenses paid trip around the world for a year. Our grandfather was concerned by Drake's outbursts and his deep interest in the chemicals we had been exposed to. Drake was convinced that if we modified the substances, they would be even more powerful if we injected them or took them orally. He thought they would make us..." Dad paused for a moment, looking down again at our mother.

"Superhuman," I said, sitting up on the sofa.

"Something like that. Drake had always been really good in science, and those skills were heightened because of the accident. He worked out some disturbing ideas about how to proceed in further developing the chemicals from the accident, and this seriously concerned our grandfather. So, our grandfather, trying to keep Drake's mind off the dangerous path he was on, sent him and his father off, indulging them in every luxury. In the end, it was probably the worst thing he could have done. While they were gone, Drake convinced his father of the potential profits of what he hoped to discover in the lab. When they returned home from Drake's gap year, they came back determined, but by that time, our grandfather had destroyed everything associated with the chemicals we'd been exposed to," Dad stopped there, because we heard the doorbell ring.

"It must be Liam," Greer said with a hesitant smile.

Greer

I was happy Liam had arrived, but was disappointed that the rest of Dad's story would have to wait. I hurried to the door as I heard the rest of my family make their way into the kitchen.

When I opened the front door, I gasped in shock; instead of looking into Liam's gorgeous baby blues, I found myself gazing into Lorcan's hypnotizing green eyes. I immediately stepped outside, pushing him further back onto the porch.

"What are you doing here?" I whispered, not trying to hide the fact that I was upset he had shown up at my house.

"I needed to speak to you," Lorcan said, matching my volume and tone.

"And you couldn't have called?" I asked, maintaining my annoyed tone.

"No, I couldn't," Lorcan said, unwilling to elaborate any further.

I kind of felt bad I was being so rude to him, so I eased off a little and asked in a slightly less agitated voice, "What do you need to speak to me about in person?"

"I wanted to warn you that my father plans to attend your choir concert and our graduation," Lorcan said, quickly looking behind me at the front door.

"Why would he attend our concert?" I asked, looking down and thinking how upset my mother would be.

"The same reason he does anything—because he wants to." I was surprised at Lorcan's directness.

Just then I heard someone calling my name, and realized it was my mother. I turned around to tell Lorcan he needed to go, but when I looked back at where he had been standing, he was gone. Mom came out and asked what I was doing out on the porch by myself, when she looked up and saw Liam pulling up in front of our house. She smiled at me and went back inside. I was still in a daze, trying to figure out how Lorcan disappeared so quickly; then it occurred to me that his arm was out of the sling and working perfectly, and his cuts and scrapes appeared much better than when I'd seen him just a few hours earlier. It then crossed my mind that maybe his father had never given up on his quest to see how far he could take his medical research. He certainly had the means to do whatever he wanted.

"Couldn't wait to see me, huh?" Liam joked, darting up the stairs onto the porch and wrapping me in a big hug. I just laughed as he picked me up and twirled me around.

Liam looked so cute in his soccer shorts and t-shirt, and I was a little sad that I wasn't going to get to spend the afternoon with him. We went inside and found everyone in the kitchen. Will was chomping at the bit to go. After a few minutes of polite conversation, they headed out. After they left, I followed Dad back into his office to finish his story from earlier. Mom was feeling tired and went off to rest, and Darcy had gone up to her room.

"Dad, will you finish telling me about what happened when Drake returned from his trip with his father?" I asked, sitting down in my favorite chair opposite his desk.

"There's not much else to tell, Greer." Dad said, sitting down behind his massive mahogany desk, which I then realized had probably been his grandfather's.

"What did Drake do when he found out your grandfather had destroyed all of the research?" I asked as I moved to the edge of my seat.

"Well, as I'm sure you can imagine, he was very angry; he became even angrier when our grandfather banned him from the labs," Dad said with a smile.

"What'd Drake do then?" I asked, imagining exactly how angry Drake must have been.

"Drake decided his best strategy would be to admit his mistake and claim to have been misguided by the greed of his father, which was all a lie. He asked our grandfather to help him get into his alma mater, Stanford. Your mother and I had begun dating just before he left for California. As a result, Drake and I had a huge fight that became physical. He swore he would never forgive me, and that I would someday pay for betraying him. I didn't hear from him again until your mother's and my wedding," Dad said, sighing at the memory of it all.

"That's when he said he wanted you all to be friends," I asked tentatively.

"Yes, but I should've known he would never forgive me. I just couldn't see what he was capable of." I could see the anger building on Dad's face.

"Do you think he has continued his medical research over the years?" I asked, trying to put all of the puzzle pieces together.

"I'm sure he has; he was studying chemistry at Stanford, and I think it became his obsession." Dad looked at me quizzically. "Why do you ask?"

"Just curious," I responded, looking down at my hands. "There's something I need to tell you, though. I spoke with Lorcan, Drake's son, and he warned me that we should expect to see Drake at our choir concert and graduation."

Dad sighed and stood up, saying, "Thank you for letting me know, but I would rather you not have anything to do with Drake's son."

"Dad, he was trying to help us," I replied, standing as well.

"Or he was doing exactly what his father told him to do," Dad said, giving me a look that told me I needed to not be so trusting. "Either way, I'd better go prepare your mother for the next few weeks."

Dad gave me a hug and left me in his study. I sat back in the chair, scooting down so I could rest my head on the back of it, trying to process everything. I heard a car pull up outside. I quickly got up and walked over to the window, and was happy to see Edmund walking up our front path.

Chapter Twenty

Darcy

I heard Greer answer the door for Edmund. When we talked at the hospital, he had asked if he could stop by and I said yes. In spite of everything I was feeling, all of the confusion and the hurt, I knew there was something between Edmund and me. I knew it wasn't just a physical attraction—there was something between us that was undeniable, and I wanted to see where it went. Greer showed him to the family room, where I was waiting. Our eyes met as he walked closer to the sofa. Greer gave me a small smile and excused herself.

"Thanks for letting me come over," Edmund said sweetly.

"Of course, I'm happy you did," I responded quickly, gesturing for him to sit down.

"I want to thank you for everything you did for Katie," Edmund began.

"I didn't do anything," I interrupted.

"Don't be so modest. I can't think about what would have happened if you hadn't acted so quickly," Edmund said emphatically. His eyes moistened slightly.

I placed my hand on top of his without reservation, and said, "I wasn't the only one there. Everyone helped."

Edmund looked down and then back at me, and with a brief sigh said, "I know I shouldn't say this—we haven't even gone out on a date yet—but there's something about you. I cannot seem to get you out of my head, and every time I'm around you, it seems to get worse."

"Thank you," I responded, to his surprise. He gave a slight laugh. I was honestly relieved that he felt that way, since I knew I did really like him. He was genuine and incapable of playing games. In my mind, that made him something extraordinary, especially given how handsome and smart he was.

Edmund and I talked for an hour before he left to go back to the hospital to help take Katie home. It was good for me to spend time with him, not thinking about the Smiths and everything I had learned. I was glad that no one outside of our family and the Smiths knew the truth, but I wondered how long that would last—and what Edmund might think of me once he learned the truth.

Greer

I left Darcy and Edmund in the family room and went into my room, where I laid down on my bed and found myself quickly asleep. It felt like an eternity; in actuality, only two hours had passed when I woke up in a daze. The recent events had left me exhausted, but if I thought I was tired then, I was in no way prepared for what the last couple of weeks of school would hold.

I had not had the opportunity to speak with Liam about everything that was going on. When I asked my parents if it was okay if I told him, they asked me to wait until after graduation. I said I would, even though I knew it'd be difficult.

Monday morning was crazy, and Mom didn't want any of us to go to school. Dad convinced her that we had to, and that we'd all be okay. I knew she would be worried all day, so we all promised to text her whenever we had a chance. Dad said he'd work from home that day, which made us feel better for her sake.

On the way to school, I asked Darcy how her visit with Edmund went, and she smiled and just said, "Fine."

"Are you two going out anytime soon?" I asked hopefully, suddenly imagining her and Edmund and Liam and me double-dating.

"Saturday night," she replied, with a slight smile.

"Isn't that the night of Mallory's graduation party? Do you think she won't have it because of the accident?" I asked. It was expected to be a huge party and, of course, I was not invited. The only people she invited that I knew were Darcy and Liam, which infuriated me to no end. I had asked Liam if he was going to go, trying to maintain an 'I don't care either way' attitude, but was seriously relieved when he said he had no desire to attend.

"If Mallory's breathing, she'll have that party. Edmund and I are just going to stop by briefly after dinner. There'll be so many people there, as long as we make an appearance, she won't care. Plus, she'll be happy I brought a college guy," Darcy said, messing with the radio as I drove.

"Careful she doesn't try to steal your college guy," I said, half-joking.

"I think she's much more interested in my brother." Darcy laughed.

My instinct kicked in, and without thinking, I laughed and replied, "Why would she be interested in Will?"

Darcy looked at me seriously for a moment, and it struck me that she wasn't talking about Will.

"Oh," I said, realizing it was going to take me a while to get used to the fact that Darcy had a brother and sister that weren't related to Will and me.

When we got to school, the only things people talked about were prom and the accident. Katie wasn't there, as expected, and neither were Mallory, Kieran, or Lorcan. Mallory returned on Wednesday, soaking up everyone's attention, and as Darcy expected, her party was still on. None of us had heard from any of the Smiths, and I was beginning to relax a bit. I had started to let my guard down, just a little, when on Thursday Lorcan strolled into lunch like nothing had happened. Everyone was shocked, because they had heard he had been injured. He showed no evidence he had ever been in an accident, and seemed his old flirtatious self as he smiled at me from across the cafeteria. I turned my head quickly away, and was relieved that Liam didn't see Lorcan looking our way. When Liam glanced up to see what everyone was staring at, I followed suit and acted surprised to see Lorcan. I was grateful that he was no longer watching me.

I resisted the urge to look over at Lorcan for the remainder of lunch. I was anxious to tell Darcy of his arrival, but knew that she would see for herself soon enough in English class. As we made our way to English, Liam pulled me off near some empty lockers and asked, "Are you alright? You got really quiet at the end of lunch."

"Yeah, everything's fine," I said, wishing it were true.

"You know, I haven't forgotten what we talked about in the car before the accident," Liam said, leaning towards me and playing with a small section of my hair.

I gave him a small smile. "What are you talking about?"

"You know what I'm talking about," Liam said, moving even closer and whispering, "about Lorcan and his family."

"Oh, that," I replied, looking down at my feet, trying to figure out what to say next.

"So, what's my mission? How can I help?" Liam said, sarcastically standing at attention.

I laughed and tugged at his shirt, saying, "I'm afraid your mission has been aborted, soldier."

"What do you mean? We made a deal!" Liam replied, starting to get a little upset.

I quickly grabbed him by the arm and said reassuringly, "There's just no need right now. My parents now know all about the Smiths, and a lot of Darcy's and my questions have been answered."

"Oh," Liam replied, a bit surprised, "so, are you related to them?"

"Liam, I promised my parents I wouldn't talk about all of this just yet, but yes, there is a connection between our families," I replied, not fully expecting him to understand.

"Okay." Liam smiled very sweetly. I thought for a moment that he was thinking that Lorcan and I might be related, which would mean obviously he could never pursue anything with me. I should have just let him think that, but I didn't want to mislead him on purpose.

"All I can tell you is that I am not blood related to any of the Smiths, but there's a complicated connection between our families. I promise I'll tell you everything after graduation. Can you wait until then?" I asked, hoping he would say yes.

Liam stared at me, a bit confused, but smiled and said, "Yes, I can wait, but I don't want Lorcan anywhere near you. I know he's up to something."

I didn't say anything as I wrapped myself in his arms, allowing him to envelop me into a massive hug. We walked silently down the hall, arm in arm. I stopped suddenly when I entered our classroom and saw Darcy talking to Kieran, who, like her brother, showed no trace of ever being in a major accident. I gasped when I saw her, and Liam looked in the direction I was staring.

"What's she doing here? I thought she was seriously injured. She looks like she wasn't even in an accident," Liam whispered in rapid succession, verbalizing all of my thoughts—except for the part where

I wondered what in the world she was up to, and why Darcy was talking to her!

When Darcy saw me, she recognized the surprised and concerned look on my face and gave me a look that said, "Don't make a big deal out of this." Kieran looked over at me with an annoying little smirk on her face. She then walked past me without saying a word, but made a special effort to say hello to Liam and touch his arm, which seriously annoyed me. In that moment, I was glad she was okay, because I thought I might physically harm her. Darcy grabbed me by my arm as I turned to confront her. Darcy pulled me to my seat, and Liam went over to his desk, giving me an apologetic look. As I sat down fuming, I looked up and saw Lorcan watching everything that had just happened from the doorway, with a small smile on his face. I was trying hard to give him the benefit of the doubt, but he was making it very difficult. Maybe Dad was right about him, and he was just his father's puppet.

Luckily, class went by quickly, as did the rest of the day. Kieran and Lorcan made no attempt to speak to me, but I never lost the ominous feeling of their presence. I also never found out what Kieran and Darcy had talked about in English class. I found it worrisome, as did our parents, that Darcy spent a lot more time in her room than usual that week. When I asked her about it, she said, "I just need time to process everything." I tried to respect her wishes, but I wanted her to open up to me. I wanted to help her, but I didn't have a clue how to go about doing that.

The next day was a big one. Since Lorcan returned to school, our debate was back on for that afternoon, and that night was the choir concert. I was anxious all day for both events. Luckily, the speech went over very well, and I made a pretty convincing argument, even though I didn't believe one word I said. The same could also be said for Lorcan. The class voted on who won our debate, and I was surprised when it came back tied. Our teacher was happy, and I was fairly certain we would both get an A.

As I was packing up my books for the day, Lorcan came over to congratulate me. It was the first time he had spoken to me since he had shown up unexpectedly on my front porch. "You were very impressive in your arguments, Greer. I almost thought you believed what you were saying." Lorcan smiled, picked up my notebook from my desk, and handed it to me.

I grabbed at the notebook and replied flatly, "I wasn't really left with much choice, now was I?"

I pulled on the notebook, which Lorcan held firmly in his hand. He leaned in towards me and looked me right in the eyes and said, "There's a choice in everything, Greer."

It seriously wreaked havoc on me when Lorcan said my name, and somehow, I thought he knew that. He smiled at me and let go of my notebook. I threw it in my bag and lobbed my heavy backpack over my shoulder, and said in an irritated voice, "I suppose we should still expect to see your father at the concert tonight?"

"Our whole family, actually," Lorcan said, appearing amused by my annoyance. What'd happened to the vulnerable, nice guy that had warned me to never be alone with his father and seemed to actually care about me?

"Great!" I said sarcastically, and started to walk towards the open classroom door.

"Wait!" Lorcan quickly grabbed my arm, more tightly than I think he meant to. I instinctively flinched and pulled my arm away from his impressively strong grasp. "I'm sorry. I didn't hurt you, did I?" Lorcan said. At once, I started to see a small part of the guy I'd seen the weekend before, the one that I thought was worth giving a chance.

"No, you didn't hurt me," I said, even though I was still touching the sore spot where he'd grabbed me, certain it would bruise.

"I need your help with something," Lorcan asked, in more of a pleading tone than I expected from him.

"What is it?" I said, trying to be nice. He sometimes made it difficult, with his multiple personalities.

"I need you to go out on a date with me," Lorcan asked, like it was the most normal thing in the world.

I couldn't help but laugh, out loud and for much longer than he appreciated. I could tell he was starting to get pretty irritated when I finally composed myself. "Are you finished?" he asked, visibly annoyed.

"Are you insane?" I chuckled. He just looked at me like he thought I was the crazy one. He, clearly, was not accustomed to being turned down.

"Let me be clear—I could never go out with you. First of all, my parents can't stand your father, and for good reason. Secondly, we're kind of related, and even though it's not by blood, it would be highly inappropriate. Finally, I'm dating Liam, whom I am absolutely crazy about." Lorcan continued to look at me with pleading eyes. "You know all of this, so why would you even ask me out?"

"My father wants you to go out with me, and won't leave me alone about it," Lorcan replied, and I detected that he was at least partially telling the truth. I wasn't surprised at what he said, but was at the fact that I was a little hurt that he didn't say that he wanted to go out with me.

"Is that why Kieran is so set on stealing Liam away from me, because it's what your father wants?" I asked, setting my heavy bag on the floor and crossing my arms across my chest. I looked around and realized that everyone had already left class, including the teacher. Lorcan and I were alone.

"That might be part of it, but more of a bonus for her. I think she actually kind of likes your Mr. Nice Guy; plus, she can't stand the thought of you with him," Lorcan said, moving a little closer to me. I wasn't sure if he was trying to flirt with me or try to intimidate me.

I stood my ground and asked seriously, "And why's that? Why can she not stand me?"

"Oh, she has a plethora of reasons in her own mind, but mainly I think she's jealous of you," Lorcan replied, inching a little closer.

"That's ridiculous! Why on earth would she be jealous of me?" I laughed.

"Oh, so many reasons," Lorcan said. He stroked the back of my cheek with his hand, the way Liam had done a hundred times, and my reflexes made me jump back to where I almost tripped over my bag.

Lorcan laughed and grabbed my arm to steady me. I yelled at him, "What do you think you're doing? I'm not falling for this little act of yours. You know I would never go out with you, and certainly not just because you need help getting your seriously twisted father off of your back!" I was furious with him for putting me in such a strange position, but I was more so with myself, for allowing myself to be put there.

Lorcan laughed and let go of me once I was stable on my feet again. "Relax," he said, "I didn't really expect you to say yes, but it is nice to know..." He stopped himself from saying anything else; of course, I fell right into his little trap.

"It's nice to know what?" I asked, the anger in my voice crystal clear.

"It's nice to know that you were offended when you thought I was only asking you out because it was what my father wanted," Lorcan replied, with his charmingly cryptic smile.

"I don't care at all if that's the only reason you asked me out," I yelled, trying to make my words as believable as possible. I could tell from his sparkling eyes he didn't believe me, and I wondered for a moment why I was allowing my pride to control me.

"But it's not the only reason, Greer," Lorcan said, reaching for my hand.

"Don't touch me!" I yelled, making sure I was steady on my feet as I braced myself for what I knew I had to say. "I don't really care what your reasons are. I'm beginning to think I was wrong about you. I thought you were different than Kieran and Drake, but you might just be the most manipulative one of all. The thing is, I can't tell when you're lying and when you're telling the truth, which means that I can't trust you, and I can't have anything to do with you." I grabbed my bag and started towards the door again. Lorcan just stood there, staring at me with an indiscernible look. I couldn't tell if he was hurt, mad, or impressed.

I was almost to the door when he spoke. "I'm sorry you feel that way, and I'm afraid that you might have to reconcile yourself to the thought that my family and I are going to be part of your life, one way or another."

I turned on my heel and replied, surprisingly unafraid, "Is that a threat?"

"I would never threaten you," Lorcan said. I expected him to smile, but he didn't.

"I wish you would never lie to me," I replied, and turned and walked out the open door.

As I left, I was startled to see Liam standing just outside the doorway. I was sure he had heard everything Lorcan and I had just said to each other. He smiled at me as I grabbed him by his arm and pulled him down the hall. We remained silent until we rounded the corner, and then he stopped me and grabbed me up in his arms, heavy backpack and all. He set me down, and gently moved the hair out of my face.

"What were you doing outside my classroom?" I asked, happy to see him, but a little unnerved that I felt like he was spying on me.

"I knew you had your debate with Lorcan today, and I had a feeling he would corner you after class. So, I wanted to get there and walk you to your car. I didn't want you to be alone with him," Liam said, still smiling at me.

"How long were you listening?" I asked, crossing my arms over my chest.

"Long enough to hear you call him a liar and a manipulator and tell him you want nothing to do with him," Liam beamed.

I relaxed a little and continued, hoping he didn't hear the part about Lorcan asking me out, "So exactly where did you come in on the conversation?"

"You were saying something about how you thought he was different than his sister and father, but you realized you were wrong, or something like that," Liam was still smiling, and he grabbed my hand after taking my bag from me. We started to walk again.

I sighed in relief that he had only heard the very last bit of the conversation. After a moment, Liam stopped and looked into my eyes. "You know, he really is the bad guy, and you shouldn't be around him. I'm so proud of you for saying so to his face."

"Thanks." I said, even though I wasn't so sure I'd done the right thing.

Darcy

"Are you alright?" Greer asked, as she approached with Liam, as I waited by our car.

"Yeah, I'm fine, but we need to get going. We have a lot to do before the concert tonight." I smiled slightly at Liam and opened the car door.

Liam and Greer walked around to the passenger door, and he opened it for her. She stood just inside the door and turned to give Liam a hug and then a quick kiss. As they separated, we all saw Kieran and Lorcan walking towards his SUV, parked a few spaces away. They just stared in our direction, both with plotting smiles. I watched them for a moment, and I heard Liam tell Greer, "You should go home now."

"You should too; don't talk to them, please," Greer insisted.

"I won't, but just go," Liam ordered.

A moment later, Liam was walking in the opposite direction to his SUV, and Greer and I were speeding out of the parking lot. I asked Greer if she had told Liam what we found out; to my relief, she said she hadn't, but that she couldn't keep the truth from him forever. I didn't need forever, just a little more time. We drove the rest of the way home in silence, and I thought about what I was going to do to protect my family from the Smiths. When we got home, I went upstairs and thought about all of my options until it was time to get ready for the concert. We had to get back up to school by 6 p.m. for a final run-thru before the concert began at 7 p.m.

As I was walking down the stairs in my sleeveless little black dress, I heard Mom, Dad, and Greer whispering in the kitchen. Will was still upstairs getting ready. I walked into the kitchen and saw Mom and Dad were dressed and ready for the concert. Dad looked so handsome in his dark blue suit, and Mom was wearing a striking sleeveless grey dress.

"Are we all riding together?" I asked, assuming we were.

"Yes, we want to keep an eye on all of you at all times tonight,"

Dad said, wrapping me into a side hug. How he could love me so much, I would never understand, but I was grateful to him nonetheless.

"Greer told us about Kieran and Lorcan's return yesterday," Mom said.

"Yes, they seem quite miraculously recovered, not a scratch on them," Greer said, looking directly at Dad and then at me.

I could tell that concerned Dad.

"How do you think that's possible? Do you think Drake is trying out some of his medical experiments on his own children?" Greer asked, knowing that was the most likely explanation.

"That could be the case, which is why it is so important that we all stay away from them as much as possible," Dad said, squeezing me a little tighter.

Greer then told them about her whole conversation with Lorcan after class, and that she couldn't hold off telling Liam everything much longer. They asked that she still wait until after graduation. I was grateful for that; it gave me a little more time to figure out what I was going to do. Our parents didn't appear shocked by anything she said regarding her fight with Lorcan, but did appear a bit impressed and relieved that she recognized him for what she thought he was—a liar and a manipulator. I wasn't sure what he was up to, but I certainly planned to find out.

Will soon joined us, and we all grabbed some sandwiches Mom had made, and ate them in the Suburban on the way to the school. Our high school auditorium was packed with parents, grandparents, and students. The concert went off without a hitch. I had not seen any of the Smiths, but the auditorium was crowded. I knew they were there. Their presence felt like a chill in the air. After the concert, Greer and I came down from the side of the stage and found our parents and friends waiting for us.

Our mother was the first to hug Greer and said, "That was just the most amazing thing I think I've ever seen. You sounded wonderful!" Greer blushed and everyone smiled.

Dad wrapped me in a hug and told me he loved me. I whispered, "I love you, too." I saw the tears in his eyes and he held me tighter.

Mom led Greer over to us, and she then hugged me as Dad and Greer hugged. It was a moment I wanted to freeze in time. Right then there were no Smiths, there was just us, our family and those we cared the most about. I knew, however, it would not last for long.

After chatting for a while with everyone else that was there, which consisted of our entire prom contingency (minus Katie and the random boys that were in our group, whose names I still could not remember), everyone started to leave. Greer said goodbye to Liam, and I to Edmund, whom I had been pleasantly surprised to see there. Mom and Dad were leading us up the aisle to exit the auditorium when I saw the three of them standing a few rows over, near one of the exits. My mom grabbed my dad's hand, and he immediately looked up and saw them as well. Dad stopped for a moment, and he and Drake stared at one another.

Drake looked over at Greer and me, as we were standing next to each other, and he raised his hands and gave us a slow, silent clap. His devious smile made Greer visibly shudder; she grabbed my hand, and I started pushing Will, who was in front of me, to move.

"Let's go!" I said forcefully, which snapped everyone out of the trance we all seemed to be under.

Dad grabbed Mom's hand, and she grabbed Will's. We headed for another exit, and I couldn't help but look at them one last time. Kieran had fixated her wicked little smile on Will, who just stared at her as he was dragged out of the auditorium by our mother, and

Lorcan stared, expressionless, at Greer.

I was the last to get into the Suburban. As we left, I knew I would have to do something soon that would keep the Smiths away from my family permanently, and I knew who I needed to talk to make that happen. When I got home, I went straight to my room and called Mallory, who gave me Kieran's cell phone number. I dialed her number and waited.

"Well, well, well," she said, with a smile in her voice. I took a breath in, and said what I needed to say.

Chapter Twenty-One

Greer

There wasn't much any of us had to say on the way home from the concert. When we got home, I noticed Mom and Dad went straight into his office, and Darcy went straight to her room. I also made my way up to my room. Just before I was about to close the door behind me, Will knocked lightly and said, "Can I come in for a minute?"

"Sure, but I need to call Liam soon, and then I want to go to bed," I replied, opening the door so he could come in.

Will sat down in my chair, and I sat on the edge of my bed. "Greer, I need some advice," Will began, and I could tell that he was really worried about something.

"What is it?" I suddenly felt anxious.

"Kieran Smith has been texting me," he replied with an embarrassed look.

"What?! Have you been texting her back?" I yelled. I was not even trying to hide the rage that started to build inside me, as I thought of that insane girl trying to mess with my naïve little brother's mind.

"Not at first, but I have sent her a few texts." Will looked down at his clasped hands.

'Will, you can't communicate with any of them. They're dangerous, just like Dad said," I railed, hoping he would hear the anxiety and seriousness in my voice.

"I know," he said, looking back up at me.

"You have to tell Mom and Dad," I said, before I realized I hadn't even asked what she had said in the texts. The truth was that it didn't matter. Kieran was up to something devious, and I had no doubt it was at her father's bidding.

"Really? What if I just don't talk to her anymore?" Will pleaded.

"No, it's not a good idea to keep anything from Mom and Dad when it comes to the Smiths; trust me, I learned the hard way," I joked, but Will could also see the seriousness in what I was saying.

"Okay, I'll tell them, but you can't say anything. Let me do it," Will demanded, standing to leave my room.

"Alright, but do it soon!"

Will walked the length of my room and opened my bedroom door. Just as he was about to close it, he turned and said, "G, you and Darce were really great tonight."

"Thanks." He had no idea what that meant to me.

I quickly changed into my pajamas and got ready for bed. Afterwards, when I picked up my phone to call Liam, I saw I had a missed call from Lorcan. Why would he call me? I had made it perfectly clear how I felt about him. I debated on whether or not I wanted to check my voicemail, and decided I had better. I hit the button to listen to his message, which said, "Greer, I know you don't want to hear from me or have anything else to do with me, but I had to call. You and your family need to be really careful this next week. My father is up to something. I'm not sure what it is, but I have no doubt it has to do with all of you. I know you don't trust me, and I have given you little reason why you should. Please trust me now. All of you need to be very careful."

It scared me, mainly because of the tone he used. If he was lying and his father had put him up to calling me, which I knew was possible, then he was, by far, the best liar I'd ever met. On the other hand, if he was telling the truth and really warning me, then I felt the need to be scared for my family. My gut told me I should be scared.

I thought for a few minutes on what to do. I decided to wait to tell my parents in the morning about the message. We were all in for the night, and there wasn't any need to make them more upset. It could wait until morning.

I tried to calm my nerves, and I picked my phone back up and called Liam. We made plans to hang out at my house the next night, to have pizza and watch a movie. I was sure my parents would be thrilled, because they could keep an eye on me. Then they would just have to worry about Will and whatever he was doing, and Darcy—but she was going on her date with Edmund, whom they really liked.

The next morning, I did tell my parents about Lorcan's message. Will told them about his recent texting with Kieran, which prompted them to keep him home the rest of the weekend. They knew that they couldn't keep Darcy home, but did urge her to be very careful, and she assured them she would. After Edmund picked up Darcy, Liam came over, and we pretty much had a family date night, which was actually a lot of fun. It was even better when Darcy and Edmund unexpectedly joined us, well before her curfew. At first I was afraid their date hadn't gone well, because Darcy appeared shaken when they arrived. She did her best to mask it, and no one seemed to notice but me.

When I was able to pull her away to the kitchen for a minute and ask what was going on, she said coolly and rather unconvincingly, "Everything's fine."

"Do you not like Edmund as much as you thought or something?" I whispered.

"No," Darcy replied quickly with a raised voice, before lowering it to match my volume, "he's great, really great."

"Then why are you home so soon?" I asked, a bit confused. "I thought you were going to Mallory's party after dinner."

"We need to get back in there. I don't want Edmund to think we're talking about him," Darcy replied, classically avoiding my question. She began to walk away, and I grabbed her arm.

"Darcy, what's going on? What are you not telling me?" I begged, still whispering. The last thing I wanted was for our parents to overhear us and get concerned, or for Edmund and Liam to hear and get even more confused.

"Nothing. Everything's fine." Darcy gave me a small smile. As much as she tried to act like everything was okay, I knew it was far from it. Darcy grabbed the bag of chips we had both come into the kitchen for, and I followed her back into the family room.

Although I was worried about Darcy, I managed to hide it, and we all had a good time. In fact, it was the most fun we had had as a family since Darcy's and my birthday. We all laughed so hard playing charades and Taboo, and Liam and Edmund seemed to fit right in. Mom and Dad were especially happy to have all of their children safe and sound in one place, at least for the night.

It started to get late, and I walked Liam out first. "Thanks for letting us hang out here tonight," I said, still laughing a little at the thought of Liam doing the sprinkler move when trying to act out the word combination 'lawn care' in charades.

"I had a lot of fun. Your family is really great." Liam wrapped his arms around me and pulled me closer to him. I rested my head on his warm chest.

"Yeah, it was fun. I'm glad Darcy and Edmund joined us," I said, my mind wandering back to her again, as it had done a lot of the night.

"Yeah, apparently Mallory's party was pretty crazy," Liam said, sounding not at all surprised.

"What do you mean?" I asked, leaning back and looking up at him.

"Edmund told me there were a ton of people there, and just as much alcohol. Apparently it was insane, and Mallory's house was getting completely trashed."

"Really?" I replied, wondering why Darcy wouldn't want to tell me that.

"Apparently Mallory didn't even care. Edmund said she was hanging all over Lorcan when he and Darcy arrived."

"Hmm." That didn't surprise me. "Did Edmund say anything else?"

"He said that when he came back from breaking up some fight between two guys, he couldn't find Darcy anywhere." My eyes widened and Liam could tell I wanted to hear more, so he continued, "He said he found her in the corner of the backyard alone, and as he approached her, he passed Kieran."

I could just picture the wicked little look that she had given Edmund, and I wondered what she had done to my sister. "What happened then?" I asked quickly.

"Edmund said that Darcy asked if they could leave, and when he asked her where she wanted to go, she said home. Is everything okay, Greer?" Liam asked. I was not even trying to hide the very worried look on my face.

"Everything's fine," I heard myself echoing the same words Darcy had spoken to me earlier in the evening, and I knew Liam did not believe me any more than I had her.

"Did my parents hear all of this?" I asked, thinking that if they had, they probably wouldn't have been in such a good mood all night.

"No, that was when they went off to find that crazy Taboo game," Liam said. I could tell from his worried look that he wanted to know what was really going on with my family and the Smiths.

I tried to divert his thinking by leaning in and giving him a kiss, which he happily reciprocated. After a minute, I pulled back and laughed, saying, "You know, we really should work on your board game skills."

"Ha, ha!" Liam said, leaning down and kissing me again to silence my teasing. I did not object.

"Excuse us," I heard Darcy snicker as her and Edmund came out onto the front porch.

Embarrassed to be caught kissing, I quickly wiped my mouth and said, "Oh, sorry."

"No problem," Edmund said, smiling at us. Liam and I walked to his SUV, and Edmund and Darcy walked towards his. I gave Liam a quick hug and said goodnight, and noticed that Darcy did the same with Edmund; they lingered a moment longer in theirs, and I saw he whispered something in her ear which made her smile.

As we walked back up to our front steps, I asked her hopefully, "So, do you think you two will go out again?"

We turned around and waved to our boys as they drove away. "I hope so," Darcy said, and gave me a smile I didn't quite recognize on her. It was almost one of someone falling in love. I thought I had better keep that observation to myself, and see where it all went.

The next week was a whirlwind, with final exams and everything that happens the last week of high school. I have to admit, I was thrilled it was ending, although I was sad that some of the great friends Darcy and I had made would be leaving for different colleges at the end of the summer. In what felt like a flash, it was Friday, the last day of school and the day before graduation.

Kieran and Lorcan had kept their distance from us all week. Kieran had continued her habit of giving me creepy looks, but it was the way she had begun to look at Darcy that troubled me more. Darcy avoided her, but the few times I saw her glance Kieran's way, I could tell she was worried about something. Once that week, I pleaded with Darcy to tell me what was going on, and mentioned what Edmund had said to Liam at our house.

"Just let it go, Greer, it's nothing. It's just Kieran being Kieran. After this week, you'll never have to see them again. Let's just enjoy this week and graduation, okay?" Darcy replied sharply to me.

"How do you know that we'll never have to see them again?" I asked, wondering what she wasn't telling me.

"I don't...I'm just assuming, since we won't be in school with them, then you won't have to see them," she backtracked a little. I wanted to continue the conversation, but I could tell from Darcy's tone that she was ready for it to be over. We didn't speak of it again for the rest of the week.

On the last day of school, I said goodbye to my favorite teacher, Ms. Abrams. She got a little teary eyed as she wished Darcy and me well. I would miss her quirky sense of humor and her demand for excellence.

I had no plans to say goodbye to my least favorite teacher, Mr. Ellsworth, but that changed when he asked Lorcan and me to wait after class. I waited in my seat, and Lorcan in his. We did not look at each other when Mr. Ellsworth began to speak, saying, "I want you to know that I have never seen two more naturally skilled debaters in a high school classroom. I hope you will consider pursuing debate team when you're in college. I'm afraid debate is a dying art, and could use some wonderful young blood like yourselves."

To say I was shocked would be an understatement. I knew Mr.

Ellsworth had liked our debate, since I had received an A+ on it, but I was truly taken aback by how nice he was at that very moment, giving us probably the highest compliment he had ever given a student.

"Thank you, sir. Your class has been very..." I paused for a moment, searching for the right word, "enlightening."

Out of the corner of my eye, I saw Lorcan snicker. He stood and shook hands with Mr. Ellsworth. "Thank you, I will consider what you said."

"Good. What about you, Miss Hagen, will you consider it?" Mr. Ellsworth asked imperiously. And there was the Mr. Ellsworth I knew.

"Yes, I'll consider it," I said with a smile.

"Good. It's a shame you two aren't going to the same college. What a debate team you would make! Well, off you go," Mr. Ellsworth said, and gestured towards the door.

How relieved I was that Lorcan and I were not going to the same college, I thought to myself; then I realized I didn't know where he and Kieran were going. I quickly grabbed my bag and bolted for the door before Lorcan had taken two steps towards it. I wanted out of there as fast as possible; part of me was surprised when Lorcan made no attempt to catch up with me.

Darcy

The next morning was graduation. I awoke early to the smell of Mom's blueberry muffins and something else I wasn't quite able to identify. I threw on my robe and house shoes, and headed down the stairs to find Greer already sitting at the bar, drinking orange juice. It wasn't long before Will was down as well, and we all sat at the table enjoying the delicious breakfast Mom had made. I smiled through my sadness and no one seemed to notice, except maybe Greer, who had been suspicious of me all week. I savored every bite of the muffins and freshly made croissants, and every moment with my family around the breakfast table.

Everyone had a wide range of emotions, except for Will, who was just happy to be eating. The significance of our graduation and what it would mean for our family had not really dawned on Will. As I sat there, laughing with everyone as we rehashed the highlights of the family game/movie night the five of us had the evening before, the doorbell rang.

"Who could that be, this early?" Greer said anxiously.

"I don't know. Darcy, Greer, why don't you go check and see who it is?" Dad said with his charming smile. Mom looked happy, but also like she was about to jump out of her skin in anticipation. Whatever or whoever was at the door was a good surprise, and our parents were a part of it.

Greer and I went to the front of the house and gave each other a quick look and shrug of the shoulders; we didn't have a clue what to expect. She opened the door and we screeched (even me) with delight. We heard the laughter from our parents behind us, as we threw our arms around our grandparents' necks—me around Grandpa, and Greer around Grandma.

"Oh my," Grandma smiled as she looked Greer over, "you look more like your mother every day! You're so beautiful! I've missed you so much, my sweet Greer," and she wrapped her into another hug. Grandma herself was quite striking. She was in her mid-sixties, but I thought she could easily pass for fifty. She was tall, like all the women in our family, and was very fit from a lifetime of being athletic. She was still an avid golfer, which was how she and Grandpa had met well over forty years earlier. She had her gorgeous silver hair pulled back, and was dressed to perfection in a striking black and cream pantsuit.

Greer and I switched, and Grandma held me tight as she said, "Look at you, you're breathtaking! I've missed you as well, my darling Darcy."

Grandpa gave Greer a hug and told her how happy he was to see her, just like he had done with me. I had always thought Grandpa was a handsome man, and I imagined my grandparents were a stunning couple when they were young, a real-life Ken and Barbie of their generation. They were attractive still, and Grandpa was the perfect complement to Grandma. He was tall as well and in shape just like her, but he was a little older, in his later sixties. He wore a dark suit that was cut flawlessly, and his full head of silver hair was perfectly combed. If there was ever a man to be called debonair, it was our Grandpa.

Mom, Dad, and Will were soon in on the greetings, and we all moved into the entryway. Mom spent a long time hugging each of her parents. It was sweet to see, and I heard Grandpa refer to Dad as son, which I didn't think I had ever noticed before.

We went back to the table, where our surprise visitors joined us in finishing breakfast. We caught up and talked about everything that was going on with graduation and our plans for college. I told everyone I was still deciding between SMU and UCLA, and, surprisingly, no one questioned me any further about it. We talked about everything except the Smiths, and I wondered if my grandparents knew the truth. They had shown no evidence that they knew in the past, but maybe that was for our benefit.

The rest of the morning was a rush, with everyone getting ready so we could get to Moody Coliseum, the SMU basketball arena, on time for graduation. We all went together in our packed Suburban. Will was less than thrilled about having to get there an hour early, the time Greer and I had to be there to get in line. Mom insisted that we all go together, under the pretense that they would get better seats that way.

Graduation itself was uneventful, yet still memorable. Ella, our good friend and valedictorian, gave an 'Ella-esque' speech. It was smart, funny, sweet, and at the end left Greer and others drying a few tears from their eyes. I didn't see Kieran or Lorcan until their names were called and they crossed the stage. I looked over to where my family was seated, and saw my grandmother gasp and grab my mother's hand when she saw them. Mom patted her mother's hand to reassure her, but I could see the worried look on Grandma's face—she knew everything.

Greer

After graduation was over and we had thrown our hats in the air, Darcy and I searched for our family. We soon found them waiting near one of the exits, and were pleased to see all of the Dobrys standing with them, laughing and chatting. Mrs. Dobry had allowed Katie to return to school for her finals, and she was all smiles as Will did his best to flirt with her. Edmund's face lit up when he saw Darcy, and I couldn't help but smile. Grandma noticed Edmund's look as well and whispered something to Mom, to which she nodded in response.

"There they are!" Dad said, and we were bombarded with hugs from everyone.

We moved outside where we could take some pictures, and began to make plans for lunch. Mrs. Dobry said she had caterers at their house at that very moment, and that she hoped we would all join them. All of Katie's friends and their families were planning to come. It sounded like fun, but apparently Mom had arranged for us to have lunch with Liam's family, which was a pleasant surprise for me. When she told Mrs. Dobry, she insisted that they come as well. Mrs. Dobry could be very persuasive and, as nice as she was, was used to getting her way.

Liam and his family found us outside and, after however many hundred pictures we all posed for with various groupings of our friends and family, we were all ready for lunch. The Alexanders were happy to join us at the Dobrys' home.

We were one of the last to arrive at the Dobrys, because Will insisted we stop and buy some flowers for Mrs. Dobry, since she was so kind to host all of us. Mom thought it was a good idea, although everyone knew that Will's motive was to make a good impression on Mrs. Dobry, in the hopes of gaining Katie's attention.

When we arrived, we were led in the house by Edmund, who seemed very happy to see us. Will went straight in to find Mrs. Dobry and give her the flowers Grandma helped him pick out. He was no doubt going to do his best to make sure Katie saw his grand gesture. When we walked into the main family room, we could see a lot of familiar faces visiting, and through the windows we could see some others out on the patio. All of our friends and their families were there, including Ella, Rebecca, Sloan, Mia, Elliot, Nathan, and, of course, Liam. I thought it was the perfect way to celebrate graduation day.

My family and I all spread out, with Mrs. Dobry coming to speak to my parents, and Darcy and Edmund going to talk to Ella and Elliot and their families by the fireplace. Will was talking to Katie, Rebecca, and Nathan in the kitchen, where Katie was putting her mother's new flowers in a beautiful crystal vase. I led my grandparents over to the large leather sofa so they could chat more with Liam and his family, whom they had only briefly met earlier. We were enjoying a wonderful conversation when I heard my grandmother gasp, as she grabbed my grandfather's arm. I looked up and, to my horror, saw Kieran, Lorcan, and finally Drake walk in through the patio door.

Drake locked eyes with my grandmother and gave her his most charming smile. I soon realized why my grandmother had grabbed my grandfather's arm—it was to keep him seated. The look that crossed his face when he saw Drake, the recognition of danger and a resolve to protect the ones he loved, closely resembled the one my father had during his last two encounters with Drake.

Before I knew what was happening, the wicked trio split up. Kieran went into the kitchen to speak with Katie and Will. Lorcan walked over and began to chat with Ella and Elliot's families, as well as Darcy and Edmund. Drake, thankfully, left the room with Dr. Dobry and Mia's father. I looked over and saw my mother was about to jump out of her skin, that our father was furious, and Darcy was looking anxiously at Will.

"This is bad, isn't it?" Liam whispered to me.

I quickly nodded in the affirmative. I looked over at Darcy, who I could tell was heading over to protect Will, who was now completely cornered by Kieran. To my surprise, Katie looked none too happy about it. Suddenly, I thought of something that could get us out of the mess we were in. It had to work, before all of the weirdness between our two families led to some awkward questions that could not be answered. I stood up quickly, paused for a moment, and then allowed myself to fall back down on the sofa. Essentially, I fainted— at least I pretended to faint, although I do think I blacked out for a split second. My grandmother quickly reached for me, and Liam stopped me from sliding down off the leather sofa.

"Greer!?" I heard Liam yell. My eyes were still closed, but I could hear almost everything that was happening around me. I could tell people were hovering, as I could feel their presence and the absence of air it created.

"Sweetheart, open your eyes," I heard my grandmother say, in the most concerned voice I had ever heard from her. I kept my eyes closed for a moment longer for effect. My plan had to work, I thought. I was not one to really ever lie or try to be manipulative, but I had to do something, or else things were going to get crazy really fast.

I could feel my parents were both now near me, and that Darcy and Will were also close by. I opened my eyes slowly, just as my mother began to wrap her hands around my face and say, "Greer, sweetheart, are you alright?"

"Yes, I think so," I whispered. I could see that I was right, I was surrounded. "What happened?" I asked, as if I had no idea.

"You fainted, love," Liam said, sharing the duty of holding me up with my mother.

"I did?" I asked, in my best confused voice. I looked over at Darcy and tried to communicate with just my eyes. I saw a small smile escape her lips. I saw Lorcan's look of great concern turn to one of amusement, when he saw the look I gave Darcy. He knew it was a farce as well. When I looked over at Kieran, she appeared anything but amused, as she rolled her eyes and crossed her arms over her chest.

"Here darling, drink some water," Mrs. Dobry said, bringing me a glass. I quickly took a small drink.

Finally, after a moment, Dad said exactly what I was hoping to hear, "We should take you home so you can rest."

Everyone agreed that I must have been exhausted and overwhelmed by the excitement of the day, and that a nice quiet afternoon at home with my family would be best. I couldn't believe how perfectly my plan had worked. We were soon leaving the Dobry's, with a ton of food Mrs. Dobry insisted we take with us. My only regrets were that Liam and his family would be left behind with the Smiths, and that Darcy had to say goodbye to Edmund so soon.

I knew Liam understood as he helped me out to the Suburban. He gave me a gentle hug and told me he would stop by later to check on me. I whispered, "Please stay away from the Smiths as much as possible. I'll tell you everything soon, I promise."

Liam nodded that he would do as I asked. I overheard Edmund ask Darcy if he could stop by later as well. She said yes, but I could sense there was some sort of sadness in her eyes that I didn't quite understand. Finally, we were all loaded into our Suburban. As I looked out the passenger window, I could see Drake looking out at us from one of the upstairs windows. I was sure that I had ruined whatever malicious plans he had towards my family for the day, but as I saw him smile, I feared he would not be held off much longer. I knew that whatever it was he wanted, he would soon find a way to get it.

Chapter Twenty-Two

Greer

No one said anything on the car ride home, not even Will, but I did notice Darcy messing with her phone, which I found odd. Once we were home, Dad asked everyone to go into the family room. We all did as he asked, taking seats around the room—the three kids on the sofa with Will in the middle, Grandma and Grandpa on the love-seat, and Mom in a chair with Dad standing beside her.

Dad began, "We…" He paused to clear his broken voice before continuing, "I should have been prepared that Drake would pull something like this today. I'm sorry, but I think this proves that they're not going to leave us alone, which means we need to be alert at all times. If they're ever anywhere near, it's best to just leave, like we did today." I saw Grandma nod in agreement. Grandma and Grandpa definitely knew everything, which explained why we saw so little of them over the years, and why they had never come to our home. It was all because of Drake.

"Well, it was good timing on Greer's part to faint then." Will laughed, trying to break the tension in the room.

"I wouldn't say it was exactly good timing," I replied with a small smile.

"What do you mean?" Mom asked, leaning forward in her chair.

"She means she totally faked it," Darcy said, leaning back against the sofa and crossing her arms over her chest as she looked away. I was confused by her attitude. At the Dobrys, she had appeared impressed by my quick thinking; now she just seemed mad or worried, I couldn't tell which.

"You did?" Mom asked, and I saw she was genuinely surprised.

"Well done, Greer." Grandma smiled. I looked around and saw that everyone else was also smiling—everyone except Darcy.

"That may have worked this time, but Greer, and the rest of us for that matter, can't go around pretending to be sick every time one of the Smiths are around. We need to just give Drake what he wants. That's the only way he will leave anyone alone. You all know him, and you know I'm right," Darcy said sharply to Mom, Dad, and our grandparents.

I leaned back so I could see around Will and speak directly to Darcy. "Who knows what his demented mind wants now? He may just want to mess with us as much as possible."

"No, he wants something particular this time," Darcy replied, quickly looking at me and then down at her hands.

"How do you know that, darling?" Dad asked, as I could see the concern growing on his face.

Darcy looked up at him. "Kieran told me what he wants, and that if he gets it, then he will leave our family alone for good," Darcy said. I could tell that she was struggling with what he wanted.

"What does he want?" Mom asked reluctantly.

"Me," Darcy replied quietly.

A look of rage flashed over my father's face, and Mom literally leapt to her feet and began to pace. "That will never happen!" she said. "None of you will go anywhere near him. We will move again. We will stay together and keep moving, until we find a place where he can't find us," Mom said, waving her hands in the air as she spoke.

Darcy and the rest of us said nothing, as Grandma rose to comfort her daughter. "Arianna, it'll be okay," she said, stopping Mom from her pacing as she grabbed her hands and placed them in her own. Mom soon laid her head on Grandma's shoulder, the way I had hundreds of times on Mom's, when I needed comfort.

"Darcy, you cannot have anything to do with Drake. You know enough about him to know that he can never be trusted. Even if you were what he wanted and he got you, which can't happen, then it wouldn't be long before he changed his mind and wanted something else from us. We are his obsession. That will never change. We just have to find a way to fight back, and be prepared for anything that might come our way. Unfortunately, I don't think moving again is the answer," Dad said seriously.

"David," Mom exclaimed, as she lifted her head off of her mother's shoulder.

"Arianna, David's right," Grandpa said, standing up. "You have run for too long, and he has always found you. It's time for a new approach."

"I think we should stay too. They say the best offense is a good defense." Will joined the other men by standing.

Mom sat back down in her chair. She knew she was outnumbered, as the rest of us thought staying was the best option. "Fine, we can stay here, but we all have to stay together," Mom demanded, looking at each of her three children.

"We can't all live like prisoners. That's not fair to any of us. We have to live our lives, free from the fear that one of the Smiths is going to show up and wreak havoc. The only way that's going to happen is if I go and live with them this summer." Darcy looked directly at our mother, and I could tell by the look in her eyes that she had already made up her mind.

"I will never allow that!" Mom yelled. Our mother had never raised her voice to one of us until that very moment, and the significance of it was not lost on any of us.

Darcy

I stood up and walked over to Mom. Everyone waited in anticipation of what was going to be said next. I knelt beside Mom's chair and placed my hands on hers. I could tell from the remorseful look on Mom's face that she already felt horrible for raising her voice to me, but I could also see that she was more scared than I had ever seen her before.

"Mom, I have to go, and not just so you all can live free of the Smiths; I have to go because I have to know this side of me. I have to know where I come from. He's my biological father, and I have to get to know him and his other children. I can't move forward until I do this. I've always known that I was different, and now I have the chance to understand why I'm the way that I am. Kieran told me that if I agree to spend the summer with him and his family, then they will leave all of you alone," I said in a calm and reasonable voice, as I masked the pain inside. It was in that moment I realized our mother's worst fear had come true. Drake had finally found us, and there was no more running. He was going to get what he wanted—me—and he was going to do everything he could to try and influence me. He was going to try and use our similarities to make me more like him than my incredible mother, and he was going to do it just to try and hurt her and Dad. I knew that, but I would also do whatever I could to not let that happen.

"You can't trust him. He's dangerous, and he will hurt you," Mom said, as the tears rolled down her face.

"That's a chance I have to take. If it means that the rest of you can be free of them, then I'm willing to do it," I replied.

"You're not going to sacrifice yourself for me or for any of us," Greer said, standing up. Her tone and stance demonstrated the severity of her anger.

"You can't go with him, he'll be the ruin of you," Mom said softly through her tears, as she touched my face.

I looked at Mom for a long moment and then I slowly stood up and straightened my dress. "I'm sorry, but I'm eighteen and I've graduated from high school. I don't need anyone's permission. I have to do what I think is right," I stated firmly, and the silence in the room was deafening. Everyone was in shock. I had made up my mind and it was obvious there was no changing it. They all had learned a long time ago that I was one of the most stubborn people they knew, and the only way they could stop me now would be to physically hold me down, which was not going to happen.

"Darcy, please don't do this," Dad begged, reaching for my hands.

I hugged him and whispered through my tears, "I can't thank you enough for everything you've done for me. No matter what happens, you'll always be my dad."

Greer

I had sat back down, but everyone else was on their feet when the doorbell rang. I knew who it was. It was perfect timing, of course. Darcy would tell us she was leaving and then, before any of us could think of a way for her to stay, she'd be gone. The Smiths were good in their planning; whenever one plan failed, they always had a backup, and eventually they got what they wanted.

I didn't move. Darcy quickly hugged Will and then Grandma

and Grandpa, who were all in shock. She hugged Mom, and whispered loud enough that I could hear, "I'm sorry. I have to do this for all of you, but also for me. I'll be safe, I promise, and I won't forget the person you raised me to be." Mom buried her head in Darcy's red hair and cried, holding her tightly. I thought she would never let her go; then the doorbell rang again.

Mom finally released Darcy, and Dad came over to hold onto Mom, who looked like she was about to collapse. Darcy walked over to me. I refused to look up at her and stayed seated. "Please don't be angry with me, Greer," she said in a soft voice. I stared at my clasped hands and said nothing in response. I was *so* angry. I was angry at the Smiths for causing all of the chaos in our lives, I was mad at our parents for keeping everything a secret, I was mad at Darcy for making the colossal mistake of going to live with them for who knew how long. She said it'd be for the summer, but what then? She still hadn't made up her mind about what college she was going to. When would we see her again?

Darcy saw how upset I was, that I had no intention of looking at her; after a moment, she said she was sorry and walked away. All of our family, apart from me, followed her to the front of the house. I heard the hall closet door open and close, and then the front door open. I was left sitting in the family room alone. I heard Lorcan ask Darcy if she was ready to go. Suddenly, I was out of my trance, and raced to the front of the house and onto the front porch. When I got there, I saw Lorcan loading Darcy's large suitcase into the back of his Land Rover. Kieran was standing by her father by the passenger side doors, both with wicked smiles on their faces.

My whole family was standing together, with Darcy in the front and my parents just behind and to her sides, each holding one of her hands. Will was a little further back behind them, and I could see that our grandparents were holding on to him. I'd never seen Will look so distraught. I stood on the porch, trying to figure out what to do. Suddenly and surprisingly, I saw Mom step forward and begin to speak.

"Why are you doing this, Drake? Allison has already given you two beautiful children. Why do you have to come after mine? Why can't you just leave us alone?" The anger in Mom's voice rose as she spoke. Drake said nothing. He just smiled. Lorcan and Kieran looked at Mom curiously, as did I. Was this Allison the same best friend Mom had in high school? Mom continued, "Oh, that's right, I forgot: you stole these children from Allison, just like you are trying to steal Darcy away from us now!" Her anger and grief bubbled over. Kieran and Lorcan looked at their father and then back at our mother.

"It was you who stole Darcy away from me," Drake growled at Mom. I noticed Dad, Will, and Grandpa all stand up straighter and more defensively.

"No, you willingly gave up all of your rights to her for more money. Then you used that money, and who knows what else, to rip those babies out of Allison's arms when you had her committed to that institution," Mom yelled. The look of horror that crossed Kieran's face was unmistakable. Lorcan just looked down, like he wasn't all that surprised.

"Father?" Kieran said, reaching for Drake's arm.

He shrugged her off, and his coldness towards her gave me a chill. "Don't listen to her. She'll say anything to try and keep Darcy away from me, but it's too late. Darcy has made up her mind now, and will come and live with me, where she belongs." Drake's victorious smile made me cringe. Kieran was hurt by his rebuff and still looked confused.

Darcy turned to Mom and gave her one last hug. She moved back slowly, looked right into her eyes, and said, "Mom, listen to me, everything will be alright in the end. Please try not to worry. I love you."

The tears fell freely from our mother's eyes again; as Darcy began to walk towards Drake and Kieran, I ran down the stairs and across the lawn towards her. "Darcy, wait!" I screamed. She turned around and I threw myself into her arms. "Come back to us, please come back to us!" were all the words I could muster.

"I will," she whispered in my ear, and then she leaned back. With her bravest face, she smiled at me as she grasped both of my hands tightly.

"Oh, that's so sweet. Greer, you're welcome to come with us if you'd like." Drake laughed, but I could sense that he wasn't completely joking. I ignored him and didn't take my eyes off of Darcy. I imagined that Mom and Grandma were doing everything they could to hold the men in our family off of him. I must have been right, because I looked up to see what I thought was a trace of fear on Drake's face. He began to get in the SUV and said, "Let's go, now!" He then slammed the passenger door.

I held on tightly to Darcy's hands and tried to memorize everything about her, just the way she was right then—because I knew that no matter when she came back to us, she would be changed. I wanted to remember the Darcy I had always known, and hoped that the one who returned would resemble her in some way. Lorcan walked over to us and whispered, "We'd better go Darcy." He turned to me and continued, "I promise I'll look out for her and won't let anything bad happen to her." He took Darcy's right hand from my left and, in the same moment, placed a note in the palm of my hand, which I quickly grasped and held to my stomach with my other hand covering it. I didn't want Drake to see that Lorcan had passed me a note, in case it was supposed to be a secret, which was what I thought was Lorcan's intention.

Lorcan and Darcy walked over to the SUV, and she turned as

Lorcan opened the rear passenger door for her. She gave us a small reluctant wave and then she quickly got in. Lorcan closed the door. Suddenly, she was lost to us behind the dark tinted windows. Who knew what was being said in there, and who knew what would happen to her while living with them. As they drove off, I felt like part of me was leaving with them. I'd never been apart from Darcy for any extended period of time before, and I could already feel the ache in my heart from our separation. She was my twin, my sister, my best friend—and then she was gone.

Once Lorcan's SUV was out of sight, it took all the strength I had to turn around and walk towards the rest of my family, standing there feeling emotions similar to my own. In our shock, we walked inside the house slowly. Will went straight to his room. Grandma and Grandpa followed Mom and Dad into the family room. I stopped just inside the door, sat down on the bench in the entryway, and slowly and quietly opened the note from Lorcan. I had already decided that if it was anything that would further hurt my parents, I would keep it a secret, but if it was something that would bring them some small comfort, then I would share it with them.

Dear Greer,

I can't imagine how upset and angry you must be right now. Please know that I am truly sorry about everything my family has done to cause yours harm. I knew that it was always my father's intention to somehow convince Darcy to leave your family for ours, but now I am so very sorry that I played any role in making that a reality. All I can do now is promise you that I will do everything in my power to protect her and keep her safe.

I know my father better than anyone, and I know that he will forbid Darcy from contacting your family for the next few months, as a way to make all of you suffer even more. I think I know Darcy well enough to know that she will agree, in order to protect you. The truth is you need to be protected. I just wish she didn't have to make such a huge sacrifice in order to do so.

I understand that you want nothing to do with me or my family, but I also know that you love your sister and are going to be worried about her. I promise I will find a way to get you updates on Darcy without our father knowing. In the meantime, I urge you and your family not to try and locate us or try to bring Darcy back. That is exactly what my father is hoping for, and the end results would be more devastating than you can imagine. Please believe me when I say this: my father is extremely dangerous. While I do not believe he would ever harm Darcy, because she is his daughter, I believe he would not think twice about harming anyone else, especially a member of your family.

I am sorry it has all come to this. I will do what I can to rectify the situation by protecting our shared sister as much as possible. I want to, at least, be able to give you that.

Yours,

Lorcan

I began to cry again. The whole crazy situation had become even more real. I knew I had to show the letter to Mom and Dad; I slowly stood up and walked into the family room, where I found everyone sitting in silence. I handed the letter to Dad and then sat down on the sofa next to Grandma, who wrapped her arm around me and pulled me close to her. I laid my head on her shoulder and closed my eyes. I wanted to wake up from the nightmare we were all in, and for everything to go back to the way it was before the Smiths had ever come into our lives.

I opened my eyes when I heard Dad sigh after reading the letter. I looked over at him and Mom, who were sitting together on the loveseat. She had read the letter over his shoulder, as I had expected. They both looked at each other and said nothing. The pain of their loss was written all over their faces.

"What are we going to do?" I asked, feeling defeated.

"I'm not sure yet, but we'll think of something," Dad said reassuringly, as he walked over and handed the letter to Grandpa and Grandma.

"I believe what Lorcan said in his letter," I replied quietly.

"I do too. It appears he has more of his mother in him than his father," Mom replied, looking at me with sadness in her eyes.

"Maybe," Dad said reluctantly. I studied his face carefully, and I knew he didn't believe Lorcan to be so good-willed towards us. He did not want to say anything in front of Mom that would cause her further pain, so he kept the rest of his thoughts to himself.

I heard the clock chime and realized that it was 3 p.m., and that Liam would arrive soon. I mentioned it to Mom and Dad and asked what I should tell him. To my surprise, Mom said to just tell him the truth. "Liam's a nice boy. He'll keep our secret until we can figure out what to do next and bring Darcy home."

I nodded and ran up the stairs to my room to change and try to put myself together somewhat. I had cried most of my makeup off, and didn't bother to put any more on. Instead, I just washed my face, put on some moisturizer, pulled my hair back into a ponytail, and then changed into jeans and a tee. As I sat down on my bed, I heard something crinkle underneath me. I quickly stood up and saw two envelopes lying there. One had my name on it, and one had Edmund's, with a sticky note on top that read, "Please make sure he gets this."

I sat back down and slowly opened the envelope meant for me.

Dear Greer,

I know you are very upset with me, upset that I didn't tell you everything I have known for a while now. I am sorry. Please know that. I am also sorry if what I am doing now hurts all of you. You have to trust me that this is for the best.

I promise that I will come home. I may not know when that will be, but I will come home. In the meantime, please look after Mom, Dad, and Will. They will need your strength now more than ever.

I do want to ask you and our family to please not try to contact me or find me while I am away. I am afraid it might be dangerous for all of you, and your safety is what I am so desperately trying to protect. I will be in touch when I can.

Greer, please know that I love and admire you so much. I will miss you while I am gone.

Love,
Darcy

My tears flowed freely yet again. I sat there, wanting to be angry with Darcy, but how could I be? In the end, she was doing all of this for us. She was trying to protect us the only way she knew how. As I sat there, staring at the letter, I heard a car door shut in front of our house; I ran over to the window to see if maybe, hopefully, she had changed her mind and come home. I wasn't surprised, however, when I saw it wasn't her. I knew, from then on, I would always be looking for her until I did see her again. I ran down the stairs, still clutching my letter from Darcy and the envelope addressed to Edmund. I reached the front door before Liam even had a chance to ring the doorbell. I flung the door open and threw myself into his arms, sobbing deeply.

"Greer, what's wrong?" Liam demanded, as he grabbed me and held on tightly. He led me over to the iron bench on our front porch and we sat down. I was still crying when he gently cupped my face with his hands and asked again, "Greer, what's wrong? You're scaring me."

I shook my head from side to side and tried to catch my breath. I wiped my tears; after a minute, I composed myself enough to speak. I told him everything, from the very beginning. I didn't leave anything out, not even the night of our first date, when I was stalked by Drake at the Jackopierce concert. I told him everything I could remember about my conversations with Lorcan. I told him everything I could think of that involved the Smiths. He listened, and while he appeared angry at various points through my long monologue, he remained silent. When I was finally finished, I felt like a thousand pounds had been lifted off my shoulders. "I know this all sounds crazy," I said, and then I waited for him to speak, afraid of what he might say. The truth was that I was afraid he would run from our house, never to be seen again. Any sane person would, I thought. Who would, in their right mind, want to get involved with a girl whose family had as much drama as mine?

Liam just stared at me with his bright blue eyes that told me he wasn't going anywhere. "I'm so sorry, Greer. I can't imagine how difficult these past few months have been for you and your family. I wish you would've told me so I could have helped in some way, but I understand why you couldn't. I'm very sorry to hear that Darcy has gone to live with them, but I'm glad that you are free of them for now. I never trusted them and always thought they were bad news, but I had no idea to what extent. I know you think you can trust Lorcan, but I don't believe that you can. Whether it's for his father or for himself, he is playing some sort of game, and you, my love, are at the center of it."

"I have no choice but to trust Lorcan now, and hope that he provides updates about how Darcy's doing," I replied, knowing it would not make Liam happy.

"Just promise me this: from here on out, no more secrets. Always tell me everything, even if it's not easy to do. I can't help you if I don't know what's going on." Liam clutched both of my hands in his.

"I promise." I stared deeply into his eyes.

"Greer, I love you and I will do anything to protect you…" Liam looked away, like he was going to say something else but had stopped himself.

"What is it? What else were you going to say?" I asked, turning his head back towards me.

He hesitated for a minute, but then said, "It's far from over. From what you've told me about Drake, I don't believe he will be satisfied until he has destroyed your parents, and the best way to do that is through their children. He has Darcy now, and he will be coming for you next." Liam's words sent chills down my spine, as I couldn't necessarily disagree. I looked down and said nothing, as I wondered when that would happen.

Liam wrapped me in his arms, and I rested my head against his chest for a long while. I closed my eyes, wanting to wake from my horrible nightmare.

Epilogue

Daveney
December 2033

I closed the last page of the journal. The mixture of emotions I felt was overwhelming. Mainly, I was in shock to learn so much about my family in one sitting. Who knew my quiet, normal, sometimes boring (in a good way) family had such a dramatic past! My instinct was to go to the closet and get the next journal and begin reading, but I was exhausted, and I knew my mom wanted me to get her as soon as I was done. After looking at my watch and seeing that it was well past dinner time, I laid my head back on the chair; I had closed my eyes for a moment, trying to process everything and quell my rumbling stomach, when I heard my mom come in the room. I quickly opened my eyes, and looked at her anxious face.

"Have you finished the first journal?" Mom asked, with some trepidation.

"Yes," I responded, unsure I wanted to elaborate any further.

"I'm sure you have some questions for me," Mom inquired, coming into the room a little further.

I nodded in the affirmative, although I had no idea where to start. Mom could sense my mixture of emotions, which really consisted of fascination and curiosity to know more of what happened; mainly I felt sad for many of the people that I knew from the story, and even some of those I didn't. To go through all of that must have been so incredibly difficult, I thought.

Mom walked over to me and picked up the journal, and began to flip through the pages. I just stared at her beautiful blue eyes, which were beginning to moisten. She held the journal close to her; shaking off the brief sadness that crossed her face, which I sensed had to do with my Aunt Darcy. She reached out her hand to mine and said, "We can talk over dinner."

I placed my hand in hers, and she helped me stand up. My legs and back were sore from sitting in one position for so long. I followed Mom out of her room; as soon as I reached the stairs, I could smell our scrumptious dinner. My growling stomach took notice as well. Mom had made her famous homemade pizza, which was one of my favorite meals.

We settled in at the table in silence. After we said our traditional mealtime prayer, I took a bite to calm my angry teenage stomach and the butterflies that arose from the conversation looming ahead.

"I know you must have a lot of questions," Mom said, staring at me as if she was trying to read my mind.

"I was quite surprised by what I read," I joked. Humor was my way of trying to deal with tense situations, something I had in common with my Uncle Will.

"I'm sure you were," Mom replied with a small smile.

"I can see now why you never told me much about how you and Daddy met," I said more seriously.

Mom laughed. "Yes, our relationship began at a very complicated time."

I asked Mom a series of questions and follow-ups, to help me process everything I had just learned about our family history. To my surprise, she answered them candidly. Finally, after a long while of back and forth conversation, I asked my most important question, "When do I get to read the next journal?"

"Tomorrow," Mom replied, to my great satisfaction.

May 2034

"Daveney is waking up," I heard my mother say as I slowly opened my eyes. With my head pounding and my eyes starting to refocus, I was instantly relieved to be lying on the sofa in my own home. How I got there was a complete mystery. As I looked at my parents, I saw the great relief on their faces that I was, in fact, alright. I knew I had to tell them the whole truth regarding the secret I had been keeping from them about the Smiths, and I knew they were not going to be happy.

To be continued...

Acknowledgments

I want to thank God, the Author of ALL things, for the gifts of His love, patience and forgiveness and the wonderful family and friends He has given me on this earth.

My incredible husband is my best friend, biggest supporter and confidant. I so appreciate his unwavering love and support in everything I do.

My sweet children bring so much joy to my life. They have taught me so much about love and they make everything in my life more beautiful.

My parents have always been there for me and I am so grateful for their love and support.

Many thanks to some close friends and family members (Kris, Sara, Melissa, Ali) who read early drafts of this novel and were encouraging throughout my journey. Thank you also to some other wonderful friends/family (Kim F., Kristi G., Beth J., Charlie, Rosie, Mary, Tori, Holly) who were supportive in my pursuing this dream—thank you for your faith in me.

Finally, a big thank you to my publisher, Mascot Books, and its fantastic staff. I am very lucky to work with such great people.

K. M. Roberson is a native Texan who lives in the Midwest with her husband and children. For more information, visit her website at www.kmroberson.com.

Coming Soon

Greer and Darcy's story continues in an unforgettable
adventure around the world in *The Hagen Family Curse*.